Anyone for Me?

FIONA CASSIDY

POOLBEG

This novel is entirely a work of fiction. The names,
characters and incidents portrayed in it are the work of the
author's imagination. Any resemblance to actual persons,
living or dead, events or localities is entirely coincidental.

Published 2011
by Poolbeg Press Ltd
123 Grange Hill, Baldoyle
Dublin 13, Ireland
il: poolbeg@poolbeg.com
www.poolbeg.com

© Fiona Cassidy 2010

for typesetting, layout, design
© Poolbeg Press Ltd

The moral right of the author has been asserted.

1

A catalogue record for this book is available from the British Library.

ISBN 978-1-84223-465-5

Typeset by Patricia Hope in Sabon 11.5/15.5
Printed by CPI, Cox & Wyman, UK

www.poolbeg.com

Note on the Author

Fiona Cassidy is more locally known as Fionnuala McGoldrick. She still retains the Christian name given to her by her birth mother before she was adopted at four months old. She is an only child and grew up in Galbally, Co Tyrone. She currently lives in Donaghmore with her partner Philip and their collective children. She has recently given up work to pursue a career in writing and teaches creative writing classes and facilitates workshops when she can. She enjoys reading, collects quirky unusual jewellery and loves anything to do with angels.

You can visit her at www.fionacassidy.net. or follow her blog at www.cassidysez.blogspot.com

Also by Fiona Cassidy

Anyone for Seconds?

Published by Poolbeg

Acknowledgements

I am a writer but first and foremost I am a wife (nearly . . . woohoo!!) and a mother and I would be nothing without my wonderful family. Philip, I love you more than words can say. You are an amazing man, a fantastic partner and a brilliant father! Thank you for your incredible support throughout the past nine years and especially since the publication of *Anyone for Seconds?* when life became very mad indeed. Every writer should have a 'hubby' like you in the wings! We have six children between us and love them all very much. Colm, Úna, Ciarán and Áine thank you for making our home such a happy and enjoyable place to be and showing us each and every day how much you love us! Since the release of *Anyone for Me?* in trade paperback in August our family has been blessed with a new addition in the form of baby Orán who arrived safe and well on 7th February this year (four weeks early in a very dramatic fashion . . . it's going to end up in a book so I'm not telling you any more!). He is a very special little boy who gave his mammy and daddy something to look forward to during some very dark days within the last number of months when life was hard for various reasons. I want him to know that I will always appreciate his comforting little kicks and nudges which reminded me that life is too short to spend time mourning what you haven't got when, in fact, you should be counting your blessings and thanking God for what is in front of you!

I owe a massive debt of gratitude to my very supportive friends who are the best cheerleading squad anyone could ask for. Noeleen, Katrina, Carrie-Ann, Rachel, Joanna, Rosalind and Denise, you are always there no matter what happens. Thanks, girls, for helping me celebrate the good times and picking me up and putting me back together again when life is challenging which it very often is in my world – but, hey, you'd all be bored stiff without the drama and the laughs we get! Thanks also to Paula (on-call hairdresser who I hope to move in one day!), to Tina for being a good friend in difficult times and Gary Hamilton for his contribution to the book with the word 'dander'.

I'd also like to mention Melissa Mellon, who was brought into my life for a reason at the right time and has been a very good friend to me and given me a lot of comfort with her uplifting messages of hope and insightful chats!

Thanks to Adrian Kelly (and his wife Ciara) for sharing his story with me and giving his shoulder to cry on when I found it hard to cope with my circumstances. Heartfelt appreciation also to Doctor Maureen Crawford for being an understanding and sensitive confidante all down the years and to Ann and the wonderful Brigeen who more recently have helped me more than they will ever know.

I would also like to acknowledge my extended family, namely the Cassidys, McGearys (Clarksons and Grahams in America included) and McAllisters (Glengormley and Australia) for their love and good wishes and for promoting me abroad and tripping to book signings and events where possible, which means the world to me! I promised my future brother-in-law Stephen a special 'shout out' in the next book and true to my word would like to thank him for providing plenty of craic and leaving a trail of teabags behind him wherever he goes! I would also like to mention Edel Woods and Brigid-Ann McGoldrick who are the best sisters-in-law anyone could have!

To my 'writer' friends, I thank you for being there in good times and in bad, i.e. when deadlines are looming or when a pickaxe is required to hack through the writer's block! Claire Allan . . . just exactly where would I be without you? You have been a rock to me in more ways than one over the last number of years and have gone from simply being a fellow writer to a very special friend (as well as the reason I like Cosmopolitans so much!). I'd also like to mention Sharon Owens who has been incredibly kind to me and gave me the great honour of not only attending her book launch last November but allowing me to fulfil a lifelong dream by meeting Brendan and Declan Murphy from The Four of Us while I was at it! Thanks also to Emma Heatherington for all the laughs on the library tour along with Mrs Allen and to all the library staff from across Northern Ireland who made us so welcome!

As always thanks to the 'Write-On' girls, especially Jacqui, Megan, Oonagh, Angie, Claire, Jo and Susanne – I know you have the PR for my books well covered south of the border as well as further afield. And congratulations to Shirley Benton who has just had her first novel published and become part of the Poolbeg gang!

Gratitude also to all the organisations both north and south of the border for allowing me to do what I enjoy most by giving me the opportunity to promote myself and teach Creative Writing to others. Special thanks to Geraldine Quinn and the staff at The Peace Factory in Dungannon, Catherine McInerney from LitNet NI and Carol Doey (who is as daft as a brush . . . but sure all mad writers are . . . I should know!!).

Thanks to the people of Galbally for their ongoing support. I couldn't be part of a more close-knit or special community and I am very grateful for the good wishes, cards, presents and general encouragement! The launch of *Anyone for Me?* in August which took place in Tally's Bar in Galbally was a fabulous night and I'd like to extend particular thanks to Paddy Tally, Rose, and local band Daybreak (AKA David McCrory and Kevin Christie) who all helped to make the evening the success it was. Thanks also to our friends and neighbours in Donaghmore especially Jim Hamill (best photographer in the world) and his wife Rossi, Malachy Comac and Gary McKay.

I am deeply indebted to all the media locally, regionally, and also in the Republic. Thank you so much for the television and radio interviews, book reviews, features and news articles which I will hoard indefinitely.

Thanks also to Chick Lit Reviews for inviting me to blog on

their website and to Malachi Cush who not only has compered my last two book launches but who promotes me where possible! Appreciation also to TP and Madeleine Sheehy from Sheehy's Bookshop in Cookstown and Lisa Blevins from Eason's Craigavon for allowing me to have signings in store and promoting me as a local author!

I'd also like to give special thanks to the National Lottery, Damien Smyth and the Arts Council of Northern Ireland who have all shown faith in me and demonstrated that by awarding me funding as an individual artist. Thanks as always to my personal proofreader Ruth Daly and her husband Finbarr. I must also acknowledge my friend and solicitor Kieran Quinn who allowed me to wreck his head with endless questions about wills and Irish land law in order to tweak a storyline within the book!

Immense gratitude to Paula Campbell and Sarah Ormston for their support and hard work in relation to my writing (it's no wonder you get referred to under the umbrella term 'the lovely people from Poolbeg'). Thanks also to my eagle-eyed editor Gaye Shortland for caring enough to make the book perfect for publication! Huge appreciation must also go to my dear friend and extremely hardworking and genuinely lovely agent Emma Walsh, whose advice and guidance are always spot on and ability to promote me in the right places superb – thank you for everything (including the motivational kick-starts and therapy sessions) – hopefully I'll make it all worth your while one of these days!

I'd also like to give a special mention to Frances Nicholson from BAAF Northern Ireland who has been very kind and empathetic towards me. Gratitude also to Anna Reynolds and to Patron Nimmy March who it was a pleasure to meet during the celebrations for National Adoption Week in Belfast last November. The British Association for Adoption and Fostering do great work in placing children, who find themselves within the care system, with foster families as well as with adoptive parents. Without organisations such as these many children would find themselves without a place in this world and as an adoptee I would like to extend my thanks to them for working so hard to make a difference. I gained a lot from being an 'Adoption Champion' for BAAF and raising awareness of a subject that is very close to my heart and hope that I can continue to help and promote this cause as much as possible in the future!

You're probably wondering why I'm being a bold child and neglecting to mention my parents until this point but my reason is quite simple . . . I wanted to save the best for last. Writing *Anyone for Me?* has been a journey, not only into the world of being a published author, but also of self-discovery. Being born into difficult circumstances and subsequently put up for adoption could have had any number of outcomes for me but thankfully I was one of the lucky ones who was placed in a good home with the most fantastic parents any child could wish for. My parents, Peter and Eileen, have been wonderful and I owe them dearly, not only for always being honest about my parentage, but also for supporting me in everything I do and giving me an identity to be proud of.

Part of the reason why I wrote this book was because I wanted to give my central character the storyline I had often hoped and dreamed of for myself but have never had and never will have. Although it is important to know where you come from it is also just as vital to be aware of what you have and as far as I'm concerned I have it all! I wish my birth mother well in her life as I now finally realise that I am at peace with 'who I am' and look forward to the years ahead with the best family in the world!

For Mammy and Daddy
(Peter and Eileen) . . .
I'm so glad we found each other and
am proud to be your daughter

And

For Baby Orán
whose recent arrival has made me
appreciate the good things in life!

WITHDRAWN

Chapter 1

'*Wedding Belles.*' I looked at the sign in distaste, whilst Frankie (my best friend and highly excitable bling-loving bridesmaid) stood beside me and hugged herself with glee.

"I never thought this day would come, Ruby. Imagine, in less than a year you'll be an old married woman!"

What she really meant to say was that she was shocked to the core that I was actually getting married (that anyone would be brave enough to take me on) and that she was even more amazed at the fact that I wasn't insisting on taking my vows in my combats and T-shirt (although now that I thought of it . . .)

I looked at myself from every angle, cursed the unforgiving lighting which showed up every freckle and imperfection I possessed (of which there were many) and swiftly decided that if I had a piece of kiwi fruit perched on my head I'd be every meringue-lover's idea of a treat!

"You look marvellous," trilled the bridal-shop assistant. "Although you could probably benefit from a bit of padding in the boob department," she added whilst groping my person.

"Oh God! Don't do that!" Frankie muttered before asking the

stupid woman (who quite obviously had a death wish) to excuse us. Frankie was petite and pretty with big blue eyes and blonde hair. She was immaculately dressed as always and usually had a large grin on her face but right now for some reason she was looking terrified.

"There's no need to attack her, you know," she whispered to me, the assistant having discreetly withdrawn from the fitting area. "All that probing and touching is part of their job – a bit like the way they feel the top of your toes to make sure your shoes fit properly." Frankie was looking nervously towards the door in case the assistant appeared and I pounced – and my unsuspecting victim lost her hair extensions and went home minus a few porcelain tooth-veneers.

"She just copped a feel. I am nearly a married woman but does that stop an opportunist with a fetish for corsets and horrific-looking net skirts from trying it on? Quite obviously not. Please unzip me from this monstrosity and take me home. Now."

"But that's the first dress you've tried on, Ruby! You didn't think it would be as easy as all that, did you? It's not like going shopping for a pair of jeans, y'know."

"That's an idea actually," I muttered. "I wonder would anyone mind me turning up in my 501s? I am the bride after all so I think that should give me the right to wear exactly what I want, don't you?"

"I am not even going to dignify that with an answer," Frankie said in a stern tone whilst peering round my shoulder and struggling with the zip. "Days off and childcare are hard to come by and I am not wasting this opportunity to see you in a posh frock."

"'Frock'," I repeated disdainfully. "What era do you think we live in, Frankie?"

"The era where brides actually care about looking nice on their wedding day and are not difficult when their friends try and help them."

I sighed as I stepped out of the dress. I had come a long way in

2

the last few years. Before I met Luke I had hardly worn make-up at all but now found that I didn't mind wearing a little lip-gloss and using kohl eyeliner to accentuate my eyes. I had forgotten that getting married entailed wearing a dress, however, and was less than impressed with the idea. I simply didn't 'do' skirts and hadn't donned one since the day I left school.

"I made out a list," Frankie wheedled. "If you don't like it here, there are three other bridal boutiques we can try. Come on, Ruby! Do it for me and do it for Luke. Imagine his face as you walk down the aisle looking radiant in a gorgeous dress with flowers in your hair!"

I opened my mouth to protest that there wouldn't be so much as a stem getting near my head but found I couldn't speak as I had an image in my head of Luke's reaction. I really did love him, and he was so good about accepting me the way I was (narky and stubborn most of the time) that the idea of surprising him really appealed to me. I couldn't imagine ever being described as radiant, though (not unless you count the fact that my hair looks like a bright red beacon).

There was a time that I didn't like Luke Reilly very much. On our first meeting he was lucky to escape with his vital organs still attached and in working order. When we met he was employed by a local newsrag and had taken photographs of Frankie and her partner Owen from a video still which showed them in a rather compromising position on student prize day in the college where we all work. It was, in fact, a very innocent kiss which got blown completely out of proportion but on a lighter note is the funniest graduation-day anecdote in Redmond College history. Well, everyone with the exception of Frankie and Owen thinks so. You can actually see them twitch when it's mentioned (which the rest of us do with wicked regularity). We soon got over that little hitch, however, and are now *getting* hitched (pardon the pun).

"How are we getting on now?" The saccharine shop assistant had tentatively reappeared.

"*We're* getting along just fine," I answered. "Just leaving."

"But you've only tried on one dress," she said in confusion.

"And *you* are still in possession of your good looks so be very grateful," I answered whilst staring menacingly at her.

It was the month of June and my wedding was still eleven months away. I couldn't understand what all the panic was about. Preparation and organisation were not my strong points anyway and I especially hated anything that involved too much fuss. To date, the only other arrangements that had been made for the wedding were the booking of the chapel and the reception venue. But there was plenty of time to do the rest, surely? We had decided to have our meal and party in the Swiftstown Arms. It was our local hotel and probably wouldn't have been everyone's first choice but it satisfied me. The food was nice and I knew the manager well and it was handy to home which meant that after my big day was complete I could be carried over the threshold and into my own bed. We were hoping to go on a honeymoon but (you've guessed it) nothing had been put in place as of yet. Maybe we'd get a last-minute deal.

Three exasperating hours, two more bridal shops, more hideous dresses and one measly cup of coffee later and we were no further forward, aside from the fact that I now hated everyone who was employed in the bridal fashion industry. They were all horrible, mean people who acted like your body was an extension of their own, which meant that they could poke and prod you at will. They were also rather suspicious and hostile towards you when you first entered their sacred domains.

"Were you looking for anything in particular?"

"Well, as I'm in a fecking wedding-dress shop I think it's fairly obvious what I want, don't you?"

I had to be escorted out of that one by the ear after the assistant wouldn't let me try on a particular dress as she thought it was beyond my price range. Cheeky cow. (Big mistake. Huge. The saleswomen in *Pretty Woman* weren't the only snobby cows in town!)

I looked sideways at Frankie who at this stage looked like she was sucking a pickled lemon.

"Frankie."

"Yes, Ruby."

"Are you annoyed with me?"

"Me annoyed with you? And why would I be annoyed with you, Ruby Ross?" she said in a low growl. "We've had a wonderfully exhausting day of insults, sarcasm, endless complaining and still no bloody dress. Honestly, if I had known it was going to be this tough, I would have suggested that you go to a dressmaker and get it made to your precise instructions in the first place."

That was a light-bulb moment for us both as we suddenly realised that Frankie had stumbled upon the answer to all our problems.

"Brilliant!" I said in delight.

"So what do you want?"

"A dress that doesn't make me look like a moron would be a good start. No frills, no ponce, no mad heavy nets that you would need legs like a heifer to carry, no ten thousand jaggy sequins that itch the crap out of you and no ten-foot-long train for every eejit to stand on whilst your boobs pop out the other end from the strain."

"A bin-liner."

"Pardon?"

"I was just thinking out loud, Ruby. Why don't we fashion you a dress out of a bin-bag?"

"Ha ha."

"What exactly is there left?" Frankie threw her hands up in aggravation and annoyance.

"A good dressmaker will take one look at me and know exactly what I need."

I thought I heard my best friend and future bridesmaid mutter something about eye-poking and sharp sticks but I could have been mistaken.

"How'd you get on?" Luke asked when I eventually arrived home that evening empty-handed apart from a family bucket of Kentucky

Fried Chicken and a box of beer which I intended to scoff with urgent immediacy. (Comfort food, as I felt victimised.)

I tapped the side of my nose and tried to look mysterious as I watched him transfer photographs he had taken that day from a memory card onto his computer, where he would spend the rest of the evening working on them.

"You didn't get anything, did you?"

"What makes you say that?"

"I met Frankie at the shop earlier and she told me that if I had any sense I'd get you a wedding planner as a present as nothing would be organised otherwise."

"Okay, so I didn't get a dress but it's no big deal. I'll just get one made instead."

Luke gave me his one-eyebrow-raised look and then kissed me tenderly on the nose. I ruffled his dark hair and put my arms around his neck, looked into his face which I found highly attractive as he had a gorgeous smile and expressive blue eyes which were surrounded by faint lines (created by constantly laughing at me as opposed to with me).

"I don't care if you turn up in a bin-liner, honey," he said. "I'll marry you anyway."

"Hmmm . . . funny you should say that."

Chapter 2

I went to work the following day as normal and was delighted by the sight of my untidy desk which made Frankie hyperventilate every time she looked at it – she had a clear case of obsessive-compulsive disorder that hadn't been properly diagnosed yet. It was stacked with papers (I could no longer see my 'in' or 'out' trays), had pens and other stationery scattered indiscriminately over it as well as editions of the *Yellow Pages* dating back to the caveman era. I viewed it as my sanctuary (a place where I was safe from demonic shop assistants and even scarier friends). My habitual doodles were also dotted around the area.

I had worked in Redmond College for nearly eleven years as a Placement Officer which required me to put our students into the industry in which they wished to pursue a career. I loved my job (mostly because I could continue to act like an eternal student myself and also because they invited me on all their beer-and-kebab-fuelled nights out which were much more appealing than anything the staff had to offer). I had recently been given my own office which totally exasperated Frankie as she thought the perk was completely wasted on me. In truth I would probably leave it looking in the same state as my home (which would be Kim and

Aggie's worst nightmare if Luke wasn't a dab hand with a duster). It wasn't that the house was dirty or that I didn't have personal hygiene standards, it was just that I thought life was too short to try and constantly emulate Mrs Mop, so I employed the philosophy that I'd let it get really mucky and then do all the chores at once.

"Good morning," Frankie said as she appeared, looking her usual spruce self.

"Please don't mention the word 'shopping'. This is a wedding-discussion free zone as far as I'm concerned."

"Would I?" Frankie said with a mischievous twinkle in her eye. "I tell you what – I'll make a deal with you."

I hated deals as they usually required me to agree with something I clearly disagreed with just to keep the other party happy.

"Pick a wedding-dress designer who we'll go and visit next week and then I promise I will act as if you're still single and spinsterhood, faded jeans and Doc Martens are the order of the day."

"Designer?" I said, feeling distinctly unimpressed at the thought.

"Dressmaker then," Frankie said, sensing my disgruntlement.

She looked so optimistic and hopeful that I didn't have the heart to burst her bubble. I knew that even if I wasn't prone to getting excited about such occasions, Frankie was, and the thought of wearing a bridesmaid's dress filled her with joy. Also, my little goddaughter Carly was going to be my flower girl and I could hardly make her wear dungarees (or could I?).

I reached across and lifted the most up-to-date *Yellow Pages*, opened it at the appropriate page and proceeded to do what I did every time I needed to pick a name and didn't know where to start.

"Please tell me you're not going to do what I think you're going to do," Frankie said from behind her hand as she cringed and made faces.

"Frankie, do you want me to do this or not?"

"Ruby, you are the only person in the world who would pick the

8

future maker of their wedding gown by closing their eyes and stabbing a list of phone numbers with a finger!"

I opened one eye, closed it again and pointed downwards.

"'*Rose Malone. Dressmaker specialising in Bridal and Fine Evening Wear.*' There you go. Go away and leave me to my Doc Martens."

Frankie spluttered and came over for a closer look.

"Ruby, she's based in some back street in Belfast! I have a bad feeling about this." She picked up one of my doodles and waved it at me in a desperate fashion. "You could design your own dress. Why don't you give it a go and then we'll have another look for a designer – dressmaker, I mean. I shouldn't have rushed you into this."

"I draw people and pieces of scenery, Frankie. Donatella Versace needn't start shaking in her designer boots yet. The Finger of Fate has spoken. Now get lost and go and annoy somebody else."

Frankie raised her eyes to heaven and sighed. She knew when she was beaten.

"Ruby, you are the most irritating person in the world but I still love you." With that she plopped a kiss on my forehead and walked out the door.

I stared after her fondly and thought back to when we first met. We had started working in a local recruitment agency on the same day thirteen years ago and had regarded each other with distaste for the first six months or at least until we had got to know each other a bit better. (In other words when I stopped thinking she was a blonde airhead and she had ceased believing I was a psychopath. Me? As if?) At that stage Frankie was married to Tony – please let it be noted that I have a dartboard with the weasel's much-punctured picture on it. Of course, things aren't as bad as they used to be as he now sees his children a couple of times a week and thankfully bestows his attentions on another gullible female. He treated Frankie really badly and left her high and dry for an American stick-insect called Stella when Ben was five and Carly was two. Things were horrible for a long time. Frankie lost lots of weight and hardly ever smiled but gradually things improved, especially when she met Owen (I introduced them – move over, Cilla, there ain't room for the two of us). Owen is the loveliest man on earth (apart from my Luke, of course . . . I am occasionally sentimental . . . just don't tell anybody). He treats her well, is a wonderful father to all the children, including Angelica (his sometimes wayward teenage daughter) and Baby Jack (their joint effort) as well as Ben and Carly. You can just see when you look at the two of them that they love each other completely (it would make you barf really). I couldn't think of anyone I would rather have accompanying me down the aisle but I also knew that she would have me looking like the proverbial blushing bride and dressed like a blancmange on the day. Somebody save me, please, I prayed.

"Ruby," Mr Reid, the college principal, had come into my office clutching a piece of paper and looking thoughtful, "I need to see you for your ten-year review at some stage this month. They've introduced a new policy which says that you have to go for a medical as well, so make an appointment as soon as you can."

I groaned. If there was anything I hated more than wedding-dress shopping (and there wasn't much, I can assure you) it was going to the doctor's. Nosy feckers that again loved to violate your person by shoving you around and asking intrusive questions, most of which I didn't know the answer to. Questions about family history were a constant source of aggravation for me and were always answered with the tick-box: *don't know.*

You may be wondering why I couldn't comment on my heritage or give information about my family's proneness to various health complaints. It's not because I wasn't interested or that I never bothered finding out – it was a lot simpler actually. I didn't know because I'm adopted.

I knew I might find out some useful information one day, though, and once I'd eliminated breast and bowel cancer, heart disease, diabetes and epilepsy, I was then going to ask the questions that had been bugging me for years. Who the hell was responsible for my greasy skin, why was my arse so big and worst of all whose wonky genes held the key to the most annoying, unmanageable reddest hair in the country?

I had always known that I was adopted. My daddy used to bounce me on his knee when I was little and tell me about how special I was and how long they had waited for me (personally I would have been looking for a refund once I hit puberty but that's a whole other story).

It used to crack me up when people commented that I looked like either of my parents but they soon shut their mouths when I enquired if they were being accompanied by a Labrador or were in need of a white stick. Honestly, I couldn't have been more different if I had tried. I have short sticky-outy mad red hair (which as I'm sure you've guessed will be mentioned a lot), am of average height, have hazel eyes and I suppose am quite striking in a weird sort of way. Frankie thinks I'm very attractive (her words not mine) and always comments that people give hairdressers hundreds of pounds to have my colouring but I'm not sold on the idea. I try to adhere to the philosophy that you have to make the best of what you're given but often feel I've been short-changed.

I felt a slight lump forming in my throat which always happened when I thought of my parents, my father in particular. My precious daddy died a few weeks after my eighteenth birthday and I can say that that was the day my heart broke in two. I loved my father dearly, idolised him completely and viewed him as a great friend. As a tomboy through and through, I had grown up in my father's shadow and loved watching football and boxing matches with him and talking about everything and anything and took his opinions very seriously (which wasn't easy for someone as strong-willed and stubborn as me).

He was only fifty-seven when my mother tried to get in our front door one evening and found that she couldn't get it opened properly. He was slumped behind it with his mouth contorted to one side. They said that he'd had a massive stroke and that it was a clot in his brain that had killed him. My mother was completely devastated but being the positive person that she is, she threw herself into her work as a cook in the local school until she had a nervous breakdown and was told she needed a break. It just so happened that at that time my great-aunt died and left Mammy some property in Donegal. So the suggestion of a break became a reality and she now lived there quite happily and ran her own home country store which provided the locals with home-made jam, chutneys, freshly baked bread and meat pies.

I hadn't actually visited my mother for a while but it was on my list of 'things to do' within the next few weeks as I didn't want to leave her out of the wedding arrangements (I'd gladly have handed them over if I had the choice and if Frankie had stopped calling me a wuss). I closed my eyes and let my mind drift to my mother's little cottage by the sea and suddenly the idea started to appeal to me very much. A few days of peace, quiet and home cooking sounded like a good plan and with that I lifted the phone, dialled the number and prepared to be interrogated for the next twenty minutes as to how I was looking after myself.

Chapter 3

"Sweet Jesus, you'd think they'd get these roads fixed," breathed Luke in annoyance as my beat-up Renault Clio slid into yet another pothole. Luke also possessed a set of wheels – commonly referred to as 'the good car' – so needless to say it was safely at home. When you come from the North of Ireland, the best way of knowing that you've crossed the border (aside from the signs written in Irish and the mad currency) is the way you no longer glide on tar but instead slip into moon-sized craters in the road. (Slight exaggeration but I do value the suspension in my car, such as it is.)

Some counties are famous for their football teams or their great landmarks or shopping attractions. Donegal, however, is most renowned for its breathtaking scenic beauty and the god-awful state of its feckin roads which must keep Kwik Fit in work all year round.

We were en route to spend the weekend with my mother and I was viewing the trip with both trepidation and excitement. I was always nervous about visiting Mammy, mostly because our time together was too short and I hated leaving her again, although having a mother on the other side of a land border can be useful sometimes. Poor Frankie would cheerfully put an entire body of water between her mother and herself, so fractious is their relationship, but for me the old saying must be true – that absence makes the heart grow fonder.

Smugglers' Bay was not a big place. It was hard to ascertain whether the title of 'village' could be applied to it or not. The main focal point of the area, apart from its beautiful scenery and sea inlets, was a little square which was bounded by a pub called the Smugglers' Inn, the local post office, a little grocer's shop and another establishment that sold fishing equipment and anything else that the proprietor could get his hands on, it would seem. Wellington boots were strung up at the door by a piece of string and buckets and spades were sold in net wrapping. Wall pictures, tools, luminous workmen's jackets, fishing tackle and dinner sets had all been placed in the window and made a most peculiar display.

"Let's go and have a look in the shop that sells everything in the world," I said. I had looked through the window several times on past visits but had never actually ventured inside and curiosity had got the better of me. "I'm sure I'll be able to get Mammy a treat for her sitting room in there."

"Your mother has enough ornaments gathering dust," Luke complained. "She'll just be happy to see you."

"I like bringing her things. It's not as if I'm there all the time. At least this way she knows I'm thinking of her and when she looks at her mounds of dust they'll remind her of me."

"Like she'd forget you in a hurry. Okay, okay," he relented as I glowered at him and got out of the car.

We were greeted by a very grumpy old man wearing slippers and a waistcoat who peered at us suspiciously over the top of his glasses when we entered his little shop, making the bell attachment on the door ring noisily.

"You break anything, you pay for it!" he barked as I lifted an ornamental cottage that took my fancy (or rather which I knew Mammy would like – painted china wasn't really my style). I decided to buy the cottage and also lifted a jar of boiled sweets and a magnetic notice for the fridge that said, '*I'm a lover not a fighter so I never fight the urge to eat.*' My mother is permanently on a diet so it's an in-joke at this stage.

"That'll be thirty euro," the old man said gruffly.

"'Pleeeeaasse,'" I said as Luke started to groan.

"Pardon?"

"'Please.' It's a word that most shop owners who are grateful for business use with their customers especially when they're charging extortionate prices for crappy old bits of tat."

I glared at him and he glared back until he turned away and I heard a gurgle emanating from his person. When he turned round to serve me again he was pulling his mouth into all sorts of strange shapes.

"Is there something wrong with you?" I enquired as the door opened again and a younger man came through.

"I got those fishing rods that you were after, Dad. Got a good bargain too. I think you'll be pleased."

I looked at the speaker and registered that he must be in his mid to late fifties. He was a rather cheerful man (which was a bloody miracle given his parentage – maybe he was adopted too) and looked like he took good care of himself and I supposed he was quite attractive and distinguished in an older-man sort of way. He smiled broadly at us after shouting out a greeting, which Luke responded to, and disappeared into the back of the shop.

I brought my attention back to the matter in hand as I waited for Mr Grouchy Slippers to exchange pleasantries before I paid him.

"Thirty euro, young lady," he said slowly. "Please."

"There you are," I answered in the same slow tone of voice. "Thank you."

We surveyed each other for a further while until I thought I might go cross-eyed and then I prepared to leave.

"Do call again," he said in a sarcastic tone.

"I would but I'd be afraid of catching whatever bug it is that turns you into a grumpy oul git," I muttered under my breath.

"What did you say?"

"Not a thing," I said cheerfully. "Have a nice day now."

Luke eyed me as I got into the car and then burst out laughing. "I'd say that's the first time he's cracked a smile in years, Ruby."

"Hmmph! God love that poor son of his. He must have his work cut out for him. It's a wonder he's as happy as he is. He must have a good woman putting a smile on his face in the background. It's surprising what a bit of action in the bedroom can do for your spirits."

We arrived at my mother's little cottage some ten minutes later. I sighed with contentment as the sun had come out and I knew it was going to be a glorious day. The cottage was situated in the grounds of a seaside manor which had been converted into a hotel by its late owner, Lord Bartley Monroe. No one was more shocked than Mammy when she discovered that it had been bequeathed to her in her aunt's will. My great-aunt Kate Kennedy (who had the wits to stay single) had been the housekeeper in the manor for almost fifty years and the cottage had been her living quarters. On her retirement, however, Bartley Monroe made the grand gesture of giving it to her in appreciation for her loyalty and hard work.

No one could have believed that the grounds of the Big House had hidden such a treasure as the cottage. It was quaint, the outside of it alone being truly charming, especially at this time of year – late spring. The mottled stone walls at either side of the building had trellises, one bearing bright beautiful yellow roses and the other fragrant wisteria. The cobbled back yard was covered in a carpet of cherry blossom as the tree, situated at the gate, had begun shedding its blooms, leaving the ground pink and soft and aromatic. A wooden summer seat with wrought-iron antique legs sat at the front of the house whilst a wooden garden gazebo occupied the back of the property.

On entering the house (if you could tear yourself away from the outside of it) you were greeted with bright and airy rooms which boasted antique furnishings and had a lovely old-world feel about them. In the sitting room there was an open fire in the centre of an ornamental stone fireplace, always flanked by a wicker basket of freshly dug turf. A dresser with plates propped side by side and cups hanging from hooks occupied another wall. There was also a sideboard that my mother had adorned with an arrangement of family photographs (mostly me in various states of gap-toothed youth with horrendous hair). With lace curtains at the window and an armchair to view the garden, Mammy could contentedly sit there for hours if she felt inclined – but sitting still for any length of time was alien to her.

There were two rather large bedrooms and an additional room which she used to house her impressive collection of books. There was also an old-fashioned bathroom with a free-standing bath and an airing cupboard. In short it was perfect and Mammy had aptly named it 'Ripples Retreat'.

"Hello, darlin'!" my mother shouted through an open kitchen window where she was snipping the stems off an assortment of flowers before arranging them in a vase.

My mother is a rather large woman. She maintains that it's the result of regularly trying out the produce she makes for her shop, although she has slimmed down a bit in recent years due to trying many mad and whacky diets (low calorie, low fat, light, I-can't-believe-it's-not, no bread, no dairy, no feckin fun . . . the list was endless). I thought she was cute and cuddly with a very pretty smile and had the loveliest blue eyes. She also had a twenty-four-carat heart and made an impression on everyone she met. With a raucous laugh and a witty repertoire, she was popular with her neighbours and had already made many friends in her new area. She looked particularly nice today as she was wearing what looked like a new dress and she also seemed to have had her hair done.

"I hope you're both hungry. I've made a chicken and ham pie and there's baked potatoes and salad as well. Come in and make yourselves comfortable and I'll fix you both a drink."

"Aaaaaahhhhh," Luke sighed contentedly as he took his first sip of chilled home-made lemonade. "People should forget about going further up the road to that hotel. They wouldn't get any better treatment there than you give here."

"Too bloody right," I announced loudly in response. "You'd get looked after better here any day of the week and you wouldn't have to pay through the nose for the privilege either."

"Mmm," Mammy said, looking thoughtful for a moment. "There's something funny going on up there at the minute and I have a bad feeling about it all. A Harry McQueen and his daughter – some sort of far-distant relatives of Lord Bartley but his only remaining ones – inherited the place from him when he died recently and took over the running of it. They may be relatives of a sort but they're nothing at all like the old man and they've been stirring up no end of trouble – half the staff have walked out and the ones that stayed are about to embark on a mutiny. They've been snooping around here too, asking all sorts of nosy questions."

"What?" I said, spitting out half my drink. "Who's been sniffing round you?"

"No one's been sniffing around me. But it seems the McQueens are interested in this place. I think they look at it and see euro signs."

"Why?"

"Well, think about it logically, Ruby. If I wasn't here they could rent this out as a summer cottage or let it to a permanent tenant or knock it down and turn it into something."

"Over my dead body or actually over theirs if they so much as dare to look at you in the wrong way! Who do they think they are, treating you like that?"

"*Rubbeee*," Mammy said in a warning tone (everyone speaks to me in that voice at some time or another. It's like something a lion tamer would use. I never understood why, though. I am perfectly calm. Honestly).

"We'll take a walk around there sometime soon and check it out," Luke said with a frown. "We'll not let anyone sniff anywhere they shouldn't be sniffing."

He was very fond of my mother and I knew he would go to the ends of the earth just to make sure she was happy.

"How are your mother and father doing these days, Luke?" Mammy asked whilst still bustling around fixing napkins and straightening the tablecloth.

I looked nervously at Luke who had stiffened and was doing a good impression of someone who had just had a poker shoved up their arse.

I slowly shook my head and tried to look inconspicuous but obviously didn't succeed as Luke was now glaring crossly at me. Mentioning the delightful (I'm joking) Mr and Mrs Reilly was enough to create this reaction in both Luke and his sister, Mandy, and was warranted when you took into account the fact that his father was the most irritating, smart-arsed man in the world and an alcoholic who had drunk the family savings. His mother was no better. She was a lush who would snog the face off a teenage boy given half the chance and chances had indeed presented themselves – there were enough embarrassing and cringe-worthy stories to prove it. They were both currently living in Spain (thank feck) and we tried not to mention them if at all possible. Although Luke tried to maintain contact with them, his gestures were not reciprocated, and they only ever rang if they wanted something – usually money. How they were surviving was anyone's guess and perhaps we were better off not knowing.

"They're fine, I think," Luke answered stiffly. "This looks like a lovely spread, Isobel. I can't wait for lunch."

Mammy took the change of subject as the hint it was intended to be and said no more whilst I finally started to breathe normally again.

I was looking round the room when I noticed that the dinner table had been set for five as opposed to three.

"Are we expecting guests?" I asked, surprised. "You never said anything. Who's coming over?"

"I'd like to introduce you to a good friend of mine, Ruby, and I thought that today might be as good a time as any."

"That's nice," I commented uncertainly.

"They'll be here shortly," Mammy said as she peered round the sitting-room curtain. "Actually they're here now."

She practically ran from the room (which is no mean feat for someone carrying an extra four stone in weight) and started to smooth down her hair and smack her lips in the hall mirror.

"God, this friend must be a complete glamour puss when Mammy's going to all this trouble," I laughed as Luke craned his neck to see who was coming in.

"Some glamour puss," Luke muttered a few seconds later but it was only when he threatened to go purple from trying not to laugh that I realised that something was amiss. I turned round and nearly suffered organ failure when I was faced with none other than my slipper-wearing sparring partner from earlier and his son who had his arm around my mother.

"Guess we know who's keeping the smile on his face now," Luke murmured.

My own mammy was a floozy with a thing for middle-aged Lotharios (note the way he had ceased being a distinguished older man now I'd got wind of the notion he might be porking my mother). How could she do this to me? How could she do this to Daddy and his memory?

Chapter 4

Everybody stood rooted to the spot with the exception of Old Man Humpy Hole who seemed to find the whole situation very amusing and kept sucking in his cheeks and making chewing movements as if he had something in his mouth. It would be my feckin boot if he wasn't careful.

Mammy was entirely oblivious to the uncomfortable situation I now found myself in and gaily looked at us all whilst making introductions.

"Ruby, I'd like you to meet Donal O'Donnell. He and I have been good friends for a while now but have become quite close. Donal, this is my daughter Ruby."

"And how close is close exactly?" I enquired through gritted teeth.

Mammy coloured and frowned, Donal shifted his feet and played with the button on his shirt and Luke grabbed me by the arm and steered me into the kitchen before I could say another word (which was rather unfortunate as I had quite a lot to say).

"Ruby, darling, you don't think you're overreacting just a tad, do you?" he whispered, still holding me in a vicelike grip.

"I never overreact, *darling*. I just tell it like it is and the way I see it my mother has obviously been carrying on with that cretin and not told me and all the time I've been fretting that she was putting a brave face on it but feeling lonely and still missing Daddy!"

"And you'd like her to continue being lonely and have her constantly hankering after your father, would you?"

Luke was looking at me sternly now and I was wondering why I was being cast in the role of bad guy. I wasn't the one putting myself about at an age where people shouldn't even be considering such things.

Mammy came bustling into the room two seconds later and fixed me with a penetrating glare.

"Ruby, when I said 'close' I didn't mean that I was having sex with him."

I jumped three foot in the air, covered my ears, closed my eyes and began to sing loudly whilst trying not to gag. My mother had just said the word 'sex' and was referring to it in the first person which indicated that she thought it was still a possibility (Yuck. Yuck. Yuck. Yuck . . . you get the general idea . . .).

When I opened my eyes my mother had gone back to her 'guests'.

"Is she always this highly strung?"

Now *he* (the devil incarnate who was leading my mother astray and having her talk dirty) was talking about me in the third person as if I wasn't living, breathing and contemplating blue murder within earshot.

"It's a bit shocking for her, I think. She was very close to her father. My Albert was a wonderful man, y'know, but eventually you learn to accept the things that are laid out for you and move on."

"Speaking of getting laid, Mammy," I said, making a big re-entrance, "your close friend and I met earlier when I stopped to get you these."

I thrust my bag of treats into her hands and proceeded to march out of the house but not before I heard the old goat in the sitting

22

room say, "Make sure and thank her now or you'll have her taking the nose off you for having no manners."

I roughly wiped my eyes and blew my nose. I had been so looking forward to seeing Mammy. Things weren't meant to turn out this way and I had a nasty feeling that I had gone too far and stuck my big DM boot in it as only I can. Daddy would soundly whip my ass if he knew and he'd be right. It was just that I still missed him so much and could never imagine my mother with anyone else. It seemed wrong and disrespectful to his memory although I knew instinctively that if Daddy could speak from beyond the grave he would want Mammy to be happy and have a companion of sorts. Who was I to dictate who my mother was friends with? She had the right to speak to and socialise with whoever she wanted and I had no right to interfere (note I was no longer referring to the 'S' word, for purely self-preservation reasons). I was still sitting out of view and cross-legged in the gazebo at the back of the cottage when Luke came to find me some time later.

"Are you all right?" he asked tentatively, handing me a glass of wine. "Courtesy of your mother. She thinks she's upset you and that you won't speak to her so I'm only the messenger and I'd appreciate not getting shot, thanks."

"I think if I had a gun I'd probably shoot myself as opposed to you," I muttered, feeling thoroughly ashamed of myself. "I suppose everyone thinks I'm a complete nutter now."

"I think it's more a proven fact and not just a mere thought, Ruby darling. You *are* a nutter."

"*Uuuugh*!" I wailed as I hung my head in my hands and wished for the millionth time that human beings had the capacity to kick their own arses as my big toe would be firmly jabbed in mine. Why was I so stupid and insensitive and so unlike my loving, giving, selfless mother? Well, the answer to that question was glaringly obvious, wasn't it? It was just another rogue gene making an entrance at an inopportune moment (and it wasn't the first time) and the sooner I knew what else was ahead of me the better.

"I'll be in, in a minute, Luke. Just leave me on my own until I decide what's the best way to take my foot out of my mouth without losing too much credibility in the process. I bet that old grouch is just loving the fact that I've made an eejit of myself after me trying to prove a point to him earlier."

"He's actually quite nice when you give him a chance and aren't chewing the head off him, although by his own admission he came tonight primarily to check your mother out and see that she was good enough for his son."

"He did fecking *what*?" I roared, sloshing wine round my feet and making Luke jump up in fright.

"Ruby, calm down before you go making another scene out of nothing. He thinks your mother is lovely. A brilliant cook. A lovely, kind and gentle person and an all-round lady. He made her blush – you should have seen her smiling in delight when he was complimenting her. Donal also seems like a good man and not the roving Casanova that you've branded him. Your mum and he only got friendly because they're both volunteers down in the Senior Citizens' Club and have been working together now for a few years. It's hardly a sordid affair and it's not as if they're hurting anybody."

"Thank you, Luke. I already felt like a prize twat but feel free to continue to make me feel worse if you must. I suppose it's no less than I deserve for getting the wrong end of the stick as usual."

"My fiery redhead . . ." Luke murmured as he kissed me on the forehead. "Always quick to jump to the defence of anyone who might be in trouble."

"Pity I don't pick people who are most in need of my fiery help then, isn't it?" I said miserably. "Tell Mammy I'll be in. Thank her for the wine and tell her I'll be eating humble pie as opposed to chicken pie for my dinner."

I sat for another few minutes and contemplated the future. Was

I always going to wonder what unfortunate traits I had inherited from the person responsible or was I going to do something constructive about it and find out once and for all? I was thirty-four and I knew that time was bound to be running out. I already had some information and would look at it again before I made any fixed decisions but something told me that before too long the answers might just be within my grasp.

Chapter 5

I awoke the following morning to the unfamiliar yet hypnotic sound of the sea. I could hear it swishing as it met with the rocks that were situated not far from where I lay, wrapped snugly in a hand-embroidered eiderdown, with Luke snoring gently beside me. I cringed when I thought of my behaviour the evening before. Mammy had been surprisingly forgiving, given the fact that I had embarrassed the life out of her, but she said she had expected me to react in a not altogether rational manner which is why she hadn't told me in advance. I had acted like a spoilt child who needed to be humoured and felt even worse after speaking to Frankie about it in a hushed late-night phone call the evening before.

"Maybe we should change your name to Angelica," she said, referring to her teenage stepdaughter, when I told her what I had done.

"Don't say that," I remonstrated. "Surely I'm not that bad."

"No, you're worse. You're an adult and you should know better. What do you want – for your mother to turn into a hermit because you don't like the idea of her having relations with anyone else? Your mother is one of the nicest people I've ever met, Ruby, and she deserves to be happy."

"Okay," I said contritely.

Frankie was the only one who could have got away with speaking to me so bluntly but, as our friendship was based on honesty and respect, we had always told each other exactly what we thought. Frankie also had first-hand experience of knowing what it's like trying to conduct a relationship under the strain of dealing with an unhappy daughter – the not very suitably named Angelica who once upon a time I could have cheerfully strangled for her troublesome behaviour towards Frankie's relationship with her father. (Pot calling kettle black, anyone?)

"I feel terrible. What should I do to make it up to her?"

"Why don't you suggest taking them out for a meal tonight? Your mammy would enjoy that. She's always cooking so it'll be a treat for her to have someone else doing the donkey work for a change."

"That's a good idea actually," I said thoughtfully. "I hear that the Smugglers' Inn has a new chef and changed their menu so maybe we'll go there – they say the hake is out of this world and the monkfish is great too, not that I like fish . . . don't worry, I'm just talking to myself."

"Yet another sign of your madness," Frankie commented. "It's understandable that you mightn't be thrilled, Rubes," she continued in a softer tone, "but you'll have to let go of your daddy some day."

My eyes had filled with tears. (I don't cry easily but any mention of my dear departed father had the capacity to turn me into a snotty wreck.)

"Angelica didn't fully accept me until she discovered the truth about her mother," Frankie went on, "and then I didn't seem so bad. We get on great these days. Still have the occasional row but at least I know it's just caused by two opinionated hormonally imbalanced women living under the same roof and not because she hates me with a vengeance."

I had come off the phone with plenty of food for thought. Perhaps if I did a bit of investigating of my own I wouldn't be so annoyed about my mother feeling the need to have a companion. Not that anyone could ever come close to Daddy in either her eyes or mine but maybe if I occupied myself with tracing my own background I wouldn't be so possessive – or rude to her potential suitors.

I already had all the information I needed hidden away in a box under my bed. Mammy didn't know it existed; not because I didn't want to tell her but more because I simply couldn't tell her. I had gone to the Births, Deaths and Marriages Registry Office in Belfast two days after my eighteenth birthday and had been thrilled to leave with the details I had gone for. They had given me my birth certificate which had named my birth mother and given her address but sadly my joy had been short-lived as less than a week later my daddy had died and I could have died with him from torturing myself with the notion that I had somehow been trying to replace him with someone who hadn't wanted me in the first place.

The pub was quiet when we first entered it. I had taken Frankie's advice and asked Mammy if I could treat them all to dinner as an apology for my behaviour the evening before. I had even made the ginormous, massive, selfless (really really hard) gesture of going back to the old ramshackle shop and personally asking Donal O'Donnell and his father Robbie (AKA Grumpy Slippers) if they would come too. My offer was accepted readily by Donal but I had to say please thirteen times before Robbie would even consider it. (I could just tell the old goat got a kick out of it.)

The Smugglers' Inn was beautiful inside with rustic designs and cosy seats that had been arranged to make the large stone fireplace the centre of the room and not the bar. A friendly barman ushered us close to the fire and brought us menus. It was obvious that the recently revised, allegedly improved menu specialised in seafood from the variety of fish that was available to the newly appointed chef, all freshly caught and prepared that day according to the promotional posters around the walls. I sighed and wrinkled my nose at the pungent aroma. (I hated fish with a passion. Karma at its best. Served me right, I supposed.) My mother on the other hand was thrilled and positively delighted (having obviously fallen off the diet wagon yet again) when the waiter asked her to choose her own delicacy and showed her a tank filled with fresh lobsters and crabs.

"Please tell me you're not seriously going to eat one of those," I said as I attempted to control my increasingly disturbed stomach whilst I watched the creatures as they wriggled around with claws and pincers snapping.

"She doesn't get out much, God love her," Mammy told the barman.

"I get out plenty," I snarled. "I just don't believe in feckin cannibalism."

"The young are so uncultured," Mammy said as she pointed to a large black lobster that was nestling to the front of the tank.

"And the old," I retorted, "are totally disgusting." I turned to the waiter. "I don't suppose you have a field of cows and an abattoir out the back, do you?"

"No, but I can tell you that our chef prepares his beef dishes with only the purest and finest Irish beef and that the chicken used in our menu comes from farms where the birds are fed corn and treated –"

"Like their own feckin children until it comes to electrocuting them and cutting their heads off. I'll have a vegetarian stir-fry, thanks."

Luke put his head in his hands and my mother raised her eyebrows and looked at me whilst Tweedle Dum and Tweedle Twat tried to keep straight faces.

"Whaaaaat?" I asked in exasperation when they all wouldn't stop gawping.

After several minutes of awkward silence the locals began to drop in, shouting their usual orders to the barman. They were a mixed bunch, with a crowd of young people dressed to go clubbing at one end of the bar and a group of elderly men in the corner, in for their evening constitutional, discussing the football results and the rising price of tobacco.

The barman brought us a tray of drinks and I knew that my eyes lit up when I spied my vodka and lime. "Lovely," I said, taking a mouthful and sighing in contentment.

"I do believe that came from your toes, Ruby," Mammy said, wryly.

(No kidding – when I was surrounded by complete eejits that liked nothing better than to indulge their caveman side by eating things that had been alive and happily running around a tank five seconds before they ate them.)

"Why don't we sit outside after the meal?" I said, for once trying to diplomatically change the subject. "Look, see the tables and chairs and oh my God . . . look at the sea!" I waved for the others to look out at where the tables were positioned to give the onlookers a perfect view of the ocean and the mountains beyond.

"It's breathtaking," whispered Luke to nobody in particular.

"It's one of our best features but I suppose we're used to it so we take it for granted now," said Donal.

"Yes, I suppose we're all guilty of doing that at one time or another," I answered quickly.

Mammy was scrutinising me so I thought I'd better make the effort to get on with her boyfriend (there was something so terribly wrong with referring to your sixty-year-old mother as being with her boyfriend).

"We've lived here all our lives but I count my blessings every day I'm alive for the beautiful surroundings I have on my doorstep," Robbie said quietly.

I looked at the old man, surprised that he could speak with such passion about anything. He seemed to read my mind, from the look he returned. Then he gruffly asked us to excuse him as he went outside, clutching an old pipe that was held together with a Band-Aid and looked in danger of falling apart.

"He won't get a new one," Donal said as he followed my line of vision. "My mother bought it for him the Christmas before she died and it might as well be made of gold as far as he's concerned. I know he can be a bit grumpy but that's more to do with his aching joints than it is anything else."

I looked out the window and felt my opinion of the elderly man soften slightly.

"Hmmm," Luke said, "some of us are grumpy most of the time lately and our joints are in perfect working order." His eyes were fixated on me for some reason as I took a large gulp of my drink and grinned back at him whilst letting the alcohol create a warm trail to my stomach and a more relaxed space in my head.

"Yes, I don't know where she gets it from," my mother answered him, jerking me into reality and bringing my thoughts back to what had constantly been in my head for the past few days.

"Somebody somewhere certainly has a lot to answer for," Luke said jokingly.

I smiled at them but knew that it wasn't reaching my eyes as I felt the familiar flutter of uncertainty penetrate my stomach muscles again. Was I doing the right thing? Should I even be contemplating this course of action at this moment in time or should I leave well enough alone and be content with my lot?

I looked over at my mother. She seemed very content. She was always happy but this was a different sort of happiness: the kind that is created by the merging of two people who gel together well. She had moved on so perhaps that was my cue to do likewise. I still had the crumpled birth certificate that had been obtained only a short time before my world fell apart and the only difference now was that there was nothing to stop me from pursuing the intentions I'd had all those years ago.

Chapter 6

Apparently I had to be undressed and put to bed that night. My mother and Luke discovered (in no uncertain terms) that copious amounts of vodka and a delicate mind were not a good combination. In the space of three hours I had joked, laughed, been loud and raucous then quiet and depressed, before finally bursting into floods of tears and telling anyone who would listen that I wanted my mammy before demanding to know if anyone knew 'Sheena'.

"And I was there all the time," Mammy said as she relayed the details of my (yet again) embarrassing behaviour the next day.

At this rate it would be a long time before I would be invited back for another trip. In fact the Smugglers' Inn would probably put up a poster advising people not to approach me as I was dangerous and I would most likely be banned from setting foot in the place in future.

"Funny the way you want your mammy when you're upset, isn't it? It's just a good job I was on hand to give you all the hugs you needed."

I cringed as I listened but didn't argue. I had a strange suspicion that I had indeed wanted my 'mammy' but that it mightn't have been the one sitting in front of me now.

"And you kept saying someone's name. I couldn't make it out but you went on and on."

"Yes, it sounded like Sheena," Luke said. "Or maybe it was Justina."

"Or Helena. Do we know anybody called that?" Mammy asked, her face frowning in concentration. "I don't think I do. In fact, I don't think I've ever met anybody called Helena."

At that point I stood up abruptly (too abruptly as it happened) and promptly was sick exactly where I stood.

"Well, that's just feckin charming," Luke said as he surveyed me in horror.

"That's the Demon Drink for you," Mammy said. "Of course there wouldn't be a problem if people took it in moderation and didn't behave like animals."

By 'people' I think my mother was referring to me and the reference to animals was quite fitting as I was currently lying on the floor wailing like a cow in labour and wondering how the hell I was ever going to make the journey home to Swiftstown in time to go to work in the morning.

"Put her back in bed, Luke. I'll clean the mess – it's a good job I'm her mother or I'd find it very difficult."

I was finding it feckin difficult. What was with the two-hundred-and-forty-four reminders that she was my mother today? Was the woman telepathic? I wouldn't be surprised actually. I had often thought it was quite funny really but Mammy was always brilliant at knowing when there was something wrong. She always said that even though we weren't related by blood I was like an open book to her. Daddy had been good at assessing my moods as well and I always felt a million times better after talking things through with him.

Oh God, now I was bawling like a banshee and making Mammy and Luke regard each other in concern and dismay.

"I didn't know whether you'd approve of my having a male friend or not, Ruby, but I never expected you to carry on like this. Honestly, you'd think I was about to frogmarch him up the aisle and demand that you call him 'Daddy'."

I stopped howling for long enough to laugh (my emotions were changing at a rate of knots and I wasn't sure if it was due to my hangover or the state of my very confused mind) at the thought of calling Donal O'Donnell 'Daddy'. Dear God, it was more than I could bear to think about!

"Now she's laughing." It was more of a statement than a question and Luke was starting to look very pissed off.

"I'm sorry. It's just the thought of calling Donal O'Donnell 'Daddy'."

"What's the matter with him?" Mammy demanded, hands on hips.

"Nothing's the matter with him, Mammy. Look, we got off on the wrong foot but I think he's quite nice." I was loath to admit that I actually meant this and wasn't saying it to placate her. He was growing on me. A bit like fungus.

Mammy didn't look convinced and the two of them continued to glare at me.

"I'm going to need sunglasses soon if you two don't stop flashing me looks," I said peevishly. "I just had an off-night. I've a lot in my head."

Mammy threw her hands up in the air before pinching Luke on the arm. "I should have realised it sooner. It's the wedding. She's stressed out because of the wedding."

I feckin well was not. I couldn't give a stuff.

"I'm her mother. I was a bride. I should have realised sooner. My poor girl is about to take the ultimate step and I haven't even asked her about it. I've been very selfish. Can you ever forgive me, Ruby?"

"Forgive you for what exactly, Mother? For not bending my ear about wedding-dress designers, whether or not I wear a veil and what colour of flowers may or may not clash with my hair? It's okay. Believe me, when I have Frankie within shouting distance every day it's a welcome relief. Although I do want you to be involved."

"Of course I'll be involved, darling. You're my only daughter. How often does one get to be Mother of the Bride?"

Could she possibly mention that she was my mother any more in the space of an hour? And could I behave any more like a neurotic eejit who had totally lost the plot? Laughing and being sick after leaving the bar dry of alcohol was one thing. But I did not do crying and I had been doing an awful lot of that and there really was no excuse for it. The sooner I got as far away from Smugglers' Bay as possible the better.

"Luke, let's go home," I said urgently. "I need to get out of here."

"And have you barfing at every bump in the road? I think not," he said with resolve. "I think we'll wait until your stomach is truly calm and then there'll be less reason for me to be worried that I might need to get the car upholstery refurbished tomorrow."

"You won't. I promise," I said flatly but I knew when I was beat. He wasn't going to budge and it would be an eternity before I could get home to my own cosy bed and even longer before I could lay my hands on the papers containing the information which had been the source of such drunken soul-searching the night before.

Chapter 7

"Good time?" Frankie asked me the next morning as I took a huge bite of my bacon buttie in the college canteen.

"Yeah, bloody brilliant," I muttered, not wanting to be rude but dying not to talk about the whole saga again for the umpteenth time. Luke had already performed several detailed post mortems on the weekend's events and was still wondering why I'd turned into a psychopathic emotional wreck.

"Was it that bad? What's he like then?"

"Who?"

"Your mother's . . . your mother's male . . . boy . . . her new friend," Frankie faltered lamely.

"My mother's new bit on the side, fancy piece, toy boy or whatever name you wish to give him, is all right as it happens. I'm not over the moon but, as you all keep telling me, it's not fair that she should be on her own. I reckon he's not the worst she could have and he seems to like her a lot so who am I to say anything?"

"You're her daughter and you usually have plenty to say, with or without permission," Frankie grinned.

"I think I said rather too much on Friday night when I was sober and just semi-mad and I *know* I said far too much on Saturday night when I was steaming drunk and my mouth was being controlled by an emotionally unstable Russian answering to the name Vladivar."

Frankie raised her eyes to heaven. "So what is the actual problem, Rubes? Are you annoyed because you think she's forgotten about your daddy or did the whole thing just shock you so much that you reacted really badly? Maybe she should have warned you that you'd be having company and then you'd have had time to compose yourself."

"She was afraid I'd react like a lunatic so she didn't tell me," I said matter-of-factly.

"Well, that worked out well for her then, didn't it?" Frankie said, raising her eyebrows.

"Can we please change the subject?" I pleaded.

"When are we going to see the wedding dressmaker?"

"Can we please change the subject again?"

"No, we can not. This is something you need to be thinking about now, Ruby. You have no idea how much there is to do. You're getting married in eleven months' time and there is so much to organise. Don't you care?"

I thought about the question and decided that I did care because I loved Luke and wanted to marry him but that all the trimmings were just a pain in the arse I could cheerfully do without, but would attend to because I knew they were important to Frankie and my mother and Luke. I knew that I was in a minority as most girls my age had spent their childhoods dreaming of a white wedding and a prince on a white horse but, while they were doing that, I was whipping the local princes' arses at pool and running rings round them on the football pitch.

"Earth to Ruby! Hello! Don't you care?"

I sighed. Frankie could be relentless.

"Yes, I care, Frankie. It's just that all the preparation is so much less important than the act of getting married itself. I'm delighted that Luke wants me and I'm going along with the rest of the palaver just to keep everyone else happy. I'd cheerfully get married in my jeans in a dawn ceremony where nobody else could see me just as long as I knew Luke was going to turn up."

Frankie looked misty-eyed and I was terrified that she was about to start simpering on me and go all soppy. "That's so nice, Ruby. Luke is very lucky."

Is he feck? God help him.

When I got home that evening Luke seemed quiet and pensive and I caught him studying me intently when he thought I wasn't looking.

"Is there something the matter?" I asked eventually as I felt disconcerted by his constant staring.

"I could ask the same question, love," he said. "Please tell me what's wrong and be honest about it. I don't want to make any more plans if you're having second thoughts."

"Second thoughts about what and what exactly are you planning?" I answered in confusion.

"Ruby, stop trying to be coy. I know when someone is in turmoil. I've been watching you all weekend and you haven't been yourself at all and I don't think that it's all to do with your mother's new boyfriend."

"I wish everyone would stop calling him that," I grumbled. "People have boyfriends at the respectable age of seventeen. At sixty they have –"

"Gentleman friends," Luke finished for me.

"Have I said that before?"

"Once or twice," Luke said, looking strained.

"There's nothing wrong with me," I snapped. "Stop looking at me like that. I've just got things on my mind."

"Do you want me to guess?" Luke enquired.

"Guess what?"

"What's on your goddamned fecking mind!" he bellowed in bad temper.

"Don't shout at me. I'm really confused."

"Should we put the wedding off for a while? Do you need more

38

time or do you want to forget about it altogether? We were happy enough before I proposed so maybe we should just go back to living in sin without the rings."

I felt the blood drain from my face, only to come rushing back in a flush from my toes up. I felt positively sick and couldn't believe what I was hearing.

"Is that how you feel?" I asked miserably, not able to meet his gaze. "Have you felt like this for long?"

Luke began to pace around like a caged lion (a caged lion on speed, I might add).

"You drive me nuts, Ruby. You have the most unfortunate habit of picking things up the wrong way and you do it every time."

"So you *have* felt like this for ages and I've obviously been too thick to notice."

Luke wheeled around and I thought for a terrible minute that he might have a tantrum which involved squealing and shouting and much stamping of feet.

"I love you, you silly cow, but I'm starting to think that you don't feel the same way about me. You've been totally preoccupied for days and you're hiding something from me. I'm not stupid, y'know."

The penny (a penny the size of a mortar-bomb) just dropped. Straight onto my head. I didn't think I had been that obvious but being totally transparent was obviously another 'family' attribute.

"I haven't been thinking about you or making plans to leave you, Luke, you great eejit. That's the last thing I'd ever want to do."

Relief flooded his face. "Care to share what you have been thinking about then? Please. I've been so worried."

I was torn. Torn between wanting to put Luke at ease and not wanting to expose the muddled thoughts that had been whirring around aimlessly in my head. Luke knew I was adopted but, as I had always been blasé about the fact, he had no idea of what I was feeling at the minute and I didn't want him thinking that I was doing it out of spite just because Mammy seemed to have moved on. In a funny way Mammy's actions had forced me to think about it again but I had always known in my heart that it would come back to haunt me some day. Maybe some people could sail through life without ever needing their existence to be acknowledged by the people who brought them into the world but I wasn't one of them. If I'm honest, I was also slightly afraid that Luke might accuse me of being incredibly greedy. Here I was with a mother who loved me unconditionally no matter what I did or how I embarrassed her, even though I wasn't her own flesh and blood, yet Luke's parents who had given birth to him seemingly couldn't give a damn, preferring to pickle themselves in beer on the Mediterranean.

"Please," he repeated, now kneeling in front of me and holding both my hands.

"Oh Luke, how could you ever think I could bear to be without you? If I tell you, will you promise not to be judgemental or try and talk me out of it?"

"Whatever you want, love, but make it quick as I'm getting a dead leg down here."

I pulled him up to his feet, gave him a hug and prepared to bare my soul. (God, I hated being a girl sometimes.)

Chapter 8

We were still sitting on the living-room floor at two o'clock the following morning, surrounded by a growing collection of coffee-stained mugs. I had to admit (begrudgingly, as I hated conversations which involved my feelings) that I felt better and more determined than ever after talking to Luke about what had been troubling me. He was very supportive and going to help me in whatever way he could.

"One mother-in-law isn't enough. Why have one when you could have two?" he remarked, once I had explained the situation.

"Hold on a minute, Luke!" I said fiercely. "Just because I'm going to search for her doesn't mean that she'll want to know me or that I'm going to bloody start calling her 'Mammy' either. If she had wanted that title she should have thought harder about her actions all those years ago. Besides, Isobel is and always will be my mother. We mightn't be related by blood but she's the one who bandaged my knees, tucked me up in bed, cuddled me and kicked my arse when I needed it. She is irreplaceable. This isn't about finding a new mother. This is simply an exercise in getting answers once and for all."

I took a deep breath and continued to finger the document in my hand. Its contents had been superimposed in my head for many years and I didn't have to look at it to see what was written on the parchment-type paper in bold black ink.

Surname:	*Delaney*
Name:	*Ruby Rose*
Sex:	*Female*
Date of Birth:	*16 December 1975*
District of Birth:	*Belfast*
Place of Birth:	*Royal Maternity Hospital*
Father:	*Unknown*
Surname:	_
Name:	_
Occupation:	_
Mother:	
Surname:	*Delaney*
Name:	*Georgina Elspeth*
Address:	*Mulroy Cove*
	Kerrycar
	Co Donegal
Informant Qualification:	*Mother*
Address:	*As above*
Signature:	Georgina Delaney

Date of Registration: 17 December 1975

I continued to hold the piece of paper to my chest and allowed my mind to wander back to the day when I had been given the information all those years ago.

Belfast had presented quite a colourful picture with its bizarrely dressed students, black taxis, white-collar workers and never-ceasing sirens, and I'd stared in amazement at all the people and the sheer volume of traffic in the city (you'd never guess I was a country hick who only got out occasionally, would you?).

On arriving at my destination (after three hours as I had got lost six times) I had surveyed the building before entering it, knowing that it could provide me with vital information. *Registry of Births, Deaths and Marriages*, the sign said.

The ageing security guard looked at me through the glass doors and nodded at me to approach.

"It's a cold day for standin' about, love," he had said in a fatherly voice which was accompanied by a broad Belfast accent. "Come in and sit down. The girls'll be back from lunch shortly."

Ruby Delaney . . . Ruby Delaney . . . Ruby Delaney . . . I repeated the name like a personal mantra over and over again in my head until I was called forward. My birth mother had given me the name Ruby and as it was the first and probably last thing she ever gave me, my adoptive parents had explained that they didn't want to take it from me or change it in any way. They also knew 'her' surname and as I was in possession of a great pair of ears which sprang to attention if the subject was mentioned, it wasn't too long before I overheard a hushed conversation which told me that her second name was Delaney and a plan had formed in my head that would lead me to finding out more.

"Hi there, can I help you?" The lady behind the counter looked expectantly at me.

Shit! This was it. There was no going back.

Tentatively (not a trait I displayed often) I approached the desk. "I was wondering if I could get a full copy of my long birth certificate, please."

"No problem, love, what's the name?"

"Ruby Delaney."

I had looked around me at that point to ensure that I hadn't been found out. However, everyone seemed to be going about their business as usual unperturbed (even though I had just told a ginormous lie and could now be on Northern Ireland's most-wanted list for identity fraud).

"Date of birth?"

"The 16th of December, 1975."

"Right, love. It'll be a few minutes. That'll be ten pounds, please," the assistant said pleasantly.

I wondered if this lady realised that this could be the most important ten pounds she would ever receive or indeed that I might ever spend. I could hardly contain my curiosity for long enough to extract the crisp note, fresh from the bank machine for this purpose, from my purse.

"Thanks a million," I whispered and I really meant it. One million pounds would not be too much to pay for the secrets which were about to be revealed. I had thought for a split second about the impact of my actions and how life-shattering (shit-splattering) they could be for God knows how many people but then shrugged my shoulders. This was a situation not of my making. I hadn't asked to be born (and if I had, I would have asked to be a normal regular child born into a family, preferably with the parents I had, who wanted me, and not a feckin outcast with mad hair).

I waited to look until I had got back out into the street. I went to a thick window ledge and used it as a support as I hugged the sealed envelope to my chest. Slowly and carefully I opened the flap, trying not to tear the wrapping which encased the information I had been wondering about for so long.

I stared at the page so hard that the print began to blur with the eyestrain. I had fantasised about what this moment would be like. They were only words but, for me, they represented years of unanswered questions which finally might be put to rest.

Of course, I already had an adoptive birth certificate which stated that Albert and Isobel were my parents. It wasn't that I had ever wanted to replace them, it was just that I wanted to know 'why'. Why had I been given up? Why could she not keep me? Why did she not want me?

"You look like you're miles away," Luke said as he stood up and stretched his legs.

"I was," I murmured. "I just got caught in a time warp."

"Come to bed, love," he said gently. "Tomorrow is a new day and we can make plans."

"Luke, are you angry with me?"

He looked perplexed and confused. "Ruby, why on earth would I be angry? I love you and what you're going through is terrible."

"You haven't had it easy yourself," I muttered with one eye shut, willing him not to react badly which normally happened when his parents were mentioned.

"Ahhhh," he said slowly. "You thought I'd be annoyed because my parents are a waste of space who shouldn't have had children they quite obviously didn't want."

I winced and continued to look at him with one eye.

He took my face in his hands and kissed me tenderly on the nose. "Ruby, I love the fact that you care enough to want to find out and will support you every step of the way. As for my parents, they've made their choices and it's better that they are where they are and not annoying the rest of us here. It might be useful if you were to have two mothers – perhaps you could lend me one as a surrogate."

It saddened me to hear him talking this way and my heart went out to him and it must have showed in my expression.

"Ruby, stop dwelling on it. I try not to. I hate talking about it as it only serves to remind me what I'm missing. It still hurts but, if there's one thing I've learnt in life, it's that if you don't strive to make the best of things yourself no one else will do it for you. You're my family now and I'm so thankful that I have you in my life every day."

He kissed me and I sighed with contentment and prepared to go to bed and fall into the deepest sleep I'd had all week.

Chapter 9

"Hey, Rubes." Owen grinned at me and handed me a mug of coffee and put a packet of my favourite chocolate-mint biscuits at my feet.

"Perhaps I shouldn't be tempting you," he said, eyes twinkling in amusement. "You're probably on a diet like all other brides-to-be."

"Sure I am," I proclaimed before ripping the green and silver paper off one and taking a big bite.

Owen (our best-man-to-be) was tall and good-looking with dark hair and glasses and I always called him Clark Kent (Superman minus the manky Y-fronts) . . . long story that thankfully doesn't involve him jumping off any wardrobes but rather refers to the fact that he is in fact a 'super man' who just happens to wear glasses and would swallow kryptonite to make Frankie happy, so great is his love for her.

He left and went outside and I looked towards Frankie who was still apparently trying to collect her thoughts on what I had told her moments before. I thought that since talking to Luke had felt so good, I might as well confide in my best friend as well but was now not so sure I had done the right thing.

Frankie stared at me in the manner of a goldfish, opening and closing her mouth at rapid speed.

"Why are you looking at me like that? It's no big deal," I said in exasperation when she continued to move her mouth round but made no comment.

"Why now?" she said eventually. "You have so much to do in the next few months that I'm just worried that you're taking on too much and that you'll stress yourself out. May I remind you that in less than eleven months you'll be –"

"Mention the word 'wedding' and you die. Instantly," I growled. "The world isn't going to stop turning just because I'm taking a dander up the aisle, y'know. I've made up my mind and that's it."

"Oh God, well, that *is* it then," she sighed. "I'll help whatever way I can, Ruby, but you do realise that this mightn't have a fairytale ending?"

"Yes, I do, Frankie. I'm not expecting to hear Cilla singing 'Surprise Surprise' in the background, whilst tearfully hugging my long-lost mother in front of an audience." (I never watched that show . . . I only knew because other people told me . . . . really . . .)

"But you might find out things you don't want to know," she continued in a voice that was sounding increasingly desperate.

"Frankie –"

"Okay. Okay. Your mind's made up 'and that's it'," she mimicked me in a growling voice.

We were continuing to sip our coffee in companionable silence when Angelica (stepdaughter with an attitude) sailed passed us.

"Hi, Ruby. I hear you're getting one of these," she said with a nod in Frankie's direction. "An evil step-parent, I mean," she clarified.

I was about to say something hotly in defence of my friend when I noticed that Frankie was looking at her in quite a tender and un-evil-step-parent-like fashion so I held my tongue.

"*Mwhah ha ha ha ha!*" Frankie cackled in her best evil-stepmother laugh.

I looked on and thought about the journey Frankie and Angelica had been on. They had gone from literally detesting the sight of each other, with lots of bumps along the way, to getting on not too badly, but they'd had one hell of a journey. (I'll not give you the intimate details as it would take far too long, but it makes one hell of a story.) If Oprah was ever having a quiet day, she should come looking for this pair as her ratings would go through the roof.

I heard excited giggling outside and knew that it signalled the arrival of Ben and Carly who had just been dropped off from the after-school club by a local bus.

"Auntie Ruby!" Carly squealed in delight, enveloping me in a hug and making my heart soar.

"How's my favourite goddaughter?" I asked whilst smoothing down her hair which had come loose from its pony-tail. "Want to look in my bag and see if there's anything there for you?"

She found the sweets I had brought for her and threw a second packet towards Ben when he entered the room. He grinned and put up his thumb in thanks as opposed to hugging me, as apparently it was no longer the cool thing to do.

"Excuse me. Just because Auntie Ruby's here doesn't mean you have to ignore me completely," Frankie said, feigning a wounded tone of voice. "Honestly, Rubes, you have those two spoilt rotten."

"As I am entitled to do as their honorary aunt," I said, smiling fondly at the two children I had nursed as babies, watched growing up and baby-sat.

Angelica moved away from the sofa and could be seen from the sitting-room window going outside and holding out her arms to Baby Jack who was playing in the garden under the watchful eye of Owen who was cleaning his lawnmower. The little boy dropped what he was doing and instantly ran to her, shouting her name as she scooped him up and blew raspberries on his tummy.

"I know," Frankie said as she followed my gaze to the scene outside.

"You know what?" I asked.

"You have the same look on your face as my mother has when she watches them in action. Jack has brought joy to our family in so many ways. He's a little miracle but I suppose his arrival helped Angelica feel that she fitted in and was part of things. It's probably all to do with that old adage about blood being thicker than water."

48

"Tell me about it," I said ruefully.

"Oh shit, Ruby, I'm sorry," Frankie said, shaking her head and clasping her hand over her mouth. "Now is not a good time for me to be talking about blood links, is it?"

"And since when have I been an uber-sensitive female, Frankie? I may be a little confused but don't be expecting any tears –" (what happens in Donegal stays in Donegal . . . *ahem!*) "– or high drama."

"Spoilsport!" Frankie retorted.

Jack bounded into the room, closely followed by Angelica who was on her knees and growling like a dog.

"Wuby, help! Wuby, help!" he panted as he climbed up my leg and hid in my shoulder.

"I'm going to feed you to the big dog," I said as he wrapped his plump arms around my neck and continued to giggle. He smelt of baby and outside and I loved him as if he was my own (minus the pain, the stretch-marks and the nine months without drink).

As I held Jack and he continued to bury his little head in my neck, I was suddenly overcome with a sense of sadness. Partly for myself and partly for Georgina (my wayward birth mother) as I had obviously never nuzzled her neck and she had never had the opportunity to feel the closeness to me that I had for Jack even though he wasn't my own. Why? It was my favourite word of the moment. (I felt like a nosy three-year-old always asking questions.)

"I didn't know that Luke was meeting you here," Frankie said as we heard the sound of a car on the driveway outside.

"He wasn't," I said as I jumped up, still holding Jack, to look out the large sitting-room bay window. "I thought he was taking photographs at the local council offices today. He must have finished up early."

"Were you expecting company?" Frankie asked as we saw that he wasn't on his own.

He had swung the car around and parked at such an angle that his passenger was blocked from view. All that was visible was the top of someone's head.

"Maybe Mandy has come to stay with you."

"Oh, please don't say that. There's only so much gossip-magazine talk I can take and it's minuscule at the best of times. I couldn't give a feck about the celebrities and who they're snogging or divorcing even if most of them do both at the same time."

Mandy was Luke's sister. There was a lot of history between us. The shortened version basically is that we used to loathe the sight of one another when we worked together in Redmond College. She was the receptionist and resident office gossip and as gossip (especially if it centred around me) was a pet hate of mine, we really didn't see eye to eye at all. She also made the fatal error of involving Frankie in one of her stories (nearly causing her to lose her job in the process) and to say that I was psychotic and baying for blood would be an understatement. I had been plotting to murder her but then she introduced me to Luke (who had also been involved and was also nearly killed). And then I discovered that I rather liked him. I accompanied him to a pub quiz one night, wore a Wonder Bra, answered feck all right and we had a snog and a bag of chips on the way home and the rest as they say is history!

"Is Mandy still writing that column for the magazine?" Frankie asked.

"'Tinseltown Titbits'," Angelica said, joining us at the window.

"That's the one," I agreed. "Best gossip columnist they've ever had by all accounts. What is Luke doing? Why is he not getting out of the car?"

After what seemed like an eternity Luke eventually emerged but his cohort remained in the passenger seat.

"Hi, love," said Luke as I opened the front door for him.

"Who's with you?" I asked, craning my neck and squinting past him at the car.

"It's a surprise for you," he answered. "Look, please don't be mad at me, Ruby. I know that perhaps I shouldn't have meddled but I know how much this means to you so I couldn't help myself. I've been making a few enquiries over the past few days and have found the answer to all your problems. This will make life so much easier and then we can just get on with making our plans about the other important event."

50

Frankie's hand had just flown to her mouth and I guessed that she must be thinking the same as I was. Luke had studied the birth certificate again. He must have done it whilst I was either sleeping or at work and then he had done something amazing. Something so amazing that my birth mother was now sitting in his car preparing to meet me. I was rather flummoxed as I had been looking forward to conducting my own search and wasn't prepared for such an on-the-spot meeting but looking at Luke's hopeful face and the way he was staring at me made me forgive him instantly.

"Have I told you lately that I love you?" I said in a rare public display of affection before I threw my arms round his neck.

"Whoa! You don't even know what it is yet!"

"I know I don't but I can guess. Let me do it. Let me go out and say hello to this person who's going to answer all my questions and put my mind at rest," I said, playing along with his little game of hinting but not naming the surprise.

"Okay," Luke said. "Okay, Ruby. You do that. I'll wait here as I know it will be something of an emotional moment for you. But let me give you a word of warning. The person in question is eccentric to say the least."

Why didn't that surprise me? I stepped out onto the drive.

Luke, Frankie and Angelica all looked like they were going to fall through the window as they were pressing against it so much in their efforts to get a first sighting of me meeting my natural mother. Even Owen had joined them, cradling Jack in his arms.

It was something of a shock, therefore, when I approached the car and found a man with blonde mullet-style spiky hair in a bright pink T-shirt talking rapidly into the mobile phone he held in one hand whilst waving the other hand around him in a wild and demonstrative fashion.

As soon as he spotted me he got very excited and opened the door so that I could hear the tail end of his conversation.

"Gotta go, dawling! Talk soon. Hugs!"

Then he got out of the car at which point I nearly collapsed with blinding shock. As well as the pink top he was wearing a technicolour sarong over turquoise baggy trousers which were elasticated at the ankle. His feet were encased in gladiator sandals and his toes were sporting the most luminous nail-art I had ever seen. He looked at me appreciatively before bowing in front of me with a flourish.

"Gabriel Sullivan," he announced in a strange accent which was a mixture of somewhere in Southern Ireland, somewhere in England and somewhere in a certain part of Soho if his current appearance and stance of one leg crossed over the other whilst holding his waist was anything to go by.

I had never been so confused in all my life. Had my mother had a sex change? Was Georgina now a very camp George? Was this a joke?

I looked back at the window in bewilderment and saw that Frankie had her head buried in Owen's shoulder whilst Angelica seemed to be in hysterics with Luke watching her with a worried expression.

"Hello," I said, unsure of how to continue the conversation.

"Ah, the beautiful bride!" he said with a sway of his hips which I found quite nauseating.

Who *was* this person? My mother? An aunt and/or uncle?

"Luke told you then," I said.

"Oh yes. He's filled me in on everything I need to know about you, my dawling, and I know that we're going to get along just fine."

"Really?" I said, feeling annoyed (it wasn't up to Luke to tell my story – it was up to me).

He or 'she' or 'heshe' came a step closer and instinctively I stepped back.

"You're going to have to learn to trust me," he said. "I don't bite, you know, or at least not on the first meeting." He laughed manically at his own joke whilst I looked for signs of recognition and found none (thank feck, I thought – I must look like my mother . . . father, I mean . . . I think . . . feck, maybe this *was* my father – no longer 'unknown'?).

"I suppose so," I muttered. "I'd like to sit down properly and get some answers. I have a lot of questions as I'm sure you can imagine."

"And I have all the answers you need, honey," he said. "Between us we'll give you a day to remember. Here's my business card just in case any of your friends need my services."

Services? Friends? Business card? What the hell was he talking about? I took the card and turned it over, and as I read it all became clear, and as it became clear a red mist descended in front of my eyes.

"Luke!" I roared. "Get your arse out here now!"

The pink creation suddenly seemed unsure of himself and started to retreat back to the car.

"Good idea, mate," I snarled. "Cause even if you don't bite on the first meeting I feckin do. *Luuuuuuuuuuuuuke!*"

Luke appeared at the door, looking anxious as well he might, the stupid bollocks.

"Out. Here. Now," I repeated through gritted teeth whilst pointing at a spot on the ground next to me.

"Ruby, please," he began.

"What is this?" I asked pointing at the car whose occupant now seemed to be cowering in the passenger seat, his earlier bravado in abeyance.

"It's a surprise," Luke said weakly. "Ta – *da!*"

"That is not a surprise, Luke. That is a freak dressed in a fluorescent shirt who suddenly thinks he has something to do with my wedding. Why is that? What have you done?"

"I was only trying to help," he said, looking huffy. "I thought it would take the pressure off you so that you could concentrate on finding your mother."

"What pressure, Luke? Did it appear to you that I was in any way stressed over our wedding? Did I look at all perturbed or as if I couldn't handle things? I might look as if I couldn't give a shit, which I don't incidentally, about all the fluff but if I *was* interested I think I could manage without his, her, heshe's help!"

Frankie appeared at that stage and held her hands up as I opened my mouth to continue my speech and maintain the moral high ground (and scare the shite out of the twerp in the car).

"This is all my fault," she said. "I made a suggestion to Luke that he should get you a wedding planner the day we went shopping and you didn't get a dress. I was only joking at the time but, now that he's done it, I think it's a wonderful idea. The perfect gift that most girls could only dream of."

"I am not most girls, Frankie. I am me. Actually, scrap that statement because I don't know who I am any more or where I've come from for that matter."

Yeah, sure I was upset that Luke thought I was incapable of planning my own wedding but I was more annoyed at the fact that my hopes had been raised and then cruelly dashed. I had walked across Frankie's gravelled driveway to meet my birth mother (okay, maybe I had got a tad carried away) but instead had met someone who wouldn't have looked out of place in a grass skirt with a pineapple on his head.

"Ruby," Frankie said as she came towards me with arms outstretched whilst Luke watched us, looking forlorn, and Angelica looked curiously at the pink spectacle in the car.

"I don't think so," I said as I walked away.

Usually Frankie's hugs got a more receptive response (even though I am not a touchy-feely person). On this occasion her arms were not well received, however, as she was standing in the enemy camp by trying to talk me into even contemplating having my wedding hijacked by a colour-blind eejit who had walked straight off the set of *Priscilla Queen of the Desert*.

The car door opened and the said eejit appeared again, looking less confident than before but still swaggering.

"I'm sorry, Ruby, I think there has been a bit of a communication problem and I seem to have borne the brunt of it. Your husband-to-be has already hired me to help him plan your wedding."

"Consider yourself un-hired then," I snapped.

"Not as easy as that, sweetie" (the feckwit had just called me 'sweetie'). He fumbled in his pocket and produced a sheet of paper and started to wave it in front of me. "You see, the contract has been signed and in order to cancel it the client needs to pay me a sum of money upfront."

"So you're telling me that he signed a contract with you today and that, now that it's several hours old and I think you're a tosspot, we can't all go our separate ways?"

"That's about the height of it. Apart from your comment referring to me as a tosspot because I'm not." He looked suddenly angry (or as angry as you can look dressed like a packet of Opal Fruits).

"How much?" I demanded.

"Two thousand pounds."

I heard several people gasp and although I wasn't sure I think I was one of them.

"Say that again," I said, walking towards him and wishing I had a Kalashnikov rifle and a magazine of ammunition.

"It's written here in black and white and has been witnessed by a solicitor. Look, can't we start again? I've never had anyone react this way before. People are normally delighted to have me help them. I'm very well connected and have a very exclusive client list, y'know. I had to stipulate in my contract that there would be some type of payment if the terms were broken because I work really hard on my client's behalf to make their day totally unforgettable at a lot of personal and financial expense to myself." He turned to Frankie and said in a trembling voice. "We haven't been introduced. I'm Gabriel or you can call me Gay for short."

I heard snorts and saw that Angelica had just doubled over before falling sideways into a bush.

"I think we all know what to feckin call you," I said acerbically.

Luke came forward. "Ruby's had a big shock so I think we should call it a day and discuss this again in the morning when we've all calmed down."

The last part of this statement seemed to be directed at me which only served to fuel the fire that was already blazing.

"Get in, Ruby, and we'll drop Gabriel back to his car in town and then go home."

"You can do what you like," I said. "I am not going anywhere with you, or him for that matter. You seem to have it all worked out nicely between you so you don't need me."

"Ruby, I thought you'd be pleased. I was only trying to help."

"Do me a favour, Luke. Don't help me." And with that I stormed out of Frankie's driveway, disappointment, sorrow and anger all fighting for first place in the battle of emotions that was erupting in my head.

Chapter 10

"Oh God. What's happened now?" was the way I was greeted the following evening when my mother found me sitting on the summer seat at the front of her cottage.

"Why does something have to have happened?" I asked peevishly. "Is it not possible that I could simply have taken it upon myself to come and visit you?"

Without even thinking about it for a split second, she eyed me suspiciously and said, "Noooooo."

I got up and followed her to the boot of her car where she was unloading large bags of flour and fresh fruit and vegetables and sighing loudly as if the worries of the world were on her shoulders.

"What's the matter?" I asked. "I didn't mean for you to get upset. I just wanted to come and stay with you for a few days."

There was no response and it was only when I looked directly at her that I could see her mind was obviously occupied elsewhere and that she hadn't heard me.

"Mammy, are you listening to me? I'm going to have a sex change, dye my hair green and call myself Billy Bob." (Green hair would undoubtedly be a vast improvement.)

"That's nice, pet," she said absentmindedly.

I groaned aloud. "Okay. What's wrong, Mammy?"

"Nothing, pet. Everything's fine." She forced a smile which looked more like a grimace and didn't fool me in the slightest. My mother was one of those cheerful annoying types who smile permanently, so for her to be putting on a happy front was very worrying indeed.

Just at that moment I sensed my mother tensing beside me and at the same time noticed her gaze travel to where a lone track-suited figure was strolling past the house and blatantly staring in.

"Who the bloody hell is that?" I demanded, knowing instinctively that this person was the source of my mother's discomfiture.

"No one, love," she answered unconvincingly.

"Oh, look, there's a pig flying over your head wearing sunglasses," I retorted. "Come on, Mammy. Spill. Now. What's troubling you? And what exactly is that silly cow staring at?" I clenched my fists and stepped towards the person who was continuing to peer at the cottage from the trees at the side of the road.

"Don't, Ruby," Mammy said in alarm. "Say nothing."

"Say nothing about what, Mother?"

"That's the new hotel owner's daughter. She's been walking past here a lot. I feel like she's sizing the place up for its potential value. She's quite sinister-looking and makes me nervous. But it's probably nothing. Just a case of your silly mammy being paranoid in her old age."

I didn't think my mother was being paranoid nor did I think she was being in any way silly or unreasonable and I also agreed with her as far as the sinister hotel owner's daughter (who was asking for a kicking) was concerned.

"So what's annoying you then or rather who has annoyed you?" Mammy said, swiftly changing the subject and studying me intently.

I didn't answer her (delaying tactics to put off the inevitable 'Ruby, why do you always overreact?' speech for as long as possible).

I looked away. "Luke hired a wedding planner."

"And?"

"And what?"

"So who's annoyed you then?"

"Luke has annoyed me, Mother."

"By getting someone to help organise your wedding? Why on earth has that annoyed you? I would have thought that you would have been pleased. You're not exactly the most girlie of girls and planning has never been your strong point."

I sighed and resisted the urge to lie down on the ground and kick my legs in the air like a frustrated toddler in a supermarket. Why did no one understand me? It wasn't just that I disliked the thought of being bossed around by a neon-coloured lunatic. I was also heartily disappointed that his surprise hadn't been my birth mother. Why had Luke put finding me a stupid wedding planner in front of helping me find my mother?

I had told my tale of woe (omitting the adoption saga) to the woman who had sat down in front of me on the coach on the way to Letterkenny this morning (I didn't take the car as I was afraid in my current mood that road rage might turn into road kill) and she had looked at me as if I was a possessed eejit and then moved seats to sit beside a group of women at the back who all regarded me warily before whispering and giggling together. (Obviously that was before I had also moved to the back of the bus to snarl and stare menacingly at them until they got off. Two stops early.)

Mammy unlocked the door leading into her small shop and proceeded to empty the bags of flour into a large barrel and pick through the fruit and vegetables until she had them in two piles whilst I plonked myself on a stool and watched.

"Apples for apple tarts and crumbles, plums for plum-and-almond tart, strawberries for Pavlova, lemons and limes for Citrus Surprise and blueberries, blackcurrants and raspberries for Summer Pudding," she said aloud whilst writing out a list. "I'm going to try a few new things as well," she added excitedly. "I found a lovely recipe for vegetarian bake so I'm going to try it and I'm also going to make sun-dried tomato and goat's cheese tarts as well. I had a woman in here last week giving out because I only made meat pies and apparently that's being racist against vegetarians. Did you ever hear the like of it?"

I smiled weakly and turned away.

"Ruby?" Mammy was looking at me sadly now. "Why are you so unhappy? You're normally such a jovial person. I've been speaking to you a few times this week and you haven't been yourself at all. Are you and Luke having problems? I think he's a lovely young man but I wouldn't like you to go rushing into anything only to regret it later. Did you have a fight? Is that why he got you a wedding planner? Was it a making-up present?"

I clenched my teeth until my jaw threatened to explode with the tension. "The wedding planner is not a present and if he was I'd be taking him straight back to where heshe came from and declaring him faulty in the extreme and an insult to trading standards. I've just had things on my mind lately. Luke and I are or were fine until he brought *him* near me. I think he thought he was doing something nice. I don't think he realised how hurt or upset I'd be."

"I'll bet that he'll be deeply saddened now it seems to have backfired on him. You really do have a terribly quick temper, Ruby. God knows where you get it from because you certainly weren't brought up in a cross environment. Our house was always lovely and calm and serene."

I scowled and sat on my hands lest they bunched themselves into fists which always happened at the slightest provocation.

"Rogue genes," I muttered crossly.

"Pardon."

"Rogue genes," I announced loudly. "Perhaps it's in the blood. Maybe I come from a long line of overreacters with bad-tempered tendencies, in which case growing up in a tranquil house would have had no effect. I'll find out soon enough, I'm sure."

As soon as I had said the words, I instantly regretted them. Mammy was looking at me with concern which swiftly changed to annoyance when the realisation of what I had just said sank in.

"Soon enough, Ruby? What exactly is that supposed to mean?"

"It means that you never know what the future might hold," I faltered. (Could somebody please give me back my shovel so I can dig my way out of the hole I've just dug?)

"I see," Mammy said, looking grim. "Have you been making enquiries then?"

I was going to blatantly lie but found I couldn't. Not about this and not to my mother.

"I do know some things but not a lot. I have my birth certificate."

"*You what?*" she shrieked, throwing the courgette she had in her hand down on the counter and glaring at me furiously. "Why would you do such a thing and why now?"

"I've had it for a long time, Mammy," I said gently. "There just wasn't a good time to pursue it for one reason or another but now that I'm older and getting married and feel more in control –" (who was I trying to kid?) "– I thought it would be a good time to investigate. It's nothing against you, Mammy. I just have questions. Questions that with the best will in the world you can't answer for me."

I looked at Mammy, hoping that now I had tried to explain it she might be a bit more understanding, but found that her mouth was set in a hard rigid line.

"I don't want you to look for her, Ruby. She doesn't deserve you."

"You can't expect me not to want to find out, Mammy, and what do you mean she doesn't deserve me? What do you know?"

Mammy opened her mouth whilst I held my breath and then she sharply closed it again. "I don't know anything but you've survived this long without her so I'm sure you could live another while without pursuing this. It's for your own good, Ruby. I don't want you to get hurt."

"Why would I get hurt, Mammy?"

"You mark my words. You'll be hurt."

"How do you know I'll be hurt? What are you basing this assumption on?"

I had never seen Mammy looking so furious before and her lack of understanding or empathy both shocked and surprised me and led me to the conclusion that she knew more than she was willing to say.

"You haven't answered me, Mammy."

"Ruby, you're just going to have to trust me on this."

"I'd trust you a lot more if you weren't quite obviously keeping things from me."

"Ruby, I don't wish to talk about this any more. I'm busy and I wasn't expecting you to be here this evening."

"Fine. I know when I'm not wanted," I said, feeling stung. "I'm going to go out for a walk." I was hoping that maybe, if I gave her time to think, she would come round to the idea.

"You do that and do yourself a favour and phone that poor boy and tell him you're sorry for reacting the way you did. Good men are hard to find. I should know. Your father was one in a million, the best husband in the world and a perfect father to you. You couldn't have found better if you had picked him yourself."

I felt a sharp intake of breath when she talked about Daddy in that way and knew that she was doing it entirely for my benefit, given the current conversation. I knew I was lucky. I also knew when my mother was hiding things from me and I was determined to find out why she was.

Chapter 11

When I left the shop the sun had started to set, making it a beautiful evening. A perfect night for a walk with your lover, I thought, giving in to my sentimental soppy side for a few seconds (yes, I do possess a tiny one). My stomach lurched as I thought of Luke and how horrible I had been to him. He had only been trying to help me so that I could focus on finding my mother which was something he knew was very important to me. It was unfortunate that the aptly named 'Gay' was the sort of person who made me want to dance in annoyance before turning psychotic but that wasn't Luke's fault. Even thinking about him made me shudder. I wanted a low-key wedding day where the most important event would take place at the altar. Now it was in danger of becoming a frilly circus performance. Don't get me wrong, I did want to look nice and was pleased to be giving Frankie the opportunity to dress up and to see my little goddaughter in a flower-girl's outfit, but I was dreading it being turned into one of the cringe-worthy over-the-top performances that I had scoffed at in the past. This was my day, therefore it should be done the way I wanted it and to my specific tastes (or, put like that, maybe not).

I took out my mobile and dialled Luke's number. It only rang once before he answered it in a breathless panicked voice.

"Ruby, is that you? I've been worried sick."

I felt like hanging up and running away.

"Yes, it's me. It's the silly cow who's had time to think, is sorry she upset you but who still wants the wedding planner shot."

There was silence.

"Luke, are you still there?"

"I'm here," he answered gently. "Are you all right? Where are you?"

"I'm fine. I'm in my mother's and I've just made a huge muck-up of things here."

I heard him take a deep breath (deep breathing was required a lot when in my company).

"What's happened?"

"Oh, nothing much. I just inadvertently told my mother that I intended searching for my birth mother in the near future."

"Shit."

"Yes, the fan is blowing it all around me," I muttered. "Look, forget about my current mess for a nanosecond. What has been done about Gabriel?"

"Nothing much, I'm afraid," Luke said. "But I'm working on it. I went to see the bank yesterday and I've a good credit rating so a loan might not be out of the question."

"A loan for what exactly?"

"For the two thousand pounds I need to get out of Gabriel's contract. I'm sorry I signed it without checking with you first but I honestly thought you'd be really pleased to have someone else doing the organising for you. The way I looked at it was that, if you had Gabriel's help, all you would have to do would be turn up on the day which is all I want from you."

I breathed deeply from the strain of going completely against my better judgement and willed my nerves not to implode. "Luke, don't be getting a loan. Tell Gay Boy he can stay but he'd better do exactly as I say and not be flouncing and frilling everything up. And you can also tell him to tone down his skirts and bright pink tops. Even the thought of him makes my head hurt."

There was silence.

"Luke, are you still there?" I asked impatiently.

"Yes, Ruby. I'm just trying to take all this in. You really don't mind?"

"Of course I mind," I growled. "But luckily for you I love you enough to recognise what you were trying to do and therefore am agreeing to it. But there will be conditions and, if he breaches them, a broken contract will be the least of his worries."

I knew that Luke was smiling down the phone at me. I could just sense it.

"Now what am I going to do about the other little matter?" I said.

"Leave it until I come down tomorrow," Luke said.

"You're coming here?" I asked.

"Are you walking home?" he enquired.

"I suppose not. Besides, two heads will be better than one when it comes to finding out what is going on up in the hotel. When Mammy arrived home this evening she seemed to be flustered and the new owner's daughter was skulking about making her feel nervous."

"And is she still living to tell the tale?"

"I'm not that stupid, Luke. We'll have to tread very carefully. I don't want Mammy to feel in any way unhappy or intimidated even though she is behaving like the most unreasonable woman in the world at the minute."

I continued to walk until the hotel came into view. It was still the same building but there had been obvious changes made to it. It looked quite enticing, I supposed, as the signs had all been changed to give a rustic old-world feel and it had been given a new coat of paint. An old-style horse-drawn carriage was parked at the door, seemingly to recapture the charm and ambience that the old Manor House must have once possessed.

On squinting in, I could see that there had been decorative alterations made to the foyer as well as a little landscaping to the grounds outside. It was also a lot busier than it had been, if the amount of cars in the car park were anything to go by. I felt uneasy, especially when I saw a face peering out at me from an upstairs window and realised before the netting was roughly tucked back into place that it was the same face that had been surveying me from behind the trees earlier.

Chapter 12

Mammy was nowhere to be found when I eventually returned from my walk and I could only presume that she had perhaps gone on a similar mission to clear her own head. It puzzled me that she was so dead set against the idea of me searching for Georgina as she was usually very open-minded about such things. But then again 'things' didn't usually involve the daughter she had brought up as her own child for thirty-odd years and the woman who had abandoned her. I hadn't actually meant to mention it to her. I would have chosen a good time when she would have been more receptive to such a discussion and not preoccupied with worrying about track-suit-attired nutters.

Or would there ever have been a good time?

I went to the fridge, poured myself a glass of wine and took it out to the garden where I sat cross-legged on the wooden floor of the gazebo and contemplated my current circumstances. I was thirty-four, getting married to a wonderful man, had a brilliant friend in Frankie and a mammy who I worshipped with the fringe benefits of getting a trip to pot-holed but lovely Donegal when I wanted to see her. Life wasn't bad, so why was I so hung up about finding Georgina?

I was still sitting deep in thought when I heard the front door closing. I was about to shout out a greeting and let Mammy know where I was but changed my mind when I heard a male voice as well as hers. The voices became louder and eventually came outside. I could hear the rattle of metal against concrete and the clink of glasses and knew that they were sitting on the patio furniture that was positioned at the back door of the cottage to capture the best of the sunrays during the day.

"But why is she thinking about her real mother? Have I done something wrong?"

"Of course you haven't. Ruby loves you very much, Isobel."

I bristled at the sound of Donal O'Donnell's voice. How the hell did he know how I felt? What did he know about me or my mother or our relationship?

"I don't think you fully appreciate what we went through to get Ruby, Donal," Mammy said in a clipped tone. "Ten years is a long time to wait for a child. A gift that other people get naturally and in most cases don't realise how lucky they are. When we got Ruby she made us complete and she helped to heal me after the miscarriages and Baby Albert's death."

Mammy began to cry and I could feel the blood draining from my face. I had heard this before but had been told it wasn't to be talked about outside the family. Frankie and Luke didn't even know and here she was telling bloody *Donal O'Donnell*.

"We had been married barely a year when we found that I was expecting a baby, y'see. We planned ahead, making arrangements as you do, talking about names and waiting patiently for the first kick. It obviously wasn't meant to be, though, as I lost the baby at four and a half months with no explanation to be had. I was pregnant again within the year and Albert and I silently hoped and prayed that this time things would be different. It happened earlier that time, leaving me numb and Albert feeling useless as he tried to cope with his own sadness as well as my emotional and physical pain."

There was a short silence and I could hear Mammy sniffing. I hardly dared to breathe.

"My last pregnancy is the hardest to think about. I carried our baby son full term. I was so excited and so proud of myself. I felt him kick, stroked my belly, talked to him and sang him songs. Albert used to put his head on my stomach and tell the baby how much he loved it and that was in the day when men weren't sensitive and weren't supposed to care. He lived for four hours before he died from complications caused by a heart defect. If it happened now there would probably be a cure. We buried our baby boy, named Albert after his daddy, and along with him buried a large chunk of ourselves. I couldn't possibly have gone through the trauma and loss and disappointment again so we decided to give all the love we had reserved for our own child to someone else's who needed it just as badly."

The tears were now coursing down my cheeks and I prayed that they wouldn't hear me as it felt irreverent to be eavesdropping on such an emotional outburst.

"The adoption process was so laborious. You almost felt like you were on trial with people calling unexpectedly to inspect your home and endless forms and red tape. I'll never forget the day they told us that we had fulfilled the requirements of their rigorous criteria and I will certainly never forget the day that they told us they had a baby for us. They told us that a little girl, already named Ruby, had been put up for adoption. We were told there was no hope of the mother ever changing her mind which was sad in one way but made us extremely happy." Mammy stopped talking and a strangled sob escaped from her.

"It's all right, love," I could hear Donal saying gently.

I peeped around the side of the wooden gazebo and saw him slip his arm tenderly around my mother.

"She's obviously confused and you're bearing the brunt of it. It'll have all blown over by the morning. Talk tomorrow and see what it brings."

I bared my teeth. Again, how the hell did he know what tomorrow would bring and how dare he pretend to be an expert on my emotions! He had met me once over a vegetarian stir-fry.

69

"No matter what happens, Donal, she shouldn't need to know about the drink problems and the men who were always calling and the neglectful way in which that woman behaved towards her wee baby. No child needs to think that they were the product of that sort of lifestyle."

"Hush now, Isobel, we'll not let her get hurt."

If I hadn't already been on the ground I would have fallen over from the shock. The men? The drink? The neglect? The discussion with Donal O'Donnell? How could she tell him such private things? Facts that I wasn't aware of but that were directly related to me. And what was with the "*We'll* not let her get hurt"? I didn't want his help or protection. What I really wanted was my daddy. He would have known what to do. I wanted him so much that I had a pain in my chest.

It was dark when I heard my mother yawn and Donal get up to leave.

"I'll see you tomorrow, pet. Try not to worry too much about everything. It'll all work out. You'll see."

I was glad that he could see because I certainly couldn't. I was cold and tired and stiff from sitting in the one position for too long and had never been so confused in all my life.

Chapter 13

I sat up in bed and just about managed to quell the scream that was about to come out of my mouth. I had eventually fallen into an exhausted doze, after hours of tossing and turning, only for my sleep to be bombarded with nightmares. In this one I was being chased into a cupboard by the Irish Country singing sensation that is Daniel O'Donnell (who was delivering a rendition of 'Nobody's Child' which was most frightening). I was then locked in there with a drunken woman and a crying baby who she was ignoring.

I roughly pulled back the covers and dangled my legs over the side of the bed. What the hell was I going to do? I couldn't let Mammy know I had overheard her conversation but I needed more information about Georgina or rather more specifically I needed to find out what Mammy knew.

I trailed myself out of bed and padded to the kitchen in my bare feet to get a drink of water. I then sat in Mammy's armchair by the window and watched as the first rays of sunlight painted the sky an orange-purple colour. Had I been in a different frame of mind I would probably have sketched the scene and coloured it in as a memory of the moment but my head was too full. Something was stirring in my mind. An incident that had happened years before.

I had been doing a history project for school and needed some information about my grandparents and Mammy had told me to find some boxes in the attic where she had stored old photo albums and memorabilia from the past. I had brought several boxes down and had begun the cumbersome task of looking through them all. I found exactly what I was looking for quickly but, surprisingly, was enjoying looking at the photos and mementoes so much that I had kept going for ages.

Several days after my history project had been handed in and I had put the boxes back in the attic, I had gone into Mammy's bedroom looking for her. Her wardrobe door was wide open, which was unusual, and when I went to close it I noticed another interesting-looking box which was partially hidden under a shoe-rack at the bottom. More photographs or souvenirs, I thought excitedly, and pulled it out, wondering why it hadn't been produced earlier.

Now, I curled my feet up in the armchair and closed my eyes in an attempt to concentrate as I tried to remember the 'secret' box and what it had looked like. It was leather, I was nearly sure of it, with some type of design on the lid. It certainly was unusual and not at all like the other boxes. It must hold something really special, I thought as I opened it. Inside were a small teddy bear and a rubber toy along with a photograph and some bits of paper. I had been intrigued and was preparing to give the articles a closer examination when Mammy came into the room. She had been most annoyed and gave me a stern lecture about never going near her 'private things' and swiftly removed the box from my hands, saying that it was personal and I wasn't to touch it. Ever. I asked her who owned the teddy bear and she muttered that it had belonged to somebody very special but said no more as she left the room with the box. Something about the whole episode scared me and I never referred to it again. Nor did I ever see that box again.

I sat forward and then bounced up and began to pace around. That box must have had some significance or Mammy wouldn't have been so worried about me seeing its contents. I didn't realise it at the time but had thought of it on a few occasions in the past when I hadn't cared as much. I was now sure that it would hold the key to me finding out more about what I needed to know. The only question was where it was and how to find it without Mammy suspecting anything.

I woke up some hours later with Luke smattering my face with delicate kisses and immediately swatted him off.

"Charming," he muttered, rubbing his jaw.

"Sorry," I said. "I'm knackered. I've been up half the night. Couldn't sleep. I only went back to bed at six o'clock and I've tossed and turned since."

"So I see," he said looking at the duvet cover which was wrapped round me like a strait-jacket (and, yes, I might need one of those soon too).

"I need to get Mammy out of the house for a while. Can you take her somewhere?"

Luke eyed me suspiciously. "And what the hell am I supposed to do with her? Take her shoe shopping? Buy her a new blouse?"

"Take her for a cup of coffee. Offer her a slice of cake and then she won't be able to refuse. Talk about me. Reassure her that there's nothing wrong and tell her all about the stupid wedding planner so that she doesn't feel left out."

"And why will you not be there too? Why do I need to do this on my own?" he whined, using the voice of a nine-year-old girl.

"I won't be there because I need to go looking for a certain box that might answer questions for me and I suppose the best place to start would be in the attic but Mammy won't know that because you're going to tell her that I'm exhausted and need my sleep."

"And what if she won't go?"

"Of course she'll go. It's coffee and cake. How could she refuse?"

"Erm, because she's cooking up a storm downstairs. She told me that she's making jam today and she's down there stirring a pot that's the size of a swimming pool."

"Feck," I said crossly and fell back on my pillow. "She'll be at that all day then and she'll not want to leave it in case it burns. Jam burns very easily apparently. Ugh! What am I going to do?"

"Well, if you let her make jam today then maybe she'll be in a position to be coffeed and caked tomorrow."

"I can't stay here until tomorrow, Luke. I need to get away from here and away from *her*." I jabbed my thumb towards the door while Luke watched me in puzzlement.

"I didn't think things were that bad, Ruby. You're mature adults. Surely you're both capable of sitting down and talking about the fact that you're interested in finding your birth mother without falling out over it?"

"Oh, she's interested in talking about it all right," I said bitterly. "It's just a pity that I'm not the person on the receiving end of the conversation. Did I ever tell you that my mother had two miscarriages or that she and Daddy had a baby son who only survived a few hours after he was born?"

Luke obviously didn't know what to say and was struggling to make the right response.

"You know why I never told you or told anyone, in fact? I didn't because Mammy and Daddy didn't want it talked about. They're from a generation where you sweep things under the carpet in the hope that you can convince yourself that your experiences weren't real and bad things didn't actually happen. They told me and me only, apparently, as an explanation as to why I was adopted in the first place but I was told that it was private. Well, guess what? It's not a secret any more. I overheard Mammy baring her soul to her fancy man last night and telling him all about it, as well as giving him some gory details about my birth mother which she had absolutely no right to do. When *I* asked about Georgina all *I* got was a sullen silence and a load of crap about Mammy not wanting me to get hurt. She doesn't have enough respect for me to tell me the truth even though she knows that I desperately want to find out and need answers."

Luke encircled me in his arms and I put my head on his shoulder

74

whilst he stroked my hair. It reminded me of what Mammy used to do when I was younger and couldn't sleep and I jerked my head up sharply, rubbed my eyes vigorously and lay back heavily on the bed.

"I think I should take you home," Luke said gently.

"I don't know what to do, Luke," I said in a whining tone which was uncharacteristic in the extreme as I was usually very forthright and sure of what I was doing.

"What do you mean, Ruby?"

"Well, if I leave here I might feel a hell of a lot better but at the same time I might be scuppering my chances of hearing anything more or getting more information. I won't rest until I find out the truth and this is the only place where I have any hope of getting that. She will not stop me from finding out what really happened. Am I being unreasonable? Is it unnatural or wrong that I should want to know?"

"Not at all," Luke answered gently. "It would be more unnatural if you weren't inquisitive and didn't want answers. Although I think as far as your mother is concerned that she does genuinely have your best interests at heart and that she is indeed worried about you getting hurt."

I shook my head and closed my eyes. I didn't dispute the fact that she wouldn't want me to be hurt but was cut to the bone that she would talk about the situation to other people whilst remaining tight-lipped with me, even though I deserved to know more than anyone else. She was being very unfair.

"What do you want to do, love?" Luke asked.

"I don't know. My head feels like a pressure cooker that's about to explode."

"I think you should trust your gut instincts and stay if you feel it's the right thing to do. You haven't told me what's so important about the box?"

I proceeded to regale him with details about my long-forgotten history project and my inadvertent discoveries.

"You think I'm reading too much into it, don't you?" I said, fixing him with a long look when he looked unconvinced.

"What? *You* read too much into a situation, Ruby? *You* put two and two together and make nineteen? Never!"

I poked him and tried to smile but succeeded in only grimacing, at which point Luke took me in his arms once more to let me know in the only way he could that he supported me even if my own mother wasn't inclined to.

The smell of bacon penetrated the room and I could hear Mammy calling us for breakfast.

"Tell her I'm not hungry," I said gruffly.

"Ruby, your mother will know there's something wrong if you don't appear. You are only ever not hungry if you're sick which you're not."

"Sick or being lied to – my stomach responds well to neither," I snapped.

"You're not supposed to know any details about this, Ruby. Remember? You weren't told – you overheard. So if you want to make your mother suspicious you're going the right way about it. Try and act normal. I know it's not easy but, if you do that, then there's maybe a chance that we'll stumble on something. And Ruby –"

"What?"

"Try and be understanding. Your mother's scared that she might lose you if you go looking for Georgina and she probably only talked to Donal because there's nobody else she could have confided in."

"I hate when you do that," I said, exasperated. "Why do you always have to be so rational and reasonable about everything?"

I was waiting for him to say that one of us had to be but he didn't.

"Because I can see the bigger picture and what you stand to lose. Your mother is a wonderful lady and I don't want to see either of you getting hurt."

"Breakfast's ready!" she called again. "Ruby, are you up?"

"I'm coming now," I responded in my best 'I'm feckin raging but trying not to let on' voice.

"Good girl!" Luke mouthed at me before I rugby-tackled him to the floor in a play-fight in order to let out some of my frustrations.

"Good morning," Mammy said when she saw me. She wasn't her usual twinkly self.

"Good morning," I responded in a flat tone.

Neither of us was acting normally but then yesterday had changed everything. We had learnt things about each other and our intentions and life would never be quite the same again.

I poured myself a mug of coffee and could feel Mammy's eyes boring into the back of my head as I stared intently at the swirling brown liquid.

"Are you all right?" she asked.

"Never been better," I said in a sarcastic tone, only to mentally kick myself. I was going to have to change tactics and stop being so obvious. I looked her straight in the eye and smiled. "Grand, Mammy. I'm actually really enjoying being here and so is Luke – aren't you, pet?"

"Me? Oh yeah, sure," he said unconvincingly. Then he yelped as I kicked him. Hard.

"Would it be okay with you if we stayed here another day or so, Mammy?" I asked.

Mammy looked at me in confusion and then fixed me with a suspicious stare as Luke proceeded to hobble outside, muttering about shin-guards and divorces that were going to happen before weddings.

"Look, Mammy, I just don't want to leave you under a cloud. I know that I upset you yesterday and I think it might do us both good to talk."

"I've nothing more to say," she said, immediately clamming up and making me bristle in irritation.

"We'll just spend some time together then," I said, showing Herculean strength as what I really wanted to do was roar and throw things at the wall.

"If you like," she finally agreed grudgingly, "although I'm going to be busy tomorrow as I have to go to the farmer's market in the morning and then I'll be at the Senior Citizens' Club with Donal in the afternoon."

I grinned broadly. "No worries. I'll come to the market with you and then man the fort here until you get back."

"I suppose you could look after the shop for me," she said thoughtfully.

"Yeah, I could." (Or I could leave Luke to do that and go for a wee nosey in the attic.)

"Fancy a walk?" Luke said as he limped back into the house (why do men love being martyrs?).

"I suppose we could," I said.

Outside, he nodded in the direction of the hotel. "Since we seem to be in the mood for investigation, why don't we tackle another problem while we're here? It'll get us out of the house for a while and maybe we'll find out a bit more about what's been happening and if your mother really does have cause for concern."

I wasn't much in the mood for tackling anything as I felt I had enough on my plate but he was right that I did indeed need to get out, and no matter what Mammy had done I didn't want to see her losing the house that she loved so much.

"Yes. Let's go up to the hotel and say hello to our little friend. I'm in the mood for head-butting somebody."

Chapter 14

Upon entering the premises, Luke and I registered that we had stumbled upon some type of guided tour that I had never seen being done before, which made me feel distinctly uneasy. There was also a very different atmosphere to the one I had experienced on other visits.

"Monroe Manor has been situated in these grounds since the early nineteenth century and was owned and lived in by the Monroe family. It is said that Lord Charles Monroe visited Ireland and fell in love with a local girl from Smugglers' Bay who later became Lady Tessa Monroe. They had four sons: Hector, Peter, Stefan and Philip. The manor's most famous and eccentric owner, however, was Charles Monroe's last descendant, Lord Bartley Monroe, who was legendary for his hunting skills both in the field and on the dance floor."

"Was there a Lady Bartley Monroe?" A well-dressed American lady asked the blonde and pretty tour guide who was dressed in green and looked like she'd rather be anywhere else in the world.

"I think there were several ladies who all thought they had earned themselves that title," the girl answered, raising an eyebrow.

I beckoned for Luke to follow me as we joined the tour.

"What are you doing?" he asked, looking quizzically at me.

"I want to see what this is all about," I muttered. "Mammy said she smelt a rat and that the new owners seemed to be causing trouble but we're not going to find anything out if we barge in and announce ourselves as being connected with the cottage in any way." (I'd watched enough detective dramas in my time and fancied myself as a bit of a *Columbo* type.)

Luke nodded. "So you think we should blend in and act like tourists then?"

"Precisely." (*Elementary, my dear Watson.*)

"It's not like you to be so sensible about things. I had visions of you coming in here and pinning somebody against the wall."

"Who says I won't?"

He slipped his arm around me as we stopped and waited for the guide to speak again.

"I see we have some new guests," she said as she nodded a friendly greeting to Luke and myself. "I'm Aisling and you can ask me anything." Then she continued with her spiel. "Monroe Manor was a large, sprawling stone mansion. It still retains most of the features of the original house and a lot of the hallmarks of the gentry who once lived here. The long tree-lined avenue leading up to the house provided them with privacy whilst the extensive lands surrounding the property gave them ample hunting grounds."

Aisling then invited the assembled group to come to the window where we could see the acres of land spread in front of us.

I could see Mammy's little cottage nestled amongst the trees near the entrance and felt a stab of fear. She was so happy there and I couldn't bear the thought of her being moved (which wouldn't be happening unless somebody fancied dying before their time).

Aisling set off again and we all moved on.

"The different wings of the manor were utilised for various purposes with certain parts being used only by servants, whilst guests were housed in the more plush surroundings of the main building. There was an entertainment room where a piano and harp took pride of place, a sewing room and a gentlemen's room where the Monroe men retired to drink brandy and play cards. The Piano Bar is situated where the entertainment room used to be and has retained some of its original artefacts as the piano and harp which are on display were the very ones which sat in this room." She pointed to the instruments which sat in the corner of the bar. "It is rumoured that Lord Bartley had an American entertainer shipped across to Ireland to tune the piano."

"We're the best!" a Texan man wearing a Stetson shouted out.

Aisling acknowledged this with a smile. "In his later years Lord Bartley began to run the manor as a country-house hotel. We have tried to retain the traditional ambience as best we can, as you can see here in the foyer."

I watched as the tour group nodded to each other in approval as they took in the scene in front of them. The foyer was dotted with large dark-green leather and mahogany sofas which overlooked the large grounds. Oil paintings depicting hunting scenes adorned the walls whilst a glass cabinet beside the reception desk displayed the decanters from which the Monroe men apparently used to pour their brandy.

"There are a lot of beautiful pictures here," one onlooker commented. "Are they originals?"

"Oh yes," the girl nodded and for the first time during the proceedings I stopped and listened intently. "Most are the work of Irish artists. Although some were imported from America and France. The Monroes collected art and some of the pieces that you see are very valuable. The servants' quarters were situated at the back of the house where our extensive kitchens are now," she continued. "They were apparently very nice. The Monroes had the reputation of being good employers who treated their staff well. Many young girls worked happily under Lord Bartley."

"I bet they did!" the Texan shouted again, winking salaciously at Aisling. "Maybe we could go for a drink later on, little lady, and then you can tell me more about Lord Bartley and what he did with his women?"

"I'm afraid hotel staff fraternising with guests isn't permitted," Aisling said, looking worried. She caught my eye and gave me a rueful smile.

"Darn shame," the gruff American said. "Pity there wasn't another hotel nearby and then maybe we could get friendly."

"She seems very nice," Luke muttered to me. "I know that they've done a lot of work in restoring the place to the way it used to be and that's a good thing. It certainly seems to have brought the tourists in anyway."

"Which is why Mammy is worried, you dufus!" I hissed. "The more people who come here and want to stay, the more likely they are to want to try and get rid of her. I thought she was exaggerating but I know now why she's so concerned."

Aisling ended the tour by answering a selection of questions and then gave a grateful sigh as the crowd started to disperse.

"Have you been here long?" Luke asked when she turned to walk back towards the reception area.

"I've been here around five years now," she answered. "I've always been the tourist officer but have only just started giving guided tours of the hotel."

"Why's that then?" I asked, feigning innocence.

"New management," she said, speaking between her teeth and looking furtive. "They've had lots of new ideas."

The last comment was uttered with barely concealed disgust and Luke shot me a knowing look.

"A bit radical, are they?" I said casually.

"Not so much radical as ruthless," she said. "They know they've got a right little goldmine here and they're determined to do whatever it takes to make the best profit from it." She suddenly stiffened.

The source of her reaction seemed to be standing at the reception desk, looking fit to be tied.

"I think you have work to do. Too much work to be standing around making small talk." The comment came from a woman in her late thirties who had long blonde hair, was wearing a pencil skirt and white shirt with breakneck heels (which she obviously used for breaking balls). Her mouth was down-turned in an expression of sour disdain and she had the coldest eyes I had ever seen. I recognised her instantly.

"Gotta go," Aisling muttered before waving us goodbye.

"Can I help you?" the blonde asked.

I was about to tell the fire-breathing nutcase that I could help her by suggesting a few management courses which would undoubtedly improve staff relations by teaching her how not to be so feckin rude, when I realised that she wasn't actually speaking to me.

"I'd like a room for the night," a well-dressed woman with a clipped English accent said.

"Of course," the bright-red-lipstick-wearing Rottweiler said, sweetness and light personified. Her mood seemed to dip however when she switched on the computer, checked for vacancies and falteringly told the lady to wait a moment.

She disappeared into the office behind the reception desk.

"Why did nobody put up the sign to say we're full? Are you all as stupid as you look?" we heard her screech before she came back out and gave the (justifiably startled) prospective guest a tight smile.

"I'm sorry, madam, but we're fully booked for the night."

"Oh, that's such a shame! This place came very highly recommended. Is there nowhere you could squeeze me in?"

"Unfortunately not, but we're working on expanding this place so we'll have more rooms in the future."

"Really?" I interrupted sharply. "And what will that entail?"

"Bulldozing the grounds to build chalets," she snapped.

"And what about the cottage?" Luke asked suddenly.

"Yes, it's very sweet," the lady commented thoughtfully. "Is it vacant?"

"Not at the moment but give me time," the Antichrist said, looking straight at me. "It would make a lovely wedding-night retreat for future brides and grooms so we're working on it."

My blood ran cold and I felt Luke's grip as he steered me out before I could do my wall-pinning, head-butting trick.

"Over my dead body," I hissed, looking back.

Chapter 15

"Bloody hell," I said worriedly as Luke and I walked the short distance back to the cottage. "What are we going to do? We can't allow this to happen."

"And we won't," Luke said, his face set in determination. "Look, try and not worry about it too much for the moment. Let's deal with the more pressing issue of you getting the information you need."

I looked at him. "Everything's going to be all right, isn't it?" If Luke told me everything would work out I knew it would as I trusted him implicitly.

He grabbed my hand and held my fingers to his lips. "I promise that everything will be fine, my love. I know you're confused and that you have a lot in your head at the moment but we will get through it."

"I believe you. As long as I have you I can do anything."

We came back to the house to find Mammy knee-deep in strawberry and gooseberry jam so, before I got a job (Delia Smith and Nigella were both safe), I decided to make myself scarce.

"I'm going to take another stroll," I said to Luke. "I need time to think."

"Do you mind if I stay here?" he said. "I wouldn't mind resting for an hour – besides, I'm dying to get my hands on some of that jam."

I smiled fondly at him and ruffled his hair. "Thanks."

"For what?"

"For putting up with me. I know I can be difficult sometimes."

"Well, as long as you know," he said solemnly before taking me in his arms. "It will all work out, y'know. I'll make sure of it. I won't let anything spoil our wedding day or get in the way of you finding your real mother if that's still what you want."

"It is what I want." I pulled back and looked at him. "Why wouldn't it be?"

"I just don't want you getting hurt, Ruby. I understand why you want to do it but, given the way your mother reacted and what she knows, do you not think you should give it a bit more thought?"

"I am done thinking, Luke," I said, feeling annoyed that he was putting a dampener on me. "It's all the more reason why I need closure on this and some answers as well, especially as my mother would rather talk to other people about it instead of enlightening me."

I tried to push past him but he held my arm.

"Ruby, I didn't mean to upset you. I just don't want you being too impulsive."

"Impulsiveness is another one of the many traits I inherited from my real mother, don't you know?" I snapped. "Just another stupid gene that makes Ruby act irrationally. Who knows? Maybe I'll become an alcoholic and start sleeping around too."

I left Luke flapping his arms in despair and marched out the door. I didn't know where I was going. I just knew that I was going to keep walking until I felt better.

I had only walked about half a mile when I gave it up as a bad job. I had developed a blister on my heel and my legs were killing me. (Donegal hills definitely weren't developed for those who took up stomping down the road in bad temper as a recreational activity.)

I looked around me and spied a parting in the trees nearby that led down to a small river with a pier. I could see fishing gear had been left unattended and moved further along the bank as I was in no mood to talk to anyone or be interrogated as to who I was, where I was from or what my connection with the place was.

I finally positioned myself on a rock and splayed my hands on my knees as I took in the view and contemplated my next move. I did want to find my mother. I'd had my moments of doubt where I had thought about all the trouble I might cause but reasoned that none of this was my fault and that nobody had given a second thought to the trouble *they* might cause by leaving me in the first place. I examined my hands and thought about what I had overheard. Was it possible that I could be the product of some type of seedy out-of-control lifestyle where I had been viewed as an inconvenience? A nasty accident that hadn't been dealt with in time? I didn't want to hurt Mammy either but she hadn't spared my feelings when she'd decided to share the apparent circumstances of my birth with her toy boy before telling me.

I angrily threw a stone into the river and immediately incurred the wrath of every fisherman within a two-mile radius.

"Oi, what are you playing at? You'll scare the fish! Clear off!" one shouted at me.

"Don't you be getting on your high horse with me!" I snorted, taking a good look at his waders and floppy hat. "And don't be pretending to care about the poor wee fishies getting scared when you're going to slit them open, gut them and eat them with chips later! What sort of a sad individual wants to spend their time standing knee-deep in reeds catching rotten mingin' fish anyway? *Yuck!*"

"As charming as ever, I see," I heard a voice say behind me. "May I introduce Ms Ruby Ross, gentlemen. You all probably know her mother Isobel – runs the shop down by the hotel."

I looked behind me and was faced with a glowering Robbie O'Donnell and then turned around to see the shocked expressions on the faces of the fishermen (who still looked like a pack of gobshites, I might add).

"You must look like your father," one said.

"And act like him too. Her mother's a lady," I heard another one mutter just loud enough for me to hear.

I lifted the two biggest stones I could see and proceeded to fire them into the river and earnestly hoped that they would miss the fish and hit the mouthy arseholes with the rods instead.

"She's a big hit with the locals," I could hear Grouchy Slippers saying before he left them all standing open-mouthed and followed me. "You really know how to endear yourself to people, young lady," he said. "Planning on staying long?"

"Not longer than I can help," I muttered.

"Good. Because the longer you stay around here acting like that, the more bad light it reflects on your mother."

"And we wouldn't want to upset her, would we?" I said, gritting my teeth (and wishing I had a grenade in my hand). "She's so honest and upfront and thoughtful and considerate of other people's feelings."

"Yes, she is," he said gruffly. "And you're making her look bad with your terrible attitude and big mouth."

"Listen, Robbie, you know nothing about me or what I'm experiencing at the minute so do me a favour and feck away off!"

I stomped off back in the direction of the cottage and didn't stop until I had arrived and my legs were ready to drop off.

When I opened the kitchen door Mammy, Luke and Donal were sitting at the table laughing and drinking coffee and eating huge hunks of home-made bread and jam.

"Good walk?" Luke asked.

"Wonderful. I'm knackered and going to bed."

"But it's only six o'clock," Mammy said mid-chew, looking at her watch.

"As I said, I'm tired." (And need to be sedated and locked away in case I kill somebody before the night's out. There was quite a list of would-be victims forming.)

"Okay, love."

I threw myself down on my bed in the guest room and felt hot tears prick my eyes. I was totally fed up and feeling very let down by the people who were supposed to love me. Nobody understood how I was feeling. Nobody was even interested. Nobody cared. (I was prone to self-pity when I was pissed off.)

I closed my eyes and gradually felt my eyelids getting heavier and willed myself to fall asleep because the sooner I slept the sooner morning would come and the closer I'd be to getting some answers.

An hour and a half later and I was still awake. Even though I was tired I couldn't sleep and although I was loath to go back out to the kitchen, where the others were sitting and probably having a great time, I really didn't have any other option as I was slowly going mad.

I was saved from humiliation and questions, however, as I discovered when I went out that there was nobody there. A scribbled note told me that they had all gone to Donal's house and would be back later.

I wouldn't have wanted to go to Donal's house but felt huffy anyway. Feckin cheek of them all, deserting me. I looked out the window and surmised that they must have taken Mammy's car as our clapped-out Renault Clio was still there and suddenly I had an idea. If they could go on an adventure, then so could I!

I was tempted to go up to the attic and ransack the area – eh, look around demurely, I mean – for what I so badly wanted but felt that it was too risky as they could come back any time. Although I was capable of being irrationally impulsive, I had a stronger desire not to make Mammy suspicious as then I might never find anything out. There were several ways to skin a cat, however, and there were other things I could do to help myself.

I got dressed quickly and then bustled about making sure I had everything I needed. I squinted at the map which told me that it wasn't too far away. A drive over the mountain and I would be there. I could maybe call into a shop and ask a few well-worded questions that might shed a little more light on the situation.

It was a wet and miserable night and I had second thoughts

about my plan when I thought of the warm and comfortable bed I was leaving, to go on what would probably turn out to be a wild-goose chase. However, it might be my only chance.

The drive, although not as long as I expected, was treacherous and my heart rocketed to my shoes several times while I was rounding corners where there were no markings on the roads or barriers to prevent a car from sliding over the cliff face and into the sea below. (Donegal Tourist Board was definitely going to be getting a letter detailing how people would rather not be killed going out for a drive, thanks very much.) I was relieved beyond belief when I finally saw lights in the distance and a sign welcoming me in Irish and English to Mulroy Cove, home of Georgina Delaney, and a place where I might finally get some answers.

To my dismay it seemed somewhat deserted as there were very few cars parked around. There was noise coming from somewhere, though, and as I locked the car and then walked slowly down the street I saw a small group of men hanging around a fire-exit door smoking.

"I bet she's on holiday," one of them said in a stage whisper as I approached.

"She could be one of them foreigners. There's loads of them here at the minute. She could be here to stay."

"Want to bet on it?" one of the others said.

"Ten euros says she's a foreigner."

"Ten euros says she's not."

I nearly ran away. They were all obviously barking mad around here. It was a means to an end, though, I told myself sternly.

"Or she could be hoping to bump into a crowd of smokers who might give her some directions," I said as I stopped nervously beside where they were congregated.

"I wish I'd bet on her not being foreign now," one of the men said in a disgruntled fashion, snapping his fingers as he did.

"You could argue that point," another one said, taking a long draw of his cigarette. "She is a foreigner. Judging by that accent she isn't from this side of the border."

The man who had made the bet on me 'being a foreigner' (seriously?) began to grin in delight whilst I tapped my foot in impatience. I'd heard of sleepy seaside towns before but this was feckin ridiculous.

"You were saying you were lost," one of the men said. He hadn't spoken before and had instead hung back in the shadows.

"Yes, I was visiting a friend and want to go back to my mother's house now but I took a wrong turn. How do I get back to Smugglers' Bay from here?"

Three sets of thumb-jabs later and an argument about what mountain road *not* to take and I was glad that my apparent lack of knowledge about the roads in the area was pretence or else I'd have been well and truly goosed and totally bloody lost.

"Do you know the Delaneys?" I asked, suddenly fearing that if I didn't change the conversation there could be fisticuffs over who was right and who owed who ten euros in bet money.

There was silence as one of the men pulled me by the arm around to the side of the establishment where a broken sign told me that I couldn't have planned it any better if I had tried, as the pub I had stopped at was called 'Delaney's Tavern'.

"This place used to be owned by the Delaneys but the family decided to give it up around ten years ago. The last owner sold up and moved abroad, I hear. It was always such a well-known spot though that the name stuck. It's like an old institution around here. They have live folk music and musicians gather here from all over Ireland for sessions at certain times of the year."

My heart nearly stopped as I stared open-mouthed at the sign. Talk about walking on the graves of your ancestors.

Chapter 16

I took a deep breath before entering the pub by a side door. It smelt fusty and was badly in need of a good airing. Clearly it was a pub for old men and dogs as the current clientele indicated. A row of barstools was occupied by men of various ages whilst a sheepdog and a small terrier both lay snoring contentedly in front of the fire. I sniffed the air appreciatively as I inhaled the smell of turf smoke. Even though it was the month of June it could still be cold at night and the fire was warm and welcoming.

"You look cold. Would you like a drink?" the Shadows Man asked.

"I suppose one wouldn't do any harm," I said.

"Get her a brandy," the man instructed the young lad behind the bar, "and make it a big one."

I held up my hand to protest but then changed my mind as every eye in the place seemed to be on me. Obviously men and their canine friends drank here regularly but females clearly didn't.

"You were asking about the Delaneys."

It was more of a statement than a question and I was glad that my newly acquired drink-buying buddy wasn't putting me on the spot as to why I wanted to know, as I had a feeling that it could turn into something of an interrogation.

"My mum and dad used to know them years ago," I lied. "I can't remember any names but always remembered that they were from Mulroy Cove."

"Let me put it to you this way," the man said, taking a swig of his pint. "The Delaneys are famous around these parts. They're very wealthy and well connected around here. This place is full of their history."

"Really?" I asked. I knew that my voice held a noticeable intonation of surprise but I couldn't help it. I was expecting to be told many things but not that my mother was from an apparently upstanding family in the community. Perhaps she was the black sheep.

"Oh yes. Their father was a big businessman although it was a shame that their mother died so young."

"And their grandfather and great-grandfather were famous for making the best poteen in the country," a man at the bar commented in a slurred voice (he looked like he'd had a swig or two of it quite recently).

"I suppose that explains the pub then," I said.

"There was a big connection of them. A typical Irish family of the time with fourteen children. Most of them moved out of the area, but one of the boys married and stayed in the village and raised a large family here – though a lot of them have moved away now."

"There's still one of them lives locally though," one of the bar patrons offered.

My heart skipped a beat. "Who would that be?" I asked, trying to keep my voice steady.

"One of the men, I think. The girls have all gone their separate ways. There was a big row amongst the family years ago, y'see. Something to do with land or money or something and it split them down the middle. It's a shame as their mother was a lovely woman."

"She was that," a few of the men agreed.

"And you don't know where any of the girls are now?" I asked.

"I thought you only knew of them through your mother and

father," one of the men said almost accusingly. "You're asking an awful lot of questions."

"The only reason I'm asking is because I know that my mum and dad were very sad to lose contact with them and I'd love to be able to give them some information when I get home." I took a deep breath and wondered if they could hear my heart beating or was it just me who could hear it thumping in my ears. "You don't know what became of Georgina, do you?"

The men exchanged glances and raised eyebrows.

"She was the youngest one who left before the others, wasn't she?" one of the men said. "She was a bit of a wild thing by all accounts. God alone knows where she's at now."

"Or what she's doing or who she's doing it with," another man answered whilst laughing lewdly.

I felt sick but still wanted to kick his head in for being insulting. I wished I had stayed in my bed as opposed to coming out in the rain just to hear my worst fears confirmed.

"Then there was the elder sister," they said, continuing to talk around me, totally unaware of the impact their words were having.

"Can't remember her name but she was a bitch. An evil, manipulative, poisonous cow if ever there was one. What was her name? Mary? No, that's not it. Maura? No, that's not it either."

"Marcella Delaney," another voice said. "That was her. Sour-faced battleaxe. She used to have the younger ones demented."

"Yeah – and then she went from tormenting them to that poor husband of hers who must need an award for bravery at this stage."

They all laughed while I simply felt dead inside. I wished I hadn't come out. Why hadn't I listened to my mother?

"Thanks for your information, folks," I said. "It's been good chatting with you all."

"If we happen to see any of the Delaneys, who should we say was asking after them?" the man who had bought me the drink asked.

"Nobody," I said quietly. "I'm nobody at all."

When I got back to the cottage I could see that the lights were on and Mammy and Luke had come home. They weren't on their own, however, as I could see another figure through the kitchen window. My heart sank. I wasn't expecting to see Robbie and was in no mood to deal with him either. He saw me as a loud-mouthed troublemaker whose poor mother didn't have her sorrows to seek. Well, I thought that he was a patronising permanently grimfaced old codger who didn't have the first clue about me or what I was going through.

"So you're back then?" Mammy said, looking annoyed (even though they were the ones who had abandoned me in the first place).

"I went out for a spin," I said defensively.

"In the rain," the three of them said at once as if I had broken a law and the guards were about to swoop in and charge me with venturing out in unsuitable weather.

"It's allowed as far as I'm aware," I said through gritted teeth.

"Let her be," Mammy said gruffly (not so much in my defence but more because she apparently couldn't be arsed talking to me).

Luke seemed very concerned and came over and put his arm around me and, instead of shrugging him off like I might have done in different circumstances, I felt the need to be close to him. I needed to know that somebody loved me and I wasn't quite as worthless as I felt right there and then.

He seemed to sense my unrest and tried to look directly into my face but I wouldn't let him. If the rumour was true and the eyes were the window to the soul, then he might see just how messed up my head was (more messed up than usual, that is) and I didn't want that.

"I'm grand, honestly. I just needed to get out for a while, that's all. I've a lot on my mind at the minute."

"*Harrumph!* Haven't we all?" Mammy muttered helpfully before walking in the direction of the cloakroom to put away the coats.

"Go on to bed, Luke," I said. "I'll follow you shortly. I'm just going to get a hot drink."

When I turned round I discovered that the hot drink had been made for me. Robbie handed me a mug, looked furtively around him and then produced a hip flask which I deduced must be filled with something potent and expensive, judging by the reverent way he was handling it and measuring out a precise amount.

"Thanks," I said, a little surprised that he was being nice to me. I didn't think Robbie 'did' nice so to speak. Grumpy and bushy eye-browed seemed more his style. I sipped the drink ... mmmm ... it was brandy.

"I'm just waiting for your mother to give me something for Donal," he said, which explained his presence there. "Get that into you and you'll feel better. It always helped me when I needed to think after Martha died. You only need to have the one, mind. No point in getting hooked on it and creating more problems."

I looked into his face and, even though I knew that his wife had been dead for a substantial amount of time, I could still see the hurt in his eyes and if his heart had been visible I've no doubt that it would have been encased in thorns and bleeding. (I was in a very philosophical zone.)

"Don't look so surprised, young lady," he said sternly.

"I'm not. I always knew you were capable of making a good cup of tea," I answered cheekily.

He nearly smiled before lifting his coat and putting it on him. Mammy came back at that stage and handed him a set of keys.

"Give Donal those and tell him I think they're the right ones," she instructed.

"I will," he said and then bade us good night.

I looked after him and, although I still thought he was a puke and that his son would never in a million years replace my father, I saw him in a new light.

Chapter 17

Mammy was thoroughly enjoying herself. We had got up early the following morning and as a result got a good parking space and a first look at what was on offer at the Smugglers' Market.

"Shopping here is a pleasure," she sighed. "No queues or crying children or noisy intercom announcements every five seconds."

There were definitely no queues or announcements. They had a very simple means of running their enterprise. They wrote what was available on a chalkboard, collected their money in old biscuit tins and bum-bags and threw in a bag of potatoes with every joint of meat purchased. The marketers seemed to have a silent agreement with their customers. The locals gave them their trade, pointed newcomers in their direction and they in turn looked after them all year round, Christmas and Easter included, when the large grocery chains were filled with frazzled women who would happily start a petrol-bomb riot over the last turkey.

"Hello, my love!" a man hosting a butchery display shouted at Mammy. Dressed in a shirt and waistcoat with a tweed cap slung over one eye, he looked every inch the country gentleman. He had a moustache and weather-beaten skin which was indicative of the amount of time he spent in the fresh air. "Come on up to me, what can I get you?" he said, ignoring the woman in front of him who had her mouth open to give him her order.

"I'll have a large sirloin roast, Sammy," Mammy said.

"I'll give you the best cut I have."

"Good man," she said as we watched him select a particularly generous amount of meat without weighing it.

"How are you, Isobel? I'm hearing great reports about that wee shop of yours."

Mammy glowed with pleasure. "It's going well. I'm trying out a few new recipes so you'll have to drop by and sample them and let me know what you think." She gave him a conspiratorial smile, suddenly aware that she was the focal point of particularly mutinous stares from the others in the queue. "Thanks. I must go and have a look around."

"You do that, my love. Make sure you visit all the stalls. There's a soup stall and a herbalist over there." Sammy pointed to where they were situated.

"Mmm," Mammy murmured. "I think I'll go and see the herbalist. I know someone who could be doing with a pick-me-up."

I suddenly realised that I was the one who apparently needed to be picked up and attempted to walk in the opposite direction.

"You're coming with me," Mammy said as she grabbed me in a vicelike grip and steered me towards a stall being manned by a woman wearing a gypsy shawl.

"Will you stop manhandling me and quit being such an outrageous flirt," I said grumpily.

"I am not flirting," she said.

"Yeah, you were. Batting your eyelids at that butcher, inviting him to sample your wares and seducing him into giving you the biggest cuts of meat. I'm going to have to start keeping a closer eye on you, Mother!" (And I was only half joking.)

"Can I get a tonic for my daughter, please? I think she's run down. She's very grumpy and tired as well. Went to bed at six o'clock yesterday evening intending to sleep, couldn't sleep and then gallivanted round the country in the rain – going for a spin apparently. Is that normal?"

I could feel the vein above my eye starting to twitch and roughly pulled my mother off me. "That has more to do with the rest of you than it has to do with me," I snapped.

"And she blames her bad temper on everyone else," Mammy said as if this was symptomatic of some terrible ailment that could be cured by popping a few herbal tablets.

"You could try some of this," the herbalist said, shoving a pestle and mortar which was filled with green goo and smelled revolting under my nose. "It's particularly good for enhancing the mood. Very uplifting," she added solemnly.

"Just while I'm here," my mother said, squinting at the bottles in front of her. "I don't suppose you have any magic tablets that would help me lose weight, do you?"

"You've come to the right place," the woman answered, obviously seeing euro signs and preparing to do a hard sales pitch on my gullible mother who would probably buy fourteen different types of tablets and potions to clutter her already bulging kitchen cabinet.

I waved my hands and moved away from them. "If it's all the same to both of you, I'll uplift my mood in my own way."

"It's me," I said as Frankie answered the phone.

"Well, praise the lord," she said in a short, sarcastic tone which was followed by silence.

Shit. She was more upset than I thought she'd be.

"Frankie, I'm ringing to apologise for my behaviour. I should have realised that Luke was only trying to help. I just got a shock, that's all."

"Which obviously meant that you had to run off to your mother's without so much as letting the rest of us know that you were alive and well. Poor Luke was distraught. He didn't know where you were and whether or not you were okay. Talk about being ungrateful! Any other girl would have been thrilled to be handed a wedding planner on a plate but oh no . . . not you! You have to overreact like somebody that needs to be locked up for their own safety as well as that of everybody around them." The last bit was shouted in a high-pitched tone and in the manner of an irate Frankie Howerd.

I may have been wrong but my clever powers of deduction told me that she was a little teeny-weeny bit pissed off with me. Or maybe a big bit actually.

"Frankie, I said I'm sorry. I didn't mean to hurt anyone. I just flipped and felt I had to get away from it all. In my own head I wasn't thinking about the rest of you or how my actions would make you feel."

"No, you were just thinking about yourself, Ruby Ross," Frankie snapped, "which is most unlike you as you are the kindest, most generous person I know – which tells me that you must be very muddled indeed."

"Am I forgiven?" I wheedled. "I'll baby-sit for you every day for the next month."

"That's not a proper punishment," she answered curtly. "You'd enjoy that too much. You should be made to wear a dress and high heels and bright pink lipstick for the next month. That would put manners on you!"

I couldn't help giggling at this and immediately my shoulders, which had been hunched in tension, sagged and my breathing steadied. Frankie had every right to be angry with me and I would die without her friendship which meant the world to me.

"As part of your punishment you must raise your right hand and repeat these words after me," Frankie said sternly. "Get that hand up now!" she barked. "I, Ruby Ross . . ."

"I, Ruby Ross," I repeated in a bemused fashion.

"Will start looking forward to my wedding."

"Will start looking forward to my wedding," I mumbled.

"I will stop being a pessimist and realise that this will be one of the most special days in my life."

I repeated it after her, feeling ashamed of my silly attitude.

"I want to remember it with fondness in years to come and will allow my friends and wedding planner to guide me."

"Now hang on just a minute –"

"*Repeat!*"

So I said the words reluctantly.

"I will believe what I am saying and allow myself to enjoy the experience. I will have dreams and wishes for my big day and they will all come true with the help of all the people who truly love me."

I smiled as I copied her again – as much as I could remember of it.

"And most important of all, I will transform myself and be a proper lady for the first time in my life."

That was a bridge too far. "You better be finished," I said to distract her, "because I feel like a right prat standing here with my phone tucked under my chin and my right hand in the air talking to myself!"

"I wouldn't have to resort to such tactics if you'd be agreeable," Frankie grumbled. "Promise me, Ruby, that from now on you're going to look at things in a new light and stop being difficult. I want you to enjoy this and I want to share it with you."

"I promise," I said (only half meaning it really but already feeling a slight shift in my point of view).

"Gabriel is a bit shocking all right but a complete genius," she went on. "I did a bit of research on him and he really is the best to be had. When Luke decided to get you a wedding planner he didn't use half measures. You are such a lucky girl. We're going to have so much fun with him and if you dare speak I'll jump down the phone and smack you one."

I curled my lip but quickly stopped making faces as I remembered the words I had just sworn to.

"Maybe we can catch up tonight," Frankie suggested.

"I'll not be home until tomorrow," I said. "I have a few things to do."

"Are you okay?" Frankie asked, still speaking in a gruff tone but more gently than before.

"Yes, I'm fine or at least I will be when I've got my hands on a little more information. I kind of told Mammy that I was embarking on a mission to find my real mother."

"What is it with you at the minute, Ruby? Are you on a mission to fall out with everyone around you? Was she annoyed?"

"Not so much annoyed as completely unreasonable. She's refusing to talk about it. I went for a drive last night to Mulroy Cove and found out a few things. I don't know whether they'll help me or not but, coupled with the other information I'm looking for, it might all come together to be useful to some degree. I'm not sure that I want to pursue it in the same way I did before but I do need to know. I need to finish this once and for all."

"Be careful, Ruby."

"I will."

"Ring me later and let me know you're okay."

"Are you sure you want me to?"

"Yes, you tart, as when all is said and done I love you – and, when you need to be told you're acting like a prat, I'll do it for you."

"You don't say. Okay, I'll talk to you later. And Frankie . . ."

"Yes."

"Thanks."

"Don't mention it. My toe is always here if you need it to kick you into touch."

I snapped my phone shut and walked to the other side of the market where there was the delicious aroma of home-made soup and asked for a large helping of the tomato and basil variety which was bubbling merrily on a camping stove. As I ate, I willed my mother to hurry up.

Chapter 18

"Have you calmed down yet?" Mammy enquired when she eventually found me sitting on the bonnet of the car.

"I'm perfectly calm, Mammy. I just want to go home." (And loot the attic.) "I'm tired." (Oh feck. Wrong thing to say.)

"See. See. I told you that you needed a pick-me-up. I know when you're run down. A mother always knows best."

I breathed and counted to four hundred before inviting her to put her purchases into the boot.

"You're in an awful rush, Ruby. I thought the whole point of you wanting to stay was so you could spend some time with me, but every time we get an opportunity you're running off to lie down or in a splutter to get away from me. Are you hiding something? You're not pregnant, are you? That would explain the tiredness and you do look quite peaky."

"I am not pregnant, Mammy. That would be the last thing I'd want at this precise moment in time. I know I'm not the most girly of girls but even I know walking down the aisle with a bump would be a bad look."

Mammy smiled and patted me on the knee. "I've arranged to close the shop and take this afternoon off work."

I could feel my chin dropping in shock.

"Donal can manage quite well himself at the club. He thought you were in bad form yesterday evening as well and when I suggested you and me doing something together he said he'd get someone to cover my shift. He really is a darling."

"He's wonderful. A great fella altogether. I must go and thank him. Personally." (Feckin interfering do-gooder!)

We arrived back at the cottage to find Luke making tea. "I thought you might like something before you went to work," he said to Mammy.

"What a thoughtful boy you are," Mammy said, putting her arm around him, "but as it happens I'm taking the afternoon off to spend with my daughter and her boyfriend. I don't see them that often and they're leaving tomorrow so I'm going to make the most of it."

Luke smiled tightly and I knew that his thoughts must mirror mine. Either that or he was worried he was going to be left taking Mammy shopping while I searched the house as had been the original plan.

"Do you fancy going somewhere nice, Mammy?" I suggested suddenly (desperation inspiring me with a plan of sorts). "Maybe we could take a drive into the mountains or go to Donegal town or into Killybegs to watch the boats?"

"I suppose we could. That's a great idea," Mammy said thoughtfully.

"We could make a picnic and take it with us," I pressed on.

"But I've just used the last of the bread," said Luke on cue, reading my mind and hiding the remainder of the packet.

We made a great team. (Bonny and Clyde, eat your hearts out!)

"Go and get some bread, Mammy," I said quickly. (Anything to get her out of the house for two minutes. I probably wouldn't have enough time to embark on a major search but with any luck she'd bump into half the country at the shop and that would stall her. I knew I was on to something. I could taste it. All I needed was a bit of peace and a lot of luck.)

"God but you're very bossy," Mammy said. "Sure we don't need a picnic. Why go to all that trouble when we could just as easily sit in somewhere and have somebody else make us a sandwich?"

I was starting to hyperventilate and knew that Luke could see it but instead of helping me he seemed to think that now was a good time to disappear. I was going to kill him.

The house phone rang and, once Mammy had gone to answer it, I sighed in frustration and wondered what the hell I was going to do.

The door opened and Mammy came in, shaking her head. "I'm ever so sorry, Ruby, but that was one of the boys from the club. There's been a problem and I need to go down. I might have to stay for a while to get things sorted. I know you were really looking forward to going out this afternoon but I will make it up to you, I promise."

"Okay," I conceded whilst trying to keep my gleeful anticipation of the contents of the attic in check. "You go on, Mammy. We'll stay here and look after the shop."

"I have the closed sign up on it already, pet, so you don't have to worry."

"Well, sure, we'll see," I said, helping her into her coat, dashing to open the door for her and practically kicking her out through it. (I was nothing if not very helpful and very obvious.)

I did a little dance once I heard the car tyres crunching on the driveway, signalling that the coast was clear for a bit of detective work.

"Where the hell were you?" I demanded when I saw Luke emerge.

"Making a very important phone call," he said whilst waving his mobile phone in front of me. "To the Senior Citizens' Club!"

"It was you?" I breathed in admiration.

"The one and only," he smiled.

"But how did you organise that?"

"I rang Donal and told him that you were planning a surprise meal for your mother and that you needed to get rid of her for a while and he was most helpful and said he'd organise a diversion."

"Have I told you lately that I think you're a genius and an all-round brilliant husband-to-be?"

"No. But feel free to charm me with your compliments. I can take them."

"I will, don't worry, but first I need to do some investigating. And then I need to do some cooking. Could you not have said I was decorating the house or something? I can't boil an egg without mucking it up."

I balanced on the ladder and opened the attic trapdoor with an almighty clatter.

"Ruby, it's a good job that there's nobody around," Luke hissed from below. "With the racket you're making, you'd be found out in no time."

I hunted around to my left-hand side and eventually located the light switch.

Minding my head, I climbed into the attic and began to look around, starting to feel slightly frantic as I couldn't see anything resembling what I was looking for. I couldn't even see the other old storage boxes of photos she had always had. I spent a while aimlessly wandering about, lifting random objects and haplessly looking around me. I was sure that I would find it, though, as when Mammy had first moved here she had told me that all her photographs and personal memorabilia had been put in the attic for safe keeping. I just needed to find where. The roof space was quite big and I was amazed at how much stuff there was. How one woman had managed to accumulate so much over the years was beyond me. She must have a hidden hoarding obsession I had never noticed before. We'd have to talk!

"Isobel, where have you put it?" I whispered.

Suddenly I had a thought. I knew that Mammy possessed a large old-fashioned trunk. Where was that? Dodging boxes, a bookcase, some old ornaments, a lamp and the obligatory crate of old toys which every attic must possess, I eventually found my mother's trunk. It opened easily. I lifted out clothes, photograph albums and jewellery boxes but so far couldn't see any leather box. I continued to hunt and lift things out until eventually I could see the bottom of the trunk. I sat cross-legged and started to go through everything I had just removed but to no avail as I found nothing.

Slowly and purposefully I started to put everything back in the trunk, trying to remember the order in which things had been packed away. I was totally deflated, not to mention miserable.

Once everything had been put back in its place and the trunk closed, I sat down heavily on the lid and felt like crying. Was this all fate trying to tell me to leave well enough alone? Should I take the apparent loss of the box, along with my mother's reaction and what the men in the pub had told me, and get the hint that it was all a bad idea? I fidgeted with my fingers for a short while as I contemplated life and eventually got up after saying a prayer.

"Come on, Daddy. I know that you'd help and that you'd want me to know the truth. Please guide me now."

I felt terrible but after I had emerged from the attic I went into Mammy's bedroom and opened her drawers and looked in her wardrobe in case she had hidden something there but there was nothing to be found and it was with a heavy heart that I started to wonder if she had got rid of it or destroyed it.

Luke was in equally bad form as we sat in silence in the kitchen, drinking coffee. While I had been up in the attic rooting through the trunk he'd had a phone call from his mother and his facial expression was now changing from being sombre to sad to angry to pensive. I knew he was miserable and, although I wanted to give vent to my own annoyance, I didn't as I knew he was really hurt.

"What did she say?" I eventually asked after watching him shred a piece of kitchen roll before he sat back and moodily kicked his toe against the table leg.

"Doesn't matter."

"I think it does actually, Luke. You're about to jump out of your skin so therefore they must have really annoyed you."

"I don't want to talk about it. Just drop it!" he snapped.

"If I said that to you, you'd pester me until I told you, and I've got all night," I said casually. "I feel like shit too, only you have the luxury of knowing why. Talk about it and let me help you."

"Help!" he shouted. "The only way you could help would be if you could open an offshore bank account for them to rifle. I can't believe the cheek of them. I'm the one saving for a wedding but do they care? Not at all!"

"You told them about the wedding?" I said, knowing that my voice sounded fearful in the extreme. Luke had planned on telling them only at the last minute in the hope that they'd be otherwise occupied and unable to come.

"Yes, I told them, but they're not interested at all. Far more concerned about getting their hands on more cash. 'Photographers do very well these days. You've got plenty of work. You can afford to help your parents once in a while. Remember where you came from.'" This was said in a squeaky voice, obviously mimicking his mother. "Remember where I came from? Is she for feckin real? My earliest memories involve the two of them coming in plastered and me having to look after them as well as see to Mandy who was only a baby at the time."

I thought about my childhood and realised how blessed I had been. I had always known where my parents were. I had never been left alone and I had always felt wanted and loved. And now here I was, feeling bad because I couldn't find my birth mother, when according to the stories I had heard she could have provided me with a similar childhood to Luke's if not one which was much worse.

"I'm sorry," I said, suddenly grabbing his hand.

"Why are you sorry?" he asked.

"Because I'm being selfish and stupid about everything. Maybe I should give it all up as a bad job and just be thankful that my childhood was so pleasant and that my mother still wants me even though I'm a permanent pain in her arse."

"Whoa!" Luke said, squeezing me back. "Don't you dare think like that. Take all opportunities with both hands and don't let me stand in your way. I'm probably being stupid too. You'd think at my age that I'd have got over feeling the way I do but I can't help it. They just annoy me so much."

"Of course they do," I said. "You're not like them, so you know that their behaviour is wrong. In fact, I think you should be the one searching for your birth certificate as you may well be adopted too, judging by how well-rounded and sweet and nice you are."

Luke smiled weakly, shrugged off my hand and took another sip of his coffee before taking his wallet out with the intention of helping his mother again.

I opened my mouth to protest but Luke silenced me with his hand. "Save it, Ruby," he said as he got his phone and prepared to transfer money. "If I don't do it, they'll only ring Mandy and I don't want her to be involved."

At that moment we heard the sound of car doors closing and I knew that Mammy must be home and, what was worse, I realised that I had nothing cooked.

Shit.

Donal raised his eyebrows when he came in and he looked at Luke quizzically. Mammy, however, didn't seem the least bit fazed that nothing had been done, instead jumping to the conclusion that Luke and I had been after some quality time together on our own.

"You young ones are so easy to see through. All you had to do was ask, y'know. Why didn't you just take yourselves away for the day instead of staying cooped up in here?" She looked at us questioningly and then coloured as she jumped to the staggeringly wrong conclusion that 'quality time' meant getting frisky. (In both our current states nothing could have been further from our minds or less possible.)

"Why don't you go into the shop and grab something from the chiller?" Mammy suggested in a blatant attempt to change the subject as quickly as possible. "There are some nice pies and I think there might be a lasagne and a quiche as well. I can rustle up a salad to go with it and make a few chips if you'd like."

"I'm not that bothered," I mumbled as Luke made similar noises.

"Oh go on! I'm hungry and I'm sure Donal is," Mammy said. "Go in and have a look and surprise us."

Luke and I reluctantly went into the shop and looked around. Even though I felt sad and depressed my spirits lifted as soon as I opened the door and the smell of herbs and spices and fresh bread wafted over me. The shop was like something that had been taken out of a country-kitchen cookery show with all its wicker baskets filled with fruit, gingham-covered pots and colourful crockery.

Luke opened the chiller cabinet and looked in morosely. "Well, what do you fancy?"

"Oh, just pick something. Mammy won't care. She'll eat anything," I answered absentmindedly, wandering into the tiny room at the back of the shop where Mammy kept all her order sheets and did her accounts.

There was a desk and a chair and a small filing cabinet where she kept all the papers relating to the business and, although it was usually locked, today it was open and a batch of papers was sticking out the top preventing the drawer from closing properly. I went over and opened the drawer with the intention of sliding the papers back into place but something made me lift them and when I did my heart skipped a beat as there at the bottom of the first drawer of the cabinet lay an unforgettable and familiar sight.

The lid of the box had the design of an ornate rose on it just as I remembered from all those years ago and it was made of leather.

"I've found it! Oh my God, I've found it, Luke!" I squealed (quietly). "I should have known that Mammy wouldn't have left it lying around for me to find. She's too clever for that or at least she thought she was before she left her filing cabinet unlocked. You'd think I was meant to find it. Thank you, Daddy! Luke, go and give Mammy whatever you've picked and divert her attention for a minute until I look in here and see what I can find."

The box felt very light and I hoped with a sinking dread that it wasn't empty. I placed it on the desk and, with trembling hands, lifted back the lid. "Yessss!" I hissed, punching the air when I saw the contents. I began to lift the articles out one by one.

There was a pink teddy bear with a white ribbon around its neck, a squeaky rubber Mickey Mouse toy that someone had obviously tried to eat judging by the teeth marks all over it, two pieces of paper and a black and white photograph.

I looked at the photograph but it meant nothing to me. It was of a lady, obviously posing to have a professional picture taken. She looked stiff and uncomfortable with her hand resting on the back of a chair as she stood poker-straight, wearing a buttoned-down flare coat and a hat with an ornamental hatpin at the front. I turned the photograph over to see if there was any writing on the back but there was nothing only stains and signs of discolouration.

Luke came back to join me and told me that I needn't worry as Mammy and Donal had left to go down to the Smugglers' Inn to get some wine for dinner.

"What have you found?" he asked, peering over my shoulder.

I shrugged and passed Luke the photo. "Mammy loves to talk about family history. She's shown me lots of photographs in the past but I know I've never seen this person before."

"Wonder who she is?" Luke said. "She looks like she'd be fun. I think she's trying not to smile."

Studying the photograph again I saw that the lady did seem to be struggling to keep her face straight. A slight twitch could be detected at the corner of her mouth.

I pursed my lips and put the picture to one side, then turned my attention to the rest of the box's contents. Upon opening the first folded sheet of paper I stopped short and hugged it to my chest.

"Omigod, Georgina's name's on this!" I gripped Luke's arm in excitement.

With further investigation, it appeared that the article in question was a baptismal certificate. I was transfixed. Not only did it contain my mother's name, it also gave details of people with the same surname who had been appointed as my godparents.

"Hilary Delaney and Gerard Delaney," Luke read over my shoulder. "Your aunt and uncle maybe?"

Hilary Delaney and Gerard Delaney, along with Georgina, had all attended a baptismal ceremony at a chapel on the Ormeau Road in Belfast for me when I was just five days old, according to the dates given.

I picked up the photograph again. "Do you see any resemblance?" I asked Luke who looked quizzically at me before taking the photograph from my hands and looking at it closely.

"Not instantly," he said, "but it's hard to tell. It's an old black and white photograph and she's wearing a hat. It's not exactly clear but I bet I could magically enhance it with my equipment if I took it into the office with me."

"No," I said at once. "Mammy must never know that I've found it or that I've been doing any investigating. Everything must be left exactly as it was. I don't want her to suspect anything."

"Belfast is quite a long way from Donegal," Luke said, frowning as he looked at the baptismal certificate again. "I wonder why you ended up being christened there?"

"Well, I was born there too. Look at this – there's another piece of paper here. It looks like a drawing."

The scene, which was sketched in pencil, depicted a bus stop with a variety of people standing waiting; there was a row of old houses behind this, one of which had a sign advertising clothing alterations. It was very detailed with lots of shading to convey the light and shadows of the surroundings and the patrons waiting at the bus stops all had intricate expressions drawn on their faces.

I was puzzled. "What does this have to do with anything?"

I turned the sheet over delicately, realising that it was already creased. This revealed nothing until I spotted a faded letterhead on the top right-hand corner of the page, telling me that the paper came from somewhere called St Catherine's Lodge.

Chapter 19

Two months had passed since my big discovery and life had reverted to normal (or as normal as my life ever could be which wasn't very). I had looked for St Catherine's Lodge in the phone book, searched for it on the internet and asked my well-travelled colleagues from work if they had ever heard of it but so far had come up with absolutely nothing. It seemed to be a very elusive venue indeed but that only added to the mystery of it all and made me even more curious about where it was and indeed what it was.

It was the month of September and a very busy time within the college as new students were arriving daily (with their mammies and daddies) looking bewildered and scared in the morning but vamped up, dressed to kill and ready to take on the world or at least the town the same night). The more seasoned students who were in their placement year were coming to see me to discuss their future prospects. Some knew instinctively what they wanted to do and where they wanted to go but others needed guidance and that was something I was rather good at (great at fixing other people's lives – positively shit at steering my own in the direction it needed to go).

I was trying to prepare questions for an induction quiz that was to take place that night but found my mind constantly wandering. My inability to concentrate was most annoying and people were starting to notice.

"Forgotten anything, Ruby?" Mr Reid enquired as he sauntered into my office and left student forms on my desk that needed a second signature.

Shit. I hoped I hadn't misplaced a student (stranger things have happened, believe me) or missed a deadline.

"Your medical. You were supposed to go yesterday and didn't show up. The clinic in Belfast phoned me this morning to see why you didn't arrive. Any particular reason?"

I could have given him a list, starting with the fact that I knew I was fighting fit (seriously how many muscles were you in danger of straining sitting at a desk and organising a few students) and ending with the fact that I hated feckin doctors and knew that they weren't crazy about me either. I shrugged my shoulders instead.

"Give me their number and I'll reschedule it."

"I'll ring them and tell them you'll be there tomorrow in the early afternoon," Mr Reid responded. "Are you all right, Ruby? Anything you'd like to talk to me about?"

"I'm fine," I lied and he carried on about his business and left me in peace.

Frankie wasn't oblivious to my scattiness either but unlike the rest of the world she knew what was causing it.

"And you're sure there was no address for this St Catherine's Lodge?" she asked, not for the first or even the twenty-first time. "You couldn't have missed it?"

I viewed Frankie with an impatient frown until she raised her eyes to heaven and set a cup of coffee in front of me. "Sorry, I know, stupid question, I'm sure you were far too thorough to have missed anything."

We were sitting in my office having a well-deserved cup of coffee at eleven o'clock. I usually stipulated that a sticky bun was to be had in conjunction with the said coffee, but Frankie had banned herself from eating anything more calorific than a Weetabix bar and for some reason had presumed I would be delighted to accompany her in this tasteless venture. I feckin wasn't but, as she was worse than Gillian McKeith with a sore arse, I didn't have much choice in the matter. I looked dismally into my coffee cup.

"Frankie, I keep telling you – I practically devoured the box and its contents, I was so eager to get my hands on them. I examined every item really carefully but there was definitely no address. Nothing except the St Catherine's Lodge letterhead. I presume it's somewhere in Belfast as that's where I was baptised and three members of the family who were so keen to get rid of me were hardly likely to traipse around the country looking for an ideal christening venue, were they? The only problem is that nobody seems to have heard of this lodge place. I've asked everybody. You have no idea how it broke my heart to leave the information and the photo there but I couldn't risk Mammy finding out that I'd seen anything. Things are strained enough as it is."

"Have you been speaking to her lately?" Frankie asked gently.

"No," I said shortly.

I had been thinking a lot about what happened and the more I pondered it, the more betrayed I felt. Like it or not, I was part of Georgina and she was part of me. Whether I'd been wanted or not, she had carried me for nine months and her blood ran in my veins and I deserved some answers. I wasn't stupid enough to think that I could embark on a full-scale relationship with her at this stage in my life nor did I want to, but a recognition of my being would be nice and Isobel Ross owed it to me to try and make that possible, after all these years, by sharing what she knew.

I had been a mischievous, impish child (who had the misfortune to earn herself the nickname 'Ketchup' at school – you work it out) but was good-natured along with it and totally idolised my parents. My adoption had never really created much of a dilemma for me as a youngster as I had always known about it. The trouble didn't start until the teenage years where crises of identity are rife at the best of times, never mind when you have a valid reason and really *don't* know who you are. I had asked lots of questions about my adoption, all of which my parents had tried to vaguely answer whilst sidestepping any reference to my mother as they pretended not to know anything about her or her whereabouts. I didn't get any hard concrete information, however, which never ceased to infuriate me and turned me into a rather difficult pubescent teen (yeah yeah, I know nobody's surprised). I was about sixteen when a plan formed in my head which involved going to get my birth certificate and tracking down my birth mother once and for all. I spent the next few years romanticising about what our first meeting would be like and how we would relate to each other. I wanted her to tell me about the circumstances before and after my birth and also wanted the name of my father so I could track him down too.

Frankie had obviously tired of her own company as she had drained her cup and was on her feet and ready to leave.

"I'm sorry," I said. "I don't mean to be rude or anti-social – it's just that –"

"You've a lot on your mind. I get it, honey," she said, giving my hand a squeeze before letting go, then taking a deep breath. "Look, Ruby. It's nice to be able to be there for you for a change instead of it always being the other way around. It gets a bit daunting being the Crisis Queen after a while. You've always been there for me through thick and thin and we'll get through this too. I know I wasn't very understanding about your need to find your birth mother when you first talked about it and rather cross when you absconded in a confused state but I've been thinking and, although my mother annoys the feckin shite out of me, I don't know where I'd be without her. Isobel is and always will be your mother but I do realise that you have a need to know who you really are and where you came from. It's only natural. I can't imagine how you must feel and the questions that must be tormenting you."

She put her arm round me and gave me a little hug, before going out and closing the door gently behind her, leaving me to my thoughts.

She was right. I did have loads of questions and they *were* tormenting me. I just wanted silly bits of information that other people never think about. Who did I look like? What were my grandparents like? Did I have any brothers or sisters? Had Georgina loved my father or was I the product of a fumble in the back of a car? Why did she not keep me? Would our meeting mean that the empty void, that had been in my life ever since I could remember, would be filled? It was strange: I was usually a very jolly, sociable, inexplicably mad person but even though I could be surrounded by a thousand people I could still feel bereft and abandoned and be the loneliest girl in the room.

Chapter 20

I finished work and made plans to go to the butcher's on the way home to purchase the two biggest steaks available as I wanted to cook ('cremate' would probably be a better word but God loves a trier) something special for Luke and have a romantic night. He really was one in a million and I didn't show my appreciation often enough. I had printed out a recipe from the internet earlier and was going to attempt to make teriyaki steak (a fancy way of saying steak dipped in sauce in my book) and surprise him. And astounded and shocked he would be as my culinary abilities usually only stretched to heating the oven and shoving something in and even then I usually forgot about it and it ended up burnt (on reflection I wondered if Luke was mad in the head, wanting to spend the rest of his life eating takeaways).

I also wanted to cheer him up as he'd had yet another encounter with his parents over the phone a few days before. Once again asking if Luke could be a good son and give them a hand. (Translated this meant that they had fecked up whatever their latest wackiest venture happened to be and expected Luke to bail them out.) They were prone to starting 'get rich quick' schemes but could never see them through and they didn't do it so that they could support their children either. It was simply a way of funding their mad existence.

It never ceased to enrage me how two people could be so selfish as to behave this way but, although Luke liked to give off about them, nobody else was allowed to. He liked to explain their actions by describing them as 'free spirits'. ('Freeloaders' would have been a more appropriate term, methinks.) We'd had a bit of a falling out as I didn't agree with him lending them any more money but he had hotly protested, saying that when all was said and done they were still his parents (an insult to loving mammies and daddies everywhere) and he had a duty to look after them.

I grimaced as I thought about them. I had only ever met them once and that was quite enough. His father, Fred, was a grotesque character who had a colourful array of swearwords which he aired regularly in a loud booming voice. He stank of beer, sniggered at his own jokes and enjoyed nothing more than to annoy anyone within his unfortunate company by commenting on all their shortcomings. He had nicknamed me Tommy (short for 'tomato head') on his last (it very nearly *was* his feckin last) visit home and I was seriously unimpressed. His mother, Beverley ("Call me Bev, babes") was an extremely irritating woman with a nasal voice who thought that she was God's gift to men (younger men especially) and was deluded in the extreme. She had brassy blonde hair, wore clothes that were too tight (and not in a good way) and put her make-up on with a gardening implement. She had absolutely no maternal instincts whatsoever and did nothing except embarrass her poor children when she was in the vicinity. I felt particularly sorry for Mandy. Although I wasn't my own mother's biggest fan at the minute, I didn't dispute the fact that every girl needs a good female role model in her life and Beverley Reilly certainly had never been that.

"Hi, Seamus," I said by way of greeting when I entered the little butcher's shop in Swiftstown.

"Hi, Ruby, I don't often see you in here," the butcher answered. (Don't get excited – he only knew me because he used to play cards with my daddy and had kept in touch with me after Mammy left for potholes new in Donegal.)

"Is it a special occasion?"

119

"Very special, Seamus. I'm cooking for a change."

"I see. What can I get you?"

"Can I have two of your biggest juiciest steaks, please? I'm going to treat my man tonight and convince him that he has made the right choice in a future wife." (Oh feck, perhaps I was setting the bar too high?)

"Well, in that case I'll give you two of my best fillet steaks. Take this bottle of soy sauce and some onions and mushrooms as well."

"I've got a recipe here, Seamus," I said, gesturing at the sheet of paper that was sticking out of my pocket.

"Start small, Ruby, and then you can experiment. Coat the steaks in soy sauce, then sear them on each side on a high heat, then turn the cooker right down and let them cook slowly and tenderise. Do the onions and mushrooms in a separate pan and cook them in butter. I can give you some nice baby potatoes as well if you like."

"Might as well go the whole hog while I'm at it," I agreed, scribbling down notes on what he was saying.

He put everything in a bag for me, charged me only half the price he should have and wished me good luck.

"You won't need it anyway, Ruby. You'll be fine. Your fella will know that he's landed on his feet with you whether you burn his dinner or not."

"Oi!" I said with a laugh. "Don't be writing me off just yet. I stayed with my mother last weekend and you never know what might have rubbed off."

"How is she?" Seamus asked with a smile. "Tell her I was asking for her. Your mother is a lady."

"I will," I said, the smile fading on my face. I wondered what everyone would think if they knew that she was consistently lying to me about my birth mother even though it was my right to know the truth.

When I arrived home I tidied up (by this I am referring to washing the breakfast dishes, making the bed and lifting a week's worth of clothes from the floor). Frankie is not allowed upstairs in my home because of my fear that she might suffer a heart attack as the result of an obsessive-compulsive inclination to want to scrub.

I love my house. It is situated in the middle of a terraced row on a side street in Swiftstown. It has a cosy sitting room and kitchen downstairs and three bedrooms and a converted attic (a bomb-disposal site might possibly be less messy) upstairs. It also has a small garden at the front and a bigger space at the back which is perfect for sitting out on hot summer days (but as this is Ireland and the weather is crap, this has only been accomplished about three times in six years).

I hummed as I took Seamus's advice and poured soy sauce on a plate and then proceeded to make sure that the steaks were well coated. I left them to soak while I chopped onions and mushrooms, popped the baby potatoes into a saucepan and left out the tub of pepper sauce that I was planning to use as an accompaniment.

The phone rang just as I was about to start cooking the steaks and I mentally swore at the caller's lack of consideration (a military operation might have been viewed as less important than this experiment).

"Hello."

"Hi, honey. I just wanted to make sure that you were okay." I smiled as I heard Frankie's voice. "You were very preoccupied today and I've been worried about you."

"I'm grand, pet. Just cooking some steaks for tea."

There was silence and I was presuming that Frankie must have been reeling from shock.

"Are you feeling okay, Rubes? You do realise that it's been that long since the cooker's been used that it's liable to blow up from sheer excitement?"

"Ha, ha," I drawled. "I decided that Luke deserved a treat." (I used the word lightly as there might be a risk of food poisoning.) "God knows what he sees in me as it is but I know that I've been very confused and out of sorts lately so I just wanted to let him know I still have time for him. We're going to have a meal, afterwards maybe go for a walk and then I plan to drag him up the stairs and rip –"

"I get the idea," Frankie laughed. "If I see him walking like John Wayne without his horse, I'll know that you've given him lots and lots of your time. By the way, don't forget about your appointment in the morning. Don't be exerting yourself so much that your blood pressure will be jumping off the dial."

"With what I've planned it's more likely to be Luke's blood pressure that'll be dancing," I said grinning, looking at myself in the mirror and deciding that I needed to take a shower, put on some make-up and generally look more appealing.

"I'm out in sympathy with you tomorrow, Rubes. I have a doctor's appointment in Swiftstown at ten o'clock. Pity your appointment's in Belfast and not here and then we could have gone together. I really don't want to go and am contemplating cancelling it."

"What's wrong?" I asked, immediately feeling concerned. Frankie and I shared similar sentiments when it came to the white-coated profession, in that we both hated all of its members.

"Oh nothing, I just have to go for a stupid smear test."

I snapped my legs shut and grimaced. When God made the world he really did have it in for the girls. I didn't see men having to go to the doctor, lie down with their legs in the air and try to be all casual whilst somebody shoves a metal device into their nether regions and talks crap about the weather.

"Lovely," I said, shuddering.

"I'm still in two minds about whether or not to go. God, but I hate those things."

"We all do but it's better to be safe than sorry. Just go and get it over with. They'll just keep pestering you until you do. Bloody relentless they are. I bet that blonde bimbo of a receptionist down in the medical centre gets a real thrill out of calling us for those."

Frankie laughed. "I suppose you're right."

"Of course I am. Be grateful at least you don't have to go for a medical where the end result will be that the doctor will be no further forward at the end than he was at the start. When they start droning on about family history, I'll just have to stop them in their tracks or perhaps I should refer them to my mother who seems to know everything but tells nothing."

"You should tell her what you know, Ruby," Frankie said in a serious voice. "If she knew that you'd overheard her then she'd have to come clean."

"And have her yelling at me about ear-wigging on a private conversation? No, thank you. I'd rather take my chances and find out myself. That's the only good thing about going to Belfast tomorrow. Sherlock Ross is going to do some investigating and find some clues."

"Let me know how you get on and good luck. Try not to be too difficult with the doctor. Remember he probably only went to medical school in the first place to please his mammy and not to deal with the likes of you."

"I'll try and remember that. Now go away. I'm very busy, y'know."

I hung up the phone and returned to the kitchen to put on dinner before trying my best to make myself marginally attractive. I intended to show my man exactly how much I loved him and there would be no half measures tonight.

Chapter 21

I woke up the following morning with a spring in my step and a (probably tuneless) song in my heart. I'd had a wonderful evening with Luke who had indeed been very impressed with my efforts (even though I had undercooked the potatoes, burnt the mushrooms and given the term 'caramelised onions' a new meaning . . . *ahem!*). My steaks had been a bit on the chewy side but Luke had eaten every last morsel, then taken my face in his hands afterwards, kissed me tenderly and proclaimed himself the luckiest man in the world. (Obviously he had drunk two glasses of wine at that stage and was viewing life through a grape-fuelled happy haze.)

We had then relaxed in contentment and talked into the early hours, all former plans of a bodice-ripping bedroom session forgotten in favour of enjoying some time together (where I wasn't acting like a deranged lunatic and so preoccupied with the different issues whirring around in my head that I forgot about poor Luke).

He had tentatively brought up the subject of arranging a meeting with Gabriel which had tested my good humour to the max but resulted in me agreeing to it as long as the said Gabriel a) refrained from calling me 'sweetie', b) didn't arrive looking like a canary and c) didn't expect me to look like one on my wedding day.

I had been about to phone Frankie to tell her that I had made this arrangement and fulfilled the terms of the oath she made me take, but remembered that she was probably in the doctor's by now gluing her legs together and brushing up her small talk as it would no doubt come in handy to distract from the task in hand or 'in fandango' as the case might be.

I left the house in good time to drive to Belfast and arrive at my appointment for twelve o'clock. I wanted time to go to the church where I was baptised, to see if by some small miracle anybody remembered either Georgina or any members of my 'family' who attended my rushed baptism.

When I arrived in Belfast some forty minutes later, I saw with dismay that the traffic was at a standstill as the result of yet more roadworks (that were there apparently to ease traffic congestion but didn't fecking half-create enough of it when they were in progress). I would never be able to get to the Ormeau Road to make the type of thorough enquiries I wanted and be in time for my appointment which was to take place at a private practice on the Lisburn Road. I had no choice but to drive to the clinic, park my car and then plonk myself in the nearest coffee shop with a frothy cappuccino until it was time to visit the doctor.

The doctor's office was a very plush affair with a waiting room boasting brown leather sofas and furry scatter-cushions that looked like they had just been plucked from the pages of an interior-design magazine. It didn't at all resemble the doctor's surgery in Swiftstown which smelt of bleach and boasted its very own smart-arsed receptionist who thought she had all the answers (except she didn't, a fact that I was going to make her very aware of one of these days).

"Is it Miss or Mrs?" the young doctor asked as he filled out a form.

"Miss at the moment but soon to be Mrs," I answered chirpily. (I was giddy as opposed to aggressive as I was in a good mood and needed an outlet for all the nervous energy the stress of this visit was causing.)

"That's nice," he answered in a mundane 'I couldn't give a feck' voice.

"Now we need to weigh you, get your height, take your BMI, do cholesterol and blood-pressure checks and have a general look at your health and family history . . ."

(Oh joy.)

"I also need a sample of urine and then I'm going to get you to breathe into this machine to measure your lung capacity. It's just a matter of seeing how far you can blow the balls up the tube."

I gave the young doctor my most sultry look and pouted.

"My ball-blowing technique is just fine, doctor. I get no complaints in that department."

An hour and a half later and I was on my way to the Holy Sacrament Church on the Ormeau Road, all health-related discussions a distant and annoying memory, as I now had more pressing issues to confront. When I arrived at the church I was disappointed to see that it was locked and when I went to the adjoining parochial house it also seemed to be devoid of any life.

"Bollocks!" I said aloud before jumping out of my skin as a voice boomed in my direction from on high. I wondered for a millisecond if lightning was going to strike me for daring to blaspheme on sacred ground but then looked up and clocked that a window cleaner perched on top of a ladder was looking down at me.

"There's nobody here, love. Father Joseph's gone to Cork to visit his mother and the housekeeper's off for the week."

"Thanks anyway," I said, dejectedly shrugging my shoulders. "Don't suppose you've ever heard of a place called St Catherine's Lodge, have you?"

"Can't say I have, love. Is it a convent or what?"

"It's a . . . erm . . . a . . . you know, I don't actually know what it is."

I nonchalantly turned around and walked away. I had also asked the doctor, his receptionist and several people in passing in the street if they had ever heard of it but was constantly greeted with blank stares and questions as to whether it was an old people's home or a school. I only wished I bloody knew.

"So you're not in danger of popping your clogs whilst looking after the students then?" Luke asked when he saw me that evening.

"Fortunately not. No high drama or tragic exits for me are on the cards at the minute. I'm fighting fit and ready to take on the world and do you know something? The doctor paid me a very big compliment today which I just know you're going to greatly appreciate in your future wife."

He encircled me in his arms and kissed the end of my nose. "And what would that be then?"

"He said my lung capacity was outstanding which in your language and mine means that I have the best ball-blowing abilities for miles around."

Luke was halfway up the stairs and pulling my arm out of its socket before I even had time to take my coat off and I reckoned that tonight just might be the night where he realised that he was blessed in his choice of partner after all.

Chapter 22

It was Monday morning the following week when I plonked myself on Frankie's desk and waved a packet of pineapple iced doughnuts under her nose. We hadn't had a chance to catch up since we spoke on the phone the evening before my doctor's appointment, as she'd had a busy weekend with the children.

"Get away from me, you tart!" She squeaked. "I told you I'm on a diet and not eating any of that crap!"

She was looking at me in terror and waving a cereal bar, which looked like it was comprised entirely of sawdust, in my direction as if it might have the same powers as a clove of garlic on a vampire.

"Why the hell are you on a diet?" I demanded, wrestling the bar from her hand and throwing it over my shoulder. "You are lovely the way you are."

"I have a bridesmaid's dress to fit into."

"And?" I asked, taking a ginormous bite of my doughnut and letting the oozing cream remain on my chin where she could see it.

"You are a tyrant from hell," she snapped before producing a bottle of water and glugging thirstily.

"What have I done?" I said, opening my eyes wide.

"How did you get on with the doctor last week?" she asked, deliberately avoiding looking at me.

"I got on wonderfully well. I'm going to live, thank God."

"You'll not live very much longer if you continue to ply your belly with that rubbish – and I'll make sure you don't, if you don't stop gorbing in my face!"

"My body is not a temple and I don't care. I am, however, very talented in other respects. My culinary skills are much improved and as for my bedroom activities . . . well, it would make you blush."

"Did you want something?" Frankie hauled a file from under my bum where I was still sitting on her table.

"I don't have to specifically want something to come and talk to you these days, do I? Actually I was wondering if you'd like to come out for lunch today?"

"Oh sure, and have you take me to the nearest greasy spoon and feed me something with a fat-content reading that would kill a horse. I think not."

"I was not about to suggest any such thing. There's a new coffee house open on the main street and I thought we might try it. Luke got a treat for putting up with me last week so now I'd like to show you my appreciation as well."

"Now, Ruby, I know I said I loved you but that doesn't mean that I want to –"

"Ha, ha," I said. "One o'clock. Be ready."

When I came back to look for Frankie at one o'clock she wasn't ready. She was instead talking animatedly on the phone to her sister Ella.

"That's brilliant," she chirruped. "I can't wait to see you. The children will be so delighted and when you're home we'll arrange to go and see Ruby's wedding planner."

"Oh goody," I said. "Let's all go to the circus and visit Gabriel the Clown!"

"Yes, that is her you hear and, yes, she's still very unimpressed but I'm working on her." Frankie held the phone away from her and mouthed at me. "Ella thinks you're the luckiest girl on the planet. She was looking Gabriel up on the internet and he has the most wonderful website."

"I'll bet he has. I bet it gets lots of hits from men of a certain persuasion who strangely enough aren't planning any weddings."

"Yes, she's still as sarcastic as ever," Frankie responded whilst I sighed and willed her to hurry up.

My stomach was rumbling and I was dying to get a break for a few hours before any more students came banging on my door.

"You're going to have to stop thinking about Gabriel like that, Ruby," my one and only bridesmaid advised me once she'd hung up and stopped gossiping. "Look on him as an ally. He will help you create the most wonderful day imaginable. Why don't you give him a ring and we can organise to meet with him soon."

"I will agree to anything as long as you start moving your butt towards that door. I have been dreaming of a big luscious salad burger all day, and so far the only thing coming between me and it is you."

"I hope they have a few low-fat options on their menu. I like the idea of salad. I just don't want the burger or the bun."

Frankie decided that now would be a good time to start applying lip-gloss and my patience (which was in limited supply at the best of times) was wearing tenuously thin.

"Yeah. Whatever. I am starving. Will you stop faffing about and come the feck on!"

Just as I was finally getting her to leave, her phone rang.

"Leave it," I commanded. "It can wait. My stomach thinks my throat's been cut."

"It can't wait. It's from an outside line. It could be important."

If I'd had a cat it would have had its arse soundly kicked, so great was my frustration at still being in the building at ten past one. The bloody coffee shop would no doubt be heaving and we'd have to wait to get seated and then I'd have a disorganised queue of bizarrely dressed students waiting at my door on my return. (But seriously, what is it about students? Once they define themselves as college-goers they immediately lose all sense and bedeck themselves in the oddest-looking clothes made from tweed and tartan and the likes and then shave half their hair off or else dye it purple. Even the boys looked peculiar.)

"Okay, I'll come down when I finish work," I heard Frankie say. Then she sat down.

I looked at her and noticed that her face had lost its colour.

"I understand," she said. "I'll see you in about ten minutes then."

She hung up the phone and flicked her fingers, which was a sure sign of anxiety or aggravation.

"What's the matter?" I asked.

She didn't answer me but was instead typing something into the search engine on her internet home page and it was with shock and concern that I registered that she was looking up the symptoms of cervical cancer.

Chapter 23

"Frankie, what the hell was that all about?"

I could feel my mouth getting dry and my palms sweaty with panic.

"Frankie, please speak to me."

"I have to go back for another smear test. The results came back and they seem to have found something abnormal. They wouldn't even let me wait until I finished work. They're insisting that I come down now and get another swab taken. That can't be good. They don't rush anything in my doctor's office. I usually have to wait a feckin week before I get an appointment and it's like a day's work trying to order a repeat prescription but now all of a sudden they're in a splutter to get me back in for another smear test. I don't like this, Ruby. I don't like this one little bit. Look at poor Jade Goody."

"Okay, Frankie, please stop getting carried away. This probably happens all the time but you just don't hear about it. Why would you? Nobody likes to talk about their fandango being put under the spotlight."

I sounded giddy and beside myself even to my own ears as I tried to process this information. It was probably just routine. Abnormal cells didn't have to indicate a major problem – or did they?

Frankie shook her head and finally switched off the computer.

"I'll have to go, Ruby. Sorry about lunch. You go on and get a sandwich and I'll meet you back here later."

"I think not," I answered quickly. "You seriously think I'm going to let you go to the doctor's on your own? I'll take you down to the surgery now and I'll either wait for you or I'll come in with you and hold your hand whilst you kick your heels in the air and think of Owen."

Frankie smiled weakly at me whilst I fished in my bag for my car keys and held the door open.

"After you, madam, and please stop looking so worried. They're just being cautious which is a great thing."

"I've been really lax, Ruby. They've tried to arrange an appointment with me three other times and three times I've either made excuses or ignored them completely. If anything happens to me as a result, it's entirely my fault for being so casual about it all."

"Don't talk rubbish, Frankie," I said quickly. "Nothing's going to happen to you. You're going to live to a ripe old age and give Methuselah a run for his money, so stop stressing."

The traffic was thankfully quite light and we arrived at the doctor's five minutes later and I waited as Frankie gave them her details and then sat beside me. She was called into the nurse's office a few moments later and while she was gone I said a silent prayer that I would be right in my casual but uneducated summation of the situation. I just hoped that it wasn't anything serious.

"Job done," Frankie said as she reappeared, looking pale but marginally happier. "They'll have the results back within ten days and then we can take it from there. They just wanted a second swab in case the first one was contaminated in any way."

"And if the second one shows up the same?" I asked tentatively.

"Then there are several avenues they can take. I might be called for a procedure called a colposcopy which means that they'll have to take a closer look at my cervix in hospital."

"More poking and prodding. Lovely. Men don't know they're alive. What do you want to do now?"

"Go back to work, I suppose," she said unconvincingly.

FIONA CASSIDY

"Nah," I answered quickly. "We don't want to do that. We want to go for a cup of coffee and a nice sticky bun because everyone knows that sugar is good for shock, so don't be arguing with me and trying to eat that cardboard rubbish again. Then we're going to go to your house to wait for the children to come home and after that I'm going to take them out for a while and you're going to have a nice bath and relax and not worry."

"I'm okay, Ruby, really. It just scared me, that's all. You take everything for granted until you're told that there's a possibility, no matter how slight, that something might be wrong and then you think about all you could stand to lose."

"Yeah, when you put it like that you do realise that life is too short to waste. It's so short in fact that just to cheer you up and put a smile on your face I'll agree to phone Gabriel and arrange an appointment just as soon as he's free."

Frankie clapped her hands together and I got a massive smile as my reward.

"When is Ella due home?" I asked, remembering the conversation Frankie had with her sister.

"She's coming home next week with Baby Celia Rose and Hammy in tow so it'll be great fun."

Ella, Frankie's sister, is one of the loveliest girls I know. She works as a midwife in a hospital in Edinburgh and had been having fertility problems until I introduced her to an old country faith healer called Thaddeus McCrory on one of her visits home who she maintains single-handedly helped her get pregnant (although I'm not so sure Hammy would agree . . . *ahem!*). I was really looking forward to seeing her and her baby daughter who was now nine months old and thriving like a gosling by all accounts (of which there were many if you happened to bump into Frankie's mother).

"Okay, I'll make an appointment with him for next week and if Ella's good you can tell her that she can come too and have a mighty laugh at my expense."

"We'll not be laughing at your expense," Frankie said, trying not to snigger (the cow).

134

We arrived at the coffee shop and, while we were there, we rang Owen to tell him to pick Baby Jack up from the nursery and also contacted Mr Reid to tell him that we would both be missing in action for the rest of the day.

"We don't do this often enough," Frankie said as she bit into a caramel square and practically had an orgasm once her taste buds registered that they were no longer being subjected to hamster-cage litter. "I've just had an idea," she said quickly. "Why don't we organise a night away before the wedding?"

"I thought that we were just going to go for a few drinks locally?"

"Bor – ing. Life is what you make it and I reckon that we should go all out to make this a really special time. It's not every day you get married."

"Thank feck," I muttered.

"And, Ruby, can you also do something else for me. Please try and make things up with your mother. I know you haven't mentioned it in a while but it's still bound to be hurting you. Try and get the situation about your birth mother resolved soon."

I briskly nodded and concentrated on sipping my coffee. She was right. I had been hiding my feelings very well but deep down it was still troubling me and I hoped and prayed that I would get a sign soon that would tell me whether or not I was on the right track.

Chapter 24

Another week had passed and although no bolts of lightning had hit me or no messages had been relayed to me from 'on high', I was still convinced that I was doing the right thing as my birth mother was the last thing I thought about before closing my eyes and again on waking up. I had got a shock the night I'd gone to the pub and heard the men there speaking about Georgina in the derogatory way they did, but I reasoned that she was still my mother and whether it be good or bad I still needed to know. I had briefly spoken to Mammy on the phone and she seemed to have mellowed slightly, even though there was still an atmosphere between us. We studiously avoided any mention of the events that took place around my last visit and had instead concentrated on the wedding and my forthcoming meeting with Gabriel at the weekend (which I was dreading but Frankie was waiting for with bated breath between explosions of laughter. The trollop.).

Frankie had also stipulated that there was to be no further mention of her smear-test results as there was no point in meeting trouble halfway and having everyone else worrying about it. So we agreed to forget about it for the moment although I kept sending up prayers to my daddy that everything would be okay.

Ella had arrived two days previously, positively glowing with happiness. Her little daughter was beautiful and it was obvious that being a mother suited her completely. Ben was overjoyed that there was now a third football fanatic in the house as he and Owen regularly cheered on Arsenal and were delighted to have Hammy join them. Carly and Angelica were excited to see their aunt and Jack was simply transfixed that there was someone smaller than himself in the vicinity and spent all his time staring at Baby Celia Rose who cooed adorably and blew bubbles at everyone.

"Hello, chicken!" I shouted at Carly who had run out to greet me as I arrived at Frankie's house on the morning that we were all heading to Belfast to meet up with Gabriel.

"Well, if it isn't the blushing bride herself," Frankie's mother commented as I walked through the door holding Carly's hand.

"Hi, Celia," I said. "Are you baby-sitting today then?"

"Yes. I'm going to look after Ben and Jack while you all go and meet the homosexual wedding-fixer. You better be careful that he doesn't have too many meetings on his own with Luke. You never know what he could be proposing for them to get up to."

"Yes, thank you, Mother," Frankie said as she came bustling into the room shaking her head, rolling her eyes and indicating generally that I wasn't to take any notice, which I didn't, as years of experience had taught me well.

Frankie's mother was a lovely lady but suffered from a permanently pessimistic point of view and a severe case of foot-in-mouth disease. Frankie's long-suffering but lovely father was nowhere to be seen as he had decided to stay at home to take the dog for a walk. (Frankie's parents had the fittest Scottish terrier in Ireland. It could beat a greyhound any day of the week it was so well exercised.)

"I'm just saying, Frankie. You can't be too careful these days. Good men are hard to find so, when you get one, you want to be sure that he won't be persuaded to start kicking with the other foot and scoring goals for the other team. God knows Ruby's waited long enough for this day. There was a time when I had my doubts it would ever happen but happily I was proved wrong and there was a man out there for her."

Celia had the good grace to go into the kitchen and put the kettle on while I concentrated on scraping my bottom lip from the living-room floor where it had landed as a result of my shock at being branded such a hopeless case.

"Jesus Christ," Frankie growled, "that woman gets worse by the day. I'm going to get a muzzle specially made for her and get it fitted at the earliest opportunity before she alienates our entire family from the rest of the population."

Ella was next to appear with the baby in her arms, all the while shouting instructions to Hammy. Hammy is a big burly gentle giant with twinkly eyes and a moustache, who at that moment was looking quizzically at his wife and answering her in soft and calming tones.

"Nappies?" said Ella.

"Check."

"Bottles?"

"Check."

"Dummy and teething ring?"

"Check."

"Change of clothes?"

"For both of us, yes." Hammy sighed. "Ella, will you please just go and enjoy yourself. Tootsie will be fine with me. We're going to have a lovely father–daughter day while Mammy goes shopping and has a nice girlie day, aren't we, hen?" He kissed Baby Celia Rose on the nose and got gurgled at in response.

"Okay, but you will keep your mobile switched on and –"

"And yes, I will ring you if there is the slightest problem which there won't be. You'd think I'd never looked after her on my own before."

"Good God, it's like a military operation just getting out of the house," I said. "This is why I like being Auntie Ruby. That way I can hand them back and go on my merry way."

"Are you not going to have any children, Ruby?" Celia asked, poking her head around the kitchen door. "Ah well, never mind, I suppose you need time to get to know your husband first. You older brides are probably just grateful that you'll have a companion to share life with."

She didn't get to say any more (thankfully, as although I was thick-skinned even I had my limits) as the microwave pinged and made her go back into the kitchen.

"Ruby, I'm so sorry," Ella said, shaking her head and looking at Hammy. "Sometimes I am so grateful that there's a fifty-minute flight separating us from here."

"Okay! That's us – we're all ready to go," Frankie said as she applied a spray of perfume to her wrists and then put on her watch. "Bye, Mammy!"

"Bye, girls!" Celia called. "Ella, make sure you keep your mobile on. You know what men are like. Anything could happen to that child when you're not here."

"Out!" Frankie ordered, glowering and trying to ignore the stricken look on Ella's face.

Once we were in the car everyone breathed a sigh of relief. I started the engine, manoeuvred out of the drive and then headed for the first sign for the M1 which would take us to Belfast.

"Okay, so let's talk weddings," Frankie said, clapping her hands and looking excited. "What are the arrangements? Where is everyone meeting?"

"I can't wait to see my new dress," Carly lisped as she sat in the back of the car holding her Aunt Ella's hand.

"There won't be a dress there for you today, darling," I explained, "but the lady will take your measurements and design something for you."

"So what is the plan then?" Frankie asked again.

"We're meeting Gabriel in Café Zen in the city centre," I said, "and Mandy is also going to meet us there for lunch. I've already had her on the phone twice this morning. I don't know what she's more excited about – talking about the wedding or seeing how many celebrities she can spot and what stories she can pick up before her next deadline. Café Zen is very exclusive apparently. They even have novelty cabaret acts during the day."

"Wow! That sounds amazing!" said Frankie and she and Ella exchanged glances and smiled.

I grinned as well, finally relenting and allowing myself to get into the spirit of the occasion.

"It sounds very strange to me," I said. "But I'm not surprised. Strange and Gabriel go hand in hand together."

"We're meeting in Café Zen and then what?" Frankie asked.

"We're going to have lunch first and maybe a wee drink to get into the mood and then we're going to discuss plans and go to some of the shops where Gabriel has contacts."

"Have you anything organised yet?" Ella asked.

"Well, to date I've booked the church, the Swiftstown Arms for the reception, and Luke has organised for one of his photographer friends to take pictures on the day. He also knows someone who works for a wedding-car company so he has that sorted out as well although he's handed all the details to Gabriel who is acting like a feckin sergeant major and insisting on taking charge of everything."

"Today we're going to look at wedding cakes, wedding stationery and then go to some dress shops," Frankie told Ella.

"And I've already told Gabriel that I'm only going to one dress shop and that's the one I picked myself out of the *Yellow Pages* in my office."

"Ruby is insisting on going to a dressmaker in a back street in Belfast and is refusing point blank to be talked out of it." Frankie rolled her eyes and sighed.

"I am a big believer in fate, Frankie. You know that. If my finger landed on Rose Malone it did so for a reason and I'm not changing my mind."

"But Gabriel is bound to have contacts in the best shops and I'll bet he could get you good discount too."

I gave Frankie my most ferocious look and she finally shut up and waved her hand in surrender.

140

When we arrived in Café Zen, I stopped and stared in wonderment. I had been told that it was quite plush and a haunt favoured by the great and the good but hadn't been expecting the exquisite grandeur and opulence that met my eyes. It had high ornate ceilings from which chandeliers hung down, sparkling and glinting in the light. The layout gave the impression of a maze as there were so many enclaves and corners, some of which were closed off behind velvet drapes and others which were decorated with large blood-red and forest-green sofas and massive cushions.

Café Zen had its own roof-top beer garden and boasted a cocktail bar where the daytime cabaret act was in full swing as a jazz singer wearing a jaunty bowler hat and a waistcoat was walking casually through the crowd and singing the blues. The bar was packed and I found it hard to see. I squinted around looking for someone resembling a packet of fruit pastilles but couldn't see anyone.

"He mustn't be here yet," I said. "But then again we are forty minutes early. We should probably just get a drink first and wait for him by the bar. He said he had a bit of work to finish here and he would meet us as soon as he was done."

Just at that moment there was a huge round of applause as the jazz singer finished performing and the spotlight centred on a corner from whence the next act would approach. A voice boomed and asked everyone to welcome to the bar 'Fifi Von Tease' and it was with horrified fascination and shock that I realised that the drag queen singing in a deep voice with a platinum-blonde wig, a tight burlesque costume, stockings and staggeringly high heels was none other than the person who was being paid to be responsible for the organisation of my wedding.

Chapter 25

"Sweet suffering mother of fu–" I began before Frankie stepped in, covered Carly's ears, and took charge.

"Can I have a large gin, please?" she shouted at the barman. "It's for medicinal purposes," she said to Ella who was looking around in confusion.

Frankie tried to discreetly point to the new act as he travelled around, singing and being cheered on by the crowd who obviously were big fans and saw 'Fifi' perform regularly. "It's . . . that's . . . erm . . ."

"That, Ella, is my wedding planner," I said in a very controlled voice. "That person dressed in a red basque and suspenders is the one who apparently will be advising me on how to dress tastefully for the day in question and helping me to plan my wedding. There might be a slight problem though. No wedding can take place if the groom has been hung up by his goolies."

"You're joking!" spluttered Ella.

"Luke is a dead man," I snarled before finishing my drink in one gulp and marching outside with my mobile phone in my hand.

"Ruby, wait!" I heard Frankie call but I wasn't listening. I had things to sort out.

Luke had left the house to go and take photographs at a local school that morning and usually I wouldn't have disturbed him but this was an emergency.

"Hello, you," Luke said on answering his phone. "Everything going according to plan?"

"Oh pretty much, I suppose," I answered. "We've just arrived in Café Zen and we're waiting for Mandy to arrive."

"Have you been speaking to Gabriel yet?"

"Have I been speaking to Gabriel?" I repeated slowly. "Well, here's the thing. It's a very funny story actually. I agreed to come and meet with Gabriel and have been doing a great job of talking myself into getting excited about this wedding and planning ahead. It had been working too, up until now. I came here today in the hope that we would be able to work something out but dear Gabriel seems to be hell bent on trying to get me hauled in *on an assault charge*!" I shouted the last bit and could hear Luke starting to breathe heavily.

"You've got to calm down, Ruby. Whatever it is, I'll speak to him about it. I asked him in the nicest possible way to try and tone himself down a bit because it was making you uncomfortable. He's not turned up looking garish again, has he?"

"Garish? No. He's wearing black and red today."

"At least he's making the effort," Luke said.

"Oh sorry, did I forget to mention that it's a red corset, with black suspenders teamed with a wig that's the same colour as a canary's feckin feathers? He is also wearing more bloody make-up than Frankie, Ella and me put together and is currently walking around warbling into a microphone and being quite the little entertainer. He's even got an alter ego. She is called Fifi Von Tease. Luke?"

"Yes, Ruby."

"Have you any last requests?"

"Ruby, please calm down. I didn't know that he was going to do that and if I had known I wouldn't have been long talking him out of it."

"*I am going to kill you!*" I howled into the phone, startling a few passers-by who obviously thought that I was a few sandwiches short of a picnic.

"I'll ring him now, Ruby."

"You'll have a job," I spat. "He's in the middle of his bloody act and at this precise moment in time is singing 'Hey, Big Spender' and relieving some poor bloke of his tie. I am a simple girl with simple needs – therefore how the hell have I ended up in this predicament?"

"Ruby, I promise I'll make it up to you. Just please go along with it for now. I've heard that he's a complete genius and that he does a very good job which is all I want."

"Why won't anyone take my feelings on board?" I asked, getting more upset by the second. "I know he's supposed to be a genius and that he's got a fabulous website and that he's wonderfully well connected but I am not impressed by any of that. I'm not homophobic either. I think under other circumstances, although we wouldn't be best friends, Gabriel and I could get on quite well but under the current ones I have to truthfully say that he is annoying the shite out of me and making me twitch." I continued to pace up and down the pavement, breathing heavily. "You are going to be making this up to me for the rest of your life, Luke. You better start practising how to grovel as you'll be doing an awful lot of it."

I snapped the phone shut and turned to find Frankie looking at me sympathetically. Ella had taken Carly to another part of the bar to buy her a Coke (and take her out of my way in case my seething rage scarred her for life).

"Not a word," I said as I stalked back inside where 'Fifi' was finishing her act with a flourish before disappearing back in through the door she came out of.

Two minutes later and Mandy arrived and was terribly upset to have missed all the excitement.

"Fifi Von Tease is your wedding planner?" she said, her mouth in a perfect O shape. "Wow! That's amazing. Fifi is quite a high-profile character on the Belfast social circuit. I've written about her a few times in my column. I can't wait to meet the man behind the mask."

"I'd use that term very lightly," I snapped.

Gabriel appeared about fifteen minutes later, looking a little less like a drag queen and a little more like a Christmas tree in yet another bright and colourful ensemble and I had to count to five hundred and nip myself hard in case I lost all control and battered him with the ice bucket sitting on the bar. I would be the laughing stock of the entire population of Swiftstown shortly because of him (or her . . . delete as appropriate) and his antics.

After he had been introduced to Mandy, Ella and Carly (who looked at him in total amazement) and given Frankie an over-demonstrative hug and kissed the air around her head forty times, Gabriel turned towards me.

"I wasn't expecting you to arrive so early, Ruby. Did you enjoy my act?" he asked, smiling sheepishly.

The deluded eejit actually thought that there was a chance that I might be impressed.

"Oh yeah – you're a real ace card," I said through gritted teeth. "Would it be possible for us to get on with the matter in hand and get this day over and done with once and for all?"

"Of course. I have an itinerary here to help us along. After we've had lunch there's a cake shop I'd like to visit. The chef there is French and he makes the most divine wedding cakes and has an extensive catalogue for prospective clients to view."

"It's a cake," I said in disgust. "It's made with eggs, flour and sugar and I do not need a bloody catalogue to look at. As long as it has three tiers and a bride and groom on top, that'll do me fine."

Gabriel laughed and spoke to the assembled group as if I wasn't there and he hadn't heard me.

"Three-tiered cakes are so last season," he said. "All the society brides are getting cakes made to their own specific instructions. I had a bride last week who is a milliner by trade, trained at the London School of Fashion, you know, and her wedding cake was chocolate gateaux made in the guise of two hats, one pink and one black with feathers flowing. The guests were so impressed. I also had another bride who had her cake made in the shape of the Egyptian pyramids as that was where she and her husband were going on their honeymoon. I can't even begin to tell you how fabulous it was!"

"Good. Then don't," I snapped. "Three tiers and a plastic bride and groom will suffice. Although I suppose I could compromise and ask the chef to make the groom out of marzipan. That way it'll be easier for me to lob bits off him when he annoys me and makes stupid decisions."

"What about the stationery?" Frankie asked, intervening quickly.

"Yes. I have another contact in the trade," Gabriel said. "He designs the wedding stationery after the dresses have been chosen and gives a very subtle hint as to what the guests can expect the bridesmaids to be wearing on the day. He doesn't give away colours – he just uses a certain design and gives a little taster. He is totally fabulous. That brings me to the dresses."

Gabriel looked at me as did everyone else.

"I have a few wonderfully talented people in mind," he said. "Vera Wang and Femme Couture as well as a few Irish designers such as Helena Quinlan and –"

"Rose Malone," I said. "She's fabulous. Don't know where she trained but her design studio is based on a street not far from the city centre."

Gabriel opened his mouth but quickly shut it again when Frankie slowly shook her head.

"Fine," was all Gabriel said in a clipped tone before we were all shown to a table where we would be having lunch and where I hopefully would manage to eat something without feeling the need to poke Gabriel with my fork.

Mandy was only able to stay for lunch and then had to report back to her station as magazine gossipmonger. There had never been much love lost between Mandy and me but, as I was destined to marry her brother and would be compelled to refer to her as

146

family in the near future, I decided to try and include her in proceedings. Luke had tried to suggest that I have her as one of my bridesmaids (obviously that was before I told him we would be divorced before we got married). A gossip columnist wouldn't exactly be the ideal person to keep details a secret. Not that I cared but I knew that if word were to escape about the colour of the bridesmaid's dress that Frankie was to wear, it might just be enough to start another civil war in Ireland.

"Thanks for coming," I said as I walked her to the door once we had finished eating.

"It was nice to get out," she sighed.

Once we stepped outside I noticed that her eyes were encircled by dark rings and that she looked very tired.

"Is everything all right?" I asked, studying her.

"Grand," she said, avoiding making eye contact with me.

"What is it?" I demanded. "Speak now, woman. You look terrible."

"Thanks," she said weakly. "Look, I'm not sure I should be telling you this but I've had Mum and Dad on the phone. They're talking about coming home in the run-up to the wedding and being there for the day itself. I don't know how to tell Luke. You know what he's like."

"He's like any other child that has been treated like crap by their parents, I would imagine," I answered with barely concealed hostility. "There is no way that they can arrive just before the wedding. It's supposed to be a happy time and I don't want it ruined. It's bad enough having Gabriel involved, wanting to flounce everything up, never mind bringing your drunken layabout of a father and slapper of a mother into the equation."

Mandy looked like I'd just hit her (subtlety was never my strong point, not that you'd guess).

"I'm sorry but there's no nice way of putting it, Mandy. Parents shouldn't abandon their children and use and abuse them at will. It's not right and I will not allow it to happen again. Next time you're speaking to them, tell them from me that they're not welcome. I'll have a bouncer installed at the chapel door to ensure they don't come anywhere near us if I have to."

"So you'd rather they didn't attend then," Mandy said, raising her eyebrows.

"In a manner of speaking," I muttered. "Your brother won't appreciate it and believe me neither will I."

"I don't want to spoil anyone's day but they asked me to speak to Luke and see if they could come. Call a truce, if you like."

My blood started to boil. Call a truce, my arse. A free day out, a slap-up meal and being feckin treated to drink all day because their son had just got married was more like it. His mother was probably hoping for an opportunity to get down and dirty with some of the single male guests (who would have to be blind, deaf, dumb, stupid and not at all fussy about who they were seen with).

"I'm sorry, Mandy, but I don't think it's a good idea. A truce might be possible one day but our wedding day won't be it. Everyone, including you, has been hurt quite enough."

"They're phoning me back later in the week to find out if they can come. I'll probably be shot for shouting my mouth off and letting the cat out of the bag. It's innate in me at this stage though. It's my job to expose things, so keeping secrets was never going to be my strong point."

"Take care," I said as she looked at her watch and took several steps back, indicating that she had to go. She looked incredibly sad and I felt very sorry for her.

Chapter 26

As it transpired the dressmaker's was situated on a side street behind the City Hall. Rose Malone was a small little lady with auburn hair that was streaked with grey. She was dressed in an old-fashioned overall peppered with pins and needles of all shapes and sizes which covered a very plain jumper and skirt. She greeted us with a wide beaming smile and spoke with a broad Belfast accent and I immediately knew that I liked her. The fact that Gabriel (who was dressed in a bright green rig-out that would make your eyes water) was appraising her with mounting horror only served to increase my pleasure.

She showed us lots of designs which Gabriel snorted at whilst picking his nails (which were painted black, no doubt to co-ordinate with his earlier fancy-dress costume).

I told Rose exactly what I wanted which was the direct opposite of what Gabriel would have chosen and he humphed and puffed just to let me know that he was unhappy (good!).

"Okay, so you'd like something understated with the least detail possible, no train and you're sure that you don't want a veil?" Rose asked.

"That's it in a nutshell. I might concede and have some type of headdress but I don't want a veil. I hated it when I was making my Holy Communion and my thoughts haven't changed any."

"Understated I like but you need some type of detail and you simply must have a train!" Gabriel interjected. "You can pin it up after the wedding itself but it would look so elegant when you're walking down the aisle."

"No, thanks." I said. "I know what I want."

"And resistance is futile," Frankie said wearily. "I've already been here with her and it's pointless arguing. You're better off just agreeing if only for your own mental health."

"I don't get paid enough for this," Gabriel declared before reaching into his pocket, producing a packet of very fancy brown-tipped cigarettes and scooting outside.

"Errrrrr . . . I think you'll find you do!" I shouted after him.

I watched as Rose did a rough sketch on a piece of paper, her hand flying and her mouth set in concentration as she shaded in areas and drew lines.

"This is only an idea now but I think we can do simple and elegant without being boring or unfashionable."

I looked at the drawing and my mouth transformed into a smile. I looked at Frankie and could tell that she was also pleased.

"That's a really nice idea," Ella commented, looking over our shoulders while Carly leaned into her side, "and very Ruby-ish. I would never have thought of that but I know that it will suit you."

"Do you see anything you like?" Rose said to Frankie. "Look for a design that tickles your fancy and I can do something to suit you in whatever colour you want. And we must also get you sorted out, wee woman," she said kindly to Carly who blinked shyly and smiled. "When is the wedding again?" she added.

"The wedding is next May," I answered.

"I'll have a lot of work to do in a rather short space of time but I do like a challenge," Rose said in a friendly voice and I knew, although I'd only just met her, that she would make me a dress that I'd like and keep my (very fussy) bridesmaid happy as well.

The only person left to convince was the sour-faced leprechaun who had gone outside.

I opened the door of the shop and looked right and left and finally found Gabriel walking around the gardens of a large sprawling building on the other side of the road.

"Do you want to come and see what Rose has drawn for me?" I asked.

"If you're happy then that's all that matters," he answered, being very non-committal.

"I am happy and I do like it. I dislike fuss. You and I will get along a lot better in this arrangement if you don't try to force me into things because there's no surer way of getting me to do the direct opposite."

"I insist that you should have a boring dress with no train and no veil," Gabriel announced. "You should complement that by having a three-tier cake with plastic figurines and plain white wedding stationery. I also think that you should have no music in the chapel, shite-looking flowers and that smiling or having fun should be banished for the entire day."

I looked at Gabriel and felt my mouth twitch. "Nice try, love, but you've just described my perfect day apart from the fact that I happen to like flowers (shocking, I know, but blame my mother) and that smiling and laughing shall be pre-requisites to attendance because I intend to crack my face that day."

"You really do love him, don't you?" Gabriel said matter-of-factly.

"Yes, I do," I said, half-expecting him to turn around and say 'poor fella' but he didn't.

"As long as you don't end up in the same predicament as the poor sods that wind up in there," he said, gesturing towards a sign that told us that we were in the grounds of a refuge centre for victims of domestic violence.

"I think that's quite unlikely, don't you?" I said.

"Hmmm," Gabriel responded. He was probably thinking that if the situation ever were to arise Luke would come off worse. (What he didn't realise was that my bark was infinitely worse than my bite, scary though it may be. I just wasn't going to tell him that.)

"I suppose we should go back in and see the others," I said. "Frankie and Ella have to get home to their children and we still need to go and visit the cake shop –" (and their vast array of plastic figurines) "– and go and look at the wedding stationery."

"Okay," Gabriel agreed.

As we walked back across the road I was taken with a sudden feeling of *déjà vu*, as if I had been there before. I decided that I must be imagining things however and put it down to a very distracting day.

"Are we ready to go?" I asked as we walked back in to find Frankie, Carly and Ella gathered around Rose who was working her magic again and transfixing them with her drawings.

Frankie held up a finger and then gasped. "Wow!" she said.

"I saw something similar in a magazine this week," Gabriel said, peeping over their shoulders and trying to feign disinterest but failing. "Do you follow the trends at London Fashion Week, Rose?"

I stifled a smile as Rose gave Gabriel a bemused look.

"No, dear, but I am a great believer in developing dresses that will suit the wearer and her figure and make the bride happy. That's the only trend I'm interested in and it's worked for me this past forty-five years."

"It's a good trend," I agreed.

Rose showed me the drawings for the bridesmaid's dress and I looked at them in delight (yes, delight . . . I think I was finally getting into the swing of things . . . just a wee bit, mind!).

"Look at this one," Frankie said, displaying another picture in front of her chest. "Isn't it amazing? Our wee flower girl is going to look stunning."

I looked at the sketch and imagined Carly (who was grinning from ear to ear) and her blonde ringlets and smiled. It would be perfect.

As we prepared to leave and I made my way past the wedding

dresses and evening gowns that were on display at the door and walked out into the afternoon air, I again experienced the strange notion that I had been there before.

"Frankie," I said.

"Yes, Rubes?"

"Have I ever been here before?"

"What do you mean?"

"Have we ever been on this street before?"

"No. Sure, there's nothing here. No shops or anything that would bring us here."

"Perhaps you were here in a past life," Gabriel suggested helpfully. "You were probably a founder member of one of those terrorist groups who went round annoying everyone and being totally disagreeable."

I stuck my tongue out at him, linked arms with Frankie and bade Rose goodbye.

"I'll give you a wee call in a few weeks, love, and you can come back and talk about it some more after I've had time to put some designs together properly," Rose smiled. "And maybe by that stage you'll have remembered. These streets all look the same. You're probably just mixing it up with another one."

"Maybe I am," I said, feeling sure I wasn't but now wasn't the time to ponder over it. I had people to see and things to do and a wedding to plan.

Chapter 27

As it turned out Frankie, Ella and Carly ended up going home on the bus on their own after we had visited the man who would be responsible for making my wedding invitations. I had to admit that he was very good and that I loved his work. Luke had decided to come down to Belfast and meet me (grovel and beg forgiveness) and we ended up going back to Café Zen with Gabriel for a drink.

Obviously the place had the same effect on all country bumpkins, as I had to tell Luke to close his mouth and stop dribbling after five minutes of standing in everyone's way at the door, gawping around him like he'd never been let out before.

"Well, you lot certainly know how to live the high life here," he said, once we'd got some drinks and sat down. He had regained his composure and looked slightly less shell-shocked by that time.

"It hasn't been open that long," Gabriel explained. "I know the guy who runs it and he's done a superb job on the décor. He enlisted my help in promoting it and I've helped to organise a few functions here."

Luke gave me a knowing look as if to say "told you he was a genius" and smugly continued to drink his beer.

"God, there must be no end to your talents, Gabriel," I said and he looked at me as if he didn't know whether or not I was being sarcastic (which was exactly the way I wanted to keep him).

"I hear that you're quite talented in your profession too," Gabriel said, addressing Luke. "I know a friend of a friend who runs a little art gallery in Belfast who was very impressed with some photographs you took at the launch of her latest work."

"Ah yes," Luke said smiling. "That was a really enjoyable night. Remember, Ruby?"

I nodded. I did indeed remember and had loved every minute of it. There were few things in life that I was truly passionate about but Luke and art were two of them and, as I'd had them both around me that night, I had been in my element.

"I have a little proposition for you," Gabriel said, leaning in towards Luke and tapping his arm.

Frankie's mother's words about my future husband and Gabriel and propositions and what they could consist of suddenly came rushing back to me and I took a firm grip of Luke's shirt sleeve and roughly tugged him back.

"*Owwwww!*" he said, rubbing his arm. "I swear to God, Ruby, you are seriously unaware of your own strength."

"Yep. Wonder Woman, that's me, and you better believe it," I said, looking at Gabriel who was wearing a bemused expression.

"Anyway," Gabriel continued slowly (this time refraining from touching Luke), "I wanted to ask you a favour. I have a friend, Caitlin O'Donnell, who's an artist based in Letterkenny in Donegal, and she is launching her latest exhibition there in another few weeks and I was wondering if you could do the needful and take some photos for her."

"Only if I can come too," I answered before Luke had the chance to utter a word.

"Only if she can come as well," he grinned. "Yeah, sure, I'd love to do it and we could stay with Ruby's mother that night."

I immediately stiffened and lost all interest in the event. I had been trying not to let thoughts of my mother invade my mind as inevitably it resulted in me questioning everything she had ever said or told me and I ended up in bad form.

I sat quietly and tried to gather my thoughts for the next forty minutes whilst taking in everything that was happening around me. A girl had emerged from the same side door from which Gabriel had appeared sporting his stockings and lace, and was belting out a Gloria Gaynor track in a husky voice.

"That's Gina," Gabriel explained excitedly. "She works part-time in the pizzeria at the end of the street but has a voice to die for. We keep telling her to audition for *The X Factor* but she's determined to stay here. Her mum's not well, you see."

I looked around me. I still couldn't believe what was happening. My life had changed so much in the last few months and now, shock of all shocks, I was sitting at a table in one of the fanciest café bars I had ever seen with my future husband and my wildly dressed wedding planner who turned into the campest man in the world when he was drunk.

"So tell me, Ruby," he began, flinging his entire self around in the chair and doing the best Kenny Everett impression I had ever seen by wildly throwing his legs around. "How did you find today, sweetie?"

"Rubbbeeeee. Her name is Rubbbeeeee," Luke slurred whilst leaning over me and waving a straw in Gabriel's direction. "Cut out that 'sweetie crap' or she'll have your guts for garters or worse she'll have mine."

"That'll be one less thing for me to worry about then, won't it?" I said. "I'll have a garter to match my wedding dress."

The two of them looked at me for a minute and then fell about laughing. (Drunken laughing, I might add, which goes on far longer than necessary and is high-pitched and annoying especially when you're sober.) I had consumed a few drinks but found that I couldn't relax because something was niggling me and had been all day, except I couldn't put my finger on what it was. I had a feeling that it might have been something to do with Rose Malone's shop.

"I'm going for a walk," I said, although neither of them was paying any attention to me.

I walked out through the front door and into the night air. I saw a summer seat directly opposite me and decided to position myself there and look into the sky. I was in mid-thought about the day's events when my phone rang and I registered with some surprise that it was Mandy.

"Hi, Mandy, are you okay?" I answered, remembering the rather bizarre conversation that we'd had earlier in the day concerning her parents.

"I'm fine. Just feeling a bit lonely, I suppose," she said.

I was shocked. Mandy gave off the aura of being a very popular girl-about-town with a glitzy job that most girls would love (apart from me, that is) except that it suddenly appeared that maybe it wasn't as glamorous as everyone thought.

"Why are you feeling lonely?" I asked gently. "What's the matter?"

"Maybe it's not so much a case of feeling lonely as being alone," she said.

I could hear the crack in her voice as it began to break.

"Have your mum and dad been in touch again?" I asked.

"They rang this evening," she said.

I turned my nose up in disgust. Typical. Useless, selfish, good for nothing, lying, cheating, drunken feckers (the list was endless). Could they not see what they were doing to their children? They should never have left in the first place or behaved the way they did, but now that they had gone it would have been kinder to just stay away and not keep rubbing salt into the wounds. Why could they not be content with tormenting the poor Spaniards that had the misfortune to be in contact with them now?

"I'm still in Belfast," I said suddenly. "Why don't you come and meet me? I'm sitting on a summer seat outside Café Zen and Luke and Gabriel are inside getting rat-arsed."

"You're joking me?"

"I am not. I don't joke about such matters. I shouldn't even be leaving the two of them on their own as Frankie's mother would have you believe that they could get up to all sorts. Luke could be getting propositioned and start wanting to join rival teams as we speak."

"This I have to see," Mandy declared. "I'll be over shortly."

I hung up and continued to look into the sky which was filled with stars.

Feckin families. Who'd have them? They were all nothing but trouble, I thought. If they weren't abandoning you immediately after giving birth to you, they were giving birth to you, lumbering you with a rotten childhood and then having the cheek to abandon you. Worse again, however, was them then having the bigger cheek to come looking for you just so as they could embarrass the shite out of you on your feckin wedding day, no less. I moved from my position on the wooden bench and started to walk up and down the street (that is, charge about in a bad temper due to nervous energy created by the mere mention of the dastardly in-laws-from-hell).

I had been pacing for around twenty minutes when Mandy was dropped off by a taxi.

"You look all hot and bothered," she observed.

"Your mother and father and their antics would make anybody feel bloody flustered," I said hotly. "Tell me exactly what was said."

"Nothing much. Mammy said that she had bought a new dress especially for the occasion and she couldn't bring it back because the tags had already been removed." In other words she had probably nicked it and was now on some Spanish store's most-wanted list for theft.

"What did your daddy say?"

"He was looking forward to catching up with everyone and having a good old Irish knees-up. He says that the Spanish beer is nice enough but that it's hard to beat a pint of the black stuff."

Translated, this meant that he'd like to come to a good old Irish wedding where he'd be fed Guinness by the barrelful, get drunk and behave like an arrogant, obnoxious twat all night.

"And what exactly did they say when you told them that they weren't welcome and that I'd have Sylvester Stallone on standby to remove them if they appeared?"

"Well, that's the thing, Ruby, you see. I did try and tell them that you didn't want them there but they wouldn't take no for an answer. They say that they want to surprise Luke and that they have a very special wedding present for him."

The feckers had ignored me and were going to come anyway. Bloody brilliant. Just what I needed to add to what was already turning into a circus. Not only did my wedding planner have nicer knees and wear more make-up than me but now I was going to have to worry about the fact that Luke's lunatic parents could turn up and give the proceedings a fireworks display that nobody wanted or needed.

"I did tell them what you said," Mandy said earnestly. "Honestly I did. But you know what they're like. They'll suit themselves no matter what."

"Don't worry," I said in a determined voice. "If I say that they won't be there, they won't, and believe me I mean it."

Chapter 28

"Where did you disappear to last night when we were still in Café Zen?" Luke asked, propped up on one elbow and looking at me as we lay in bed late the following morning – after he had managed to sober up.

I had discovered that Gabriel and Luke were quite a mischievous handful when they were drunk and a bad combination to contend with. Luke had booked us into the Holiday Inn near the city centre and after he and Gabriel had howled every verse of 'Staying Alive' at the entrance (complete with all the "Ahh – ahh – ahh" bits that were sung at four-hundred-tone-deaf decibels which turned the hotel doorman into a bad-tempered maniac), I had eventually persuaded him to shut the feck up and come inside.

"Hey? Where did you go?" he repeated now when I didn't answer.

"I went for a walk to chill out," I said, "and then Mandy arrived and we sat and talked for a while. Thanks for coming down though. It was a nice thought."

"I just wanted to try and make it up to you," Luke said quietly. "I didn't realise that you were going to stumble upon Gabriel in the middle of a drag-queen act and was afraid that you'd never forgive me so I decided to surprise you."

"And surprised I was."

"Mandy was in peculiar form last night too. I thought that she would have been in her element and doing her usual celebrity-spotting routine but she seemed totally distracted. There must be something in the air with you women at the minute."

"She was just tired," I lied. "It must be very wearying being a professional busybody. You and Gabriel didn't need us anyway. You must be the new addition to Fifi Von Tease's act."

"Yes, I have a vague recollection of using a Corona beer bottle as a microphone," Luke said sheepishly. "Was I that bad?"

"No, you were bloody worse," I answered, laughing as he threw a pillow at me while I swung my legs out of bed.

"You have to admit that Gabriel's not that bad when you get to know him," Luke said. "He's very good at what he does and he's getting me a job into the bargain. If I play my cards right I could get plenty of photography work through the contacts that Gabriel has."

"Well, I will admit that I'm looking forward to another gallery exhibition," I said.

"We can take a trip down before the actual launch. Maybe make a night of it. Stay at a hotel where I won't serenade the doorman – badly and nearly get thrown out – and go and visit a few other places." "Sounds good," I said, feeling my excitement mount. "Let's do that soon. I'd love to get away but just don't be telling my mother about it or she'll be insisting that we go and stay with her and I just couldn't be arsed at the minute."

Luke opened his mouth and went to speak but wisely changed his mind as I was in no mood to be remonstrated with.

"If that's what you want," he sighed.

"It is," I said. "In fact, I think we should ask Frankie and Owen if they want to come with us as well. I'm not the only one that has had a lot to contend with lately. Frankie hasn't had it easy either."

"Why, what's wrong?"

"Nothing for you to worry about," I said, pointing at my nether regions. (Why do women always do that? Between pointing at our crotches when discussing medical problems of a female nature and referring to our bits as "down there" in ominous tones as if they were a million miles away and living on a planet all of their own, men must think we're mad altogether.)

"Oh right," Luke said quickly in case I might elaborate further and actually start telling him details. "Of course we'll ask them along. It's a long time since we've been out with them."

"Good. That's settled then." I finally removed myself from the edge of the bed and went and switched on the shower and got myself a large fluffy towel from the pile beside the bath.

After a basic continental breakfast we went for a walk before going back to the hotel to collect our things and head for home.

The receptionist bade us farewell and asked if there was anything else she could do for us.

"Are you from around here?" I asked, suddenly inspired and seizing the moment.

"Yes," she said, smiling.

"Have you ever heard of St Catherine's Lodge?" I asked in the hope that finally somebody might give me a positive response.

She shook her head and looked thoughtful. "Have you any idea where it is?"

"None – although I think it must be in Belfast somewhere but strangely nobody has heard of it."

"Hold on a minute and I'll ask some of the others. Some of the older women might know."

She came back several minutes later with a woman who had greying hair and was wearing a pair of overalls.

"St Catherine's Lodge," she said slowly and purposefully. "I used to hear my mother talking about that place but it was known locally as 'The Baby Convent' because it was where women went to get rid of babies they didn't want."

Her words cut through my heart like a knife and I could feel Luke's grip tightening on my arm as he looked at me sadly.

"Where is it?" I asked, my voice devoid of all emotion as I was incapable of feeling anything.

"Well, that's the thing, you see. Nobody ever knew where it was. It was the best-kept secret in Belfast because the mothers who went there never talked about their experiences and their families most likely wouldn't have known that they were there and, as for the nuns, well, they were bound by the church to keep quiet."

"Right," I said. "Thanks for everything. You've given me more information than anyone else has and for that I'm very grateful."

I turned and walked out of the hotel with my legs shaking and threatening to buckle beneath me.

Luke came out quickly after me. "At least it's something," he said. "As you said, it's more information than you've had so far which is good."

"Oh yeah. It's great, Luke," I said angrily. "I've just had it confirmed that not only was I not wanted but that she was so ashamed of the fact that she was pregnant with me that she had to hide away in a convent that's more elusive than the Scarlet Pimpernel himself!"

"I'm sure it wasn't that she didn't want you. It was probably more circumstantial than anything else. It was the mid-1970s, Ruby – girls who got pregnant would have been practically ostracised in their own communities. It's not like now when every other mother with a pram is a Lone Mother and it's just accepted. It was a different era back then. Keeping you could have ruined her life."

"Or her lifestyle. From what I heard it wasn't so much that she had to give me up. It was more that she didn't want me in the first place for fear that I'd get in the way of her socialising and her men. I am so sick of this shit. What am I? A bloody masochist. I can't do this any more."

I stomped to the car with tears threatening to spurt in a projectile fashion from my eyes.

Twenty minutes later we were driving home with both of us in a sombre frame of mind. Luke was quiet for fear of sticking his foot in his mouth and making my already volcanic mood worse and I was so deep in thought that I had transported myself to a different world of self-loathing and worthlessness.

My phone began to vibrate in my pocket but once I registered that it was my mother I threw it onto the dashboard of the car in a fit of pique and refused to answer it.

"That could be important," Luke said. "Your mother doesn't usually ring your mobile, Ruby. You should have answered that."

"If she wants me I'm sure she'll leave a message!" I snapped, at which point my phone beeped to let me know that I had a voicemail.

Wearily I lifted it, rang the number for my mailbox and impatiently listened and waited for the mundane message which would consist of my mother asking how I was because she felt guilty. Except that wasn't what I heard. The message was indeed from my mother but she sounded frantic and frightened.

"Ruby, you've got to come and help me. I'm so scared. Please help me, love –" and I didn't get to hear any more as the phone became muffled and fuzzy as did her voice.

"Turn the car around, Luke," I said, panic-stricken. "Mammy needs me and I'll never forgive myself if anything happens to her."

Chapter 29

We arrived in Smugglers' Bay less than two hours later and my distress increased tenfold when I discovered a Garda car and an ambulance sitting in my mother's drive. I had tried to ring on numerous occasions on my way down the road but to no avail as the house phone didn't seem to be working and her mobile kept referring me to the answering service.

I burst in through the door and then into the sitting room and saw Mammy wrapped in a blanket being comforted by a female Garda officer whilst her male counterpart took notes. Donal was sitting beside her looking anxious and I could see his father through the window, standing out in the back yard smoking his pipe.

"Mammy!" I shouted, going to her and throwing my arms around her. She wept into my shoulder and appeared so fragile that I was afraid I might break her if I held her too tight.

"What's happened to you? Are you hurt? Has someone done something to you?"

My voice was high-pitched and annoyed and the female officer motioned for me to follow her out of the room.

"What's happened?" I asked, nearly afraid to hear what she had to say.

"Your mother was burgled last night. Two intruders got into the house and tied her up. They obviously didn't get what they came for as nothing is missing. Then they messed the place up, no doubt looking for cash, and took off, leaving her still tied up on the floor."

"Last night? Why wasn't I informed?" I said in confusion. "Why are you all here now if the incident happened last night?"

"She was only found this afternoon," the officer said gently, making me recoil in horror.

My poor mother had been tied up all night, was in the house on her own, probably terrified that whoever it was would come back, and hadn't been discovered until after midday.

"Who found her?" I asked quietly.

"Aisling Redmond. She works up at the hotel."

"She's the tour guide," I said, remembering the name. "Thank God she did. It just doesn't bear thinking about if she hadn't."

I put my hand over my mouth and turned away from the guard who gently rubbed my arm, before leaving and returning with Luke who immediately enveloped me in a hug.

"Your mother's okay," he said. "She's shocked and frightened but she knows it could have been a lot worse. They didn't get away with anything and they didn't hurt her as such. Nor did they threaten her to tell them if valuables or money were hidden – which is what usually happens in such cases."

"No, they just left her lying there tied up like a sack of rubbish to fret until she was found. What if she'd had a heart attack or a stroke or something? What if Aisling hadn't found her when she did? She could have starved to death."

"I think I'd have been able to live off my ample hump for a while, sweetheart," Mammy said as she joined us in the room, looking pale and strained but trying to smile. "A bit of starvation would probably do me the world of good."

Donal and Robbie also came in with their coats on, as they were leaving, and Donal gave me a pat on the arm while Robbie awkwardly gave me a conciliatory nudge with his elbow and I smiled weakly back at them both.

I gave Mammy another hug and rubbed her shoulders. "Why don't you go and lie down, Mammy," I said. "You're so pale."

"Lying down is the one thing I don't want to do, love. I was lying down on the floor up until two and a half hours ago and that was quite long enough."

I grimaced as I thought of what she must have gone through.

"Where were you when you rang me?" I asked.

"I had managed to get my arm free, you see, and was within reach of my mobile. It had been in my pocket but slipped out while I was being tied up so I managed to get it easily once I manoeuvred myself in the right direction. I tried to ring Donal first but he had his phone switched off and then I rang you. I didn't want to ring you at all, love, but I was left with no choice."

"You sounded so scared," I said.

"I was in the middle of leaving you a message but then I heard someone at the door and got frightened and dropped the mobile. I thought it was them coming back for me but thankfully it was that lovely wee girl Aisling. She untied me, got me a glass of water and phoned the guards and the ambulance, and then went back to the hotel to report what had happened – but I haven't seen her since. I don't even know why she was here."

"Where are the paramedics?" I asked, suddenly remembering that they had been there when I had walked in.

"They've left. I'm fine. They were going to take me to the hospital in Letterkenny and were trying to tell me that I was suffering from shock but I told them I didn't want to go anywhere. As long as I have my girl I'm happy," she finished, giving me a squeeze and putting her head on my shoulder.

The door knocked and Mammy froze in my arms.

"Who is it?" I asked.

"Oh God, it's that cross-looking diva from the hotel along with an older man," Luke said, peering through the side of the curtain.

"That must be her father," Mammy said, looking more strained than ever.

"I'll get rid of them," I said as I went to open the door. "You go into the other room, Mammy."

I opened the door.

"I'm Judith McQueen, Assistant Manager in the hotel, and this is my father Harry. He's the new owner," Bag Features said with a sullen face. "Is your mother here?"

"She is but she's in no fit state for visitors," I said. "Any message you'd like passed on?"

"We were just sorry to hear about the incident that occurred last night," the older man said, speaking for the first time. He was tall and quite handsome with greying hair and a tanned face. His hands were perfectly clean and soft-looking and his nails looked like they'd been manicured every day of his life.

"I'll be sure to tell her that," I said, going to close the door.

Judith stuck out her arm and, leaning against the door, prevented me from closing it properly.

"We'll need to speak to your mother as soon as she's well. This has raised some security issues which we need to address as this cottage is situated on our ground."

"Really. Well, I'm so glad you're taking the matter seriously," I said.

"We're taking it very seriously," she responded sweetly. "It's happened once and we wouldn't like it if the intruders came back again. Your mother needs to think about her own personal security. She's in a vulnerable position living on her own in the grounds of a hotel with guests passing through daily. Anything could happen. Anything at all."

I wouldn't have minded but she accompanied her final words with a menacing sneer that aggravated me beyond belief and that, coupled with the rest of the day's events, became too much. I lunged forward but Luke intervened just in time to stop me from smacking the silly cow in her sanctimonious face.

"If you think that you're going to use this situation to your advantage by trying to scare my mother you've picked the wrong woman," I hissed. "She's lived here quite happily for years now and has a booming business and she's not about to run away from anything."

Judith looked nastily at me and I maintained her stare until her father decided (very fecking wisely) that it was time to leave.

"I'm sorry if we've upset you, Miss Ross," he said. "I can assure you that it wasn't our intention. Please give your mother our best regards."

I slammed the door but Judith continued to scowl in through the glass at the top and only removed herself after I'd stuck up my middle finger at her and loudly threatened to go and sort her out.

"Ruby, the guards are outside looking for clues. Control yourself, will you?" Luke said, chastising me.

"There's something very funny going on here," I said, "and I am going to find out exactly what because my mother is happy where she is and will not be forced out by anyone."

I turned away from the door and saw that Mammy had come back into the kitchen, ashen-faced and pensive, wringing her hands and making me doubt my own words. Where did we go from here?

Chapter 30

"What the hell am I going to do, Luke?" I whispered as we sat in Mammy's kitchen sipping tea and talking quietly. "I can't leave her like this. It's not as if I'm just down the road if she needs me. I wonder should we offer to take her back home with us. But wait, no, that's a bad idea. They'd think they'd won then and I'm not having that."

"What's with the whole 'they'd think they've won' philosophy', Rubes?" Luke asked in puzzlement. "It's not as if *they* came into the house dressed in balaclavas and ransacked the place."

"Humph!" I said in response. "That Judith one has it totally in for Mammy. Did you not hear her? 'Vulnerable – a woman on her own – anything could happen'!"

Just as I finished my rant I heard a knock on the back door and opened it with such force that I nearly left Aisling, who was standing there with a bunch of flowers, reeling on the spot.

"Hi," she said nervously. "Is this a bad time? I just wanted to see how your mother was. I haven't been able to get her out of my mind today and wanted to bring her something." She handed me the flowers.

"Aisling, I'm sorry," I said in a much calmer tone. "Please come through and have a seat. I'm just a bit frazzled. This has been quite a shock and I'm worried about Mammy. I don't like leaving her here on her own and I want to get to the bottom of what's going on. Judith and her father were here earlier."

"That would frazzle anyone," Aisling said, pulling out a chair and sitting down. She looked at me, narrowing her eyes and sighing. "Things have been so different since Bartley Monroe's manager left and *they* took over. There are hardly any of the old staff left. Half of them walked out of their own free will because they couldn't handle what was happening and the other half were sacked on the spot for showing resistance. It's ridiculous. She's horrible to everyone. Barks orders and instructions like she's a dog-handler, screams at the staff in front of guests and treats everyone with pure disdain – but yet the hotel is booming."

"If you don't mind me asking, why were you here this afternoon? Do you usually call in with Mammy because I've never heard her mention you before?"

"I stopped because, while I was passing the cottage, I saw that the gate and door were both open and the lights all on which I thought was strange as it was daylight. The shop wasn't open either which was unusual and I just wanted to check that everything was okay. To be honest, I very nearly didn't stop as I didn't want your mother thinking that I was a nosy cow but I'm so glad I did."

"So am I, believe me."

"What did Judith and Harry say when you told them about what had happened to Isobel?" Luke asked.

"They didn't say a lot. Just closed ranks like they normally do and kicked me out of the office so they could talk."

"Did they seem shocked?" I looked at Aisling and raised my eyebrows.

"Not really but then they're not known for showing any type of emotion over anything, let it be good or bad. You could have the hotel booked for six months in advance, the place spotless and offer to entertain them by doing double-pike somersaults to a band playing and they'd still have the same indifferent expression on their faces. Why do you ask? What are you thinking?"

171

"I don't know," I said truthfully. "I just can't help feeling that it's all rather convenient for them. They've made no secret of the fact that they regard Mammy's presence here as a nuisance and now something has happened that may or may not result in her deciding to move away. She hasn't said anything to that effect but I know she's thinking it. Who wouldn't be at her time of life and in the position she's in? She's a widow living on her own with different people passing through here all the time. Who wouldn't be scared after being broken into and robbed?"

"But she wasn't robbed," Luke interjected. "The police already told us that nothing was touched which seems strange to me. Doesn't your mother keep a float for the till in the shop here somewhere?"

"I think she keeps it upstairs with her. I don't think it's a big float either. A hundred euros I think is the maximum she has in it."

"That would still be useful to a burglar," Aisling said thoughtfully. "And I'm sure she has some nice jewellery and valuables here and if she was tied up everything was there for the taking, so to speak."

"It's very strange," said Luke. "Especially as they didn't even question her about possible stashes of cash."

My mind flew back to simple concern for Mammy. "I really do hate the thought of her being alone after this."

"I thought she had a male friend," Aisling said, obviously referring to the lovely Donal O'Donnell who had returned and was at present upstairs keeping a vigil over my exhausted mother.

"She does but he can't be here all the time. He has an elderly father at home. Besides, they're not young things. Living in sin wouldn't be quite her scene, I don't think."

"I can keep an eye out for her if you'd like," Aisling offered. "I know what it's like. My parents live just down the road from me and I worry about them all the time, living on their own in a big farmhouse. I wouldn't mind looking in on her in the evenings just to make sure she's all right and feeling comfortable."

"You're very kind," I said. I liked Aisling. She seemed like a sincere and genuine girl who wanted to help.

"Would you like some tea, Aisling?" Luke asked, standing up.

He looked at me and I stuck my tongue out. I felt like a human teabag. I had done nothing but drink mugs of the stuff since I arrived (must be the old Irish coping habits kicking in – if you're in any way depressed, drink copious amounts of tea to feel better and if that doesn't help look for the answer at the bottom of a whiskey bottle).

Aisling smiled and nodded and took her coat off.

"So tell me some more about yourself then," I asked. "You said you didn't live far from here."

"No, I don't. I only live about two miles away. I was still living with my parents up until about a year ago but decided to cut the apron strings once and for all and I have my own flat now. That's part of the reason why I'm trying to be on my best behaviour up at the hotel. I can't afford to lose my job. I've just signed mortgage papers and need to stand on my own two feet and make sure the bills are paid every month."

"It must be hard," I sympathised. "Although I think you're very patient I'd say I'd have clocked your woman by now with one of her own pointy-heeled shoes. How she walks I'll never know."

"She doesn't walk, Ruby. She flies on a broomstick, don't you know?"

"So what's the deal with her father then? I wasn't sure what to make of him earlier when they were here."

"To be honest, if it was just him running the hotel we wouldn't have half the problems we do. He doesn't seem that bad when he's on his own, although he's generally not there very much. He's a big business tycoon by all accounts and this isn't the only hotel he owns. Buying and selling property and businesses is his hobby. Unfortunately he's a besotted father as well and must still see Judith in ponytails and ribbons as she can do nothing wrong in his eyes."

"Is there not a hotel in Outer Mongolia he could send his lovely daughter to manage then?"

"I wish," she said ruefully. "She really is vile in the extreme."

"I can't believe she showed so little sympathy today when it was apparent that my mother had been through a horrendous ordeal. She was more interested in talking about what security issues needed to be addressed and about how the intruders had been here once and she wouldn't like to think that they'd do it again."

"Has it been confirmed that there was more than one then?" Aisling asked.

"I thought you knew the full details?" I looked at her in confusion.

"I didn't really take time to find out the details, to be honest," Aisling answered. "I came in, untied your mother, got her a cup of tea, made a few phone calls and then left."

"So you didn't know how many people were here then?" I said. "You didn't know that there were *two* intruders who you would naturally refer to as 'they'. Very interesting. So if you didn't know, how did the lovely Judith know?"

Chapter 31

"I'm going to have to take a few days off work, Mr Reid, and I'm sorry if you're annoyed but if you don't like it you can shove it up your –"

"I don't think you'll get very far talking to him like that," Luke commented when he came into the room and witnessed my rehearsal.

"He's going to kill me. I am going to die. Feckin students are only back and need their feckin placements sorted out and where am I? Done-feckin-gal. This is not funny."

We had stayed for two nights already and I was in a state of panic. Mammy had declined to leave the house, was jumpy and nervous and I still hadn't got to the bottom of why Judith had acted the way she did. I had been up at the hotel several times but she had never been there.

"At the end of the day, Ruby, there are some things in life that are just more important than work and your mother is one of them. She needs you more than the students do and I'm sure that in your absence the college will be able to sort something out. They're not that helpless. What would they do if you died?"

"Thanks," I said glumly. "Cheer me up with that thought, why don't you?"

"Tell him that you'll keep your mobile on and make calls from here if necessary. You can't say fairer than that and if he gives you any grief direct him to me."

"Why? What are you going to do, Rambo?" I asked.

"I'll zap him with my laser beam," Luke said. "Or maybe that was Superman."

"Right, wish me luck," I said as I went outside to make the call I'd been dreading all morning. I didn't know what was happening to me. I usually wasn't prone to worrying about things but lately I seemed to be stressing about everything. I was starting to turn into the type of person who usually annoyed the crap out of me which was most irritating.

"Can I speak to Mr Reid, please," I asked nervously. Stop it! I inwardly commanded. If I had been in front of the mirror there would have been lots of stern looks and much finger-wagging.

"Ruby," Mr Reid said in his smoothest tone, "are you all right?"

"I'm okay but unfortunately my mother isn't."

I went on to explain what had happened and was amazed when his reaction was not one of gnashing of teeth and angst but instead was one of concern.

"Take as much time as you need, Ruby. We can manage."

"I'll keep my phone on," I gabbled, "and then if you need me you'll be able to reach me."

"Don't worry. We'll try not to disturb you. Give your mother my regards and, Ruby, while you're there please try and sort yourself out. It's been very obvious that you haven't been yourself lately. I don't want you to come back until you're ready and when you are back I want all of you here instead of just your body whilst your mind is elsewhere."

I was stunned and shocked. Had I been that obvious? It would appear I had. Was everyone talking about me? Were they pitying me which was a sentiment I couldn't abide? Not that anyone knew what was on my mind but still I didn't like the thought of people wondering what was wrong with fun-loving, mad Ruby and feeling sorry for me.

"How'd you get on?" Luke enquired when I went back into the house.

"Great," I answered grumpily.

"So why are you in such a bad mood then?"

"He more or less implied that I needed to pull myself together, Luke. Do I look like I need to do that? In fact, don't bother answering that."

"Why don't we take your mother out for a while today, Ruby?" Luke said in an obvious effort to change the subject. "I was thinking that we could maybe go and visit that art studio Gabriel was talking about where I have to take photographs. We have an excuse to go so she won't feel that we're coming up with ways to amuse or distract her. And it might cheer other people up as well . . . *ahem!*"

"Do they have a bar there?" I asked grudgingly.

"No bar. Just lots of pictures. Go and get ready."

It took us a while to persuade Mammy that going out was a good idea. I knew that she was feeling very vulnerable but was also afraid that, if she didn't get out of her nightclothes and leave the safe confines of her bedroom while we were all still keeping her company, she might never do it.

"It'll do you good to get out," I reasoned. "Dress up and put some make-up on and you'll feel better. You've been hiding away here for far too long."

"I've been here for two days, Ruby," Mammy answered. "That hardly makes me a hermit."

"Not yet," I muttered under my breath.

"Okay okay. I'll go and have a shower and get ready. Anything to get you off my back. You're very heavy to carry."

I rolled my eyes and left her to it and went to tidy myself up.

An hour later, after much fussing, we were finally in the car and heading towards Letterkenny. I let Mammy sit in the front beside Luke (of course I wasn't allowed to drive when Mammy was a passenger because I was too impatient and might kill us all apparently).

It took us longer than it should have (because I wasn't driving and Luke was an eejit with an even sillier co-pilot) to find the gallery, mostly because Luke thought it was in the town itself when it was actually on the outskirts. (Considering both he and Gabriel were drunk when they had the conversation, it was no wonder that his memory of the directions being given was hazy.)

Eventually we arrived outside Caitlin O'Donnell's Art Studio. Once inside I could see what the fuss was about. The artist in question was certainly very talented.

Mammy saw a watercolour that she fell instantly in love with.

"Oh look! It's called *Sunset Across the Bay*. Isn't it lovely? I have the perfect spot for it in my cottage."

"Are you all right, folks?" asked a well-polished gentleman who had just emerged from the back of the gallery.

"Well, that very much depends on what you would charge me if I were to tell you that I would like to buy this painting," Mammy said, pointing out the one in question.

"Ah, yes," he said approvingly. "That piece is not actually one from this studio but one which was taken from another exhibition. You're lucky to have seen it here as we're about to box them up and send them back to the artist."

"Really? What's her name?"

"Sarah Larkin."

I pursed my lips and nodded with interest.

"We actually know very little about her and have never met her. One of our associates happened to see her work and liked it and brought it here, thinking that it would complement some of the work that Caitlin has done."

"That's nice, although you still haven't told me the price," Mammy said.

"I'll give it to you for one and fifty hundred euros and I'm being very kind but I know you'll be back," he said with a twinkle in his eye.

"Do you accept sterling?" I asked quickly. "I'll buy it for you, Mammy. I want to," I said firmly, looking in my purse and eventually fishing out some notes. I had been armed with a wad of cash for my wedding expedition with Gabriel and the girls but hadn't really spent anything.

"We accept anything as long as you promise to thoroughly appreciate the painting," he answered with a genuine smile.

"I promise I'll do that and so will my mother," I answered. "There really is some beautiful work in this collection."

"She's a wonderfully talented lady!" a female voice butted in. "Luke?" an elegant blonde woman asked, offering her hand to him.

"The one and only," he answered. "I take it you must be Caitlin."

She nodded with a smile, shook hands with Mammy and me, then walked over to straighten some information cards about the gallery which were on display.

"Gabriel Sullivan has been in touch with me and he speaks very highly of your work," she said. "I'm so glad that you've agreed to take some photographs for me. I'm very excited about launching my new exhibition."

"What's the subject of your collection?" I asked with interest.

"They're quite abstract paintings," she answered thoughtfully. "Lots of designs on different textures using strokes and implements I've never used before. I can't tell you any more though as I'm keeping it a secret." She turned to Mammy. "I see you've bought one of Sarah's."

"I've fallen in love with this painting," Mammy said, looking lovingly at her new purchase. "I could climb into it."

"You'll perhaps get to meet the artist the night of my launch, as will I, and you can tell her what you think then. I'm sure she'll be delighted with such complimentary feedback." She turned to me. "Are you an artist yourself?"

"God, no. I just scribble a bit but what I truly enjoy is looking at other people's work and appreciating what they've created."

"That's like saying that I'm not a photographer," Luke said incredulously.

"Or that I don't cook," Mammy said. "She *is* an artist. She's just

179

too modest to admit it. Some of her work is very good, you know."

I bristled with annoyance and motioned at Mammy to keep quiet. Compared to these people I was no artist. I was simply a wannabe with a penchant for doodling. Nothing more. Nothing less.

"Why don't you bring some with you the next time you're here and I'll gladly take a look at it for you. I could put you in touch with some people who might be interested in commissioning paintings from you if they like what they see."

"Honestly I couldn't," I responded. "They're not good and anyway I only do it for fun. It's like an escape for me sometimes. I find it quite therapeutic in ways." (Basically I draw when I feel like smacking someone for annoying me, then find that the urge to vent frustrations isn't as strong.)

Caitlin looked thoughtful and indicated that she agreed with me.

"Art gives those of us who are inclined to express ourselves through brushstrokes a unique outpouring for whatever issues we have lurking beneath the surface."

I thought of the untidy jumble of sketches lurking in my office drawer. They certainly were an outpouring of something although I wasn't sure that Mr Reid would have been entirely impressed had he seen the way I had characterised him (think Scrooge with big ears, whiskers and a cane).

Caitlin excused herself, saying that she had to go out, and after we had spent another half hour wandering around the gallery commenting and exclaiming in response to the art that was on display, we decided to leave and go and get something to eat. There were a few lovely restaurants that specialised in fish and I wanted to treat Mammy (I could go vegetarian again if necessary).

"Ruby, honestly, you'll be broke before you get home. You don't have to keep paying for everything."

"I don't *have* to do anything, Mother. I'm doing it because I *want* to. I do love you."

"And I love you too, darling. It's nice to have you back. I know things were a bit strained between us for a while."

"Shhh," I whispered. "I don't want to talk about it right now. We'll discuss it later."

Mammy looked perplexed and seemed uncomfortable with the suggestion that it was ever to be mentioned again, but said nothing.

It was after five when we returned to the cottage and, when Luke hung Mammy's newly purchased watercolour up for her, I took the time to view the painting. Looking at the scene depicted reminded me of the Smugglers' Inn where Mammy had eaten her lobster and we had sat outside and looked at the mountains and the sea. I had made enquiries as to the body of water in the painting and the man in the art gallery had given me lots of information. The artist had captured the sun setting over a bay known locally as the Jeweller's Lough, the name derived from the fact that in years gone by it was used by smugglers to get in and out of the country. It was such a quiet, idyllic spot that no one imagined that such activities were in operation until much later when the thieves were long gone and laughing their legs off at the authorities.

The artist had captured every detail to perfection, the lines and swirls and use of colour making the watercolour appear like a transparent window looking over the scene as opposed to a picture painted on paper. I was transported from Mammy's sitting room in 'Ripples Retreat' to the water's edge. I could smell the seaweed, feel the breeze on my face and watch the sun fade in all its magnificence, casting sparkling, bejewelled shadows over the water, making its name come to life.

Luke came into the room and smiled at me.

"It really is beautiful," he said. "The artist has obviously put her heart and soul into it. You're going to have to tear yourself away from it, though, as Frankie's on the phone."

I went to pick up the phone.

"Hi, babe," I said.

"Hi, love," she said quietly.

"Frankie?" I said questioningly. "What's the matter?"

"I got my results back today, Ruby, and it's not great. I have to go to hospital next week for a biopsy as they found cells which showed signs of severe change. I've been looking it up on the internet and I'm so scared. I just have to hope and pray that these cells haven't spread as then I'll be in big trouble."

"Oh Jesus," I said. "Sit where you are. I'm coming home."

Chapter 32

Luke agreed to stay in Donegal with Mammy whilst I went home to be with Frankie. Mammy was distraught to hear what had happened and was insisting that I should leave first thing in the morning. I, on the other hand, had different ideas and decided to leave there and then because if I drove at my usual rate (Speedy Gonzales) I reckoned I'd be there before nightfall – besides, the sooner I left the sooner I'd be back.

"You're coming now?" Frankie said in surprise when I rang from my hands-free kit and was already halfway down the road.

"Don't tell me that you're unhappy or have a problem if you don't want me to act on it," I answered. "Of course I'm coming, you eejit! Where else would I be?"

"What about your mother? She needs you too, Ruby."

"She's got Luke staying with her. Besides, it's not good for her to become dependent on me. She's had a scare but all the best self-help books tell you that you must confront your fears in order to conquer them."

"And where do you keep your stash of self-help books hidden, Ruby?"

"Shut up, you tart! I don't need any. I just read it somewhere and remembered it."

"Okay, okay. Ring me when you're close by and I'll put the kettle on."

"Feck the kettle," I said, indicating and pulling up beside an off-licence. "What we need is a bottle of wine."

Seventy miles, a lot of cursing at slow drivers and one lukewarm bottle of wine later, I eventually arrived outside Frankie's front door. I could see her curled up on the sofa with her laptop and knew that she was bound to be looking for information on her condition whatever that might be.

Frankie threw her arms around me in the hall and I could tell that she had been crying. Owen appeared as well, looking anxious even though he was trying desperately to be upbeat.

"She'll be fine," he said with forced cheerfulness. "I've told her to put that damn laptop away as she's making herself a hundred times worse by reading things off the internet. Every individual person and case is different after all."

"Sorry, doctor, I didn't realise that you were such an expert in these matters," Frankie answered acerbically, shrugging him off as he tried to comfort her.

"She's been like that all day," he said wearily after she'd gone back to sitting on the sofa in the sitting room. "She didn't want to annoy you but I'm afraid I made her phone you. You're the only one who can talk some sense into her. She thinks I don't understand because I'm a man and don't have –" Owen took this opportunity to point at his nether regions and then scratched his ear (perhaps men do point after all). "You know what I mean," he finished.

"Yes, I know what you mean and, yes, I'll sort her out. Don't fret, she'll come round. It's just a big shock for her. I know that you think it's probably just a few cells and not much to worry about but psychologically it's much more. I'm sure it'll be fine but Frankie's probably thinking – God forbid – about what might happen if it's not. I'm sure you would both like more children and she's most likely afraid that her fertility could be affected."

Owen ran his hand over his head before taking his glasses off and rubbing his eyes. "She's annoyed as well because she missed three previous appointments. She was always too busy to take the time off work or was just putting it off because of the inconvenience. Now she's really beating herself up about it."

"They are highly unpleasant and we're all guilty of doing that one time or another," I said. "At least she's had children. They always tell you that after having a baby you can deal with anything but unfortunately I haven't and my coping skills aren't the best. Smear tests are horrible but very worthwhile it would seem. She'll be grand. Everything will be fine. They're just being cautious – that's all." I was babbling uncontrollably but at least it was masking the fact that I was scared out of my wits.

I didn't know who I was trying to convince more: me or Owen. I couldn't bear the thought of anything happening to Frankie. She was my best friend in the whole world who knew all my secrets and inadequacies. She was the one I talked to when I felt down and the one I laughed uproariously with when I wanted to share good news. She was everything to me and I simply wouldn't allow anything to happen to her.

"Right, you," I said cheerfully, going into the sitting room. "Shove up a bit on that sofa and talk to me."

"I think maybe I'm being a bit of a drama queen," Frankie said. "It's probably nothing. Nothing in the grand scale of things anyway."

"The small scale is important too," I murmured. "I'm with you all the way, pet, no matter what."

We were sitting beside each other with our feet resting on a bean bag and I put my head on her shoulder and we lay back in companionable silence as only best friends can and then I heard snoring (she had only fallen asleep on me in the most uncomfortable position possible).

I gently eased her off me and pulled a blanket over her. I then went in search of Owen who had gone to attend to the children. I could hear Baby Jack gurgling and singing along as the musical mobile above his cot played a gentle lullaby, and the children laughing at a DVD. Angelica was away on a school residential trip and was unaware of what was happening at home. It was past the kids' bedtime but the house had obviously forgone its usual routine as Frankie was preoccupied, which only served to prove how lost we'd all be without her. I furiously shook my head and told myself to wise up. God, we were all acting as if she'd been given really bad news and that the big C had actually reared its ugly head. It wasn't that bad. It was simply a wake-up call and I was going to phone the doctor first thing in the morning and book myself in for a smear test (the snotty receptionist was going to get some shock).

The following morning I got up early and went into the children's bedrooms and gently woke them.

"Auntie Ruby!" Carly started to scream before I clamped my hand over her mouth and motioned for her to be quiet.

"You can squeal at me the whole way to school, pet, but not before then. Now where does your mother keep your uniform?"

"It's hanging in the wardrobe," she answered. "Daddy put it there last night. We hardly saw Mammy at all yesterday. I think she must have had a sore head. Auntie Ruby, why are you here and why are you taking us to school? Mammy always does that."

"You're right, darling. Mammy's head is very sore and she's very tired so I'm going to take you to school instead to give Mammy a wee rest. You don't mind, do you? I'll even stop at the shop and get you something nice for break-time if you like."

"We have to eat fruit at break-time and drink water and there's lots of water in the fridge and fruit in the bowl downstairs," she answered gloomily.

"So no chocolate bars or crisps then?" I said. (Flippin' schools take the pleasure out of everything these days! Playing Swap Break would be hard without Monster Munch or Curly Fries, that's for sure.)

"Well, Auntie Ruby will just have to get you treats later on then," I said.

"Will you still be here when I get home?" she asked in surprise.

"Would you like me to be?" I asked and got my reply as she hugged me tight and buried her head in my shoulder.

I then woke up Ben who was just as surprised but a lot less cheery (not a morning person at all – not dissimilar to myself).

"What are you doing here?"

"Oh well, that's just charming," I said, faking annoyance. "I'll just go home then, shall I?

"Is Mammy all right?" he asked with a frown. "She seemed really upset yesterday and kept on telling us to go out of the room so she and Daddy could talk and then I heard her shouting at Daddy and him saying he was sorry."

"Did you actually go out of the room or did you just pretend to go out and leave your ears behind?" I asked, bemused.

"I sat on the stairs," he said. "I was just worried, that's all."

I ruffled his hair and he immediately reacted as if I'd bitten him.

"Where's the hair gel?" he asked as he went straight to the mirror and started to pull all sorts of odd faces whilst tweaking his hair into funny shapes with his fingers.

"You look like Bart Simpson," I commented and got a sideways poke of the tongue in response.

Owen appeared, looking dishevelled, with Baby Jack in his arms.

"I slept on the floor in his room last night," he explained. "I didn't want him crying and wakening Frankie. I took her up to bed after she fell asleep on the sofa but she woke pretty soon afterwards and tossed and turned half the night."

"I'm going to take the children to school," I said. "And I'll take Jack to nursery. I think you should stay with Frankie today."

"I have to teach this morning unfortunately," he said, "but I'll be cleared up before lunchtime and then I'll take a half day."

"Don't worry about a thing. I'll be here and I'll make sure she's okay."

"I know you will, Ruby," he said. "Every girl should have a friend like you."

"What? A loud-mouthed, opinionated redhead who detests all things girlie?"

"They're the best sort, didn't you know?" he said, which made me feel fuzzy and warm in one respect but desperately helpless in another.

Chapter 33

I had been keeping in close contact with Luke while I was away and had heard that, in the two days since I'd been gone, quite a few unusual things had been happening at the hotel. Firstly Bitch Features had returned after mysteriously disappearing for several days and appeared to have had some type of personality transplant.

"What do you mean she came to the cottage and left flowers?" I demanded, speaking to Luke over breakfast on the morning I was due to go back to Mammy's, and thinking he must have been hallucinating.

"Firstly she sent Aisling down to say that her father would like to have dinner with your mother tonight and then she arrived with a bouquet."

"Had she been at the brandy decanter, do you think?" And I wasn't joking. I'm a great believer in the old adage which suggests that a leopard can't change its spots and this leopardess certainly didn't appear the type to do so, therefore I smelt a very large rat.

"Tell Mammy to meet him," I said thoughtfully.

"What?" Luke said in a surprised tone.

"Well, how else are we going to find out what's going on?" I

189

demanded. I am also a big fan of whoever thought up the idea of keeping your friends close but your enemies closer.

"She can hardly interrogate him, Ruby. This is your mother we're talking about. Not you. Besides, he's not likely to tell her anything if he is up to something."

"I'm not asking her to interrogate him! But he's hardly asked her there on a date, has he? There's obviously a motive behind it. Trying to scare her didn't work so they're going to try and butter her up now. Well, it'll take more than a bunch of poxy flowers and a meal to do that. I'd love to be a fly on the wall. Can you not send her out with a Dictaphone in her pocket or put a wire on her?"

"Put a wire on her?" Luke repeated slowly. "Ruby, have you been watching old reruns of *Spooks* again?"

"No, I have not," I said crossly. "I've been far too busy with Frankie although I think she's feeling a lot more positive now."

"Well, that's no wonder. She's been spoilt rotten since you went home. Chemists should bottle you and sell you as a tonic, Rubes."

I had to admit that I was about to declare myself bankrupt as I had been putting all my efforts and my bank balance into keeping Frankie and the children happy, and I was also officially knackered. I had been staying in my own house (which I was going to have to tidy before I left, in case Luke had forty heart attacks on his return) and going to Frankie's every morning in time to take the children to school so that she could have a break. Frankie and Owen both protested at the start but I am quite difficult to argue with so they simply let me get on with it. Owen was teaching at another campus and had to leave early each morning and Frankie was working on an event for the college and had decided to work from home and was grateful for the opportunity to lie in her pyjamas whilst I sorted everything out.

"You're going to go back to your mother's tomorrow," she had commanded the evening before. "I'm fine. I just overreacted a bit, I think. I've been in touch with the doctor and he says that they get lots of abnormal smear results although he did say that only a small percentage of them showed up severe cell changes. I'm not going to dwell on it though. I'm going to be positive and hopefully next week will bring good news. I'm going to have a procedure which involves scraping away cells for a biopsy. They can treat it there and then too, if it's not too bad, which is good, I think."

There was nothing good about anything that suggested your fandango needed to be scraped but I wasn't going to share that gem with Frankie. I was simply going to do a lot of praying in the hope that my daddy was paying attention.

I had agreed to leave as I wanted to get back to Mammy, but would miss the children. Carly had been heartbroken when she heard that I was going and I had to beg Owen to make sure and take her to the shop in my absence.

"Auntie Ruby is a menace and we'll have to tell the dentist to chase her if all your teeth fall out," he said whilst Carly grinned broadly at me.

"He wouldn't chase Auntie Ruby," she said confidently. "Because Auntie Ruby would bust him!"

"She knows you so well," Frankie said, fondling her daughter's hair and hugging her close.

"Brush your teeth loads," I said, pretending to do mine with my finger and making faces at Frankie and Owen.

"I love Auntie Ruby," I heard her say. "I wish she could live with us all the time."

Owen stifled a laugh and Frankie hid in Carly's hair to hide her own amusement.

"Shut up, both you tarts," I said to Frankie and Owen. "I wouldn't want to live with you lot either. It's like being on holiday with the feckin Brady Bunch."

I arrived back in Donegal in time to see Mammy getting ready to go out. She seemed much more relaxed. The word around the village was that several other people's homes had been broken into and two men had been apprehended.

"Oh," I said, totally taken aback.

"It kind of puts paid to your theory of the break-in being a ploy to scare your mum then, doesn't it?" Luke said thoughtfully. "I'm glad, though, as your mother seems much happier. I think she's relieved at the fact that people were arrested. It makes her feel safe which hopefully means that we can go home soon." Luke put his arms round me and nuzzled my neck.

"Did you miss me?" I asked, putting my head to one side.

"I did actually," he said. "I'm looking forward to getting you home and having you to myself for a while, Ruby 'Nightingale'. Always quick to go and help others. It's one of the things I love about you."

I felt myself blush (oh great, now my face was the same colour as my hair!).

"It's nothing," I said. "I was only doing what anybody else would do. My mother needed me and my best friend was upset. Although I'll be grateful when everything settles down again and they all quit having problems. For me, trouble seems to come like buses – all at feckin once."

"Yes, well, I think this bus is about to leave," Luke said. "I think we should go home tomorrow. Your mother will be grand. Besides, it's nice to know that Donal and Robbie are only down the road if she needs them."

"Have they been here much?" I asked.

"Donal has hardly left and Robbie has been up and down too. They're both full of concern and genuinely do care."

I nodded and made a mental note to thank Donal the next time I saw him. I also wanted to call into the shop to see Robbie as I had found myself increasingly warming to the elderly man. He was very like me. (Yes, unfortunately for the rest of mankind there are two such creatures in the world.) He called a spade a spade and said exactly what was on his mind which wasn't always a good thing but compared to some of the underhand activities that had been going on lately it was a welcome change.

Luke and I decided to open a bottle of wine and sit outside in the gazebo after Mammy left, looking lovely in a red dress and matching pumps. She reckoned that her intruders had done her one favour as all her clothes were looser and her waistline seemed to have reduced.

"It's called the Stick-up Diet," she had joked. "Although I wouldn't recommend it to the fainthearted even though it seems to totally wilt your appetite. I think I'm going to have a salad tonight."

"Sure you will," I said, smiling at Luke and knowing fine well that as soon as Mammy spotted the menu that salad would be the very last thing on her mind. "It's more of an accompaniment than a main meal, don't you think?" she had been known to say in the past.

Donal and Robbie arrived a short time later and I went straight to the cupboard, brought out two more glasses and invited them to join us.

"I always come prepared," Robbie said, producing his famous hip flask containing brandy. "Will you boil the kettle for me, Ruby, and I'll make myself a cup of tea and add a splash of the good stuff to it."

I went back into the kitchen and he followed me and closed the door, making me feel slightly perturbed. I hoped he wasn't going to tell me off.

"I wanted to give you this," he said, producing a little box.

I was intrigued and took it from him tentatively. I took a knife from the cutlery drawer and snipped the Sellotape that was holding the lid down and carefully removed an object that was encased in bubble wrap.

I looked quizzically at Robbie. "What is it?" I asked.

"Well, it would spoil the surprise if I told you," he said. "Go ahead and open it. We got a collection of these in the other day and when I saw them I thought of you."

That sounded ominous. It was probably a gargoyle or one of those signs that said '*The dog's all right – just beware the owner doesn't bite.*'

I unravelled the wrapping and revealed a small angel made from crystal. It glinted and sparkled in the light. I examined it closely and held it reverently.

"It's lovely," I said, at a loss to fathom why he was giving it to me.

"It's a guardian angel," he said gruffly (obviously embarrassed as when he and I were together we were more likely to be sparring partners as opposed to people who exchanged gifts). "I thought you might like it as a reminder of . . . as a reminder of your – your father, God rest his soul. My wife, Donal's mother, used to collect angels. She loved them and I gain great comfort from their presence."

I resisted the temptation to loudly say "Aahhhhh!" and started to think that I'd spent too long with Frankie this week and as a result had turned into a soppy git.

"That's a really nice gesture, Robbie," I said. "I'll put it pride of place on my mantelpiece and it will indeed remind me of Daddy who no doubt is smiling down and laughing his head off at me at this present moment. He really was a gentleman, you know."

"I know he was," Robbie said. "Your mother talks about him all the time. It's hard to move on after a death. I never could. I just turned into a grumpy old goat who forgets his manners and shouts a lot."

Luke came in, looked from me to Robbie and down to the crystal in my hand, then walked straight back out again with a bewildered expression on his face.

My mobile rang at that moment, preventing any further conversation. I answered the call, listened intently, felt the colour drain from my face and then got angry.

Luke and Donal came hurtling into the room when they heard my raised tones and when I came off the phone three people were staring anxiously at me.

"Harry McQueen has only offered to buy Mammy's cottage for two hundred and fifty thousand euro," I said weakly.

Chapter 34

"I hope that you're going to deliver for me this morning," I said, wagging my finger and speaking intently. "No half measures today. I want you to go and speak to The Boss and tell him that I expect his full co-operation in this matter. This is a very important day and it's imperative that everything runs smoothly for all our sakes. Don't let me down now."

I regarded my subject and dusted its head. My little angel had become an integral part of my life. I spoke to it every day, stroked its head, cleaned it (yes, I know you're all in shock but Daddy always looked his best when he was here so his representative was going to be no different) and occasionally shouted at it when I felt the need to let off some steam.

Luke and I had been back for a week and today was the day that I had been both dreading and looking forward to with nervous anticipation. Frankie was going to the hospital this morning for her procedure and we were all on tenterhooks.

I had spent the previous evening with her and, although she seemed relatively calm, I knew that she must be very frightened but determined not to show it. Angelica had returned home from her school trip and was being particularly agreeable which meant that she also realised the enormity of the situation. Owen had thrown himself into his work and had been teaching the part-time students the evening before and was glad of the distraction.

Frankie's appointment was at eleven o'clock and I had been up since six as I couldn't sleep and was totally restless (so much so that when Luke emerged, rubbing the sleep from his eyes, I had cleaned the kitchen, mopped the floors and washed out the shower).

Luke came straight over and enveloped me in a bear-hug. "It's all right, sweetheart," he said, gently stroking my head. "Everything will be fine."

"Get off me," I ordered. "Why are you talking to me in that stupid tone of voice?"

"Because you're obviously very disturbed," he answered in a high-pitched tone. "You cleaned."

"Feck off!" I said and threw a duster at him.

I had brought my angel to work with me and was happy to report that all of me was here. Mr Reid had been right. It was no fun for anyone when Ruby Ross was only half there so she decided to pull it together. In the short time that I had been back, I had put ten students into placements, made four new contacts with employers who were willing to take placements on and had scheduled countless students with fifteen-minute time slots to discuss their future.

"Nice to have you back," Mr Reid had commented one morning in passing. "The place just wasn't the same without you."

"Glad to be back," I had responded with a smile.

Even though a lot had happened over the last few weeks, and I would have had every reason to have gone into a meltdown, I didn't. Instead I had decided to apply the philosophy that 'That which does not kill us can only make us stronger.' (If it didn't kill me, that is.)

I hardly let the phone ring once before I answered it, hoping that it was Frankie ringing to tell me some good news but was disappointed instead to hear an older woman's voice.

"Is that Ruby?" she asked softly.

"Yes, it is."

"Ruby, it's Rose Malone here. I have put together a design for your wedding dress, bridesmaid's dress and the outfit for the little flower girl and was wondering when would suit you to come down to Belfast and view them, as I'd like to get started as soon as possible and let you see some material samples so you can choose the colour and fabric."

"Oh right," I said. I hadn't expected any of this to be happening so soon and nothing could have been further from my mind but suddenly the idea of going back to the homely side street that seemed to have a magical quality all of its own appealed to me greatly.

"Give me your number, Rose, and I'll get back to you after consulting with my bridesmaid."

"That's fine," she said. "I'll talk to you soon."

I looked mournfully at my phone and wished that I could ring my bridesmaid and tell her the good news but I couldn't. Decisively I took my mobile and scrolled down to look for Mandy's number. Talking to someone else for five minutes would occupy me and stop me from panicking over Frankie ringing or not ringing as the case might be.

"Hi, future sister-in-law," Mandy said brightly on answering.

"Hey, you," I said in a chummy voice. "I've just had the dressmaker on the phone summoning us back to Belfast to look at dress designs."

"Oh, how exciting!" Mandy said and I could hear her clapping (probably in the manner of an excitable seal). "What's wrong with you? You sound grumpy. Are you okay?"

"I always sound grumpy this early in the morning, Mandy. If I was you I'd do a bit more research and get to know your in-laws better."

"So when are we going then?" she asked.

"Who said anything about *you* feckin going?" I asked in mock horror.

"Well, you wouldn't have told me if you weren't wanting me to go," she argued.

"We'll go as soon as possible. I still have to speak to Frankie." At the mere mention of her name my heart started to race. Depending on what the doctor said this morning, bridesmaids' dresses and colours and fabrics which were things she adored could be the last things on her mind.

"I've got to go, Mandy, but I'll speak to you soon. Okay?"

I hung up the phone and it rang again straight away.

"God, you're quick off the mark today," my mother said. "Any news yet?"

"No," I said through gritted teeth. "I thought that you were Frankie to give me news."

"What time was she due to be seen at?"

"Eleven o'clock." I looked at my watch and the time was half past eleven.

"She'll probably be a while yet," Mammy said helpfully. "You never know what hold-ups there could be at the hospital and then she'll have to get the procedure done and have a chat afterwards."

I knew she was probably right but my patience was wearing very thin and my nerves were on edge.

"Have you had any more thoughts about what you're going to do about the McQueens' offer?" I said, needing to talk about something other than Frankie and hospitals.

"I don't know what to do, Ruby. I'm going to see my solicitor next week to discuss it but at this moment in time my gut instincts are telling me to stay where I am."

"Part of me is glad that you're happy but another part of me wants to take you home with me," I said with a worried frown. "I don't like you being on your own there, especially not after what happened."

"Stop worrying, Ruby. Sure, there were two arrests made for other burglaries and the police have indicated that chances are it was the same crowd. Besides, Donal is taking care of everything for me. There's a burglar alarm being installed as we speak and, trust me, it would wake the dead so I don't think anyone is going to be stupid enough to try that again. Donal and I have also been talking and he might stay with me one or two nights in the week just to make sure I'm safe."

"Oh, I see, just to make sure you're safe. I believe you, Mother. Thousands wouldn't."

"Ruby, I have no idea what you're insinuating."

"I'll bet you don't," I said, feeling more confident and comfortable about her staying where she was. "Maybe it is better that you stay," I said thoughtfully. "Don't give in and do what they want. That's making it too easy for them. Besides, you're happy where you are, aren't you?"

"It's not about making life easy or giving in, Ruby," Mammy said solemnly. "It's about doing what Aunt Kate would want and I know that she would hate to think that I was giving the cottage away to have God knows what done to it. It would be different if they were going to preserve it and keep it as an attraction but I have a feeling that isn't part of the plan. I'd say that they're more likely to demolish it or at the very least change it so much that it won't bear the slightest resemblance to what it is now. And I love it."

I thought of the roses growing up the side of the cottage and the turf by the old-fashioned fire and couldn't have agreed more. It was a very precious family heirloom and all the money in the world couldn't recompense for destroying any part of it.

"Say no then," I said. "Go and tell them that it's a very generous offer but that you're not interested. No deal, Mr Banker."

"I can't just say 'no' outright, Ruby. I need to know my rights. What if there's some kind of loophole in the contract Bartley drew up when handing the deeds of the cottage over to Aunt Kate? Something that gives the owners of the manor some rights over the cottage?"

"Don't be silly, Mammy," I said impatiently. "The cottage is legally yours and they have no say in anything to do with it. In any case, as for demolishing it, surely the Manor House and the cottage have to be some type of listed buildings that are preserved by the State? They've been there forever and are part of the history of Smugglers' Bay. People just can't go willy-nilly knocking down houses that have been there for centuries!"

"You're probably right," she sighed. "In any case, I just want to be sure that when I'm declining their offer I have the right information to back it up."

"Sounds like you've made your mind up," I commented.

"I think I have – but a quarter of a million euro is still a lot of money and I have to think of you as well."

"I'm happy, Mother. I've got everything I need, so don't be worrying about me. Besides, I like the thought of being a permanent thorn in the lovely Judith's side."

"I better let you go," Mammy said. "Ring me when you know how Frankie is."

I hung up the phone and five minutes later it rang for a third time and my mouth dried as I answered it.

"Hello."

"Hi, honey."

"I seriously wish that anybody and everybody who does not answer to the name 'Frankie' would break their phones and stop feckin ringing me!" I shouted.

"I love you too," Luke said in a huffy tone. "I only phoned to see if there was any news."

"Don't phone me. I'll phone you," I snapped. "And by the way I do love you. I'm just worried, so be patient with me."

"I'm always patient," Luke answered. "I'm very lucky that God gave me patience in abundance. He must have known that I was destined to meet up with you in my future and would need a good supply."

I hung up and tried my best to fill in forms for the next half hour, between manically looking at the clock, checking for emails, and picking up and banging the phone down to ensure that the college telephone system was still in working order. I gave up as the clock approached half past one and my nerves approached well past shattered.

I tried to ring Frankie's mobile but couldn't get a connection. I tried to ring Owen but he didn't answer either and the house appeared to be empty. She had been given bad news; that was the only explanation.

I looked witheringly at my angel who apparently hadn't done his job properly, switched off my computer, locked my office and then headed out to the car park. With a heavy heart I opened the car door and threw in my bag, sat down and laid my head on the headrest which was precisely when I spotted Frankie's car in my rear-view mirror.

"Jesus Christ," I said loudly before going to investigate.

Frankie was sitting motionless in her car with her eyes closed, listening to music, and jumped when I gently opened her door.

"Was it terrible?" I asked.

She didn't make any response and I hunkered down at her side and took both her hands in mine.

"I'm here for you, love. No matter what, I'm here for you."

Frankie turned to me and nodded. "He told me that if I hadn't gone for the smear when I did that I could have had full-blown cancer, Ruby. Can you imagine how I feel knowing that? I could be sitting here now with something growing inside me that could have killed me but for some reason I went to the doctor that day. I really wanted to cancel the appointment but I didn't. Somebody up there must like me." She breathed heavily and pointed to the sky. "They did a really close examination today and found that some of the cells looked cancerous. They explained that, if they're contained within the skin covering the cervix, then it won't be a true cancer – unless the cells break through the top layer of skin and spread into the tissue underneath." Frankie took a deep breath and sniffed. "Thankfully they were able to tell me that it hadn't spread but that I was very lucky. Who knows what would have happened if I'd neglected it for any longer? It scares me so much and just doesn't bear thinking about."

I could feel the colour draining from my face and I felt light-headed with stress. "You had a close call then," I murmured.

"Too close for comfort, Rubes. I have to go back in another three weeks and see them again, but the doctor seemed confident that he had got it all. When I think about these last few weeks, Ruby, the one thing that it has taught me is to appreciate what you have and to grab life with both hands, as you never know the day or the hour when it could all be taken away. I look at my children and Owen and Mammy and Daddy and Ella and you and I realise how lucky I am. There are things I've always wanted to do but I've put them off to another time. Time? What's that? It means nothing if you're not going to be here to enjoy it. I know what I have to do from now on and I also know what you have to do. You must find your birth mother, Ruby. She's out there somewhere waiting for you. I just know it. Don't give up this chance of finding out who you are. You need to know so don't leave it any longer."

I got up, leaned into the car and gave Frankie the tightest hug she'd ever been on the receiving end of. Then I stood up and looked at the sky and thanked my father for what he had done.

Finally I had my sign.

Chapter 35

"That's fantastic," Mammy said happily, once I imparted the news that Frankie was marginally happier even if she did have to go back and have another check-up.

"Yes, it's a lesson to us all that we must make the most of life," I said cheerily. "We're only here once and we shouldn't waste opportunities for happiness. We should take lots of chances and risks as they might never present themselves again."

"You're not going to do anything daft and book yourself in for sky-diving lessons or start bungee-jumping, are you?" Mammy asked in a worried tone.

"I'm not talking about adrenalin-rush extreme sports, Mammy. I'm talking about life in general. I'm talking about spending time with your loved ones and appreciating the good times and I'm talking about me wanting to find my birth mother. I don't want to die wondering whether she's good or bad, whether she wanted me or not. I still want to find out. It's my right to know where I came from."

There was silence on the line although I could still hear Mammy breathing (which no doubt would turn into heavy spasms any minute, given her reaction to earlier conversations on the subject).

"I wanted to talk to you about this in person, Mammy, but I couldn't wait. This is very important to me and please believe me when I say that I don't want to hurt you."

"Hurt?" Mammy said. "It's not about *me* getting hurt. It's about *you* setting yourself up for a major fall. You talk about wanting to enjoy life. Well, enjoy it then. Be grateful for what you have and stop looking for things you haven't got. You were adopted for a reason which is precisely why you should content yourself. If I thought that there was the slightest chance of you getting a happy outcome from this, I would give you my blessing and help you look myself but trust me when I say that there won't be."

"There you go again," I said angrily. "Predicting the future when you haven't a clue what you're talking about. How can you say there won't be a happy outcome? How do you know?"

"I can feel it," she said. "A mother's instincts are very strong. Their main concern is to protect their young which is what I'm trying to do, only you're too headstrong to accept that. You want to go galloping into things head-first only to come out the other end more hurt than you've ever been in your life. I don't want to see you reduced to a sorry mess when you discover that the romantic image you've conjured up in your own head doesn't match reality."

"Back this up!" I shouted. "You told me that you were going to see a solicitor next week in order to be clear on your facts before you gave an answer to the McQueens – so do me the same courtesy and explain why you feel so strongly about this! What do you know? Stop hiding things from me. If you want to protect me, let me hear it from you and not from a stranger."

It took me all my willpower to stop from blurting out that I had overheard her conversation with Donal. An exchange which told me all I needed to know about my darling birth mother. I just wanted her to be honest with me and tell me what she knew and how she had found out.

There was a short but awkward silence.

"I can't do this over the phone, Ruby," Mammy said in a weary voice. "We need to meet and discuss it more."

204

"So you're at least willing to talk about it instead of lying to me and hiding things?"

"I would suggest that if you want my help, young lady, you should speak to me in a more respectful tone. I am still your mother, you know."

I stood chastised and felt like a six-year-old.

"Well, it so happens that we'll have reason to meet," I said then. "We're going to Belfast on Saturday to see the wedding-dress designer and look at the designs she's made for us and I'd like you to come."

"I'd like that very much, Ruby," she said in a gentler tone. "How about I come and stay with you on Friday night and we can have a chat then."

"I look forward to it."

As we had received good news that day, Frankie and I did what any other self-respecting set of best friends would do and went and got roaring drunk that night to mark the occasion. (Slight exaggeration as Frankie sipped two drinks but was relieved beyond words and acted like a drunk lunatic anyway. I drank enough for both of us.)

I had rung her after I got off the phone from my mother and we had arranged to go to the Swiftstown Arms for a drink (which turned into numerous G&Ts and a hefty hangover). The boys had joined us whilst Angelica baby-sat and it felt like old times again (minus all the stress and hassle of recent weeks).

"Hi, Ruby," the manager, Bobby Laverty, greeted me when we arrived. "Looking forward to the wedding? I'm sure you're on the countdown now?"

"Are you joking?" Frankie demanded. "You really don't know her that well, do you?"

"We'll have to get together and discuss menu plans soon and talk about bands and DJs. I have a list somewhere, I think."

"That's great," I said, not feeling pressurised to talk about it but happy to do so as I was actually starting to look forward to it.

Two hours and a number of half'uns later and I would have

discussed anything with anybody, I was feeling so mellow and relaxed. If Gabriel had been in the company I might even have agreed with him on whatever convoluted point he would undoubtedly be trying to make. (Maybe I should be pissed as a pre-requisite to our next meeting?)

"We should do this more often," I announced with a demented grin on my face whilst I manhandled Luke (in the manner of a PSNI officer frisking a suspect) and searched his pockets for change to put music on the jukebox. "This is what life is all about. You have to enjoy it. Enjoy it, you hear!" I said. (At this stage I was not only speaking to my own company but addressing the entire bar, much to their apparent amusement allegedly.)

"You must come to the art gallery with us next week," I instructed Frankie and Luke. "It's an order. Get Angelica to baby-sit and we'll make a proper night of it. Stay somewhere nice and indulge ourselves."

"Oh Jesus," Frankie said, "here she goes!"

"Yeah, well, we all have little fetishes. Yours is horny lecturers where you work. Mine is art." This was said with much arm-waving and sniggering.

"Oi!" Owen said. "Don't drag me into this. It wasn't me who initiated snogging on camera in front of the students on graduation day. Look at your mate and lay the blame squarely at her door. It's all her fault for being so irresistible and gorgeous."

"Oh yuck," I said. "Get a room, you two!"

"We will," Owen said and pulled Frankie to her feet, whereupon they both said goodnight, and left soon after, holding each other's hands and looking blissfully happy.

"They're so in love," I declared with a sigh.

"Excuse me, but I don't actually dislike you either," Luke said. "In fact I happen to think that we should get a room too."

"Do you really?"

"Yes, I do. We should go home right now. I'll even carry you over the threshold in preparation for when I do it after we're married."

"I'd like you standing at the altar unaided, Luke," I said. "Traction and a morning suit would be a very bad look."

"Fair enough but I happen to think that you and I are a very good look. Now get on your feet and let's leave. We have about a week's worth of snogging to catch up on and the sooner we start the better."

Chapter 36

I spent the Thursday evening before Mammy was to arrive on the Friday tidying the house (stop laughing – I know it's something I don't normally do but, as I was keen to extract information, I didn't want Mammy distracted by feeling the need to polish every surface in sight).

"Is this where I live?" Luke said jovially when he came in from a photography job. "I must be in the wrong house. The one I left this morning needed bomb-disposal experts to sort it out."

"Ha feckin ha, funny boy. My mother is arriving tomorrow and she better tell me everything I need to know or there will indeed be an explosion and it will involve me having the mother and father of all fits."

"I think Owen might need me to keep him company," Luke said quickly. "He's washing his hair and might just require me to hold the shower nozzle for him."

"That's a good idea actually. Make yourself scarce and I'll give you a ring and let you know if it's safe to come home."

"If? That sounds ominous. I'd like to sleep in my own bed tomorrow night if it's all the same to you."

"Well, you better hope that Mammy is in an honest and

approachable mood then because I don't intend to waste any more time faffing about over this. I want to know the truth. End of story."

"Ruby –"

"Luke, don't say another word. I know that you're all trying to protect me and wrap me in endless layers of cotton wool, but honestly I don't need it. I'm a big girl and I'm quite capable of handling whatever she has to tell me. What I can't handle is being constantly fobbed off with lies. If Daddy had been here he would have insisted that I be made aware of the facts."

"Fine. Would you like some help with the cleaning?"

"No, actually. I'm doing all right on my own. I'm finding it quite therapeutic in a way. It's helping to take my mind off things. Don't get excited though," I said, noting the hopeful expression on his face, "I'm sure it's just a phase I'm going through and it'll pass."

"Well, thank God for that," the resident housekeeper said sarcastically. "I wouldn't like to be usurped from my position of cleaning lady."

"I know," I said brightly, leaving the room whistling, with a floor-brush in my hand.

Mammy arrived the following evening and immediately congratulated Luke on his capabilities in the house-cleaning department, much to my amusement and Luke's nervousness.

"Well, actually, Ruby cleaned the house last night."

The sound of Mammy's laughter pealing through the house suggested that she thought he was joking and as I had more important fish to fry I didn't argue with her.

"Coffee, Mammy?" I asked as she made herself comfortable on the sofa.

I had bought a coffee cake and cheesecake (my belief being that sugar would loosen her tongue) and was in the middle of putting them out on plates when my phone beeped with a message from Frankie.

Hope all goes well this evening. Life is too precious to waste.

Love you loads xxx

I read the message and grinned and then snapped my phone shut before going to order Luke to get out.

"Are you still here?" I demanded, walking back into the sitting room where he was talking to Mammy.

"Good grief, there's no need to go kicking the poor fella out of his own home," Mammy said, looking a bit on the desperate side and giving Luke pleading gazes which when translated meant that she would rather he would stay and protect her from the wrath of her impulsive question-asking daughter.

"Oh, I think there's every reason, Mammy. We have wedding plans to discuss which he is not privy to –" (did you see what I did there – very clever, I thought) "– and there are a few other little issues that need to be addressed as well which we might be better doing on our own. Tell Owen I said hello, Luke, and I'll give you a ring later."

Luke kissed me on the cheek and gave me a squeeze to let me know that he was in solidarity with me and then he left.

I made sure that Mammy had a full mug of coffee and all the delights she could cope with in front of her before I joined her on the sofa and pounced.

"Okay, Mammy. So tell me what you know about Georgina."

"Eh . . . erm . . . Ruby, you're putting me in a very difficult position here. I was told years ago, just shortly after you were adopted, that if this situation was ever to arise I was to firmly steer you away from it. No good can come of this."

"Mammy, if you don't tell me, I am simply going to go and find the information myself anyway. So you have a choice. You either help me or you don't and if you don't I will never forgive you."

"That's not fair, Ruby!" Mammy cried, noisily banging her coffee mug onto the tray it was carried in on. "You make it sound like I'm being deliberately awkward or wilfully hiding things from you but I promise you I'm not. God, I wish your father was here!"

At that point she seemed to break down and I felt marginally guilty for putting so much pressure on her but reasoned that I didn't have any other option.

"I wish Daddy was here too, Mammy, because he would tell you like he always did that there's no point in arguing with me and prolonging the inevitable. I know that I'm impulsive and headstrong but those are traits that are obviously innate in my character and I'd like to know who they're inherited from. What's the worst that can happen? Nobody will think badly of you for telling me, if that's what you're worrying about. They'll only have to meet me to realise why you were left with no choice."

"I wish it were that simple," Mammy said sadly, at which point I started to lose the will to live.

How many of these useless statements was I going to have to listen to before she actually told me something that would be of some benefit to me?

I began to impatiently jiggle my leg and tap my foot until Mammy put her hand up, signalling for me to stop.

"All right, Ruby. Here it is." She paused and I held my breath. "Your mother didn't want you, Ruby. It pains me to have to tell you that but I've been left with no choice. She never wanted you and treated you badly when you were in her care. She gave birth to you in an institution for unmarried mothers, then took you home until you were forcibly taken from her. She neglected you terribly. There was talk of alcohol and drug abuse as well as men constantly calling to the house."

I felt sick to my stomach as I listened but a horrified fascination made me want to know more.

"How old was I when I was removed from her care?" I asked quietly, all my earlier bravado gone.

"You were around six weeks old, I think," Mammy looked at me with tears in her eyes and held out her hand to me. "I can't bear to think of what you might have gone through in those six weeks, Ruby. You were so special to your father and me and we loved you so much. You were such an adorable baby with your tufts of red hair and a smile that simply lit your face up." Mammy looked wistful.

"If she was so bad why did they allow her to keep me for those six weeks?" I asked. "Surely if she had a tendency to behave in that manner, it would have been a kinder thing to remove me right away?"

"Perhaps they didn't know how bad she was. As far as we know, the authorities only became aware of her afterwards. They received complaints from several worried sources who were highly concerned for your welfare and their information was acted upon quite quickly."

"Do you remember the box?" I asked tentatively. "I caught a glimpse of it one day when I was in your room when I was younger. You took it from me and wouldn't let me see it. But not before I noticed the black and white photograph and the toys and the drawing."

"You've certainly got a good memory, Ruby," Mammy said in a strange tone. "You remember all that from a five-second fleeting glance at something I took from you almost immediately, do you?"

Shit.

I squirmed awkwardly in my seat and squinted at her.

"Ruby, I know you found it. I knew it had been moved when I went to the filing cabinet the next day."

"Why didn't you say anything?" I demanded.

"What's to say?" she shrugged. "I've kept it all these years because those things are part of you and I did want to give it to you one day. There just never seemed to be a right time and I was always afraid of what I might create as a result. I needn't have worried though. You're good enough at making things happen all on your own with no help from me."

I was starting to feel very annoyed. My mother was a very honest person (usually) and I couldn't understand why she had suddenly started playing so many games.

She seemed to read my mind.

"Ruby, try to understand things from my perspective. I don't want you to get hurt. You're right. I do know things. I know terrible things that no child should ever need to hear about their mother. The one person in the world who should have their best interests at heart. The world is a strange place. People who don't deserve children seem to be the ones who are presented them on a plate and those who would die to have a family get nothing but grief and heartache."

Mammy stopped and looked at her hands and I knew that she was thinking about the babies she lost, my siblings. I felt desperately sorry for her and my anger faded.

I moved closer to her and took her hands in mine. "I'm sorry, Mammy. I know this isn't easy for you but can *you* see it from my point of view? I didn't ask to be born or to be a burden to anyone. But here I am. I've had the most wonderful parents and a fantastic childhood but, when all is said and done, I'm still curious and why shouldn't I be? The person who brought me into the world is out there somewhere and, like it or not, I have a right to know who she is – just like I have a right to know about my father. Please try and understand. All I want is some answers. I'm not planning on disowning you or denouncing your role in my life. You have been and always will be my mother. Nobody can ever take that away from either me or you."

I sighed and let go of Mammy's hands and moved back to where I had been originally sitting. I felt tired and weary and wondered why life had to be so bloody complicated. Why couldn't I just be normal?

"Is the photograph in the box of my mother, do you think?" I asked suddenly.

"Truthfully, I'm not sure who it is but she must be connected with you somehow. You've got her eyes."

I put my hands on my face (as if I was going to remove my eyes and examine them) and looked at her in wonder. "That's the first time I have ever looked like anyone," I said before promptly bursting into tears.

Mammy held me for a long time after that as I continued to ask questions between sniffs.

"We let you play with the Mickey Mouse toy and the teddy bear for a while but then we put them away for safe keeping," Mammy explained when I commented on them.

"Where is St Catherine's Lodge?" I asked. "I know it's in Belfast but I don't know where."

"I haven't the faintest idea," Mammy responded.

"The drawing is interesting," I said as I closed my eyes and remembered the shading and the intricately sketched people.

"I often wondered about that too," Mammy said gently. "It's possible that your mother, like you, was fond of drawing."

"Why didn't you change my name?" I said, continuing to fire indiscriminate questions.

"If it had been up to me you wouldn't have kept it at all," Mammy said. "Ruby is a beautiful name which does indeed suit you, but I would have preferred a fresh and untarnished start to our life with you. But your daddy wouldn't hear tell of it. He always was very set in his ways and kind-hearted to boot."

I felt my eyes fill with tears as I nodded in agreement.

"I wish he was here to share this experience with both you and me," I said in a broken voice. "It's not that I want a new mother, y'know. You know that you're irreplaceable as far as I'm concerned."

"The same goes for you, Ruby. You were a precious child and still are and, even if your birth mother was foolish enough not to recognise it, your father and I certainly did. I've told you all I know now, so it's over to you. If you wish to pursue the matter, then that's your decision to make."

"Thank you, Mammy," I said, hugging her. "Thank you so much."

214

Chapter 37

I awoke the following morning and got out of bed quietly so as not to disturb Luke who was still asleep. He had come home after I had rung him and held me in his arms until I must have eventually dozed off, as the last thing I could remember was having my head stroked whilst he told me over and over again how much he loved me.

He had been shocked when I relayed details of my birth and subsequent adoption and did nothing to hide his disgust upon hearing of my ill treatment.

"It just doesn't make sense though, Luke," I'd said in a moment of clarity. "She had me baptised and there was the photograph I found and the teddy bear. Where did they all come from? Could someone who was so callous and cold-hearted have had the thought to put that little box together for me or was it done by someone else?"

"I don't know, darling. All I know is that I love you. I can't imagine how you must be feeling but at least you know now and you can continue with the rest of your life."

I had sat up and stared at Luke as his words sank in.

"You don't think I should look for her, do you? You think I

should just leave well enough alone and forget all about it, just because I have a bit more information now than I did yesterday."

"It's not that I think you shouldn't look for her, Ruby. It's more that I would question your reasons for wanting to. Isobel told you that she neglected you and didn't look after you properly, so why would you want to? Whoever this Georgina person is, she doesn't deserve to get to know you now. Not now that all the hard work has been done by your mum and dad and you're all grown up and no longer a helpless child that can simply be ignored."

Luke's voice was raised and I could see the anger and hurt in his eyes and at that moment my love for him grew stronger. I cuddled into his chest and he put his arms tightly around me as if to protect me.

I lay there for a while and listened to the sound of his heart beating and it calmed my mind, which was whirring to process what I had been told, at a rate of knots.

After a time I sat up and switched our bedside lamp on and whilst we both squinted in an effort to adjust to the sudden light I told Luke my thoughts.

"I know that you don't want me to look for her and that Mammy feels just as strongly about it all. But I have to. I need to know why all this happened because I still don't think I've been given all the facts. I don't know whether it's because Mammy knows more but isn't telling me or whether there were pieces of the story missing when she was told. Something about it all just doesn't ring true to me and I want to find out why."

"You can't argue with the actions of social workers and authorities, Ruby," Luke said imploringly. "They obviously had your best interests to the fore when they removed you and if there were complaints by members of the public, well, then, that just goes to prove that there was cause for concern."

"Maybe that is the case, Luke, and maybe I'm feeling the way I am because I don't want to believe it but either way I want to know and wild horses wouldn't stop me, so save yourself a lot of time and trouble and don't even try. Don't get me wrong. I'm under no illusions and I'm not making any excuses for this woman. I just want to know the truth and I want to hear it from her."

I let the water from the shower run over my face as I soaped my hair and continually thought about the revelations of the night before (although I wasn't exactly shocked, given the fact that I had already heard half the conversation before . . . I just wasn't going to tell Mammy that). I was very confused and in the midst of a myriad of feelings – anger, sadness, curiosity, wonderment. The most pressing of my emotions at the moment, however, was anger and I had a desire to find Georgina for the sole purpose of confronting her and asking her what the hell she thought she was doing getting pregnant and having a child she obviously didn't want. Had she any idea of the legacy she had left behind? Did she know what it felt like to grow up knowing that you had been given up by one family who didn't want you, only to be adopted into a wonderful one who accepted you, but where you felt like an outsider some of the time especially when conversations turned to the subject of genes and family trees and who's like feckin who? I hated that . . . when anyone had a baby people were immediately dissecting the poor child's features to apportion likeness or blame, as the case may be, for a shape of face or nose or eyes. And then there was me – poor old Ruby with the mad red hair who resembled nobody and felt that she never quite fitted in. Yes, the mould was certainly broken when I was created. I would just like to know who was responsible.

After I had come out of the shower, dried off and was applying moisturiser to my skin I could hear movement downstairs and guessed that my mother must be up and preparing to line our stomachs for another mad day in Belfast. I could hear her clattering with pans (and no doubt muttering about the shocking state of my cupboards). She had obviously found what I had left in the fridge, however, as soon the smell of bacon came wafting up the stairs accompanied by the delicious aroma of freshly percolated coffee.

"We should invite your mother to stay more often," Luke

217

commented, smacking his lips and grinning as he sat up and stretched in bed.

"Are you suggesting that my breakfasts are not up to scratch, Mr Reilly?" I asked, preparing to flick him with my wet towel.

"Not at all. I love burnt toast and am rather partial to soggy cereal, but you might want to go down and watch her all the same. You never know what you might pick up. The way to a man's heart being through his stomach isn't a well-known fact for no good reason."

"Well, I should be well chuffed then," I retorted, "because obviously my other qualities make up for the fact that I can't cook which must make me very special."

"You are special, Ruby," Luke said quietly, getting up to hug me. "Your daddy always told you that and he was so right."

"Don't, Luke," I said suddenly fighting back tears with a lump in my throat. "Don't remind me."

"But you need to be reminded, Ruby. You need reminding that you weren't just some abandoned baby who was immediately forgotten but that you've played a very important part in the lives of everyone you've touched since. Georgina Delaney will be very sorry she let you go when she finally meets you."

"She'll be sorry," I said defiantly. "But maybe not for that reason."

Chapter 38

My mother couldn't contain herself. She just had to take me outside and tell me in no uncertain terms how she felt. We were standing outside Rose Malone's dressmaking shop and she had met Gabriel about twenty minutes previously.

"He is just lovely. If I had a son I would want him to be exactly like that. He's so warm and kind and so in tune with us girls and the way we want everything to be perfect."

"Well, that's hardly surprising mother as he's a big girl himself," I said. "And before you go wishing him to be your son, please note that he hasn't taken off his coat –" (which was bloody ankle-length and made him look like an extra from *Pride and Feckin Prejudice*) "– therefore you don't know what horrors are lurking beneath."

"Do be quiet, Ruby, and give the boy a chance! He really does seem to know what he's talking about and has so many wonderful contacts."

"Yes, yes, yes, I know all that but just because *he* has them doesn't mean that *I* want them."

"What about this dress? He seems to be a bit unsure as to whether or not you're making the right decision about it. He's very knowledgeable about designers so why don't you take his advice?"

"Because, Mother, I don't want to end up trussed up like a Christmas turkey which is exactly how he would have me looking! I will only wear what I feel comfortable in. I want my day to be special. I only ever intend to get married once, thanks be to feck, therefore I want to do it my way. I don't want it spoiled or ruined and I don't need to be constantly told what to do."

"Oh, I can sympathise with him there all right," Mammy said, adopting her knowing expression. "You never did like to be told what to do and I should know. I've had enough experience of fighting the losing battle since you were a child."

Frankie saved the day by literally bouncing out the door and doing a jig on the footpath. Her new-found lust for life was catching and soon even I was smiling (slightly).

"He's just great!" Mammy repeated to Frankie. "It's a pity more men aren't like him."

"If all men were like him, Mother, there'd be slim pickings for the rest of us. It's hard enough to find a good man these days without the likes of you wishing that they were all gay."

"I didn't mean that I'd like them to switch teams so to speak," Mammy said whilst Frankie sucked in her cheeks and stared very hard at the display in Rose's window. (What is it with older people comparing sexuality to five-a-side football?) "It's just that he's such a sensitive soul."

After Mammy had left, still telling anyone who would listen to her about how wonderful she found Gabriel to be, Frankie marvelled at how worldly wise and accepting she was.

"You don't know how lucky you are," she said, shaking her head in apparent disbelief. "Can you imagine my mother's reaction if she'd got to meet him? Dear God, it doesn't even bear thinking about. She'd interrogate him to within an inch of his life whilst trying to analyse what had made him gay in the first place, as if it was a disease. Then she'd be announcing that every passing male should clench their butt cheeks to avoid possible attack."

Even I had to agree that when it came to being a modern woman Mammy was up there with the best of them. She was living her own life, running her own business, back in the dating game and an official woman of the world and I had to admit that I was proud of her.

"Your mother is wonderful," Gabriel announced as he appeared outside, clutching his fancy cigarettes and grinning broadly.

"I would tell the two of you to get a room only there'd be no point," I said, shuddering. "Good God, the mutual appreciation is starting to become a bit overwhelming."

"That was supposed to be a compliment," Gabriel said, sounding weary. "I can never say the right thing with you, can I?"

"Jok-ing!" I replied. "Lighten up."

"No, seriously. She is a fantastic person. You're so lucky to have a mother who accepts you for who you are and allows you to be yourself. I wish I was as privileged."

He looked incredibly sad and I stared at him in surprise.

"Are you all right, Gabriel?" Frankie asked, suddenly concerned that the upbeat character who had been there five seconds before seemed to have disappeared.

"I'm fine really. I just wish that things were different but, no matter what else you can do in life, there's no turning back time or changing the past."

"What happened?" I asked.

"Ruby, he mightn't want to talk about it," Frankie hissed through the corner of her mouth.

"No, honestly, it's fine. It's part of who I am at this stage and it always helps to talk. Putting it mildly, my mum and dad aren't quite as accepting as your mother is, Ruby. I've been like this ever since I can remember. I never quite fitted in at school, always got picked on by the boys and positively loathed sports but the girls loved me although not obviously in a normal boy–girl way. They used to come to me with all their relationship problems and I'd hang out with them and go shopping or whatever else they were doing. I always felt far more comfortable in their company, although I got to quite like the boys in time."

I nodded, thinking that I had always been the direct opposite. I had loved sports, hated other girls and would have stuck their heads down the toilet if they'd even so much as mentioned the state of their relationships to me. Poor Gabriel wouldn't have stood a chance with me around then (not that he was faring much better as it was, mind you).

"After a period of time, most people knew I wasn't going to settle down with a nice girl and make babies. Most people except –"

"Your mother and father," Frankie finished for him whilst he nodded sadly in response.

"I sat them down one day to tell them, but hardly got to opening my mouth before they both erupted on me. According to them, I was a disgrace. A freak of nature that should have been drowned at birth. What I was doing and all that I stood for was unnatural and unhealthy and it was to stop immediately. I was the talk of the parish and they weren't having it."

"How did they find out before you told them?" Frankie asked softly.

"One of the boys who used to torment me at school took great delight in telling my father," he said.

"Vicious little fecker! I know what I'd have done with him," I responded. Gabriel wasn't one of my favourite people in the world but I could never imagine being that cruel towards anybody.

"Do you still see your parents?" Frankie asked as Gabriel hung his head, deep in thought.

"I haven't seen them since," he said matter-of-factly. "I was given a choice that day. Either I stopped what I was doing and started making amends for all the hurt I'd caused, or else I got out of the town and never showed my face again."

"That's very harsh," I said, not quite believing what I was hearing.

"It was a reality for a lot of gay people years ago, only you never got to hear about it," he went on. "We paved the way for the younger generation. People are much more liberal these days. Apart from my mother and father of course, along with their cronies who would probably re-enact the Salem Witch Hunt and burn me at the stake in my pink T-shirt if they got half the chance. I don't know why I'm telling you this. I usually pretend my parents are dead or retired to the Continent if I'm ever asked. After all, who wants to let the world know that their own parents despise them enough to give them up in favour of their precious principles?"

"Or their lifestyle and freedom," I murmured.

I looked at Gabriel and saw a raw hurt in his eyes that must mirror my own and for the first time felt that there was an understanding and empathy between us.

"Well, if it's any consolation, I think that they're the disgrace and the freaks," I said sternly.

"Coming from you," Gabriel answered with a smile, "that means a lot."

"Yeah, well, don't get too excited. I'm still not wearing a veil and if you try to persuade me that I should be wearing high heels again, I'll feckin throttle you with my bare hands."

Chapter 39

Rose took my final measurements when we went back into the shop and wrote them all down on a piece of paper whilst humming with a pin perched in the corner of her mouth.

She had done more detailed drawings of her original ideas and I had fallen instantly in love with them and hadn't needed to consult with anybody with regard to whether or not I was making the correct decision in hiring her. I knew in my heart of hearts that I was doing the right thing and viewed her shop almost like a magical kingdom which was shut off from the rest of the world. I didn't know why but every time I went there I felt as if I had 'come home' for some strange reason and still got the feeling that the place was very familiar in a weird sort of way. Although I'd stopped airing my views on the subject out loud after everyone started giving me funny looks, obviously convinced that I was imagining it.

"Ruby," Frankie had said the last time it was mentioned, "you have only ever been in Belfast a handful of times in your entire life. It's hard enough to try and get you to go shopping in a normal street that actually has shops in front of you, never mind one that doesn't, so you would never have had any reason to be anywhere near here."

Now she was looking at me accusingly. "You've got that look on your face again," she commented.

"What look?" Mammy asked.

"The one which is usually followed with her wondering why she finds it so familiar around here. She's convinced she's been here before."

"Were you a student here?" Rose enquired upon hearing our conversation.

"No," I said. "Why do you ask?"

"No reason. There's a doctor's and a dentist on this row that have been here for years and are quite popular with the students because they're near the city centre, but there's nothing else. The street was mostly residential years ago but not any more. Most of the houses have been renovated into offices now."

"Okay. I must be officially doting," I conceded.

"Too much stress about the wedding," Mammy said knowingly before she was jumped on from all angles.

"I am not stressed. What the hell would I be stressed about?" I demanded.

"Stressed? Why would she be stressed?" Gabriel enquired hotly. "That's what I'm here for. I'm like a giant stress-ball for brides to squeeze," he said, deftly stepping out of my way before I managed to strangle him with my bare hands, although for a change I was only joking.

Mammy's mobile rang as Rose was finishing with me.

"Hello. Yes, it's Isobel speaking. Aisling, how nice to hear from you!"

I immediately started to pay attention to the conversation, firstly because I liked Aisling and secondly because I knew she'd be unlikely to be calling from Donegal for a spot of idle chit-chat.

"But why would she be doing that?" I heard Mammy ask in a panicky voice. "I'll tell her right away and let you know what I'm doing," she said in a firmer tone whilst looking at me.

"What?" I said as Mammy hung up.

"Nosy cow!" she said fiercely.

"Who? Aisling?" I asked in surprise.

"Of course I don't mean Aisling," Mammy said crossly. "Aisling was simply ringing to warn me. Judith was snooping all round the cottage earlier on, looking in through all the windows and taking photographs of the house and the garden."

I felt myself immediately stiffen in response to this information. "What the hell does that interfering bitch think she's playing at?" I said angrily.

"Well, if I knew that I wouldn't be standing here wondering what I'm supposed to do now," said Mammy. "I'm rather far away to do anything. Besides, I wouldn't want to get Aisling into any trouble. I can hardly ring Judith up and say, 'Sorry, love, but would you mind removing yourself from my home when I'm not there?'"

"No, you wouldn't like to do that but I wouldn't mind," I said, grabbing my mobile and walking towards the window where I would have the best reception. "Do you have the number for the hotel?" I asked.

"I think I have a card here that has the number on it somewhere," Mammy said as she practically emptied out the contents of her handbag and eventually found it along with a pile of crumpled receipts and a broken lipstick. "Here we go," she said at last with a flourish.

I took the card and rang the number. It was answered on the first ring by Aisling.

"Aisling, don't say a word. Pretend you don't recognise me. It's Ruby here. Is that trollop in the vicinity?"

"Yes, madam, I'll get her for you now," Aisling said in a smiling voice.

"Put her on like a good girl. Thanks for warning Mammy and don't worry. I'm not going to get you in any trouble. I'm sorting it now and going to have a bit of fun in the process."

A pause and Judith came on the line. "Judith McQueen speaking."

"Judith," I said in my most cheerful tone. "Do me a favour and get your arse off my mother's property. You were spotted taking photos and acting suspiciously this morning by someone I've hired to look after the place while Mammy is away."

I could hear her bumbling like an eejit on the other end of the phone.

"What's the matter, sweetie? Cat got your tongue? I'd be very careful about what you do in future as I have a surveillance team on standby and they're recording every movement you're making. I could ask them to give the tapes to the guards right now for trespassing on private property and taking illegal photographs of the said private property."

Mammy and Frankie looked on in astonishment whilst Gabriel gazed at me with what looked suspiciously like pride in his eyes.

"I didn't mean any harm –" Judith began.

"Really? Did you not?"

"I-I'm just taking photographs of the whole estate – its features," she fumbled. "For – for a brochure – you see –"

"My mother hasn't given you an answer or signed anything so I wouldn't be too presumptuous about her intentions if I were you."

"No – I –"

"Stay away from her home. Don't go anywhere near it again or we'll take legal action."

"No – I –"

I slammed down the phone.

"Stupid feckin cow. Needs a good clip round the ear if you ask me," I muttered.

"A surveillance team?" Mammy said. "Outside my house?"

"There are so many cars parked around there that they could be in any one of them," I explained. "Sitting with a fully functional recording system which would mean that they could tape everything that happens in or around the cottage."

"Feckin James Bond, eat your heart out!" Frankie said, laughing. "I am seriously going to have to have words with Luke about allowing you to watch so many spy and espionage thrillers. They've obviously rubbed off on you a bit too much."

"And correct me if I'm wrong but did I just hear you call someone 'sweetie'?" Gabriel said slyly.

"Ah, Jaysus! I have definitely been spending too much time under your dangerous influence. Next thing I'll be wearing a corset and painting my toenails."

"Ruby, you are my child but sometimes your bullishness astounds even me," my mother said incredulously. "I cannot believe that you phoned Judith and threatened her with legal action."

"Didn't it do the trick? I don't think we'll be having any more problems with her for a while but, just to be sure, I think a wee trip to Donegal is in order just to double-check. Frankie, go and talk nicely to your mother and stepdaughter and tell them that you and Owen are going away for a few days. Mandy was supposed to be meeting us here after we're finished so I'm going to give her a ring and command her to tell her boss that the only gossip she'll be hearing for the foreseeable future will be of the seaside variety. And as for you," I said, addressing Gabriel sternly, "you can come too but only if you promise not to entice my future husband into singing any more tuneless duets. And you're not allowed to wear that basque either – too many people with dicky hearts could see you and then where would we all be?"

Mammy and Frankie looked at each other whilst Gabriel looked at me questioningly with raised eyebrows whilst chewing his lip thoughtfully.

"Any chance we could get a move on?" I said. "We don't have all day and some of us have a wedding to organise."

"Aye aye, sir!" Gabriel said, saluting me and looking for all the world like a Russian soldier in his military-style coat (all he needed was a furry squirrel on his head and he'd have played the part well).

"You're sure about this?" Frankie asked.

"Are you still standing there?" I demanded. "*Phone. Husband. Now.* We'll look on this as a mini hen night."

"But the men will be going too!" Frankie said.

"Well, then they can have a practice run at the stag night and take Donal and Grumpy Slippers with them."

"Grumpy Slippers?" Gabriel asked in bewilderment.

"I'll explain on the way," I said.

We were there for a further forty minutes, watching as Rose worked her magic on Frankie, took measurements, made suggestions and added little details here and there to the drawings she had prepared. She had measured Carly on the last visit, so she wasn't with us, much to our flower girl's disgust.

She handed me her sketches once more for final approval.

"Now you're sure that these are what you want?" she asked.

"If my bridesmaid is happy, then I'm happy," I said. "And the flower girl will be ecstatic as well. I can't wait to show her what you've designed."

"I think they're wonderful," Frankie said in glee. "I couldn't get any better if I went to a specialist designer shop and I really mean that."

Rose glowed in her praise and blushed even more when Gabriel told her that she was very talented – which nearly gave *me* a heart attack never mind anyone else.

"What? Praise? A compliment? An actual admission that perhaps I am capable of making one or two decisions on my own?" I said. "Wow!"

"Yeah, all right, Sarky Knickers, let's go to Donegal where you can introduce me to Grumpy Slippers and my happiness will be complete," Gabriel muttered with a grin whilst my mother smiled over at us as if we were both her children (heaven forbid) having a falling out.

"I know what you did in there," Frankie murmured as she linked my arm and we left the shop. Gabriel and Mammy had left before us (also linking arms, I might add).

"Made a few decisions, ordered a few dresses, tried to keep everyone happy," I said.

"No. You held out your hand to someone who needed you and I'm very proud of you."

"What are you waffling on about, woman?" I asked.

"I'm talking about Gabriel and how you've offered to take him

229

to Donegal. I feel really sorry for him, you know, and I know that in your own way you were trying to let him know that you are on his side."

"Don't be getting any ideas," I warned. "I am not about to start looking as if I got dressed in the dark and putting all my clothes on back to front in unsuitable colours. I just happen to think that his parents are a pair of insensitive, small-minded dickheads and the sooner people like that are stamped out the better."

"You're not going to stamp on anybody, are you?"

"Metaphorically speaking," I said before she started thinking that I was about to leave footprints on heads. "I'm not that bad. Besides, this is something that Gabriel needs to work through on his own, the same way I'm doing, only in his case maybe it's worse. At least I was only abandoned by the person who gave birth to me. Poor Gabriel was abandoned by the people who brought him up which must be a much harder cross to bear. I should know as I've watched Luke go through it as well and it's not pretty. The only difference is that he has his sister to share the burden with and me to pick up the pieces after every nuisance phone call."

"He'll get over it with our help," Frankie said cheerfully. "We'll take him out for the night and let him get it all off his chest."

"The Smugglers' Inn won't know what's hit it," I said as we made our way down the street in preparation for going home to pack.

Chapter 40

"Ruby, I can't just drop everything. I've got photographs to take tomorrow. The local papers are desperate for them and if I do a good job there'll be more work in it for me."

"Can you not forget about it? It's only one job," I grumbled.

"No, I can't. We have a wedding to pay for and a honeymoon to plan and I'm not leaving anything to chance. I'm going to take every bit of work that's offered and then some."

"Feckin killjoy," I said. "Everybody else is going. Even Gabriel."

I thought that this revelation might have a bit of an effect although I wasn't expecting Luke to seem quite so stupefied.

"Do I need to take your pulse to make sure you're still breathing?" I asked as he continued to stare at me open-mouthed and rooted to the spot.

"I'm alive," he said. "Completely and utterly amazed but alive. What happened?"

"Nothing happened as such. I just decided that we needed to go to Donegal and that it would be nice to make it an enjoyable time for everybody. We're due a night out with Frankie and Owen, and Mammy would appreciate the company. Plus, the gallery exhibition is on this weekend and, as you're going on Gabriel's suggestion, I just thought that it might be a nice gesture to ask him along."

"Ruby and Gabriel," Luke said with a grin. "Friends at last."

"I wonder would you ever feck yourself," I said crossly. "I just thought that it was the right thing to do."

"I knew it would happen eventually," Luke said in an irritatingly knowledgeable tone of voice.

"Knew what would happen eventually, darling?"

"Knew that you would eventually see sense and agree with the rest of the world in acknowledging that I made a brilliant decision when I hired Gabriel."

"I don't have time for this," I said. (Note to women everywhere: never tell a man he is right and definitely never tell him that you are wrong as it will lead to lifelong anguish and sentences that begin with "Do you remember the time I was right and you were wrong . . .")

"I have a bag to pack. For the two of us," I added. "Because you are going to tell the papers that your future wife has important plans for you and your camera tomorrow that don't involve them."

"I tell you what. Why don't you girls have a wee night to yourselves tonight and then Owen and I will follow you down tomorrow evening? Gabriel will have the time of his life giving you all a make-over while we're not there. Have you spoken to Mandy?"

"Yes. I did ask her to join us but she said she had plans. She was in quite a strange mood. And FYI Smart-arse Gabriel will be doing no kind of make-over on me. He's already got me agreeing to things I never thought I'd entertain, just to shut him up, but he needn't push his luck and start thinking that he can transform me into a horrible girlie-girl because it just won't be happening."

"And I wouldn't want it to," Luke said, cupping my face with his hands and pinching my cheeks. "I love you just the way you are."

"Good job too," I said. "'Cos you're stuck with me."

After I had packed a bag, given Luke a kiss and gone to Frankie's where Carly and Jack had spent half an hour climbing over me, we finally prepared to set off. Celia had been roped in to baby-sit and was doing her usual fuss routine and driving Frankie to distraction.

"I will kiss the ground when I finally get out of here," Frankie had growled as Celia went off on another tirade about how many nappies she would need for Jack and how Frankie hadn't packed enough, making me wonder did she know her child at all.

"A few days away from my mother will be a holiday in itself. Poor Daddy and the children can be the focus of all attention for her."

"Does that include Angelica?" I asked as I hadn't seen her.

Frankie gave me a quizzical look. "Angelica and my mother in the same room for an hour is quite likely to cause bloodshed. What is it you're after – another civil war? She's wisely decamped to a friend's house and is staying firmly out of the way until we come back. Owen is also taking himself off and has already left to go to Dublin and visit his mother for the night, since we're having a girlie night with Gabriel."

"I do wish you'd stop calling it that," I mumbled. The word 'girlie' conjured up all sorts of scary images that appealed to me about as much as chewing my own arm off (yeuch).

"Oh stop complaining, there could be worse ways to spend your time," Frankie said, grinning broadly. "It was your idea to go down and take the biggest girl of all with you, so you have nobody to blame but yourself."

"I am going to check that my mother's cottage is safe and secure. We will go for a wee drink tonight and then on to the art exhibition tomorrow night and nowhere in that do I anticipate doing anything pink or fluffy or Gabriel-ish."

"Whatever you say," she answered whilst quite obviously laughing at me.

We were going to meet Gabriel at the border and Mammy had already left, muttering that instead of preserving the cottage she'd be better applying for planning permission to knock in a few more rooms as she didn't know where everyone was going to sleep.

"I think some of us should stay in the hotel," Frankie suggested when I told her of Mammy's concerns.

"You just want a dirty weekend away," I said accusingly at which point I got my ear flicked.

"Noooo," Frankie said sternly. "I would love a dirty weekend but now is not the appropriate time. I just thought that if some of us were to stay in the hotel we might be able to do a little more snooping and see what the lovely Judith is up to."

I thought about her suggestion for a few seconds and then grinned. "I think that would be a very good idea actually. Have you packed your best lingerie?"

"Well, as it so happens I always like to be prepared. I never know when Superman is going to appear so I always like to look my best."

"Jezebel," I muttered.

By the time we arrived in Donegal it was already getting dark and the thought of curling up in front of the fire in the Smugglers' Inn with a drink was highly appealing.

We had driven in convoy after we'd met with Gabriel who, judging by the bags he'd packed, must have thought he was moving in with Mammy as opposed to going to stay for two nights.

"This is the cutest cottage I have ever set eyes on," he announced when he saw it. "It's like something you'd see on a postcard."

He had then stood in awe as he looked towards the hotel which was standing in all its magnificence in the evening sunshine and looking very impressive.

"Wow! That is the most gorgeous place I've ever seen and look at the amount of cars! Business must be good."

My stomach did a flip when I heard this as, the more I thought about it, the more I feared that Mammy was going to be subjected to a campaign which would result in her either having to move or wanting to move because she was no longer happy. Why else would bloody Judith have been photographing the place? Obviously she was planning to use the photos to add to the appeal of the hotel by advertising the cottage or else she was jumping the gun and taking photographs in preparation for a sale. A sale which would not be happening, I thought grimly. When I had talked about a surveillance team I had only been half joking. I would nearly camp out in the car myself just to make sure that nothing untoward was going on.

Mammy had obviously been cleaning in anticipation of her guests as the smell of furniture polish in the cottage had the capacity to make you high.

"Dear God, Mother, do you have shares in Mr Sheen that you haven't told me about?" I asked with watery eyes whilst trying not to lose consciousness from the whiff.

"Yes. They needed somebody to take your quota of cleaning products so I offered."

"Oh ha ha," I said, hands on hips. "I'll have you know that I've become quite domesticated in the last while. I don't know whether it's due to the fact that I need something to burn off excess nervous energy or because it distracts me but I've found I quite like it."

Frankie and Mammy both looked at me as if I had sprouted horns.

"Shut up," I said as I grabbed my bag and made my way to my room.

The girlie night which I had been dreading didn't happen. (Obviously I cried with vexation as I had been so looking forward to it.) Instead I was subjected to the weirdest night I've ever had in my life. Mammy had decided that it was time that Donal got acquainted with everyone who was in any way involved with her daughter's wedding, so both he and Robbie joined us for drinks in the Smugglers' Inn.

In order to be dressed for the occasion, Gabriel had decided that it would be appropriate to wear a flamboyant long purple velvet coat (complete with a pink and green corsage in the lapel), his favourite pink shirt and a pair of jeans decorated with brightly coloured beading. He accompanied these with pointy-toed boots which wouldn't have looked out of place on the child snatcher in *Chitty Chitty Bang Bang*. He had said that the jeans had cost him an obscene amount of money in Paris but to me they looked like they had been decorated by a child who had been let loose in the arts and craft box (in other words they looked like crap).

"It's a pleasure to meet you," he had said when being introduced to Donal and warmly shaking his hand.

Robbie had limply shaken his hand whilst looking at him in disbelief.

"I'm Ruby's wedding planner," Gabriel had gushed. "It's always so nice to meet the family before the wedding. I become very attached to my clients, you know!" He put his arm around me (and potentially shortened his life span).

"And what is your role again?" Robbie asked, looking very confused.

"I'm a wedding planner," Gabriel said slowly as if he was talking to an eejit (the point could be debated, I supposed). "Therefore I am responsible for putting the wedding together, so to speak. I organise the flowers, the catering, the photographer, the video, the invitations and also liaise with the hotel. I usually like to play a major role in picking out gowns for the bride and bridesmaids but on this occasion have come up against quite an obstinate bride who is insisting on choosing her own designer and designs."

"Does that mean that she's picking her own dress?" Robbie asked.

"Unfortunately it does," Gabriel said dramatically. "I can only advise. I can't force."

Robbie raised his eyebrows and turned away and I resisted the urge to burst out laughing when he gave me a double thumbs-up sign underneath the table.

"He's very bright," he commented as we went to the bar to buy another round of drinks.

"Are we talking intelligence bright or are we talking 'sore on the eyes and in your face' bright?"

Robbie clarified by shading his eyes and looking in the general direction of the snug where we were all seated.

When we arrived back with the drinks, Donal had gone to talk to some friends and Frankie had left to go the little girls' room.

Robbie had also excused himself to go outside for a smoke, looking nervous as Gabriel followed in hot pursuit, clutching his designer cigarettes. With everyone otherwise occupied, Mammy moved closer towards me.

"I declare it's a miracle," she said. "You and Robbie are actually growing fond of each other."

"We are not," I snapped. "I just needed help at the bar and he has a pair of willing hands."

"If you say so."

"Yes, Mother, I do."

"About the other little matter – have you had the chance to think any more about what you're going to do?"

"There have been so many matters lately I've had to make decisions on that you'll have to enlighten me as to which one you're referring to, Mammy."

"The chat we had on Friday night," she said awkwardly.

"I don't know yet," I said, not wanting to commit myself and have her breathing down my neck and either constantly asking for updates or trying to talk me out of it.

"When you make a decision, will you let me know? Because whatever you decide, I'd like to be part of it. Whether it's good or bad I'd like to be there to help you through it."

She looked imploringly at me and I put my arm around her and gave her a squeeze.

"I haven't made any plans as of yet," I said truthfully, "but when I do I promise to let you know."

Robbie and Gabriel came back to our company and were deep in conversation about fishing which made the rest of us look at each other in amusement. They made a most unusual pair: the old man clutching his battered pipe wearing a jumper and corduroy trousers and the spectacle that looked like he had just stepped off the set of a West End production.

"My grandfather used to take me fishing when I was young," Gabriel said. "He was a lovely man, very gentle and quiet. And understanding," he added as an apparent afterthought.

Gabriel's expression grew sombre once more as he stared into his drink whilst obviously recalling memories of happier times in his youth.

"I sell rods, you know," Robbie announced suddenly. "I'm sure I could get you one that you'd be happy with and maybe we could go out while you're down here. Just for old time's sakes. I had a grandfather who liked fishing too."

Gabriel looked like he might cry (I feckin hoped he didn't – Robbie wasn't fit enough to run out the door in a state of panic) and Mammy was patting me on the knee and looking all agreeable and not aggravated for a change and I suddenly discovered that it was when you least expected it that people could surprise you the most.

Chapter 41

The following day was spent relaxing – which I interpreted as slobbing about in my pyjamas until I was eventually prised out of them to go up to the hotel for a meal before going on to the art gallery.

Owen and Luke had arrived down in the morning and we had all spent a very enjoyable day together. Mammy made lunch early as she reasoned that none of us would want our appetite to be spoiled if we were planning to dine in the restaurant in Monroe Manor early that evening.

Gabriel and Robbie had left to go fishing at some ungodly hour in the morning. I didn't hear them leaving the house but Mammy told us all in a halting voice, in between laughing her head off, that she had heard Robbie tell Gabriel that unless he wanted to scare the feckin fish he better wear something a bit tamer that he wouldn't mind getting dirty. Gabriel had then apparently come up the stairs and was heard swearing loudly as he couldn't find anything remotely suitable. It wasn't until Donal arrived in the afternoon for something to eat that we heard the full story. Gabriel had had to borrow clothes from him and, as they were two completely different sizes, was left wearing trousers that were at least three inches too short for him and held in at the waist by a belt that was buckled as tight as possible but still too big for him.

"He must look like one of those schoolboys who has to wear his brother's hand-me-downs," Frankie said.

"Knowing Gabriel he'll make it into some sort of fashion statement," I commented. "We'll see all the celebrities sporting a similar look soon and then he can take credit for starting a new trend."

"I never saw anyone with a wardrobe quite like it," Mammy said in disbelief. "It's very bizarre. Yet he seems to have great taste in every other way."

"It's not that he has bad taste," Frankie said, quickly jumping to his defence. "It's just that he's an extrovert who likes to express himself through his clothing. He wants to be noticed and talked about."

"He wants to be loved," I whispered.

"What did you say, Ruby?" asked Mammy.

"Oh nothing. Just talking to myself again. Take no notice of me."

Gabriel and Robbie arrived back just before four o'clock and in time to make arrangements for dinner. Gabriel was grubby and tired but had a glorious smile painted on his face.

"I caught two rainbow trout and they were this size," he said whilst holding his hands out (ten foot apart) to demonstrate how big they were and staring at us all for approval. Robbie was standing behind him (holding his hands five foot apart) looking on proudly in the manner of a pleased mentor and both of them looked as if they'd had a successful day.

Frankie and Owen were getting ready to leave as they were going to make their way up to the hotel before us and book in for the night (squeaky mattresses and noisy headboards all round then!). Luke, Mammy and I were going to go to the Piano Bar in Monroe Manor for a drink. Gabriel was going to have a hot shower, clean himself up and join us later with Robbie and Donal who were going home and then calling back to the cottage to collect him. I was bloody exhausted just listening to it all.

"This must be what life is like in your house," I commented to Frankie after we had made our extensive plans.

"It's worse," Frankie said wryly. "At least adults try to be agreeable and are usually ready on time and don't need to go everywhere accompanied by a handheld computer game."

"Rather you than me, love."

When we arrived at the hotel we were greeted by Aisling who was grinning from ear to ear and gave us a very warm welcome.

"What have you done to our leader?" she asked, talking out of the side of her mouth. "She's been acting like a scalded cat since you spoke to her and there have been lots of meetings behind closed doors. She's also started to take long walks round the car park and she's been seen looking into parked cars and acting very strange."

"Really? I'm so sorry to hear that she's feeling out of sorts."

"That's maybe not a bad thing. She's so wrapped up in herself that she has no time to harass the rest of us. Life has been quite peaceful actually. It's like old times again."

"Glad to be of service, my dear. What time do you finish work? Can you join us for a drink?"

"I'm afraid we're not allowed to drink on the premises," Aisling answered. "New rules. Staff lower the tone of the place apparently."

"What a cow," I said, getting worked up again. "She really does think she rules the world, doesn't she?"

"Well, she certainly thinks she has total control over this place anyway and I'm not arguing – not with a mortgage and car payments every month."

"Maybe we can arrange to meet somewhere else another night. What about going down to the Smugglers' Inn sometime?" I suggested.

"I take it you haven't heard the news then?" Aisling said. "The Smugglers' Inn was robbed last night. Two men went in after closing time just as the barmen were counting the takings and locking up. They were tied up and the place was ransacked. It's in a terrible mess apparently. They broke all the glasses and mirrors, smashed tables and chairs and, as for the drink, I don't think they left a bottle of anything intact. It'll take them weeks to sort out the damage apparently so I'd say they'll be closed for the foreseeable future."

"That's terrible," I said worriedly. "Do me a favour and don't mention any of this to my mother. She's bound to hear sometime but I'd rather it was later rather than sooner. She thinks the culprits have been arrested and that's that. I just don't want her worrying even though she has had a burglar alarm fitted and assures me she'll be fine."

"She won't hear it from me," Aisling assured me. "It's an awful shame though. The Smugglers' Inn had just been done up and was looking really well. They were doing a roaring trade and it was a popular spot with tourists and people just passing through. From a purely selfish point of view I'm also a bit fecked off that I'm going to have nowhere to have a wee beverage of a weekend now. Not, mind you, that it matters in the grand scale of things."

"Of course it matters," I said. "You should be allowed to enjoy yourself as much as everyone else!"

At that point Judith came in. She looked uneasy at my presence and quickly walked into her office and sharply banged the door.

"That's all she does these days," Aisling said. "Always hiding behind that door and she is seriously nervy. I went in to give her a message the day before yesterday and she nearly jumped six foot in the air and swallowed her tongue. She was on the phone and writing stuff down but she practically flung herself across the table to hide whatever it was when she saw me coming in."

"Well, I'm no detective but I'd say she has a lot to hide," I said thoughtfully. "You said that her father is a tycoon and into buying and selling property and businesses. Who knows what his plans are and how legal they are, come to think of it?"

"Oh, knowing them, whatever they do they'll get away with it. Her father is a highly respected businessman with lots of contacts and there have been plenty of bigwigs hanging around lately to prove it."

"Really?" I said. "I wonder why?"

"Yeah, lots of suits coming and going and whisperings and meetings."

"What are you two talking about?" Mammy demanded, coming from the bar to find me. "Are you coming for a drink later, Aisling?"

"She can't," I snapped, looking straight at Judith who had just reappeared and was looking nastily at me. "The Gestapo won't allow it or perhaps I should call them the secret police. Only problem with secrets is that they come out eventually."

Judith held my gaze and then slowly and deliberately turned away with her nose in the air but not before I detected a slight hint of fear in her eyes. She was up to something. She knew it and I knew it and it wouldn't be long before everyone else would know as well.

I looked at Mammy and how animated she appeared as she rejoined the company in the bar and sipped from a glass of wine and laughed at something Luke had said. Her happiness was everything to me and I wouldn't let anything come between her and it. Judith had better watch out. She simply didn't know who she was dealing with or what lengths I was prepared to go to, to ensure my mother was content.

Chapter 42

"Once Ruby stops looking so ferocious maybe she might tell us what she would like to drink," Mammy said, studying me intently which annoyed the shite out of me.

"What are you staring at?" I demanded.

"I think it's more about what *you're* staring at," she said, making a face at the barman who was standing waiting to take my order.

"I'll have a vodka and Diet Coke, please, and a hurley-stick to smack that silly cow up the mouth with," I responded without taking my eyes off Judith who was continuing to strut in the reception area like a peacock, in between acting like Hitler with the staff and grimacing badly at the guests.

"The vodka and Diet Coke I can do," the bow-tied and apron-attired barman answered with a wry smile. "Don't worry. I've fantasised about hitting her a smack as well. I don't know what your gripe is but around here we have plenty."

I stared at him open-mouthed before raising my eyes and turning myself around so that I was facing him fully. "So it's not just me that she has that effect on then," I commented. "She turns me into a psychotic maniac every time I see her."

At this point everyone else around me started to snigger.

"She's usually very calm, y'know, is our Ruby," Frankie said. "She'd never be one for overreacting or acting like a madwoman in the grand scale of things."

"She'd certainly never threaten anyone," Luke added.

"Or want anyone dead," Gabriel uttered. He had just arrived looking as splendiferous as usual in a get-up you'd probably find in Elton John's maddest stage wardrobe minus the crazy glasses. Robbie and Donal positively faded into the background beside him in cords and shirts (and were trying to act as if they didn't know him by walking slowly behind him, whistling as they went).

"Feck away off, you lot," I said briskly. "I only half mean it usually but this time I'm deadly serious."

"Or just deadly," Gabriel said, batting his eyes and eyelashes (which were lined with more eyeliner than any of his three female counterparts) at the barman who was returning his gaze and grinning.

"Gabriel or you can call me Gay for short," Gabriel said, proffering his hand.

"My name's Darryl but people usually call me 'gay' for short as well," responded the barman.

I was astounded. Gabriel must have a 'gay in the vicinity' radar as the barman looked totally straight to me – but then what did I know? Once they came out of the proverbial closet they must be taught how to give off a special signal, I decided, watching as Gabriel and Darryl continued to hold each other's gaze while everyone else grinned happily.

"Are you from around here?" Frankie asked, addressing the barman with great gusto.

"No. I'm from a little village in west Donegal actually."

"Where they don't like gay boys and you were told to get out or else face the wrath of the church choir," Gabriel added.

"You know me well," Darryl commented, seemingly unshocked at Gabriel's insight.

"Have you two met before?" I asked in confusion.

"Nope," Gabriel answered confidently. "It just makes good sense to me that that would be why he had left. Small villages are notoriously small-minded and –"

"Not good at accepting that a young man wouldn't want to settle down with a nice girl and have a family and be sickeningly normal," Darryl finished in what was now becoming a very camp voice (did he sound like that from the start or was I now just imagining it? . . . hmmmm . . .).

"Oi, when you two are quite finished making eyes at each other and finishing each other's sentences maybe we could get our drinks," I said in my most important voice. "And don't knock normal. Sometimes it's good to lead a quiet life."

"If you're that way inclined," Gabriel said.

"But some of us aren't. Some of us –"

"Like playing for the other team?" my mother said.

"Yes, we play for the very happy pink team whilst the rest of you play for the –"

"Very ordinary grey team," I said. "Yeah yeah, I get it. Darryl, why don't you go and get our drinks and then come back and tell me why Bitch Features in reception annoys you so much?"

"No can do unfortunately," he said. "I'm already getting the evil eye because I've been standing here talking to you for far too long."

"But I want to hear more," I whined.

"Why don't you come to the art gallery with us?" my mother suggested, looking for all the world like the cat that got the cream (or Cilla Black perhaps). "That way you two boys can get to know each other better."

"Very smooth, Mother," I said once Darryl had gone back to the bar to fulfil our order with Gabriel skipping gaily (no pun intended, you understand) after him to apparently "help carry all the drinks down". "You're as subtle as a flying brick, you know."

"Ach sure, it's just lovely seeing him meet a wee friend."

"A wee friend, Mammy. He's gay and thirty-something not five, in case you hadn't noticed."

"Oh shut up, Ruby, and just be happy and stop glowering all the time. Honestly, you can give the dirtiest looks on the planet. God knows where you –"

"Get it from. Yes, Mother, God knows. Excuse me while I go and get some air," I snapped before marching out of the bar to the front door.

I wished that I smoked as I looked at a few others who were standing around a gas heater and enjoying a cigarette. It looked like something that might relax me. What the hell was I doing getting myself all worked up again? What exactly was I annoyed about? Was I in a bad mood because bloody Judith was being a twat as usual or was I pissed off because my mother had again reminded me that I was acting in a certain way that she didn't recognise which was obviously attributed to Mrs Desertion herself, my birth mother.

"Ruby, come back inside. We're ready to order the food," Frankie said gently as she appeared through the door.

"I've done it again, haven't I?" I said in sheer annoyance. "If I bend over could you possibly kick my arse for me? Why do I keep doing this? I'm not a super-sensitive person but any mention or hint about me being different makes me mad."

"You didn't know before what you know now, Ruby," Frankie said. "Give yourself a break."

"I keep taking things out on her when I shouldn't," I said mournfully. "Mammy'll bear a close resemblance to a human punch-bag before this situation has resolved itself, if it ever feckin does."

"Of course it will and your mammy understands. She knows how difficult it is and she didn't mean anything by what she said in there. She wasn't trying to be insulting towards you – it was just a common turn of phrase."

"I know that. I'm just behaving like a complete prat as usual. And speaking of prats, here comes another one."

Judith had just come through a side door and was deep in conversation with a balding man in a suit.

FIONA CASSIDY

"Yes, it's got a lot of potential," she said as she flicked her hair and looked engagingly at her companion, therefore not noticing us. "But it'll be worth a lot more by the time we're finished. There are a few problems that need taking care of, but I'm sure we'll have them ironed out soon."

They smiled conspiratorially at each other and then got into a fancy sports car, leaving Frankie and me looking after them in shock.

"Did that bitch just threaten to iron me?" I asked Frankie.

"I don't know but it certainly seems as if she's up to something and who was he?"

"One of the suits who's been hanging around obviously."

"I wonder if she's getting extra friendly with him to ensure she gets what she wants," Frankie said, clicking her teeth and shaking her hands like she was holding a set of reins.

"Don't," I said pretending to gag. "You'll make me regurgitate my dinner before I've eaten it. Lucky man. I wonder if he realises what he's letting himself in for."

At that point Luke joined us outside and Frankie discreetly decided to leave, after giving me another squeeze.

"All right?" he asked, putting his arm around me.

He looked weary. Probably sick and tired of me acting like a neurotic eejit all the time lately. I was sure that it must be incredibly tiring for him as I knew that I was knackered from constantly being on edge and subsequently taking the hump where none was intended.

"Top of the world," I responded with a sigh. "Look, you don't have to worry about me. I'm grand now. I've had my wee moment and now I'm going to go in and apologise to Mammy *again*. I think I'll start every future conversation with an apology and that way it'll save time. It's all I seem to do."

"It's bound to be confusing, Ruby, but we'll get through it! That's what I'm here for after all. For better, for worse, for always."

"For your sins," I added before kissing him and accompanying him back inside.

Chapter 43

I motioned for Mammy to come to the bathroom with me before I sat down again. The others were all intently studying menus and pretending not to notice that I'd just reappeared, even though I could see Robbie trying to look at me through the corner of his eye (badly, as he looked cross-eyed and not half wise)

Once we had walked into the ladies' room I stood in front of Mammy and placed my hands on her shoulders. "I'm sorry for leaving the table so abruptly. Robbie and Donal will think it's a ritual from the North that people in the Republic have never heard about."

"No, Ruby. I think they know that it's just one of your little rituals. I'm sorry for sticking my foot in it yet again. I can't seem to say the right thing around you these days. You're so sensitive and take everything the wrong way."

"It's not you, Mammy. It's me." (*Ugghhh*, now I sounded like I was breaking up with her . . . "It's not you, darling. I love you. It's me. I'm the reason why we shouldn't be together because I give lame-assed excuses for acting like a plank." Sorry, an ex-boyfriend said it to me once and I never forgot it.)

"Why are you looking at me in such a strange fashion, Ruby?"

"No reason. Never mind, Mammy. Look, let's go back and enjoy our night. I'm going to try and lengthen my fuse and stop taking everything so seriously. It's just that I've grown to hate any suggestion that I'm in any way different from my family. Maybe it's not so much that I want to find my birth mother any more. Perhaps I've just come to the realisation that more than anything I wish I belonged to you and Daddy."

As I said it I felt choked and close to tears. I hated feeling weak or vulnerable but yet that was how I seemed to be feeling a lot of the time lately. Pesky stupid Georgina. What the hell had she reduced me to? I was Ruby. Fearless Ruby who would smack you as quick as look at you if you spoke to her in the wrong tone but these days she bore more of a resemblance to a squished banana than her former glorious self.

"This was why I didn't want you to do this, Ruby," Mammy said gently. "A big part of my reluctance for you to pursue this was to do with you getting hurt, but I also hate to see you feeling so unsure of yourself. You seem to be constantly questioning whether or not you fit in, even though you are loved so much by everyone around you. None of us would be without you. You even seem to have won the affections of Robbie O'Donnell these days though he has the reputation of being one of the most difficult men this side of Donegal."

"Well, whoop de feckin doo-da, I'm delighted that Robbie likes me but I'd much rather that my birth mother had liked me slightly more before she let me go without a second thought."

"Well, her loss was our gain, Ruby, and don't you ever forget it," my mother said fiercely.

"I don't know why this keeps happening," I said in frustration. "I haven't been thinking about it all day but now all of a sudden it's back to the forefront of my mind. It's like an unwelcome invader that keeps popping up to annoy me. I don't want to think about this right now. I want to enjoy my night."

Frankie appeared just as we were coming up for air from a bear-hug.

"Wee message from Owen and Luke, ladies, which basically translates as 'Come the feck out, our stomachs think our throats are cut,' and that's the censored version."

"We're coming now and we're fine," Mammy said. "Aren't we, Ruby? Looking forward to good food, good company and no more foot-in-mouth incidents."

"Which aren't your fault, Mammy. Just ignore me or else kick me in future."

"Can I have that in writing, please?" Frankie said with a grin.

"No, you feckin can't, you tart!" I said.

"Tart?" Owen said as we reached the table. "Apple or rhubarb?"

"Or cherry?" Luke said, joining in. "We're just fantasising about food at this stage as it feels like it might take forever to appear."

"Oh shut up. We're here now," I said gruffly. "And who ever heard of a cherry tart anyway. Cherry pie maybe."

Donal and Robbie were making eyes at each other which obviously meant that they were having a full-scale conversation about the state of my head through facial expressions and the answer was that I was wired to the moon.

"Sorry to keep you all. Mammy and I just had a few things to sort out and they're sorted. Again . . . *ahem*."

"Darryl!" five voices shouted in unison, "You can take our order now!"

Darryl appeared with a notepad and proceeded to write down everyone's orders which were made at breakneck speed.

Gabriel was positively glowing and stared dreamily into space after Darryl had departed to deliver our requirements to the chef.

"Isn't he just lovely?" he said. "We have so much in common."

"He's delightful, I'm sure," I said as I played footsie with Luke beneath the table.

Frankie's phone rang in her bag, just as my big toe was snaking up Luke's calf, and made us both jump.

"Oh God, it's Angelica! I hope nothing's wrong!" Frankie said, looking worried. She got up. "Hello. Yes, love. Is everything okay?"

Frankie stood rooted to the spot for several seconds before her hand flew to her mouth and she closed her eyes and shook her head.

"Oh no," she exclaimed, making everyone turn round. "That's terrible."

Owen was on his feet demanding to know what the problem was just as I was mentally making plans to go home and forgo the trip to the art gallery.

"What's happened? Are the children okay?" Owen demanded.

Frankie said goodbye to Angelica and hung up. "Yes, everyone's fine. It's nothing to do with the children. Ruby, I don't quite know how to tell you this but there's been a bit of an accident. There's been a fire in town. The fire brigade are still at the scene and it's pretty bad."

"A fire where?" I demanded, standing up abruptly. "Please tell me that my wee house is still standing."

"Your house is fine, Ruby, but the venue for your wedding reception isn't. The Swiftstown Arms has been burnt to the ground."

Gabriel looked stricken, my mother looked horrified and Luke and I simply stared at each other.

What the hell were we going to do now?

Chapter 44

"Was anyone hurt?" Mammy asked. (Oops, I suppose that should have been my first thought but I was kind of preoccupied by the fact that the room where I was planning to wine and dine my wedding guests was now fire-kindle.)

"They got everyone out in time. There was a major gas leak and an explosion, as far as Angelica heard."

I could feel the blood draining from my face. I know I said I wasn't a girlie-girl but even *I* didn't want to end up having my wedding reception in a makeshift tent in somebody's back garden (which was the hopeless picture in my mind as my plans had just literally gone up in smoke).

"Don't panic. I have contacts. I'll get something sorted," Gabriel said quickly.

"You may have contacts, Gabriel, but we certainly don't have the money to pay for some fancy hotel," I said mournfully. "Who ever heard of a hotel burning to the ground just months before a wedding? It couldn't just be a wee fire created by an electrical fault that caused a bit of smoke damage. Oh no. This had to be a big, dramatic, destroy-all-in-its-wake fire that wreaked complete havoc. Is that typical of my bad luck or what?"

"You may not have the money," Mammy said quietly. "But I do. Or at least I know of one sure-fire way of getting it. A simple signature would be all it would take to sort this mess out."

"A simple signature signing away what?" I squeaked. "Please tell me that you are not referring to the cottage and letting that greedy pair of feckers get their hands on it? Over my dead body. I'd rather not have a reception at all if that's the case."

"Rubbish," Donal intervened. "You'll be having a reception. We'll sort something out. Sure if all else fails, I'm sure the Smugglers' Inn could arrange something."

"The Smugglers' Inn can't sort anything out. Have you not heard the news? Burglars destroyed the place last night. It was completely wrecked and will probably be closed for the foreseeable future for refurbishment."

Everyone around me looked stricken.

"We hadn't heard," Robbie said. "I suppose we've been out all day."

"Who would want to cause damage to the Smugglers' Inn?" Donal asked. "The owners are lovely and very well liked around here."

"I read in the paper recently about how bars are getting turned over at the end of the night and the burglars are getting away with the profits. A place like the Smugglers' Inn would make a tidy sum and there is a recession on and people are desperate," said Robbie.

I cleared my throat and looked towards Mammy who had paled and was staring into the distance.

"The wedding isn't until May," Luke said, changing the subject. "Surely the Smugglers' Inn would be refurbished by then? It might be all right."

"Might be? Well, that's hardly good enough, is it? I'm not that keen on switching my wedding reception from one venue that has just burnt to the ground to another one that has to go through extensive refurbishment due to a robbery. Strangely enough, it doesn't inspire me with confidence or conjure up any images of happy ever after."

"You lot are all daft," Frankie said suddenly. "You're all blind to what's sitting directly under your noses. We're sitting in a perfectly good hotel at the moment. Why not have it here? Get married in Smugglers' Bay and have the reception here. Problem solved."

I looked at Frankie and wondered had she gone temporarily insane.

"Oh yeah, what a wonderful idea, Frankie. Why don't we have our wedding reception, the most important event in our lives or so you keep telling me, in a hotel which is managed by somebody who can't stand the sight of us? I'd rather not be subjected to a deliberate case of food poisoning or have Judith McQueen gob-spit in my wine, thanks, if it's all the same to you."

"But it would be so handy," Mammy said. "And you're here now and I don't see anyone doctoring your drinks or being rude to you. She can't turn you away. She'd probably be delighted to be making money from you."

"Even if I was mad enough to consider it as a feasible option which I'm not, have you noticed how busy this place is? I'm sure it's booked up well in advance and we're getting married in eight months."

"I'll speak to Harry McQueen," Donal offered. "I'm sure we could work something out. Don't worry, Ruby, we'll find a way to still give you and Luke the wedding reception you deserve."

"Indeed we will," Robbie echoed his son's sentiments.

I forgot my troubles for a moment and looked at the sincerity that was etched on the faces of Donal and Robbie and decided that I was very lucky. But then the reality of their words sank in and I got cross again.

"I don't want to work anything out with this lot," I clenched my teeth and drew my fists into white knuckled balls. "You're not listening to me."

Frankie came and stood beside me and rubbed my arm whilst Luke held my hand. I felt drained. What calamity was going to befall me next?

"There's nothing we can do tonight," Luke said just as Darryl and two other waiters appeared carrying steaming plates of food to our table. After all the complaining, nobody seemed hungry any more and my appetite had certainly wilted. I picked at my food for the next half hour and then sat subdued as the bill was paid.

"Do you still want to go to the gallery?" Luke asked gently.

"Are you shitting me? It's the only thing keeping me sane at the minute. Of course I want to go."

"In that case your chariot awaits and I'll do the driving tonight so that you can relax and enjoy yourself."

"Thanks," I replied.

Where was the enjoyment in knowing that your wedding day was possibly doomed, especially when after a lot of soul-searching you'd come to the conclusion that it actually *was* important and you did want it to mean something after all?

Chapter 45

By the time we arrived at the art gallery I was feeling marginally more relaxed. Luke had pointed out again that there was very little I could do about it and spoiling my evening by worrying wouldn't change anything.

A lot of people seemed to be excited about the event as two traffic attendants were directing the queuing cars into a nearby car park beside the building, whilst suited waiters were giving people glasses of champagne as they entered the premises. Mammy was travelling with Donal and Robbie, and Gabriel was waiting for Darryl to finish his shift and then they were going to make their way over.

"Wow!" Frankie and I said in unison as we looked at the scene unfolding in front of us.

"Swish or what?" Frankie said with her mouth gaping. "You didn't tell me that this was going to be such a toffee-nosed affair. I feel like a tramp now."

Frankie, as usual, was dressed to perfection in a black halter-necked dress and black peep-toe shoes. Her hair was wound in a decorative bun and silver jewellery adorned her neck and wrist whilst long sparkly earrings dangled from her ears.

"Some tramp," Owen said, looking at her appreciatively and letting out a long slow whistle.

"You're slightly biased," she said, giggling as he nuzzled her neck and whispered in her ear.

"Would you two feckin lay off and get a room!" I said.

"We have already," Frankie said excitedly. "And it's magnificent."

"Yes, it's amazing," Owen said. "I usually couldn't care less about what a room looks like as long as it's clean but I have to say I was very impressed. Why didn't you take Ruby to see it when we were still at the hotel, Frankie?"

"Oh. I never even thought," Frankie said. "I'll sneak you in on the way back. It's maybe better that we didn't go before when the lovely Judith was there. She probably would have thrown you out."

"I'd like to see her try," I growled. "A sumo wrestler would have difficulty in getting me to budge if I didn't want to."

"That's true," Luke said.

I looked down at my clothes and took a quick squint in the mirror at my reflection. Compared to Frankie, I was most certainly the tramp as I was dressed as usual in my comfiest black trousers, DM boots and a long purple top with a black belt. A silver necklace with a black stone (courtesy of Frankie's massive jewellery collection) and black stud earrings were my only concession to jewellery. My hair was smoothed down in a softer style than usual and kohl eyeliner and lip-gloss had been liberally applied.

"You look lovely," Luke said as I appraised myself.

He pulled up the handbrake after parking the car near the entrance of the car park.

I smiled and sniffed the air as we approached the gallery, carrying Luke's photography equipment. A little cottage beside it obviously had a roaring turf fire inside, as the aroma was giving the evening a lovely heady traditional scent that reminded me of my grandmother and days gone by.

We came to the front door and Luke introduced himself to a young man with a clipboard who was ticking names off a guest sheet.

"Excellent. Caitlin O'Donnell is inside mingling and will be delighted that you've arrived. She doesn't want anything formal – just a few shots of everyone who's in attendance as well as some photos of her work. If you like art I'm sure you'll agree that it's a sight worth viewing."

"You can be the judge of that, Ruby," Luke said as we continued into the room.

"I'll give you a fiver if I'm wrong but I think Mr Doorman is in Gabriel's gang," I said, looking back at the man who was still greeting everyone enthusiastically and giving directions.

"How can you tell?"

"I don't know. Just call it a hunch," I said. (Oh feck, maybe spending too long in Gabriel's company had inadvertently honed my radar as well.)

As we continued to make our way through the crowd I spotted Caitlin who was talking animatedly to a group who were hanging on her every word. She looked radiant and was dressed in a pewter-coloured tulip frock with matching heels. Her blonde hair was clipped at the front whilst curls cascaded down her shoulders.

"Look, there's Mammy and her entourage coming now. I better go and meet them and let her know that I'm okay."

"For now," Luke murmured.

"I bloody heard that," I muttered.

"You were meant to," he said. "I'll go and mingle and take a few snap-shots of the crowd. See you later."

After I had spoken to Mammy and spent a few moments with Donal and Robbie I wandered around, soaking in the atmosphere and studying the pictures that were framed and on display. As Caitlin had described, they were very contemporary bold prints with large swirls of colour, dramatically framed, and each with a name that seemed to bear some significance to the piece.

I had become transfixed with one which was a series of red and black imagery set in a silver background and entitled *Celebration* when Caitlin came to greet me. She was glowing with excitement and happiness and I wished it was me showcasing my work (although I doubted very much that the crowd who had gathered would be very interested in my crumpled doodles . . . but then there was no accounting for taste . . . maybe they would).

"Congratulations, Caitlin," I said in thorough admiration.

"Thanks for coming, Ruby. Make sure you look round all the rooms. Each room is dedicated to a particular style of art and I know that you'll appreciate it. The room at the very back of the gallery contains Sarah Larkin's paintings. I agreed to let her exhibit some of her work tonight as well. I just met your mother and she was heading in that direction."

"Is Sarah herself here?" I asked, feeling my excitement grow.

"She's here somewhere. I'll introduce you if I get the chance later in the evening although I haven't managed to speak to her yet myself."

"I look forward to it," I said as we parted company and I took her advice and began to explore around me.

There was indeed a series of rooms just as Caitlin had explained. The main room, where the drinks were being served and everyone had congregated, was displaying the new collection but the other rooms played host to a variety of styles and moods of painting which totally enthralled me. There was a room solely dedicated to life drawings of faces and people in various poses and situations. Another room was filled with beautiful watercolours depicting neon-coloured landscapes, dramatic skylines and seaside views with cottages, starry skies and upturned boats. The next room had a Continental air to it with paintings of sidewalks, canopied cafés, street signs and showgirls with their legs in the air performing on a stage. Once I had emerged from this room I ascertained that there was only one display left to view at the end of the corridor and it must belong to the great Sarah Larkin whose ear would be bent listening to the gushing noises my mother would be undoubtedly making.

I entered the room and took a deep breath. All around me was a collection of the most hauntingly beautiful paintings I had ever seen. There were colourful images of waterfalls in the summer, frozen lakes in the midst of winter with Christmas lights reflecting from the ice, messy kitchen dressers, old women sitting by fires and children running along a beach laughing with the wind in their hair. Each painting was unique and the attention to detail was amazing. I thought of Mammy's painting and how we always said that it made you want to climb in and be part of the scene, and so it was with everything else that this artist had constructed.

I was lost in concentration when Luke came to find me and had no idea how long I had been there.

"They're breathtaking," I whispered reverently. "She is such a talented artist. Her work is amazing. I've never seen anything like it. I can't wait to meet her. Luke, please don't let me make a gobshite of myself. Don't let me curtsey or fall at her feet or do anything daft."

"Ruby, since when do you curtsey? Please tell me. I wasn't aware that you knew how."

"Well, I don't. But I might start. She's unbelievable."

Luke shook his head, put his arm around me and directed me towards the door.

"Well, now's your chance. Caitlin asked me to come and get you as she's with Sarah at the moment and would love you to meet her."

I steeled myself and felt strangely nervous as I wondered what she would be like. I hoped that she wasn't going to be some cocky disappointment who was full of her own self-importance and enjoyed having her head up her arse – as had been the case with a few other artists I had met.

"Caitlin, I found her," Luke called as Caitlin and a group of other people came into view.

"Super," she said, looking all around and scanning the faces in the room. "Excuse me everyone but where did Sarah go? She was here a moment ago."

A series of shrugs and pursed lips indicated that no one knew where she was.

"Her paintings are amazing. Absolutely fabulous," I said.

"Good job I'm self-assured, isn't it?" Caitlin murmured to the assembled crowd. "That's all I've been hearing all night."

"I don't think you have anything to worry about," Luke said as he gestured towards the sales desk where people were thronging to get more information and money was being exchanged for paintings.

"Oh, here she is now," Caitlin said. "Sarah, can you come over here? There's someone I'd very much like you to meet."

I looked just in time to see someone wearing a purple crocheted hat coming towards me only to be steered in a different direction by one of the door attendants.

"Oh dear, she must be needed elsewhere," Caitlin said apologetically. "She's creating quite a stir."

I had to resist the urge to stamp my feet and flap my arms against my thighs in the manner of a bad-tempered toddler as I was now desperate to meet her.

Mammy and Gabriel approached at that stage and distracted me from my annoyance.

"I just very nearly got speaking to Sarah," I said. "Have you seen her stuff? Oh my God, it is out of this world. I could move into that room and admire her work forever."

"I'm in sympathy, dawling," Gabriel drawled in an affected voice. "I could move into Darryl's room and admire him forever although I have to say that the doorman is quite cute and available as well if his flirting is anything to go by."

"Ha!" I said loudly, startling half the people beside me and making one woman slosh her wine out of her glass and onto her dress.

"Ruby, must you shout?" Mammy enquired whilst giving me the cold shoulder and smoothing down her hair (and effectively trying to let on that she didn't know me).

"Sorry. I just love being right." (Even though I didn't need it, I had a radar too it would seem. That could be a cause for concern actually.) Caitlin attracted my attention for a second time by waving at me from the other side of the room and beckoning for me to follow her.

"Come with me now, Ruby," she called. "She was about to leave but I told her to wait for a few minutes until she got to meet her newest and most fervent fan."

I practically climbed over four people and stampeded over two others in my haste to join Caitlin.

"Where is she?" I said breathlessly.

"Ruby, I'm sorry, this was obviously not meant to be." She pointed to the window and I followed the direction of her finger which indicated a car into which the same hat-wearing woman was climbing.

"For feck sake!" I said loudly, attracting the attention of the whole room. "What is she? Plain rude or publicity shy or what?"

"She is actually very publicity shy," a man answered in response to my outburst.

I recognised him as the gentleman who had served us the day that I had bought Mammy her *Sunset Across the Bay* picture. "She very rarely comes out to meet anyone."

"Oh great, so not only did I not get to meet her tonight but now you're telling me that the chances of me ever seeing her again are next to none. Great. Just great. I feel like a groupie who has narrowly missed getting a ride in the tour bus. Metaphorically speaking," I added quickly as eyebrows shot up around the room.

"Listen, don't worry, pet. I'll sort something out," Luke said, squeezing my arm.

I sighed with disappointment and then started to feel truly sorry for myself as I remembered that my wedding reception was now in tatters and that I was still a poor abandoned baby who nobody loved (slight exaggeration as my mother and fiancé were both standing beside me but if I was going to go down the road of complete self-annihilation I might as well do it properly and air all my woes).

"Have you seen everything you wanted?" Luke asked, packing his camera back into its case.

"Let me just go and have one last look at Sarah's display," I said before tearing off in the direction of the room which held the pictures that I wanted to burn into my memory forever.

Luke came to get me after fifteen minutes had passed and I was still staring open-mouthed at the splendour in front of me.

"We need to go, love."

"Okay, pet. I'm coming."

"No, you need to come now. Mandy has just arrived but she won't talk to me. She's insisting that she needs to speak to you."

"Mandy has driven all the way from Belfast just to speak to me?"

I rushed out to the entrance and grabbed my coat, before tearing out to where I found Mandy looking ashen and shaken.

"What's the matter?" I demanded.

"Luke is going to have the mother and father of all fits, Ruby," she said through her tears.

"Whatever it is, it can't be that bad," I said, linking arms with her, wondering what her parents had done now – I knew it had to be something to do with them. "You ought to have been in my shoes today. Feckin bloody hotel where we were going to have the reception got blown up and I just missed the opportunity to meet my newest art icon."

"Ruby, listen to me. It's really bad."

"What is it?"

"Mum and Dad phoned me again."

"Tell them to feck away off!" I said angrily.

"I would, Ruby, only it's a bit late for that."

"Why?" I asked slowly, hardly daring to breathe.

"Hello, Tommy," an irritating voice said behind me.

Only one person called me 'Tommy' – for 'tomato head'.

"I'm sure since your own father's dead you won't mind giving your future father-in-law a big slobbery kiss."

Chapter 46

"Please tell me that I'm in the middle of a desperate nightmare that I'll wake up from eventually, hoarse from screaming blue murder and in a cold sweat," I said in a controlled voice.

I grabbed hold of Mandy and steered her round the corner to the side of the art gallery and demanded an explanation.

"What the hell are you doing here and why did you bring them? Not exactly smart when you know how annoyed Luke is likely to be."

"I got a phone call this afternoon asking that I pick them up from the airport, and I thought it best to bring them here because Daddy has a key to your house and was talking about staying there until you and Luke came back in the morning and, no matter how annoyed you both are now, I think that that would have been worse."

"How the hell did he get a key?" I demanded.

"He said that he got one cut the last time they were here."

I blew out in frustration and could hardly believe the brass neck of the pair of them. How dare they land unexpectedly like this?

"We've had enough bad news for one day. I can do without this," I said.

"We'd better go back to them in case Luke comes out," Mandy said.

I took a deep breath and we went back.

"Well, isn't this nice?" Fred Reilly announced in a thick slightly slurred voice, roughly gathering Mandy to him in a bear-hug.

He reeked of alcohol and I was amazed that he had been allowed to board a plane in that state. The airports definitely should have been warned that they were coming and extra security measures taken. I could just imagine Luke's mother being manhandled into a secure area to be searched. Only problem was that the old lush would probably enjoy it too much (young virile men in uniforms everywhere beware).

"Nice? Strangely enough not a word I would have used," I said through clenched teeth.

"That's not quite the welcome we were expecting," sniffed Beverley Reilly. "Not considering that we're about to accept you into the bosom of our family."

I had to sit down on a nearby wall to stop myself from falling over. "Believe me, when I agreed to join your family, Beverley, neither you nor your husband were the main attractions."

I couldn't feckin believe this. Not only did they have the cheek to arrive unannounced but it seemed that they were disgruntled that there wasn't some type of fanfare awaiting them. They also appeared to be completely deluded as to their own importance.

"Where's Luke?" Fred demanded. "We must see him and talk about the sleeping arrangements."

"Sleeping arrangements?"

"We'd like to stay for a little while," Beverley chirruped. "It's not every day that your only son gets married and we'd like to be here for him."

I wondered had she undergone brain surgery (specialist surgeon required for a brain so tiny) or a personality transplant since the last unpleasant meeting, as she had never been there for her son in his life before so what exactly was the point in starting now?

"You should go away and come back again nearer the time

266

then," I snapped. "The wedding isn't for another few months."
(Mental note to self: destroy all written statements pertaining to the wedding and tell manky in-laws that the event is happening in June as opposed to May. Also ensure that there's a bomb scare at the airport the next time they try and visit.)

"That's not a problem. We're here to stay. No point in coming all this way if you're not going to make a proper trip of it."

"I beg your pardon? What the hell do you mean you're 'here to stay'?" I demanded. I could feel the panic rising inside me and was trying not to react too much as I was fearful that a) Mandy might pass out and b) that if I actually did what I wanted to do and banged their two heads together and then drop-kicked them back to where they came from, it might attract just a little too much attention.

"It's not uncommon for parents to want to come and visit their children, is it?" Beverley said in a superior voice.

"Normal parents usually try to take an active interest in their child's life the whole way through and not only when it suits them or when they need something," I hissed.

"She always was a bit of a drama queen, wasn't she?" Fred said, looking at me coldly.

"And bad-tempered and highly strung. Our Luke could have done a lot better really. Got somebody a bit more like himself."

I wondered if the smoke that I sensed billowing out of my ears was visible to everybody?

"Someone like him, Beverley?" I asked in an icy voice. "And what exactly is your son like? Please tell me as I'd be really interested in hearing your analysis of your son's personality, especially given the fact that you hardly know him and only ever show up like the proverbial bad penny when you're looking for something."

The silence that ensued was not due to an awkward intake of breath resulting from shock at being snapped at but because Fred (arsehole drunkard) was too busy swigging from a tin to respond and Beverley didn't answer because she had just clocked the hunky doorman that Gabriel had expressed a liking for and was now standing bolt upright and sticking her well-padded boobs out as far as she could.

"Go ahead, Beverley, see if you can convert him. I'm sure the poor guy will be thanking his lucky stars that he bats for the other team when he sees you staring at him with your slutty eyes and lopsided chest."

Mandy intervened before anything more could be said and attempted to persuade her parents to wait in the car.

"Why?" Beverley asked in a peeved voice.

"Are we going?" Fred asked. "Where's the party? I could be doing with another drink."

"Just come on," Mandy said, obviously upset, as she steered them towards her car.

"Ruby, what the hell is going on out here? The whole place is at a standstill in there as the party now seems to be outside and Caitlin's asking questions. Where's Mandy? Has something happened?"

I prayed that Mandy had acted in time and that Luke hadn't seen anything but of course that would have been too easy.

"Ruby, this is not a game. This is a very important night in my career. I could get a lot of work through Caitlin and her contacts and you skulking about out here whilst being heard screeching like an alley cat is not exactly the image I want to project. What the hell is wrong with you now?"

I took a deep breath and closed my eyes and wondered why God Above seemed to have it in for us all. What the hell was the deal with families and why did they have to be so troublesome? When you're small you're led to believe that your family is the most important thing in the world. They are the ones who are supposed to look after you, encourage you to do well, protect you from all harm. Yet from where I was standing all they did was lie to you, cause no end of trouble and arrive at the most inopportune times and have your fiancé blame the whole sorry mess squarely on you even though it wasn't your fault and you'd rather be anywhere else in the world.

"I'm sorry, Luke. Mandy has a few problems and she wasn't sure how to deal with them so together we're working on a solution."

"Could you try and do it quietly?" he asked in an incredulous voice. "Honestly, does everything have to be such a drama?"

"Didn't I tell you she was a drama queen?" Luke's mother chose that particular moment to pipe up and make her presence felt as she escaped from Mandy's grip and headed straight for her son.

I closed one eye and tried not to make visual contact with Luke as I wanted to avoid seeing the panic in his face.

"That's not exactly the welcome I was expecting from my boy," Beverley said as she stepped forward and grabbed Luke, pulling him to her ample bosom.

Luke stared at me, apoplectic with horror, and I put my arm around Mandy who had started to cry and was now shaking uncontrollably.

"Cheers, everybody! It's good to be home!" Fred Reilly announced as we heard the ring being pulled on another can and he continued to guzzle his beer.

Luke pushed his mother away and stared angrily at his parents.

"Did you know about this, Mandy?" he demanded.

"Luke, it's not her fault," I said in a stage whisper. "Have you ever tried reasoning with your mother and father?"

"So let me get this straight. Obviously, seeing as they are here and knew where to find us and now you're indicating that there was reasoning to be done, you all knew about this but nobody told me. Care to enlighten me as to why not?"

"Because you mightn't take it very well," I said in a dull tone, waiting for the eruption that was bound to come at any second.

Trouble only came in threes, didn't it? Or did it? Because right at that moment I saw Judith McQueen arrive with her suited gentleman friend in tow and of course she was visibly delighted to note that the world seemed to have blown up around my ears.

Chapter 47

I found myself in the unfamiliar position of wanting to calm someone else down. So this is what it felt like trying to deal with me.

"Luke, don't panic. We'll sort this mess out."

"Mess? Well, I suppose that's one word you could use to describe them," Luke hissed. "What the hell are you doing imposing yourselves on us like this?" He walked over to his sister and put a protective arm around her. "She doesn't deserve this crap and neither do I. We've been through enough thanks to your behaviour and we don't want to know any more."

Luke let Mandy go, then pulled out his wallet and dug out his bank card. "How much?" he demanded. "How much will it take to get you out of our lives once and for all? You can take it all as far as I'm concerned. It would be money well spent."

"You'd think you were an abused child the way you're carrying on," his mother commented, not seeming to notice how desperately upset her son was.

"Don't you dare try and make light of my feelings, Mother," Luke responded. "I grew up in a house where I didn't know where my father was nor what state he was going to arrive home in. It was so humiliating and embarrassing to have other kids comment on what a drunken disgrace your father was –"

"Now just you wait one minute," Fred Reilly started to bumble. "You might be a big lad now but I could still take my belt off to you if I wanted."

"Really?" Luke spat. "Do you think you could focus on it for long enough to actually see what you're doing or would you perhaps be seeing double?"

Beverley Reilly was standing stock still when her son rounded on her and instinctively she went to hide behind her daughter for protection except that her daughter didn't seem keen to get involved. Mandy stepped aside and left her mother at the mercy of her brother who was now foaming at the mouth in bad temper.

"And as for you, what sort of an excuse for a human being puts herself about so much that her children get laughed at for having the village bike for a mother?"

"How dare you!"

"Shut your stupid great mouth and listen very carefully to what he has to say, Mother!" Mandy shouted. Her eyes were wild, her hair had come loose from the clip that was holding it and her knuckles were white from the pressure of trying to control herself.

"You come here, you great hypocrite, pretending to care about my wedding!" yelled Luke. "Tell me this, Mother. What's my favourite food? Where do I work? What's Mandy's favourite colour? Where does she do her grocery shopping? Does she have a boyfriend? Do you realise that your daughter now concentrates all her efforts on writing about the lives of other people because she can't bear to think about her own? She gains great satisfaction from reporting on everyone else because then people actually notice her and pay her some attention. It's just a pity that her own mother could never do that!"

I was stunned at Luke's insight about Mandy and, when I thought back to all the years that she had spent gossiping about the rest of us within the college, I suddenly understood it.

His mother stood open-mouthed in shock as did everyone else.

We had attracted quite a crowd outside and I could see Caitlin O'Donnell looking confused and perplexed through the window. Mammy, Donal and Robbie were also peering out, no doubt wondering what the commotion was about, and I prayed that they would stay where they were. There were already too many people involved.

"Luke, I know that your father and I may not have been perfect parents but really there's no need to make such a –"

"*Perfect parents!*" Luke spat. "If there was an award for having been the worst, most useless parents in the world I think you both would most definitely be in with a fighting chance of getting the crown."

"If my parents didn't beat them to it," Gabriel whispered beside me. He was looking deeply annoyed and was rubbing my arm. Frankie and Owen had also joined us now, both looking upset and obviously not knowing what to say.

"The next time that I have the bright idea of coming to Donegal for a break, can you please shoot me or at least talk me out of it until the notion has passed?" I whispered to Frankie.

"Turn around and go straight back to where you came from!" Luke shouted. "You are not wanted or needed here. We've had to learn to survive without parents. You know, I have actually been known to tell people that my parents are dead, because it's easier to say that than have to admit to both other people and myself that I'm not wanted, was never wanted and was always treated like some nuisance whose only purpose in later life was to become a walking piggy-bank when you messed up and got yourselves in trouble yet again!"

"You ungrateful shit!" Beverley declared before turning to her husband who was wobbling on the spot like a spinning top. "We should have known that this would happen. That boy always was too sensitive for his own good."

"A big sissy," his father agreed.

I had heard all I was prepared to listen to. "How dare you come here full of drunken self-righteous shite and declare yourselves to be somehow hard done by?" I shouted. "He has done nothing but love you all down the years even though it pains him to even hear mention of your names. Have you no conscience? Do you not realise the damage that you've done? Thank God Luke is the man he is. He's kind and loving and hardworking and must have been switched at birth as he's certainly not like either of you which is a bloody miracle that we should all be grateful for."

"Oh well, aren't you just a match made in heaven?" Beverley said nastily. "You're welcome to each other. I don't have to listen to this."

"You're right. You don't," Luke said in a calmer tone. "Please do everybody a favour and feck off, and don't worry, your invitation won't be getting lost in the post, you'll simply not be getting one. My family will be with me and they're all I need." Luke waved his arms to indicate Mandy, Frankie, Owen, Gabriel and me and gave his parents a menacing stare.

"That's very nice, Luke," his mother said in an annoying nasal voice, "but here's the thing. We wanted to surprise you. We told Mandy that we had a special wedding gift for you and we came here to give it to you tonight."

"I do not want or need a single thing from either of you," Luke said, turning to look at me. "I have everything I need right here."

"Well, that's a shame because we came to tell you that we're home for good. We thought you'd be pleased and that it would be a nice surprise for you both. We decided that Spain just wasn't for us and that we'd like to come home and spend some time with our family."

"What do you mean you're 'home for good'?" Luke asked in a high-pitched squeak.

"We wanted to spend some time with our children."

"Bullshit!" Luke shouted. "What's the real reason you've come home and if you don't answer me I'll ring the Spanish authorities and find out myself."

They both looked panic-stricken.

"Let's hear it."

"Your father got into a bit of trouble recently. He owes a bit of money to a loan shark who wasn't keen on giving him any more time to pay up so we had no choice. We had to go."

"So you just thought that you'd come here and pass your problems on to us."

"We mistakenly thought that we could rely on our own children for help but obviously you'd rather that we went back and got murdered in the night."

"Chance would be a fine thing," I muttered.

"So let me get this straight," Luke said again with a look of pure disbelief on his face. "You're home for good."

"Yes. We've sold everything, packed all our worldly goods into a suitcase and now we're back to stay. How many bedrooms did you say you had?"

Chapter 48

My feet seemed to have welded themselves to the ground and Luke appeared to be in a trance as none of his facial muscles had moved in the last five minutes. Everyone else seemed just as shocked. Beverley and Fred were still standing in the same position and still looked as if they thought the whole world owed them a favour.

"We only have a small house. There's barely enough room for Luke and me, never mind anyone else," I stammered.

"That's funny," Beverley said. "I swear I can remember Luke talking to me about it in one of our phone calls and I'm sure he described it as having three bedrooms and an attic conversion. Sounds to me like you've more room than you need."

"Let me put it to you both in as kind and gentle a way as possible," I snapped. "If we lived in Buckingham Palace with forty-four bedrooms at our disposal and four separate wings which would stop us from ever bumping into each other, the answer would still be 'no'. Take the hint. We don't like freeloaders. Perhaps you should have thought about treating your son and daughter a little better in the past if you were so keen to have it reciprocated in the future."

"That's fine. We'll go to a hotel then," Beverley said.

"Unfortunately as our financial affairs aren't in order yet we may have to borrow some money from you, Luke, as I'm sure you wouldn't like to see your parents stranded on the street."

"Anybody got a cardboard box handy?" I enquired loudly before Luke shouldered me into a corner and took a deep breath.

"Maybe we could put them up just for a few nights, Ruby. Just until they get themselves sorted."

"Out of the feckin question. Absolutely not. No way," I responded, putting my hand over his mouth before he could say another word.

"You're doing what you always do. You give off stink about them, refuse to talk about them and recoil every time they phone wanting something but you still help them. They've hurt you so much. You just told them in no uncertain terms how badly you feel so why help them now? If your parents got in through our front door they'd take root there and never leave, and believe me that would not be grounds for a good start to married life. Can you imagine us all sitting around the breakfast table in the morning? Your daddy with his quarter bottle of vodka and your mother in her see-through negligee? I think not." (Even the thought of it conjured up images that would need to be talked about in a therapy session. Not that I needed one, you understand.)

"Ruby, your mother was forced to give you up at six weeks old because of her behaviour yet you're desperate to meet her. I've known my parents all my life and I know that they are awful people but they're still my parents."

"Don't you compare my situation to yours," I said in a warning tone. "They're totally different."

"Are they?" he said wearily. "Are they really?" He sighed and rubbed his hand through his hair before jingling his car keys and patting his pocket in search of his wallet. "I spied a B&B down the road when we arrived. I'll go and see if they have any vacancies."

"Why are you doing this?" I demanded.

"Because I want to get rid of them right now. I'll arrange for them to stay in a B&B for a few days and after that they're on their own."

I watched Luke as he pointed to the car and coldly asked his parents to get their stuff, before slamming the doors once they were in and sending gravel flying as he screeched away.

"Okay, people, show's over," I said as a crowd continued to hang around gawping at us.

"Why don't you come back with us," I said to Mandy who was staring at the ground with a faraway expression on her face. "You can stay at Mammy's with us tonight. Come on in and I'll get you a drink. You look like you need one."

"I'll follow you in," she said. "I'd just like to be on my own for five minutes if that's okay."

Gabriel and Frankie hung back to make sure I was all right.

"Are you okay?" Frankie enquired.

"Yes, I'm fine. Luke's not though."

"I thought only I had problems," Gabriel volunteered helpfully. "Perhaps I've been looking at it all wrong. Maybe it's better, if you break contact, that it stays broken. I might just be the lucky one after all."

"How could they do this to them both and why now?" I asked. "Ever since I've known Luke he's been hurt by the fact that his parents have never been around and now that they're here we have more problems than ever."

"My point exactly," Gabriel said chirpily.

"Gabriel, do me a favour and go and feck yourself, will you?"

"Sorry. I don't mean to offend but that experience has just put things into perspective for me. I lost my mum and dad when I chose to leave and, if I was to land at their door tonight, I have no doubt that I probably would end up on my back in the driveway whilst the old cronies down the road gathered a pitchfork-wielding mob. But you know something, it doesn't bother me because at least this way I get to be me and I'm happy. Why go looking for something that might only bring you trouble in the long run. Just be happy with what you have, that's going to be my motto from now on."

Gabriel waved at Darryl who was waiting for him at the door and left us with a nod.

"He has a point you know, Ruby," said Frankie. "People should be content with what they have and not invite trouble upon themselves, when for all they know it could lead to all sorts of heartache. In this day and age you're lucky if you have a loving family around you at all and, if you have, then be happy and count yourself privileged."

"I know exactly what you're saying, Frankie, but look at it from another angle. Sure, you're happy and everything's going well, but what if there was something else out there that could prove to be life-changing for you in a positive way? And possibly not only you but somebody else as well? But you continue just languidly trudging on, happy to be content, and too scared to find out more."

Frankie put her arm around me and placed her head on my shoulder. "You do whatever you feel is right, Rubes."

"I will, but for now I don't think we should be talking about me. I think I should be concentrating on trying to make Luke feel better because at this point in time he's guaranteed to be feeling like a villain even though he's anything but. Did I mention how much pleasure it would give me to kill his parents?"

On walking back into the gallery I immediately sought out Caitlin who was looking rather tense, to say the least.

"Caitlin, I'm so sorry about the disturbance. Luke will be back shortly. I've had a wonderful evening and so has everyone else. I hope that you won't allow that fiasco to take away from the occasion."

"I'm trying not to but it's quite difficult as you can imagine," she said in a clipped tone. "I wanted this evening to be remembered for the fact that so many people came out to support me and appreciate my art. I didn't want it associated with a squalling match outside which is exactly what that was."

"I'm so sorry," I said, hugely embarrassed. "Luke will explain." There wasn't much more I could say so I left her and went to join the others.

"I'm going to do Caitlin's photographs for free as an apology," Luke explained breathlessly as he rejoined our group some time later. "I think that under the circumstances it's the least I can do."

"You weren't long," I said. "I take it there was a room."

"Yep," Luke said sullenly. "I dumped their bags out in front of the house, paid for the rooms and left."

I knew that he was trying to be strong about it but that inside he was bound to be a trembling mess.

"Are you going to see them again?"

"I don't know and right now I don't care," he said as he left my side to go and be with his sister who had just appeared from outside with red-rimmed eyes and a worried frown on her face.

"I don't suppose you know where my mother is?" I called after him.

"The last time I saw her she was sitting down in the foyer talking to a man in a suit," he said, shrugging his shoulders.

"Oh right," I said, thinking nothing of it until I rounded the corner and saw Mammy deep in conversation with none other than Judith McQueen and her suit-attired friend who were grinning from ear to ear and looking very pleased with themselves indeed.

Chapter 49

"Well, isn't this cosy?" I commented, making Mammy jump and her two companions lose their grins. "So what are we talking about then?"

"Oh nothing at all," Mammy answered, looking at her hands and picking her nails. (And subconsciously giving out "I'm doing something I shouldn't be doing" vibes.)

Judith was looking smarmy which wasn't unusual and her friend looked like a cat that had just been dunked in a bowl of cream.

"I see. Shall we be making tracks then, Mammy?"

"Of course we will. I just have to say goodnight to Judith and Mr Humphries here."

I stood and looked from one to the other but nobody moved. Instead they all looked expectantly at me.

"Well, goodnight then," I said. "A pleasure as always to be in your company." (If I had Pinocchio's nose it would have extended dramatically.) I yawned and looked at my watch.

"I'll be with you in a minute, darling," said Mammy. "Why don't you wait in the car?"

"Nah," I said, linking arms with her and peering closely at Judith whose smarm was starting to wilt. "I'd rather wait here until you're ready to leave."

"Ruby, please. Just for one second and then I'll be straight out."
Mammy squeezed my arm and looked appealingly at me. Reluctantly I let go of her and started to walk backwards out the door, keeping my eye firmly on Judith and hoping that she could read body language as right now my every pore was shrieking 'Feck off and leave my poor wee Mammy alone!'

I decided that as I had a bit of time to kill I would go and view Sarah Larkin's paintings one last time. Her work was mesmerising and she had me well and truly hooked. I absorbed every line and curve and examined the definition and contrast in every stroke and again felt that I could have stayed there forever, quite happily imagining myself in any one of the depicted scenes.

"I told you that this is where she would be," Luke said as he and Frankie noisily bustled into the room and broke the spell.

"Have you been in here?" I asked Frankie, noting that she was staring at everything as if for the first time.

"Yeah, I wandered in earlier but didn't really get a proper look. These are quite good, aren't they?"

"Quite good? Quite good?" I repeated incredulously. "They are totally amazing. If I had as much talent as this girl I wouldn't still be stuck here. I'd be away to Paris or America or somewhere in Italy where I'd be making the European artists shake in their Continental boots."

Frankie nodded in agreement and then smirked at me the way she always did.

"Is my mother still talking to our lovely friend?" I asked Luke.

"Judith? Yes, she is."

"I don't like it. She's up to something," I announced. "And Mammy's in cahoots with her. I didn't want to leave her alone with them but Mammy insisted so they were obviously discussing something they knew I wouldn't like."

"Your mother isn't stupid, Ruby," Luke sighed. "She'll do what's best for everybody. She's a big girl and quite capable of making her own decisions, you know."

The last bit of the sentence was said with much head-shaking and eye-rolling which served only to annoy me and make me even more nervous. I didn't want Mammy having to make any decisions about anything. The cottage was her home, she was happy there and she had the right to be left in peace without a gobby psychopath like Judith McQueen sticking her oar in at every opportunity.

"How are you feeling now?" I asked Luke as we made our way back out to the main foyer area.

"Top of the world and then some."

"Luke, I'm really sorry about everything that has happened. I wouldn't have wished it for you. What are we going to do about your parents? It's one thing ignoring them and pretending that they don't exist when they're in Spain, but now that they're right under our noses we'll have to decide what to do."

"Do you believe this story about them owing money to a loan shark or do you think there could be other reasons why they've come back?"

They were *his* parents – I didn't know why he was asking me. But I tried to be helpful. "Drug-smuggling, jay-walking, numerous convictions for being drunk and disorderly, having the Spanish mafia after you?" I suggested.

As we approached the door I could see Mammy standing outside with a look of determination on her face. Judith McQueen and her cohort were directly in front of her and they had all just shaken hands.

Chapter 50

"I will not calm down," I said, shaking with uncontrollable rage. "How the hell could you do this, Mammy? Aunt Kate will be doing wheelies in her grave."

"She would only have wanted me to do what made me happy, Ruby."

I snorted, banged the cup I was holding on the draining-board, and sat down heavily on a chair at the kitchen table. For once I was totally stuck for words.

"Ruby, stop being difficult. I've made my mind up and that's that. I'm signing the agreement tomorrow and then I'll have up to three months to look for somewhere else to live. Judith said I could take as much time as I needed."

"Oh, how very thoughtful of her, I'm sure," I drawled. "Aunt Kate must have worked damn hard for her boss to turn around and make such a grand gesture as to give her this cottage. It's totally unique, one of a kind, not another one like it anywhere in the country, and you've just given it away like it's of no importance at all."

"I haven't given anything away, Ruby. In fact, I'm getting an excellent price for it considering that it's only a two-bedroomed cottage. I talked them into giving me substantially more than they intended, I think."

Donal and Luke eyed each other and let out slow whistles whilst I looked around me in disgust.

"Well, you know something, Mammy," I said tersely. "There are just some things that money can't buy. I can't believe that you've just given up and given in like this. I wouldn't have allowed them to force you out. You could have stayed here quite happily. What about the shop? You've established yourself now. Are you prepared to lose what you've worked so hard to create?"

"It's not about winning or losing or being forced or giving in for that matter. I've done what I think is right and what will most benefit everyone. This way I can go and look for another house and perhaps build a shop that will totally fulfil my requirements. That's not ultimately why I've decided to move though. My main reason is because I want to help you and Luke. You deserve to have a proper wedding and, from seeing Luke's work, if I gave him some money he could set up his own photography studio and you'd have peace of mind. I know you have your savings but you're my only child, Ruby, and I'd like to see you settled and happy and I know that's most certainly what Daddy would have wanted had he been here. All this is lovely," she said, raising her arms in the air gesturing around at the cottage, "and ordinarily I wouldn't have thought about leaving it but right now I think it would be for the best."

"So you're telling me that *I* am the reason why you've lost all sense?" I was trying to stop shaking as I spoke. "Well, guess what, Mammy, I won't take a penny. We'll still have a nice wedding and Luke and I will continue to make ends meet. You do what you want but never again let me hear you saying that you've made this foolish mistake on my behalf. There's still time to change your mind, you know. Nothing has been signed yet so it's not too late."

"Why are you being so obstinate? What difference does it make to you where I am? I was burgled in this house. Tied up and left lying for hours on end. Has it ever crossed your mind that perhaps that might also be part of my yearning to get away from here? It wasn't a nice experience and it doesn't conjure up any happy memories. I think a new start for everybody is just what the doctor ordered."

"Have your new start if it's what you want but I don't want any part in it."

The silence in the car was threatening to engulf me. Luke was lost in his own thoughts (as well as apparently being completely fed up with people being unreasonable. Whoever they were.).

Frankie and Owen had also left to go home at the same time as us and were probably sitting in silence as well. The only difference would be that they would be too wrecked to speak after having an all-night shagfest with no rugrats to disturb them.

Frankie had given me a guided tour of the room which she and Owen were sharing after I had walked up to the hotel (post-argument with Mammy) in a fit of temper which would have resulted in Judith being choked if only I could find her. The room was beautiful and tastefully decorated with period furniture and sumptuous bed linen in warm colours. From the window, a breathtaking view of the Monroe estate where stags and deer continued to roam was visible with the mountains in the distance. An en suite bathroom with a whirlpool bath, matching his and hers dressing gowns and a fluffy pile of towels completed the decadence and made me want to throw up in annoyance. Obviously, the hotel was doing well on its own merits. There was absolutely no reason clear to me for Judith to be so covetous of my mother's home. Why did she need it?

We had left Mammy's cottage first thing and were now halfway down the road and approaching the border which would lead us back into Northern Ireland and I couldn't get there quick enough.

Nobody had slept a wink during the night as the kitchen seemed to be a thoroughfare for those who thought that warm mugs of milk and nips of brandy were going to help them sleep. Mammy was obviously upset because I had been so annoyed with her.

Luke and Mandy were up half the night discussing their parent situation and, after Mandy had gone to sleep, Luke nearly wore a hole in Mammy's rug pacing about and, as for me, well, my head was well and truly fried with everything that was going through it.

I didn't know what I was most upset about: the fact that Mammy was threatening to sell the cottage, the fact that Judith, the cow, was going to get her way or the fact that Luke's parents had just gone and unceremoniously dumped themselves on everyone without prior warning.

"Are you hungry?" Luke enquired as we approached the border town of Lifford where there were several nice eating establishments that we usually stopped at.

I folded my arms and continued to stare mutinously out the window.

"Am I to interpret that as a 'no' then?" he asked in a sarcastic tone.

"Interpret it whatever way you want," I sighed. "I just want to go home. As far as I'm concerned hell will have frozen over before I ever set foot in Donegal again."

"For feck sake, Ruby, you can't go saying –"

"Luke, do me a favour and don't tell me what I can and can't say or do. Everybody around me seems determined to do whatever they want regardless of how I think or feel, so I'm just going to do the same."

"You better not be including me in that, Ruby," Luke growled.

"Whatever," I said. "Just drive."

We arrived home less than an hour later and I was glad to be able to get out and stretch my legs and get away from Luke who had heavy-breathed like a nuisance caller and driven like a raving lunatic the rest of the way home. It was just a hunch but I think he may have been a little bit pissed off with me and I suppose I couldn't blame him. I knew that he thought I was being unreasonable but I couldn't help that. I was reacting to the whole situation in the only way I knew how, and if that happened to upset a few people along the way then so be it. I checked my phone again and saw that Mammy had left yet another message in my voicemail. Without listening to it, I pressed delete again and threw my phone into my bag which I hung up under a pile of coats at my back door. (Because obviously if I hid it, it would disappear and never annoy me again.) I had also clocked up several missed calls from Gabriel which I had also chosen to ignore as his high-pitched ramblings would have got on my last remaining nerve and rendered me entirely useless.

Luke had gone out for a walk (which was obviously a clever and cunning plan to escape from me) and I had retired to our bedroom and partaken in a ritual that women everywhere will understand. As I was sad, I went in search of something that would make me feel even worse and then sat on the end of my bed and let fat tears of frustration, anger and disappointment plop onto my jeans. I gently fingered the birth certificate which was beginning to fall apart from too much handling.

"If you want to make this up to me, Georgina, you'd better start now," I whispered. "Please pray that things will start working out for your child before she finds herself estranged from her adoptive mother and no longer caring about a wedding-reception venue. The way things are looking there will be no bloody wedding as my future husband doesn't appear to want to speak to me."

Chapter 51

I lay back where I was and fell asleep. When I awoke, startled and squinting to adjust my eyes to the darkness, I was still holding tightly to the old and crumbling certificate.

My eyes were stingy and sore and I had a crick in my neck. The house was eerily quiet, Luke was nowhere to be seen and I had never felt as alone in all my life. I sat up, rubbed my head and prepared to go downstairs.

Even beneath the multitude of coats I could hear my phone beeping to alert me to the fact that I had a message or ten. Mammy wouldn't give up easily and I knew that she would probably be worried sick about me so I decided to give her a ring.

"So you are alive then," she greeted me.

"Just about," I croaked.

"I spoke to my solicitor earlier and couldn't really understand what he was talking about."

"Complicated, selling a cottage, is it?" I asked.

"No, smartarse, actually it's quite simple when you're told that you're not allowed. Lord Bartley Monroe certainly ensured that the owner of the cottage was going to take their position seriously. The solicitor explained that it was stipulated that the cottage must always remain intact as a home and must never be sold in order for anyone to gain profit. Therefore I would be going against the terms and conditions of the contract if I sold it."

I took a moment to digest her words. "You mean that you have to –"

"Yes, I have to stay so Judith won't get her way after all. I've been trying to let you know all day, seeing as it appeared to be such a bone of contention with you but as usual you do like you always do and blank me as if I don't exist."

"I wasn't blanking you. I was sleeping actually if you must know. I didn't get much sleep last night."

"Who did?"

"How are you today?"

"Wonderful, dear. Never been better, considering that I'm now going to be faced with the task of telling Judith that I can no longer sign on the dotted line. Safe in the knowledge that I also won't be in a position to help you either, I'm in great fettle altogether. I might have a party to mark the occasion. Fancy coming down? No, that's right, I just remembered, I'll have to organise for hell to get rather cold for you to show your face around here again."

"I'm sorry it didn't work out and that you didn't get what you wanted, Mammy, but maybe it's for the best. You don't know what Judith was planning to do with the cottage. She could have had it buried within a matter of days and you can't tell me that you wouldn't have been upset if that happened."

"It would have been hers to do with as she pleased, Ruby. I'd have been sad to see anything happening to it, of course, but it would have been out of my hands then."

"You sound like you'd have been glad to be rid of it. Why?"

"Because with the money I could have got for it I could have booked a grand hotel for my daughter's wedding and set her husband up properly in his career," she snapped.

"I don't need you to worry about us, Mammy. We're perfectly capable of looking after ourselves, you know."

"I always knew you were capable of looking after yourself,

Ruby. I was never suggesting that you weren't. I just wanted to make life a bit easier and more comfortable for you, that's all. I know that none of this has been easy for you and you don't half like telling the world when you're annoyed about something. I'm glad that at least Gabriel had the courtesy to stay with me for a while this morning before he went up the road."

I could feel myself starting to prickle with annoyance and indignation but was determined not to let her words rile me.

"Yes, he's very fond of you, Mammy. Not having a mammy of his own obviously makes him appreciate you."

"I'm glad somebody does," she sniffed.

I opened my mouth to make an excuse as to why I had to suddenly drop the phone like it was burning me but was too tired to think of one.

"I have to go, Mammy. I'll speak to you soon. And in case you were in any doubt, I do love you. I just hate to see people being taken advantage of."

I had dozed off on the sofa and was just waking up when I heard the front door opening and Luke padding quietly into the house.

"I'm awake!" I shouted from the living room.

He didn't look at me when he entered the room but I knew he'd been crying nevertheless. He sat down heavily and I roused myself and went and joined him.

"I'm sorry if I annoyed you, Luke. I didn't mean to take things out on you. God knows you have enough to worry about. Where've you been?"

"Mandy and I have just spent the evening together. We've been trying to work out what to do about our parents and have made a few decisions."

"Am I allowed to ask?" I said tentatively.

Luke took a deep breath and I could see that he was having difficulty speaking.

"Mandy wants to call a truce with them," he said. "She was too young to remember most of the crap we were subjected to or else

290

has blocked it out. I think her childhood has been put in a box in her brain with a big 'never to be opened' sign on it. I was like a mother and father to her as I always looked after her but I think she's just dying for a normal life and would like to give them a chance to make amends. They've been on the phone constantly to her, apologising and asking for the opportunity to make up for lost time, and she seems to think that they might be serious. Who knows, maybe the fact that we didn't fall at their feet when they arrived and wouldn't take them in has woken them up to the fact that they've really hurt us and we won't forgive easily."

"How do you feel about it?" I asked, rubbing his shoulder. "Would you like to start again with them?"

"I'm scared, Ruby. Really scared. I don't think I could face being rejected all over again but for the sake of my little sister I'll give them a second chance. Life's just too short."

I knelt down in front of him and took his hands in mine.

"If I can do it so can you," I said simply. "Let there be new beginnings all around."

Chapter 52

"Stick the kettle on, darlin'. I think we might need a wee cup of coffee to start seeing straight again!" Luke shouted with great bravado.

"You can have coffee if you want but I'll be having another beer," his father said, going and opening my fridge door and rooting through its contents like it was his property.

"We haven't got any," I said loudly.

"We haven't got any coffee?" Luke repeated after me in a stupid slurred voice that was accompanied by bloodshot eyes and eyelids that were blinking slowly.

Luke was one of the great unfortunates in this world who was totally and utterly incapable of holding his drink. He became instantly stupid and started stumbling over his words and over-pronouncing things which annoyed the crap out of me.

"No. We haven't got any beer," I said to his father.

"Run along to the off-licence, there's a good girl," Fred instructed me whilst patting me on the bottom.

I grabbed his hand, twisted his arm up behind his back and leaned him over the kitchen table until he was out of breath, panting and begging for mercy.

"Don't you ever touch me again and if you want beer go to the off-licence yourself and buy it and drink it somewhere else, you big ignorant oaf!"

"Do all guests get physically assaulted upon arrival or is that a welcome saved especially for me?"

"Just you," Luke and I answered in unison.

"We were just out for a few drinks there," Luke said, rather unecessarily.

"Really? I thought you'd gone to Mass to pray for divine intervention and a miracle."

It had been a week since Luke had made the decision to give his parents a second chance and after a stilted and awkward phone call they had arranged to meet up tonight to have a 'nice chat'. I was willing to give his parents another chance if he was big enough to do so but I hadn't expected Luke and his father to land into me legless. His parents were currently staying with Mandy as they preferred being in Belfast to Swiftstown (happy was not the word for my reaction to this arrangement).

"And you couldn't have had 'a nice chat' over a cup of coffee and been sensible? You had to go to the pub and get rat arsed."

"We didn't do anybody any harm," said his father. "Everybody's entitled to a wee drink, you know. You should try having a few yourself. Might loosen you up a bit. You're very tense. Is something the matter?"

"Nothing that a one-way ticket to the moon wouldn't feckin sort out," I muttered whilst flicking on the kettle and putting two heaped teaspoons of the strongest coffee I could find into a mug for Luke, who had just sat heavily on a chair and was starting to drool and doze off, and there was absolutely no way that I was being left on my own with his father. I could do without being taken up on a murder charge at this moment.

"Here, drink this," I said as I handed Luke the mug which he promptly spilt over his leg before shouting that I was trying to scald him.

"And what am I drinking then?" his father enquired, squinting at the wine rack that was empty except for a solitary bottle of champagne that Frankie had given me to mark my engagement and he certainly wasn't getting that.

"Plenty of water in the tap or I can scald you – sorry, what I meant to say was, I can make you a cup of coffee as well."

Luke's father began to pace around like a demented dog who had lost its tail and I half expected him to start shaking with alcohol-withdrawal symptoms. Luke had often talked about the way his father used to behave and it made me sick to my stomach to think about it. As a teenager he could never invite friends over as he was too embarrassed by what his father might say in his permanent drunken stupor. He was a tradesman of sorts when Luke was very small but soon decided that lying around drinking all day and working on developing the biggest beer-belly in the country appealed to him more than earning an honest living for his family. I wanted to forget all of that and start afresh, but his current behaviour was irritating me beyond belief and I couldn't stop the images from creeping into my mind.

"I'll just stand here and talk to myself then, shall I?" said the arrogant prick who then proceeded to answer himself. "'Yes, Fred, I'd love to get you a drink because I'm marrying your son in another eight months and I have you to thank for him being so well equipped in the trouser department.'"

"Luke, wake up now," I commanded the figure who was now slumped in the kitchen armchair and snoring like a tractor with a broken engine.

Of course there was no movement as he was pissed as a fart and totally unresponsive or at least he was until I kicked him in the shins and made him yelp.

"You get up right now because we're going to drive your father back to meet Mandy at a location that I am going to arrange now."

I lifted my mobile and rang Mandy's number. She answered on the second ring.

"Hi, Ruby. How's it going?"

"Feckin fantastic, thanks. Can we meet up please so that I can

294

give you your father back in one piece as if he stays here much longer I may be forced to deliver him in bits and I know which tiny itsy bitsy bit I'll be throwing you first."

"Oh God, I'm sorry, Ruby. Dad persuaded Luke to go out for a drink. I didn't think it was a great idea as he seemed upset. Is Luke okay?"

"Oh, nothing a good sleep and a dose of liver salts won't cure in the morning, I'm sure. Needless to say, he's not allowed out to play with your father any more. What's your mother doing?"

"She's just gone out actually. All dolled up and saying not to wait up for her."

I raised my eyes to heaven and prayed for the poor unfortunate specimen she was bound to hook up with.

"So how are you finding life, now that your parents are staying with you?" I asked, shaking my head to rid it of all horrible images of Beverley doing whatever she did once she was let loose on the country.

"It feels funny to have them staying with me. Funny but nice in a weird way. It's nice to be able to say, 'Sorry, can I phone you back? My mum and dad are here.' I know that they're far from perfect, Ruby, but it's something I've dreamt of for years."

I could only empathise with her and, after I had manhandled Luke up to the bedroom and taken his boots off, I bundled his father into the car (wishing that I had a gun and gag) and prepared to drive to Lurgan where Mandy had agreed to meet me.

Chapter 53

"The nerve of him. The absolute cheek. I swear to God I don't think I'm the only one in our house whose parentage is confusing. I don't know where they got Luke from but I thank God that he in no way resembles the cretinous, disgusting individual who apparently is his father."

"So it went well then?" Frankie said as she curled into a more comfortable position on her sofa where she was lying contentedly, wearing cosy pyjamas and slipper socks.

I had called in to vent my frustration the following evening after a particularly harrowing day at work. Luke was so hung over that he missed a photo shoot because of it and I was thoroughly fecked off because my car had broken down on the way to Lurgan the evening before which left me stranded for another two hours with the feckwit father-in-law-to-be which was an extremely unpleasant experience that nearly gave 'road rage' (side-of-the-road rage, that is) a new meaning.

"I do not need all this confusion and disruption," I said. "I used to look at you and feel real sympathy for you, what with that shit excuse for a father and husband leaving you and the children in the lurch, the nasty interfering granny-in-law always causing problems, the bitchy stepdaughter putting in her tuppence-worth and all while your mother was having a freak attack in the background. And my conclusion is that I take my hat off to you because I don't know how you did it and with children and being pregnant too. I'm exhausted just saying it."

"And I'm exhausted listening," Frankie said, putting her hands around the mug of coffee she was drinking. "Shall I tell you how I managed to cope, Ruby?"

"Please do. I need all the help I can get and my hormones are fine. I think."

"I got through it all with a lot of help from a very good friend of mine. She's slightly highly strung and very feisty. You wouldn't want to mess with this one." Frankie clicked her tongue and sucked her teeth (in the manner of a dodgy builder about to price a job). "She's the one who saw me through it all and I'm always here for her too. I don't know how much help I'll be but at least I'm here."

I smiled and knelt down beside her while she stroked my hair.

"How is dear old Nebby Peg these days?" I asked, referring to Frankie's ex-granny-in-law who was the biggest pain in the arse and the most malicious woman I had ever met

"I think she's all right. The children don't really see much of her. I think she scares them to be honest."

"Is she still in the old people's nursing home?"

"I believe they had to move her to a more secure facility," Frankie said. "I think the staff were finding her rather hard to manage."

"Well, wouldn't you wonder at that?" I said in mock disbelief which was followed by a snort.

"Ruby, it only seems bad at the minute and it's probably because everything has happened at once and knocked you for six. It could be a blessing in disguise though, as at least if it all happens now hopefully everything will be resolved by the time the wedding comes around. There have been a lot of blessings in disguise lately. Perhaps I had started to take life too seriously and worry about silly things so the Man Above decided to give me something very real to concentrate on with my cancer scare. Believe me, I'm not half as wound up as I once was. It's just not worth it."

"You were due to have another check-up recently, weren't you?" I said, my hand flying to my mouth as I suddenly remembered. "I'm so sorry! I forgot all about it in the midst of everything that has been happening."

"I think you could be forgiven, Ruby," she said. "You've had quite a lot on your plate recently. There's no need to worry anyway. They got it all and I couldn't be happier. I've actually already booked my next smear test. Can you believe it?"

"Yes, I can, actually," I smiled.

"So tell me more about your lovely father-in-law-to-be then. You're so funny on that theme."

"He is the most annoying, irritating, obnoxious, vile man in the country. Standing talking to himself in my kitchen and taking credit for the size of Luke's whatsits."

"*Yuck!*" Frankie said, her hand poised in the air still holding the cup she was about to drink from. "That's gross."

"Yeah. A bit like him then."

"Hi, Ruby," Angelica said as she came into the room. She held out her arm for Frankie to fix the clasp on a bracelet for her.

"You're very dressed up for a school night," I commented, much to her amusement.

Her hair was jet black these days and she was wearing skin-tight black jeans with long grey boots and a grey woollen figure-hugging top with a belt.

"I'm meeting the girls for a Chinese in town and then we might go and see a late film. I hear that the new vampire movie is very good."

"Jaysus, Chinese and a vampire show! If anybody had suggested that as a good night out before, would you even have contemplated it?" I said, looking at her in fascination. She had grown up terribly in the last few months.

Frankie laughed and nudged me on the head with her toe.

"Ah, I suppose I better go and attend to my husband-to-be," I said, getting to my feet with a sigh, "and show him what a dab hand I am at treating hangovers."

"Is he still suffering then?" asked Frankie.

"Of course, and I am my usual sympathetic self."

"Which means he's getting dog's abuse obviously."

"He feckin deserves it for bringing that lunatic into my home and then having the cheek to doze off, leaving me to deal with him."

"Just remember that all this is no picnic for him either," said Frankie. "I complain about my mother and you're not thrilled with yours at the minute either but at least they're normal and they care. They always looked after us well and didn't feck off to another country only to come back years later to embarrass us and act like eejits."

"Yeah, well. Water under the bridge and all that. Hopefully in time we'll not be looking at them like that any more," I said but was far less confident than I sounded.

The house was in darkness when I arrived home and I concluded that Luke must have gone to bed early. I flicked on the kettle, looked through the local paper and threw my shoes off, thinking that I might have a bath and an early night myself.

Once I had finished my drink, I headed to the bedroom and to my dismay discovered that it was in darkness with no sign of Luke anywhere. I sincerely hoped that he wasn't out with his father again as there was only so much crap I could put up with in any given forty-eight-hour period.

I quickly punched in his number and he answered on the third ring.

"Where are you?" I demanded.

"Going to the bus station."

"Eh . . . why?"

"To meet your mum. She phoned earlier and said that she was coming down but that she didn't want to drive. Believe me, Ruby, I wish you had been here as my stomach is doing back-flips and my head feels like it has been jammed full of cotton wool."

"Well, you *will* act like a gulpin and go drinking with your father who could drink a sailor under the table."

"I won't be doing it again."

"I'm delighted to hear it but, getting back to the matter in hand, why has Mammy decided to come here? What's wrong?"

"She wouldn't tell me anything over the phone. Said it would have to wait until she saw us."

"Oh God. I'm nearly afraid to ask."

"I guess you'll find out soon enough."

Chapter 54

The first thing on Mammy's mind was, naturally enough, the McQueens. She said that the solicitor she usually dealt with had intended to look up Bartley Monroe's last will and testament, in order to further clarify his intentions regarding the cottage – but then he had been signed off work with a bad back. She thought that the other fella in the office was a bit shifty-looking, so she didn't want to talk to him about it. So, instead, if he sent her a copy of the will she would bring it for us to look at.

At which point we explained that she had more chance of being bitten by a dinosaur than she had of us understanding any of the legal gobbledegook likely to be in a typical will.

"Some help you are, Ruby!" Mammy complained.

"Mother, did you ever attend my graduation from law school?"

"No."

"Well, there's your answer then. You need a specialist to look at a will, to decipher what all the different terms and references and clauses mean. God alone knows why they have to make these things so complicated!"

"Obviously so that you'll have to pay a solicitor an obscene amount of money to translate it all for you," Luke said, "and advise you on where to go next."

"I suppose I'll just have to leave it and wait until my solicitor comes back from being off sick. There's no rush really when all is said and done."

"So," I said, trying not to smirk, "what was the lovely Judith's reaction to the fact that you weren't in a position to sell her the cottage?"

"I think she was a bit upset. She gave poor Aisling a right mouthful and started shouting at the other staff. It was very embarrassing actually."

"Hopefully, now she knows that she can't have it, she'll lay off and leave you alone and let you get on with things. Mammy, you didn't really want to sell, did you?"

"I wanted to do what was best. I told you that already, Ruby. And if that meant selling up then I would have done it but, as it happens, I am glad in one way that I'm not moving as I do love my wee cottage."

I smiled a self-satisfied smile. "I knew that all along, you know. If you had sold it I would have gone mad. I know how much it means to you and seriously you're going to have to stop worrying about Luke and me and how we'll manage. We'll be fine."

"Have you booked anywhere yet for the reception?"

There was silence as Luke and I stared at one another and he chewed his lip and I shrugged my shoulders. I had barely thought about it – there had been so much else going on – but now that the subject had been raised a prickle of fear rose inside me and again the image of a tent sprang to mind.

"I thought not, so I booked it for you."

Again there was another silence as Luke and I furrowed our brows and wondered what was coming next.

"I had to pull a lot of strings but eventually we came to an agreement and it's all arranged."

"I do love a good guessing game, Mammy, but I really would

love it if you'd put me out of my misery and tell me what you've done."

"I've provisionally booked the wedding suite in Monroe Manor for you. I spoke to Harry McQueen himself and he assures me that it will be a day to remember. You can examine menus and have a look at the honeymoon suite when you next come to see me."

"Perhaps you should open your own wedding-consultancy business and give good old Gabriel a run for his money," Luke said, laughing nervously and looking at me.

I didn't know what to say or how to feel. I had the mental image in my head of a tent and then I remembered the gorgeous room that Frankie and Owen had stayed in at the weekend and how nice the food had been and could feel myself start to mellow slightly. That, however, was before I took into account the fact that Mammy had gone behind my back, essentially usurping the wedding planner who had annoyed my head for so long, and booked my wedding reception, the most important day of my life, in an establishment that was owned by the two biggest shysters in the country.

I took a deep breath, looked at Mammy's face and smiled (or maybe grimaced would be the right word).

"Gabriel's not going to be very happy with you," I commented. "You're stealing his thunder and putting him out of a job."

"Well, actually, I asked him to come down and meet me and we did it together."

"You what?" I shouted.

"Well, you would never have done it yourself."

"Feckin right I wouldn't have done it!"

Luke got up from his seat and was now pacing around like a wild animal.

"Ruby, can I have a word in private, please?" he asked in a pleading tone of voice.

We went into the sitting room, leaving Mammy sitting sipping a mug of tea.

"What?"

"Please don't fly off the handle again. It's all you seem to do these days. Your mammy has done that for us because she cares that you have a nice day. It won't be the easiest day for her, y'know. Watching her only daughter getting married and not having her husband there to share it with her. So please, Ruby, for me, go along with it and make her happy. She deserves it. She's such a good mother."

"I agree. I actually was going to relent but not before I smacked Gabriel around the head for taking liberties."

"Rubbbeeee!"

"Oh okay, just a small slap then."

We rejoined Mammy in the kitchen where she was sitting and nervously awaiting my return if the way she was wringing her hands was anything to go by.

"So when are we going then?" I asked.

"Going where, dear?"

"Well, correct me if I'm wrong but were you not the one making suggestions about going to view rooms and look at menus or did I just imagine that?"

"So you're okay with it then?"

"No problem at all. It's a lovely setting and so handy and, now that dear Judith won't be hankering after the cottage, I'm sure she'll have all the time in the world to devote to being my right-hand woman. I might request that I deal directly with her only, for all my little whims. I think Gabriel and I should arrange a meeting with her as soon as possible actually."

Luke put his head in his hands and Mammy grinned broadly.

"Why not? I think that's a very good idea. Gabriel is so talented at what he does and such a lovely boy. I wonder how he and his wee friend are getting on now?"

"Honestly, he really isn't a five-year-old and the last time I looked his little friend was a six-foot-tall, well-built, strapping waiter called Darryl."

"I know. Isn't love funny? It can come in all shapes and sizes."

"Indeed it can."

"I'm sorry for intruding, Luke, but can I ask how your mammy and daddy are getting on?"

"They're getting on all right, I think. I haven't seen too much of them and, although they're staying with Mandy, I don't think that she's seen a lot of them either."

"Any word of them moving to a place of their own?"

"I think they're still trying to get their financial affairs straightened out."

I went to my mother and hugged her tightly. "Thank you. I do love you and I'm sorry for everything."

"I love you too, Ruby," she said gently. "And don't you ever forget it."

Chapter 55

Three months had passed since that fateful night when Mammy had informed us that Monroe Manor was to be the venue for our wedding and to say that it had been eventful would be an understatement in the extreme. Luke's parents were still living with Mandy (*quelle surprise*) and making no effort to move – although Mandy didn't seem to mind. Her magazine column was going from strength to strength as her mother kept insisting on going out to all sorts of wild and exotic nightclubs where Mandy got no end of fodder for her gossip groupies. She had met Gabriel at one of these hotspots one night and informed us that his partner had a strong Donegal accent – therefore Mammy had been right – love did come in all sorts of shapes and sizes. Gabriel had been in touch a few times and strangely enough I had become fond of him. I still threatened him if he made stupid suggestions but grudgingly I had to admit that he had grown on me.

As for me, I was still the same, apart from the fact that I had decided to content myself and do no more research about my adoption until the wedding was over.

Christmas was coming (a time where I morph into The Grinch for two weeks whilst everybody around me is full of the joys of

Rudolph and cooking sherry) and work was busier than ever as we all tried to tie up loose ends before the holidays. Luke and I had decided to spend Christmas in Donegal this year and as a gigantic gesture my mother had invited Mandy and her deranged parents along too. I had protested at first but Luke had seemed so pleased that they were being included, and that we were acting like a normal family, that I shut my mouth and decided to offer it up for all my sins.

It was Christmas Eve and I was putting the finishing touches to our Christmas tree (it had literally only come out of the roof space an hour beforehand as I refused point blank to be blinded by twinkly lights and have an extortionate electricity bill just because everyone else in the street wanted to look at my tree . . . bah, humbug!). I didn't see the point in putting it up at all as I intended to be away for most of Christmas but Luke insisted that we had to get into the holiday spirit and at least have a tree up for when we returned on Boxing Day.

"Are you ready to go, love?" he asked as he carried several bags downstairs and added them to a pile of wrapped presents which were sitting at the door. I normally didn't 'do' presents but decided that I would participate in the tradition this year as I had so many people to thank (apologise to) for putting up with me. It had been a hard year for everyone.

I had already given Frankie her gift – a beautiful angel necklace – and she had been thrilled with it.

"It's just to remind you that my daddy is watching over you as well," I had told her.

The thought that things could have been very different, had she not had the life-saving smear test when she did, was never far from my mind and I wanted to let her know how precious she was to me.

I had grown very fond of the little angel that Robbie had given me and still talked to it, shouted at it and cried over it when the mood took me.

"Just coming now," I said as I added the last few pieces of tinsel to the tree (okay, who am I kidding, what I did would be best described as firing it in the general direction and hoping that it would land successfully and stick somewhere).

We arrived at Mammy's house shortly after nine o'clock and even I stopped for long enough to appreciate the enchanting scene she had created by adding tiny sparkling blue icicles to the front of the cottage and adorning the trees at the side with crystal lights. A real pine tree had been cut and decorated and was standing pride of place in the living room and a variety of beautiful baking aromas coming from the kitchen added to the atmosphere.

"Happy Christmas, love!" Mammy announced, throwing off her apron and coming to greet me with a hug.

"Are we the first to arrive?" Luke asked.

I remained silent even though I wanted to enquire if he could hear any loud mouths in the vicinity drowning out the soft music that was playing in the background. The place didn't smell like a brewery either and the whiff of cheap perfume wasn't threatening to knock me down. Which basically all went towards concluding that *no*, his parents hadn't arrived yet.

"Yes, dear. Come in and I'll get you a wee drink. What'll it be? I have mulled wine or brandy or whiskey or there's beer."

I stared at Luke long and hard.

"I think I'll just have something soft for now, thanks," he said quickly. He had been out several times with his father and the end result was always the same.

Donal and Robbie were already ensconced by the fire and I waved a cheery hello to them both.

I wasn't the world's greatest present-shopper but had decided to buy gifts for both of them as they were so good to my mother and knowing that they were only a short distance away made me feel much more confident about her security.

"I've got something for you," I said to Robbie who looked startled at first.

"I didn't know that we were going to be exchanging gifts," he said awkwardly. "I didn't bring anything for you. I just brought some wine and a bottle of brandy for us to share."

I quietened him with a wave of my hand. "Look on it not as a Christmas gift but as a thank-you for all you've done for my mother and for being nice to me when really you should have been kicking my arse for being such a cow."

He went to place the gift under the tree but I stopped him. "You can open it now if you like. You might enjoy it tonight."

He gave me a quizzical look and then began to tear the wrapping off. I was like a child watching him as I couldn't wait for his reaction.

Having peeled the wrapping paper off, he looked at the box and then slid it open to reveal its contents. He stared for a moment, took the item out, and once he read the inscription I saw his eyes grow misty although he covered it well by faking a coughing attack and then wiping his whole face with a hankie.

I had put a lot of thought into what I would give him as he had shared an understanding with me when I had been particularly confused (as well as horrible).

"What's that?" Mammy asked, coming over and squinting.

"It's a new pipe," the old man said.

"I thought that your old one was very precious to you," Mammy said gently.

"It is but just look at the message on this one."

Mammy took the box from him and read what was written in small writing on the handle.

It said: '*No matter where you are I will always be with you. An angel wherever you smoke.*'

"It's beautiful and a lovely thought."

Mammy gave me a slow smile and gazed at me with pride in her eyes. Donal also appeared to have placed me slightly higher in his estimation as he too was looking fondly in my general direction and then Mandy and the mad parents arrived and the magic was broken and replaced with much guzzling and nasal laughter.

We had decided that we would have a few drinks in the house

first and then go up to the hotel and see the delightful Judith. I hadn't been in her company since the day Luke, Gabriel and I had gone to see her to discuss menus, table layout, possibilities for a band and to get a sneaky peek at the honeymoon suite which was totally exquisite and had made me want to jump on the four-poster bed and drag Luke with me.

I had eventually got over the initial shock of having my reception there although I didn't think Judith had. Gabriel had pulled out all the stops and been the ultra-officious wedding planner and quizzed her tenaciously, telling her that everything had to be perfect as his bride was just that – perfect.

I had nearly wet myself laughing and Judith had been raging. She had tried hard to hide it but not hard enough as the corner of her mouth had curled and I could swear that I heard a low growl emanate from her person.

"Am I allowed to ask what you got for Donal?" Mammy asked.

"I'm afraid I was rather boring and just got him a new jumper and some socks and have to admit that Frankie picked them out but it's the thought that counts."

"I have something rather special for you," she said with a mysterious wink.

"Give!" I demanded. I had always had lousy patience when it came to waiting for anything.

"Nope. It's not Christmas until tomorrow and as it's a Chrissss-mas present you'll just have to wait until then. I can't wait to see your face."

"What are we talking about?" Luke asked upon joining us in the kitchen.

"Oh, nothing, Luke. I was just telling Ruby about the Christmas present I've got her which she is going to love."

"Bet she'll like mine better."

"Oh, that's right. You got her something similar, didn't you?"

"Yes, I'm sure they'll complement each other very well."

I rolled my eyes and left them to their game. It was probably clothes or a new scarf and a pair of boots or maybe they'd got me the sketch-pad and pencils set I'd been droning on about for the last six weeks. I'd even left the catalogue out and put a big black ring around the number, in the hope that when Luke would next look at it he'd get the hint. Men don't do well with subtlety. They need it spelt right out to them.

We left the cottage about an hour later and walked the short distance to the hotel. You'd have imagined that it would have been rather quiet on Christmas Eve night but in actual fact business seemed to be booming.

"Do people have no homes to go to? No children to sit and build toys for?" I asked in surprise.

"I'm sure they do but it's traditional around here to go for a drink on Christmas Eve night and, as there are no pubs left within a ten-mile radius, this would be the main attraction," Donal explained.

"Why are there no pubs left? Has business been that bad?"

"Not bad at all. They'd all be fine if the thugs with the baseball bats would stop going in and wrecking them."

"It's not exactly Mafia country around here, is it?" I commented. "So why have there been so many incidents? It doesn't make a lot of sense – and anyway I thought that the Smugglers' Inn was well on its way to being revamped again?"

"It was but then the firm who were putting in the new furniture left all of a sudden and never came back. It was all very strange."

"Then there was the bar in the golf club and the bar at the Smugglers' Bay Yacht Club," Robbie continued. "They've all been hit in some way and, as you can imagine, their owners are all very fearful of future attacks and are taking their time in re-opening to give the guards a chance to get to the bottom of it all."

"And in the meantime the McQueens are laughing all the way to the bank. Life simply isn't fair, is it?"

"Happy Christmas!" everybody shouted once the clock had hit twelve o'clock. Surprisingly I was really enjoying myself (especially given the fact that the manky in-laws were in the area). I had a feeling that Mandy had told them to behave (or perhaps threatened them with eviction). Fred was his usual arrogant self but on a much smaller scale and Beverley was trying very hard to be charming which could be quite a scary experience when you were on the receiving end of much sleeve-tugging, nudging and scarily large smiles.

There was no sign of Judith anywhere although we did get speaking briefly to Aisling.

"So what's been happening since the last time I was here then?"

"Her Royal Highness wasn't very impressed by the fact that she can't have your mother's cottage but seems to be concentrating on other things. There are still a lot of suits and hushed meetings happening which none of us are privy to but as long as she doesn't annoy me I don't care."

We left the hotel shortly afterwards and walked arm in arm the short distance home.

"Since it's now officially Christmas Day, can I please have my presents?" I begged. "Come on. It's your fault I'm like this, Luke. You kept teasing me."

"I don't know, Ruby. What do you think, Isobel?"

"I don't know, Luke – she might appreciate them better if we wait until morning. After all, Santa Claus doesn't appear on a whim just because one of his recipients happens to be just a wee bit impatient."

They both burst out laughing and looked nearly as excited as I was when they left the room.

Two minutes later I had a blindfold placed on me and was led to another room.

"You're not going to put me in front of a firing squad or leave me to the mercy of Judith or anything sinister, are you?"

"You can take it off now, Ruby," Luke said as he gently kissed me on the cheek.

I rubbed my eyes and looked at the two large packages that had been carefully wrapped in coloured tissue paper. My heartbeat increased one hundredfold as I knew instantly what they might be.

I ripped the paper from the first one and gasped as I saw what it was.

Frozen Lake Christmas was the title and it was the picture from Sarah Larkin's collection that I had been most drawn to.

"There's another one here for you to open, Ruby," Luke said gently.

"Sorry, I got lost there for a minute," I said.

Gently I eased the wrapping off the second picture which also had Sarah Larkin's name in the corner. It was a beautiful print that I had never seen before. It was called *Outstretched with Love* and it depicted a pair of hands being held out to a little girl as she ran towards the owner. They were on a beach, complete with its own path which led up into the mountains.

"Are you happy?" Luke asked.

"Nah. Take them back and ask for a refund."

Luke went to handle the painting I was holding and I pointed my finger at him. "Touch it and you die. I can't believe that you did this. I seriously do not deserve this after everything that's happened this year."

"Yup, you certainly are hard work," Luke said. "But I suppose you're worth it."

I have to say that it was one of the best Christmases I had ever had and I was hopeful that this would be indicative of a new year which would be filled with love and laughter and see me marry my true love without too much stress.

As usual I was wrong.

Chapter 56

It was the month of February and so far my year had been pleasant enough. There had been no major catastrophes and I was feeling upbeat and cheerful. My decision to call off the search for my birth mother had been a good one and I was optimistic that having taken a break I would be in a much better frame of mind to start pursuing it again when I decided that the time was right. (I should have known that the 'black cat being squished by the bus' scenario was bound to raise its head sooner or later.)

Rose Malone had been in touch with me at the end of January to ask if Frankie, Carly and I could go for a fitting and naturally Gabriel was going to come along as well. I had taken his advice about the cake and, instead of going for the three-tiered plastic-figured variety that I had first planned on choosing, I was now getting a cake made in the shape of a cottage which would have pink roses made from icing cascading down the sides. Gabriel was thrilled that I had changed my mind and thought that he was a master negotiator. (Little did he know that the biggest incentive was that I knew how much it would piss Judith off, hence no negotiating needed.) I had also decided to go for the stationery he suggested and he was liaising with the photographer, the lady he had recommended to arrange the flowers and the limousine firm. He was also a dab hand at dealing with Judith who I preferred not to talk to (unless there was something I knew I could annoy her about).

Strange things were still happening in the hotel although Aisling still wasn't sure what. I had grown to like her very much and considered her to be a good friend. She was also very kind to my mother which added instant brownie points to the situation.

"It's tomorrow that you go to Belfast for a dress fitting, isn't it?" Luke asked as he stirred a pot of soup.

"It is," I said, cutting hunks of bread from a large French stick. "I'm so excited to see what she's done with my dress."

Luke gave me a strange look, laughed to himself and took the butter out of the fridge.

"And what may I ask is so feckin funny?"

"'I'm so excited to see what she's done with my dress,'" he said, mimicking me in a voice that wasn't too dissimilar to Gabriel's.

"Shut your face," I said. "I can still arrive in a pair of DM boots and some dungarees if you'd prefer it."

"No, thanks, the dress sounds fine. It'll probably be the one and only time that I'll ever get to see you not in trousers, so from that point of view the sheer novelty factor will be overwhelming."

I threw a dishcloth at him and got cutlery out of the drawer.

"I was wondering though, when you go to Belfast tomorrow, do you think that you could arrange to meet up with Mandy and Mum? Just for a quick cup of coffee or something?"

"Yeah, sure," I said, willing myself to remember to text Mandy later on.

"You don't mind?" he asked.

Of course I feckin minded but Luke was giving me hound-dog eyes and I was in a good mood because I was looking forward to seeing my dress.

"No. As long as they don't want to gatecrash the bridal shop, then that's fine."

It was strange in a way but we had now got used to having Luke's mother and father around. They had never gone back to Spain and seemed content to be here. Another surprising turn-up had been the fact that they had just moved into a rented apartment not far from Mandy's flat. Their mother had recently started a hair and beauty course and was making very scary noises about wanting to do my hair the day of the wedding. (Please piss off. My hair is bad enough without letting some enthusiastic mature student near it just so that she can impress her tutor and then shag him.) Luke's father was still a very annoying drunk but had made a New Year's resolution to cut down on his intake and only drink beer (in copious amounts) and leave the hard stuff to everyone else. If nothing else it was a start.

I rang Frankie and she answered on the first ring.

"You wouldn't be just a wee bit excited, would you?" I asked as she squealed and I held the phone away from my ear.

"Just a bit. I cannot wait to see my dress! *And* I've another bit of news for you!"

"If you tell me that you're pregnant again and that bumps are the new look for going up the aisle, I'm going to kill you and I'm very afraid that Gabriel may have a heart attack."

"Don't be so silly! I'm not pregnant but I know somebody who is and she's coming home tomorrow and if you don't mind would love to come with us to the dress shop!"

"Oh my God, Ella's pregnant again!" I yelled. "Way to go, Hammy! His target practice is definitely much improved."

"Isn't it fantastic?"

"So what time are we meeting at then? I told Rose that we'd be with her at around twelve o'clock."

"That's perfect. We can pick Ella up from the airport and then just go ahead to meet Rose."

"Is she travelling on her own?"

"Yes. Hammy is insisting that she gets away for the night on her own. She's only coming for two days though – she says that that's all she could manage without seeing Baby Celia."

It was slightly after twelve when we arrived at the dress shop the following day. Ella's plane had been slightly late, the traffic had

316

been manic and parking impossible. We had ended up parking across the road in the car park of the big red-brick women's rescue shelter and had sneaked out the gate, hoping that nobody would shout at us for trespassing.

"Hello, girls," Rose said in greeting. "Would you like a cup of coffee before we try anything on?"

"No, thanks!" Frankie and I answered in unison whilst Carly skipped from foot to foot in the manner of an excited puppy.

"What they really mean," Ella said helpfully, "is that they would love a cup but they would rather have it after they see their dresses."

Rose smiled knowingly and beckoned us through to the fitting room beyond the shop. It was old and there were rolls of fabric and material everywhere and several mannequins decked with clothing of various shapes and sizes.

"Are you ready?" she asked before reverently removing a sheet from a hanger.

And there was my wedding dress and I knew that it would be perfect. It was the right colour and the detail was enough to make it stand out without being overpowering.

"Would you like to try it on?"

"Yes, please."

I took off my clothes, put my hands in the air like she instructed and allowed her to slip the dress over my arms and then over my head. She zipped me up, tugged here and there and made markings with pins and then she let me turn around to look at myself in the mirror.

My hand went immediately to my throat in shock. The dress looked too beautiful and too delicate to cover my frame.

"What do you think?" I asked.

Frankie couldn't speak as she was snivelling into a hankie and Ella seemed also to be having difficulty in answering me whilst Carly made a low 'Oooooooooh!' sound.

"Would somebody please say something – please?"

"You look divine, dawling," a voice drawled from behind me.

We had arranged to meet Gabriel here and as usual he had timed it well.

"You approve?"

"I more than approve. It's stunning. Outstanding. Can I please add you to my list of contacts, Rose, as you are an expert in what you do?"

Rose blushed and smiled happily. She made a few more alterations and then turned me round so that she could unzip me and place the dress back on its hanger.

"Frankie, now it's your turn."

Frankie blew her nose loudly and then took her coat off but not before she nearly strangled me giving me a hug.

We all whistled and made appreciative comments when we saw her dress. It was perfect for her shape and colouring and the shade was perfect.

"Another triumph, Rose," Gabriel announced loudly. "Haute couture, eat your heart out!"

"Exactly," I said. "You would have had me standing in some stuffy designer shop looking like a flouncy meringue. I am so glad that I'm a stubborn bitch sometimes. I always knew that there was a reason I should have come here."

"Yeah, your magic finger did the walking," Frankie said.

I emerged from the fitting room and looked around the shop whilst I waited for Frankie to get dressed. I went to the window and the ever-familiar *déjà vu* feeling came over me.

"I wish I knew why I keep thinking I was here before," I said to Rose as she appeared, looking for her glasses. "It really is driving me insane. There has to be a connection somewhere. We parked across the road today and I got it crossing the road as well. It's starting to freak me out, you know. I'm not a big believer in reincarnation but there's just something so familiar about this place."

"I really can't think of what it can be," Rose said (for about the hundredth time as she had heard this conversation on all the other occasions). "It's unlikely you've been here. It's a residential area mostly with a few accountancy firms and a doctor's office and the dentist's and then there's the women's refuge across the road. Of course, it wasn't always a refuge – it used to be a convent."

"Really?" Frankie said as she joined us.

"It wasn't your average convent, though. Unmarried mothers gave birth to their babies there."

My heart leapt and began to pound.

"You don't happen to know what it was called?" I asked with my throat drying up.

"I believe it used to be known as St Catherine's Lodge."

Chapter 57

I woke up and was surrounded by faces.

"What happened?"

"You fainted, dear," Rose said gently. "Take some small sips of water and you'll feel better."

I shakily took the glass and drank slowly from it.

"You're awfully pale, Ruby. It must be all the excitement," Ella said.

"A bride is never properly a bride unless they pass out at least once," Gabriel said.

"We can check that off the list then," I croaked.

Frankie was beside me, rubbing my arm and kissing my hand.

"Oh my God!" she said. "I can't believe we found it like this."

"Join the club. It certainly explains a lot though. It's no wonder I recognised it."

"Recognised it? How?"

"Come with me," I said to Frankie as I pulled myself into a sitting position.

"Take it easy," Ella urged. "Don't move too quickly or you might just end up on your back again."

320

"Chill out, Nurse Ella. I'll be fine. Frankie will hold on to me."

"Why? Where are we going?"

"For a little walk across the road."

The air hit me as soon as I walked out the door and I clung tightly to Frankie's arm. We crossed the road until we were standing looking at the clothes shop from the grounds of the convent.

"Do you remember I told you about the sketch? The hand-drawn picture that showed trees, a bus stop and the front of a shop advertising clothing alterations? The sketch that had St Catherine's Lodge written on the back of it?"

"Yes, of course."

"Look in front of you."

Frankie looked at the shop. Looked at me. Looked at the shop again and then clapped her hand over her mouth.

"The picture is of this street, isn't it?"

"Yes."

Every detail of the sketch had been burned onto my brain and as I looked all around me I could see where the artist had got her ideas from. I could see the old houses, the bus stop, Rose Malone's shop which no longer had its 'Clothing Alterations' sign up but which was still there nevertheless.

"I can't believe that I didn't figure this out before."

"You never would have thought, Ruby. How were you to know how important or significant this street was going to be? Your finger of fate guided you well."

"I'm going to go over there to ask a few questions," I said determinedly.

"But, Ruby, it's no longer a convent. They'll not know anything."

"Somebody might know something. Every tiny detail counts. Go back across to the shop. If you don't mind, this is something I need to do for myself."

I opened the gate which led into the grounds of the women's refuge, past the sign that told me that it was now called Haven House. I walked slowly around the gardens which were very

321

peaceful and fragrant with different varieties of flowers and shrubs planted all around. I sat down on a wall and looked at the building in front of me. It was red-bricked with lots of windows and a welcome mat at the front door. The downstairs windows were colourfully decorated with butterflies and animals and a wind-chime blew melodiously in the breeze. It was a nice place, I decided, or at least it was now. I wondered what it was like when Georgina had been here. I was presuming that Georgina must have been here at some point. And I was presuming she had drawn the picture.

I went to the door and several times attempted to press the doorbell but lost my nerve at the last minute. The people within would think I was nuts. Maybe I would ring them instead? At least I knew where it was now and it wouldn't be as embarrassing as having to explain myself in person.

No. I wasn't going to be afraid. I had waited my whole life for this and dreamed of nothing else for the last few years.

"Pull yourself together. Get a fecking grip and stop being such a pussy," I said out loud before jumping three foot in the air as somebody put their hand on my shoulder.

"Don't be afraid. Why don't you come in and speak to us? We're here to help after all," a lady said. She was petite with black hair and brown eyes, dressed casually in jeans and a shirt, and was looking at me kindly.

"I don't think you understand," I said, embarrassed (my face was probably the same colour as my hair). "I'm not here because I have any problems as such – I'm just looking for information."

"That's fine." The look on the woman's face told me plainly that she didn't believe me.

"Honestly. I just need a bit of guidance and then I'll be on my way."

"The first step is to admit that there's a problem and you've accomplished that one beautifully by coming here to speak to us. The other steps will come in time. You don't need to be afraid any more. We'll protect you and your family. We have rooms upstairs if

322

you ever feel that the situation is becoming too dangerous. Have you any children?"

"I really admire the work you do," I said in a controlled voice, "but you still don't understand. I'm not a battered wife nor am I seeking refuge here. It's information about the building itself that I need. You don't happen to know anything about St Catherine's Lodge, do you?

"I don't. But I know someone who does," the woman said, smiling.

Two hours later and I was sitting in a nursing home, having been directed there by the lady I had spoken to in Haven House.

The old nun didn't seem to understand when the nurse told her that she had a visitor.

"But it's not Maureen's day to come here and see me," the old lady said in confusion. "It's not Wednesday, is it? Am I senile already?"

The nurse laughed and patted her on the hand. "No, Sister Therese, you're not senile yet. I'll make sure and tell you when it happens. Maureen sent this young lady to see you. She thinks that you may be able to help her with something."

"That's grand then. What's your name, young lady?" She patted the armchair that was situated beside the bed in her room. "Maureen is a good girl – she's my niece, you know," she said proudly. "She runs the refuge. I helped her secure the premises for it when St Catherine's closed. Do you know her well?"

"My name is Ruby, Sister, and I only met Maureen today. She's very nice and she told me that you used to work in St Catherine's. I was hoping that you could give me some information about someone who used to stay there or at least I think she used to be there."

"You're referring to one of my girls then," the nun said, nodding and seeming to understand. "Your red hair and brown eyes remind me of someone. Once I hear the name perhaps I'll remember – my old memory isn't what it used to be but up to recently I could remember them all, every one."

"Georgina."

"Georgina ... Delaney ... the same eyes," the nun said.

I couldn't believe it. At last.

"I have the same eyes as her?" I asked gently.

"And the same nose and she was red-haired too. Tell me, do you like to draw?"

I nodded, mesmerised.

"Georgina loved to draw. She was very good at it. She was at her happiest either sitting in the garden or looking through the window and drawing. She drew exactly what she saw in front of her but she also had an amazing imagination. She was a lovely young woman and I was very fond of her."

"That's why I thought I'd been there before," I explained. "The street opposite St Catherine's was drawn in pencil on a piece of paper, you see. The paper had a letterhead on it and that's how I knew about the lodge. It was drawn so clearly and in such detail and I've memorised it so well that I thought I was there before. I've been there several times now because the lady across the street from the women's refuge is making my wedding dress. I've had her tortured every time, asking her why I ever could've been there."

"Ah yes," the nun said smiling. "I always told Georgina that she could take paper from my office when she wanted to draw. That's why you saw the letterhead. Where did you find it?"

I began to explain to the nun about my father and mother, the birth certificate and the other things I had found in the box.

"There was an old black and white photograph as well. It was of a lady wearing a coat and a hat. I'd never seen her before in my life. Do you know who that might be?"

"The picture will be of your grandmother. Georgina carried that about everywhere with her. Her mother died when she was younger and Georgina absolutely worshipped her. You obviously meant a lot to her when she sent it with you to your new parents."

I couldn't speak. I was so overwhelmed with emotion that I was content to simply stay in the company of someone who actually understood my situation and knew my mother.

"So, you haven't met her?" the nun asked after we had sat in silence for a time.

"No, but I'd like to. Do you think she'd like to see me?"

"Yes, I think she'd like that very much. I'm quite surprised that she ended up having you adopted. When she left the lodge she was more than happy to be looking after you and was very good to you. I always thought that she'd make a great little mother."

"What about the drink and the men?"

The nun looked confused which prompted me to explain what I had been told.

"Perhaps that's what your parents were told but it's not the young girl I knew. Shortly after she had you, her sister came and removed her from the lodge. She wasn't really fit to go anywhere as she'd had quite a difficult birth but her family were quite rich and most insistent that she leave. They gave a generous donation to the convent."

"What was my aunt like?" I asked eagerly.

Sister Therese made a series of facial movements that indicated that she didn't quite know how to answer this question.

"I haven't met any of them," I said. "So I'd be grateful for any information possible."

"I only met her for a very short period. I don't really remember much about her. They told me that they were taking Georgina and the baby home to be with the family and that we had nothing to worry about."

I was utterly confused. "But if she was going home to a wealthy family, how did she end up living in a house on her own drunk and with men calling all the time and being investigated by social services? My adoptive mother was told to put me off the scent if I ever did try and look for answers. She was told that I was badly treated for the first six weeks of my life and that there would be nothing but heartache in store for me if I ever was to trace my birth mother."

"Your mother was told to tell you this. I see."

She looked as if she really did see.

"Does that bear some significance to you?" I asked.

"I couldn't be sure and far be it from me to cast aspersions on anyone but I believe that your aunt worked with Social Services.

Chapter 58

I walked out of the nursing home and could hardly see because I was blinded by tears. You didn't need to be Einstein to figure it out. Obviously it had been a deliberate act. The old nun had nothing to gain from not telling me the truth and I had always questioned the fact that somebody who was portrayed as being so bad could have put together the little box which was so obviously filled with sentiment and love.

I rang Luke and told him what had happened in a halting voice in between alternate sessions of crying and kicking the wall in a rage.

"How could anyone be so cruel as to do that to their own sister? And their own niece for that matter?"

"Whoah, Ruby. You can't jump to conclusions just on the strength of what one person says. This lady is in a nursing home. She's old and her memory is failing. She could be confusing Georgina with somebody else entirely."

"I wonder would you ever feck yourself, Luke Reilly! I know in my heart of hearts that she is telling the truth because so many things didn't make sense to me!"

"If it makes you feel better to think that, then fine. I just don't want you getting hurt, that's all. And, anyway, I thought that you weren't going to think any more about this until after our wedding?"

"I did not leave the house this morning expecting to be in possession of such information which was dropped on me from a great height after I fainted like a big girl, Luke. I didn't exactly go looking for it, did I?"

"You are a girl."

"Shut up."

"What are you going to tell your mother?"

"I'm not planning on telling her anything. Why do you ask?"

"Because we're going to Donegal tomorrow. Your mammy wants to see us. She says it's very important. Apparently she's been talking to her solicitor and he had some very interesting things to say about the matter of the cottage. Aisling will also be there as she wants to talk to us in person."

"Luke, speaking of mothers, I've just remembered that I'm supposed to be meeting yours for coffee and – I'm not being horrible – but could you do me a favour as I think I'm not really in the mood for going anywhere?"

"Say no more. I'll ring her and tell her that you can't meet her because you fainted and aren't well. It isn't exactly a lie after all. Just you get yourself home safe to me."

I had instructed the girls and Gabriel to go on home without me as I wasn't sure how long I was going to be at the nursing home and was travelling home by bus. Which gave me plenty (too much) time to think.

Perhaps I should have stayed in bed that morning. Ignorance is bliss. Isn't that what they always say? But, quite obviously I was meant to go there. My angel had guided me as the last thing I had done before leaving the house was to kiss it and invite Daddy to see my dress.

"Are you all right? I've been worried sick about you," Frankie said in a breathy voice once I had answered my mobile.

"I'm fine. It's been a long day and I'm sitting on the bus and unless you want everybody to think I'm a fruitcake with a mad family I'm not going to discuss it here. Honestly, you couldn't make it up."

Luke enveloped me in a bear-hug and was delighted to see me home.

"I've been so worried," he said, echoing Frankie's words.

"There's no need to worry about me," I said, nuzzling into his shoulder and taking comfort from his arms.

"Other people should be worried though. They should be very afraid because if what I've been told is true then I'd say that I have a very strong case on my hands for malpractice. How disgustingly unethical can you get?"

I had a restless night's sleep where my dreams were plagued with images of a baby being forcibly taken away from a young woman with red hair whilst a nun, bound and gagged, sat beside her unable to say or do anything to stop it.

"What time did you tell Mammy we'd be down?" I asked Luke next morning.

"As soon as we could, basically. She sounded so excited on the phone. Her solicitor friend must have found something major in the will."

I momentarily forgot my own news. "Well, that's it then, there's nothing for it. We'll leave as soon as possible after I have a shower. One thing, though – on the way there there's a wee pub I'd like to call into for a drink."

"I know you've had a shock but showing up at your mother's legless isn't the best idea in the world, I don't think."

"I have no intention of getting drunk, Luke. It's important. You'll see why when we get there."

I was too tired and weary to start giving explanations now. I needed to figure things out in my own mind first.

The journey to Donegal seemed to take much longer than usual but I suspected that my eagerness to arrive was making it appear that way.

"Turn left here," I instructed once we had passed through Letterkenny and I saw the small black and white sign which indicated that Mulroy Cove was only ten miles away.

"We're going in the complete opposite direction from your mother's, Ruby. Will this take long?"

"For your own preservation, Luke, stop asking so many feckin questions and just drive. You'll see why I'm so keen to go when we get there."

We arrived in the main street about fifteen minutes later and it looked totally different in daylight. I got out of the car, stretched my legs and once I had got my bearings took Luke by the hand and led him up the street to where the back entrance to the pub was.

Two men were standing having a cigarette at the door and I recognised one of them as being the man who had bought me a drink and given me facts about the family the last time I was there.

I was apprehensive as I approached and didn't have a plan as such but I needed some more information and this was the only way I could think to find it.

"How're you doing, lads?"

"Grand. Lost again, are you?"

I laughed nervously and overcame the urge to kick up my heels and run in the opposite direction.

"I was wondering if you could help me. My parents were delighted to hear that I'd been in contact with people who knew their old friends and I was just wondering if you could tell me any more about them."

"She's interested in getting news about the Delaneys," the man explained to his cohort who pursed his lips, nodded and took another sip of his pint.

"What is it that you want to know?"

"I'm particularly keen to get information about Georgina. She was the youngest, wasn't she?"

"That's right. A proper little goer, that one."

The other man laughed lasciviously and I felt sick.

"Why would you say that? Did you know her personally?"

"No. But a lot of other fellas did."

They guffawed again and I resisted the urge to knee the pair of them in the goolies. That would soon put an end to their amusement. Luke put his arm around me, sensing my discomfiture, and I took a deep breath and prepared to go on.

"Seriously, did you know her? Have you ever seen her?"

"No, I haven't. But who the hell are you? Bloody Special Branch? Why so many questions?"

"It's just important. Something happened a long time ago and I think that people may have been fed the wrong information about her. You seem to think that she was some kind of disreputable character even though you've never actually met her. Why would you say that?"

"It's common knowledge. She left here years ago and there were stories about her being, shall we say, very friendly with the boys."

"So she was a prostitute then?" I said through my teeth.

"God no, but we can only go by what we were told."

"And who told you?"

"Well, her brother-in-law used to drink in here and he never had a good word to say about her. Nothing but trouble and an easy lay, he would say. His wife, who was an oul' battleaxe, was constantly having to bail her out of trouble. Of course it helped that the wife had such a good job."

"Where did she work?"

"She worked for the health department, I think."

"No, actually," the other man argued, "she worked with children I think. Took them away if they weren't being looked after properly and that sort of thing ."

Chapter 59

I stalked to the car without looking back.

"I thought that you wanted to go into the pub," Luke said.

"It wasn't a drink I was after. I just wanted to find out more about what people around here think and that little conversation has just confirmed all my suspicions."

"Which lead you to deduce . . . ?" Luke prompted.

"That she was set up somehow. Everyone has this awful opinion of her but nobody has ever met her. Her asshole of a brother-in-law was obviously loose-tongued and didn't care how he portrayed her."

"So you think that everything that has been said about her isn't true?"

"I don't think. I'm sure of it, Luke."

We arrived at Mammy's house about forty minutes later, following a journey where I was pensive and confused.

"Say nothing about any of this," I warned Luke. "I don't want Mammy knowing anything until I'm totally sure of my facts."

Aisling and Mammy were both sitting in the cottage drinking coffee when we arrived and Mammy immediately put out two more mugs and poured for us and offered us a slice of cake.

I took a large gulp of the strong sweet liquid and settled myself back in the chair.

"Should you not be at work, young lady?" I asked, wagging my finger at Aisling and noting that she was dressed in her civvies.

"I would only I don't have a job any more."

Only then did I notice that Aisling's eyes were red-rimmed and she looked totally miserable.

"She was sacked yesterday," Mammy said, patting Aisling on the hand.

"What happened? Did you finally lose your cool and smack her one?"

"No, but I wish I had now. She called me into the office yesterday morning and there she was with her father and the suit."

"Mr Humphries," I said, remembering the man who had been speaking to Mammy the night of Caitlin O'Donnell's gallery exhibition.

"That's the one. The three of them sat and told me that the hotel was going to be undergoing some changes and as such they were no longer going to need a tour guide or anyone to deal with tourism or publicity as they were going to appoint their own person."

"They can't do that!" I cried "You have rights."

"They've offered me a package to go quietly and say nothing to anybody about what has happened."

"I hope you told them where they could stick it!"

"I'm supposedly thinking about it at the moment. I have to go up later and let them know my decision but what they don't realise is that I have information about their plans."

I put my mug down and sat forward. "So there were plans. I always knew it."

"Oh, there are plans all right. Plans that don't include any of us and plans that were never going to suit your mother either. I was in the office one day looking for a phone number and noticed some papers sitting on her desk. They looked to me like architectural plans and I couldn't resist having a sneaky peek. Basically they want to knock down the hotel and build a brand new one. A horrible glass-structured modern monstrosity with its own exclusive clubs which the locals aren't going to be allowed to join. He intends to call his new hotel 'Zada's'. Research has recently shown that people like modern hotels more than they like the rustic theme that made Monroe Manor popular. Ultra-modern is what he's aiming for. He's going to have a glass lift going up through the centre of the building and a glossy glass front to the entrance which would boast a fountain and ice sculptures. The rooms would all be white or black with inset baths and balconies overlooking the cocktail bar and golf course that he's building. There would be exclusive membership and the fees he is planning to charge would reflect that. Basically it's going to be a haven for the filthy rich but more so for businessmen, with state-of-the-art conference facilities and fax-machines and laptops in every room. They're even going to provide secretaries to type letters and do their memos whilst they stay here."

"They can't do that!" I said in total disbelief. "Surely that's a listed building that can't be destroyed? It's been there for centuries. It has to be protected. People can't just go knocking things down if they feel like it. And where was the sense in doing all the refurbishment work to it if they were simply going to destroy it?"

"They were very clever, Ruby. They were already offering deals to the punters that we didn't know anything about. We could never understand why there were so many suits coming and going all the time but it turns out that they were already using the meagre facilities available and offering discount packages once the new hotel was built. The hotel refurbishment was to put everyone off the scent until they had built enough clientele to make it a viable business proposition."

"What a nasty cow!" I spat. "Business seemed to be booming for them too. Why would they want to lose all that?"

"They won't lose out. Not in the long run. There's nowhere else for people to go around here any more, so if people want to go out they'll come to the hotel regardless of what it looks like."

"I thought you said that the locals wouldn't be allowed into the clubs?"

"They won't but there will be a bar there for them and golf and boating clubs linked with the hotel that locals will be encouraged to join."

"But there were perfectly good clubs in town before they got . . ." I trailed off as realisation dawned on me.

"Yes, Ruby, there were clubs in town before vandals kept on going in and wrecking them."

"The same way as thugs came in here and scared the life out of Mammy but didn't actually steal anything."

"Correct. I'll let your mother take over from here."

Mammy had been sitting quietly sipping her coffee with an envelope in front of her. She put down her mug, slid some papers out of the envelope and smiled broadly.

"Well, after he got over the back trouble, I spoke to my solicitor about Lord Bartley's will, and he deciphered all the high-falutin' legal language for me."

I nodded and wondered where all this was going.

"Very specific instructions were written into the will. The Big House, Monroe Manor, was left to Harry McQueen but on condition that it was not to be knocked down or deliberately destroyed. The same goes for the cottage which, as you are already aware, is mine – a fact that neither Judith nor her father have ever respected. I don't want to say too much more for the moment, as I'd like to go up to the hotel and get the staff and the locals together for a little chit-chat."

"We've tipped off some of the local papers that there's going to be a community rally and they're going to be there in force to take notes," said Aisling, looking particularly pleased when she imparted this nugget of information and I knew that, for her, revenge was going to be particularly sweet.

Luke and I went out to the car to get our things after we had got up from the table. Aisling had left to go and have a shower and Mammy was preparing lunch as Donal and Robbie were both coming over.

"This certainly is the day for revelations," Luke said, rubbing his hair in disbelief. "Just when you thought things couldn't get any more complicated."

"Not a word about the other situation to Mammy," I warned. "It might take me some time but I intend to get to the bottom of it and have all my facts straight before I say a word. Hearsay will simply not be good enough for her. She'll need evidence of some description."

Chapter 60

We all left to go to the hotel two hours later. Aisling and Mammy were both carrying envelopes which were full of astounding information that would cause Harry McQueen's empire to come crashing down around him and hopefully when it did fall it would smack Judith up the face.

"What's going on?" Judith asked as we all trooped in.

"Check the booking list," Aisling said. "We've booked the main suite for a public meeting. You're more than welcome to come. Invite your father as well as this concerns you."

"You have no right to be here!" she shouted, her face twisting in a nasty sneer. "You lost whatever rights you had two days ago when you were given your marching orders."

"I hope that you're taking good note of this," Aisling said to a man behind her who suddenly produced a notebook and began to scribble furiously.

"Simon Reid from the *Donegal Chronicle*, Miss. Tell me – on what grounds was your ex-employee sacked? Do you think you made a mistake?"

Judith backed into her office with a look of pure terror on her face.

"That's it, run along to Daddy and tell him he'd better attend this meeting," said Aisling.

By the time that Judith and her father did arrive, the room was buzzing with activity. Local people had come in force and the staff were all in attendance. Aisling had been very busy and had basically knocked on doors and encouraged as many people as possible to come along as there would be some very interesting revelations. I scanned the room and everyone looked very solemn.

"That's the owner of the Smugglers' Inn," Robbie said, nodding at a man who looked pale and unshaven. "He's been through a terrible time. His wife and he split up after the inn was ransacked the second time. They've been under terrible pressure. Rumour has it that he might lose his house."

"And that's the bar manager from the golf club," Donal continued as we looked towards a man in a suit whose eyes seemed to be literally sparking with anger.

A group of gentlemen wearing T-shirts with *Smugglers' Bay Yacht Club* on them obviously were representing the bar there which had also lost its trade. I wondered if Judith and her father had ever thought about the amount of damage they had caused to people in their attempts to line their already burgeoning pockets.

Aisling stood up and went over to the side of the room where she tapped a glass with a spoon in order to get everyone's attention.

"Good afternoon, everyone. For those of you who don't know me, my name is Aisling Redmond and I've lived in Smugglers' Bay all my life. It's a beautiful place which boasts its own marina, has several well-known beauty spots as well as an award-winning restaurant, golf club and boating club. Unfortunately in the last six months we've seen thugs come in and destroy all of these businesses. Strangely, though, this hotel has never been touched."

"We have an excellent security system in place here," Harry McQueen began to explain, standing up.

"Sit down, Mr McQueen!" Aisling barked. "When I want your opinion I'll ask for it and I'll be asking for it very shortly."

Harry McQueen looked positively shell-shocked and I was glad

338

to see that Judith was shifting uncomfortably in her seat. Mr Humphries was also present but his smugness was nowhere to be seen and had instead been replaced by a worried frown.

"It has come to my attention that big plans are afoot for Monroe Manor. This hotel has been part of our community now for many years and is a much-loved attraction with tourists coming here over and over again which obviously boosts the economy of the area. It would appear that this wasn't enough for the McQueens, however, as they put together plans to knock down the hotel and build a new one – some modern monstrosity called 'Zada's'. A hotel which I hasten to add was going to be far too good for the likes of us. Exclusive membership only, apart from a purpose-built golf course and a small boating club which were only being put there as a token gesture to attract the locals and put the other clubs in the area out of business. They would, however, be far enough away from the hotel to ensure that the tone of the place wasn't brought down. Isn't that the way you worded it in one of your memos, Harry? There would also be bars attached to both these facilities but the bar in the hotel itself was going to be for guests only. The present staff were all to be sacked and new suppliers brought in."

It was with great satisfaction that I saw several of the barmen and porters flexing their hands and cracking their knuckles whilst the McQueens and Mr Humphries all looked nervously towards the nearest fire-exit door.

"Harry McQueen has insulted the integrity of practically everyone in this room. Integrity, there's a word you mustn't be too familiar with, Harry. I'll explain its meaning to you later. The biggest news, however, is that in actual fact this hotel is no longer yours."

I saw Harry and Judith look at each other in shock and then at Mr Humphries.

"I don't know where you're getting your facts from, Aisling, but I can assure you that the hotel is mine and that as such it's mine to do with what I wish," said Harry. "You talk of giving this rural backwoods an economy boost. Just you wait until I build my new hotel. You ain't seen nothing yet!"

"You don't appear to have heard me, Harry," Aisling repeated. "It isn't yours. It now officially belongs to Isobel Ross."

Judith leapt from her seat and looked around her, her eyes blazing with fury.

"What the hell are you talking about? The only thing she owns is that stupid cottage!"

"Let me read an extract from the late Bartley Monroe's will to you," said Aisling, picking up a document.

You could have heard a pin drop as she began to read.

"I hereby bequeath the Manor House and land attached thereto to my relative Harry McQueen, his heirs and assigns, subject to the condition that the Manor House remains unaltered and remains in keeping with the original building plans and specifications attached hereto. In the event that there is any breach of the above condition, then the ownership of the property will revert to Kate Kennedy, my former housekeeper, her heirs and assigns, under the conditions stated above."

Aisling fixed her gaze on Harry McQueen.

"You forfeited all rights to Monroe Manor when you concocted a plan to destroy it and actually brought in machinery and started to knock down a wall at the back of the building. The will states that, if this situation were ever to arise, ownership would revert to Kate Kennedy and her heirs. Isobel Ross's Aunt Kate was given the cottage by Lord Bartley Monroe and, by giving it to her, he made her and her heirs 'honorary Monroes' to whom he would entrust the task of ensuring the preservation of it and the Big House itself. The clause in the will stops anyone from disturbing the foundations of the house or destroying its structure. Minimal damage has been caused as yet but I have in my hand a set of plans which disclose that our beautiful Manor House was to be toppled to the ground. I've taken the liberty of inviting Isobel's solicitor here just in case you need further explanation. He's very good, very good indeed. You should speak to him and see if he's dealt with many cases of aggravated burglary in the past. I found cheque stubs that were going to a very peculiar source and have discovered that they were being paid to the head of a gang, the members of which now have thankfully been apprehended and won't continue to vandalise the other establishments in the area. They were also responsible for burgling Isobel Ross and frightening her half to death. Honestly, for two such nasty-minded individuals you are both positively crap at covering your tracks."

The journalists stopped scribbling into their notepads for long enough to produce Dictaphones and approach Harry and Judith demanding answers but not before one of the barmen waded in and caught Harry McQueen a perfect punch on the side of the nose and I had advanced towards Judith who couldn't run away in her high heels . . .

When I arrived home the following day Frankie was waiting for me.

"Are you okay?"

"Oh, I'm fine, love. It's been a very confusing few days. Some bits good. Some bits not so good."

My bottom lip was threatening to start wobbling and I galloped into the house as I didn't want my reputation of being a hard nut in the neighbourhood to be destroyed.

"Ach, pet, come here!"

Frankie put her arms around me and stroked my head whilst I sobbed on her shoulder.

"The only silver lining in this particular cloud seems to be the fact that we are now getting my wedding reception for free as obviously I won't have to pay for it seeing as my mother now owns the hotel."

"That was a real turn-up for the books, wasn't it? How is your mum going to cope, though? She knows nothing about running or managing a hotel."

"She doesn't but there are a few people that she has come to know and trust that do. Aisling is going to take over the management of it, Darryl is running the restaurant and she has just hired someone whose speciality is going to be co-ordinating events there."

"Who?"

"Let's think. Who do we know that is a dab hand at organisation, has millions of contacts, has started a relationship with the bar and restaurant manager and loves to be in the thick of things?"

"Gabriel? Oh my God!" Frankie shouted.

"Yeah. It's great. At least when he's there I have him out of my hair."

"You don't seriously mean that," Frankie said. "Admit it – you love having him around."

"I will admit to no such thing."

"Seriously, though, how amazing that so many problems have been cleared up all at once! Which leaves one big outstanding problem: what are you going to do about Georgina?"

"I'm going to keep hoping and praying that something will happen. This little fella normally helps me out." I stroked the angel on my mantelpiece and then looked lovingly at the picture of my father which had pride of place beside it.

Chapter 61

A few months had passed and the wedding was creeping closer. I had been for several more fittings with Rose Malone and looked longingly at the building across the road every time I visited, knowing that it was where my mother spent a lot of time and that in a sense I had been with her even though I didn't know her.

I was at a crossroads and wasn't sure where to go next. Should I go back and confront the old nun for more information? Should I go to Social Services and demand that I see my Delaney aunt and ask her to explain the situation – or should I go back to my original plan and leave everything until after the wedding was over and I had time to think? I felt that the latter was probably the most sensible solution, my only problem being that my mother knew me so well and kept asking me what was the matter. I hated keeping things from her and felt that she had the right to know what I had been told.

"What am I going to do?" I asked Luke for the millionth time. "This is driving me nuts. I'd love to tell her but I know that she'll think I'm exaggerating or simply not believe me."

"Who told you the facts about Georgina?" he asked.

"Sure, you know who told me."

"Well, given the circumstances and the fact that you think she won't believe it if you tell her, why don't you ask the nun to explain it to her?"

I pondered the idea and then dismissed it. Then started to think about it again.

"What do you think? Do you think it's a good idea?" I asked Frankie later.

"Well, in the absence of all other suggestions or ideas, why not? Your mother will hear it all straight from the horse's mouth, so to speak. She's only going by what Social Services told her and as far as I can gather they were more than a little biased when they were drawing that particular picture."

I looked at my angel and said a little prayer as I rang the number.

"Would it be possible to speak to one of your residents, please?" I asked the lady who answered the phone. "Sister Therese."

Mammy complained all evening about how she hated being rushed, as well as asking questions and wondering aloud why she suddenly had to accompany me to Belfast.

"Rose wants your opinion on my dress," I lied.

"Really? Well, I suppose she can see that I have a good eye for style. I don't see why it has to be right now today, though. I'm very busy trying to get things organised at the hotel. You can't expect me to suddenly drop everything just because you want me to comment on your wedding dress."

"Stop grumbling and just trust me," I said, wishing that she'd keep quiet. She was going to get the shock of her life once she realised that the road I had turned into didn't take us to Rose Malone's shop but instead to an old people's home where she would be shocked yet again at the information that would be imparted.

"Ruby, my geography isn't perfect but even I know that you're going in completely the wrong direction."

I parked the car, looked beseechingly at Mammy and put my hand on her arm. "Please come with me."

344

Sensing the gravity of the situation, she followed me without a further word.

As we entered the nursing home I turned to her and quietly said, "I'm sorry that I couldn't find the words or the courage to do this myself but it's hard. I hope that you'll understand and that you'll not be too disappointed and cross with me."

"Ruby, please tell me what this is about?"

Mammy looked stricken and I was sorry to have caused her such distress. I took her by the hand and led her down the corridor to the room where I knew Sister Therese would be waiting.

"Come in, come in," she beckoned. "Lovely to meet you, Isobel. You should be very proud of Ruby. It's not easy to do the right thing all the time."

I closed the door and went and sat in the garden, knowing that Sister Therese would be telling my mother the story of how a young girl with brown eyes and red hair had come to her many years ago desperately needing help.

Mammy came and sat beside me some half an hour later and without speaking put her hand over mine.

"I'm so sorry, love. All these years I've obviously been believing something that wasn't true but, if it's any consolation, I was only repeating it with the best possible intentions. I never meant to hurt anybody."

"I know you didn't, Mammy. You couldn't possibly have known about the corruption and lies that you and Daddy were being fed."

"I feel so guilty," she said with tears in her eyes. "If you hadn't gone ahead and tried to find out, we both would have died thinking that she hadn't cared for you which is such a cruel thing for anyone to believe. I'm your mother and love you with all my heart but I feel so sorry for her. My baby son died which was a hard cross to bear but I can't imagine what it must have been like to have a healthy beautiful little girl, only for her to be taken away. She must have been heartbroken. Probably still is. Probably wonders every day what you look like, what you're doing, what sort of life you've had. Obviously that's where you get your artistic abilities from."

"And my bad temper and my stupid hair."

We both smiled through our tears.

Mammy and I clung to each other and whispered words of comfort and regret. We stayed like that for a short time before Mammy brusquely straightened herself, wiped her tears and turned me round to face her.

"Ruby, you're getting married soon and I think that we should leave everything until after that. You want to be able to enjoy your big day and not have anything hanging over you like a dark cloud. I know it will be hard but you have Luke to think of as well."

"I think that's a very wise idea, Mammy. But after, will you help me to find her?"

"I'll swim seas, climb mountains or go to the end of the earth if I have to, sweetheart."

Chapter 62

It was the week before the wedding and preparations were under way in all shapes and forms. Gabriel had everything running like clockwork and I had to admit that he was a godsend as he had organised everything to a tee.

I had gone to collect my dress from Rose Malone's and brought her a voucher entitling her to stay in Monroe Manor for two nights. She had been overjoyed and had hugged me tightly when I was leaving and wished me luck.

Frankie and I were going to stay with Mammy the night before the wedding and Owen and Luke were being put up in the hotel. The wedding was going to take place in a small country chapel not far from where our grand reception was to be held.

"Shall we go down to Donegal earlier than planned?" Luke asked.

"Why would you want to do that?" I asked.

"You've finished work. I've nothing left to do and I think it might be a nice idea to relax for a few days and not have to worry about anything. Gabriel will be taking care of everything and it would be a nice chance for us to recover from the madness of the last few months."

"Before we jump headlong into more madness, you mean," I

said, laughing. "That would be nice. I'll go and have a quick bath and then I'll ring Mammy and see what she says."

"She says it's fine. I asked her already."

"Are you two plotting behind my back again?" I demanded in mock annoyance. "If I didn't know better I'd say that you were both up to something."

"*Moi?* Would I?"

"What about your parents? What time is their plane due in today?"

"They're coming home on the four o'clock flight apparently and Mandy is picking them up at the airport."

"Have they decided on anywhere yet?"

"I don't think so although Mum said that she liked the look of Turkey and would perhaps like to settle there."

(I bet she liked the look of it . . . lots of tall, dark and handsome Turks who have a thing for brassy blondes. What would there be not to like?)

"How does your daddy feel about that?"

"He's not crazy about the idea although he says he'll do whatever Mum wants as he'll probably be in a Turkish bar most of the time."

"Do you think they're happy living like that?" I said.

"I know it sounds weird, Ruby, but they need each other. They most certainly do not have the most conventional marriage but I think they're happy being able to do their own thing, safe in the knowledge that the other one will be there if they need them."

"Please tell me that our marriage is never going to be like that?"

"I can assure you that we'll be pillars of society and very much together but at the end of the day if everybody was like that the world would be a very boring place."

We arrived at Mammy's cottage later that day after a relaxed drive down but when we went inside Mammy was nowhere in sight. Instead Robbie was in residence and had the kettle on within minutes. I was glad to see that the pipe which I had got him was sticking out of his top pocket. I had been reliably informed that he used the box that the new one had come in to preserve his old Band-Aid-covered one which he still adored.

"I've been told to give you a cup of tea and then to bring you up to the hotel for seven o'clock and not a minute sooner."

"Why?"

"I didn't ask why," Robbie answered gruffly. "I'm just doing as I'm told."

"And where exactly do you think you're going?" I demanded as Luke walked out the door.

"The instruction was to keep you out of the hotel. Nobody said anything about me not being allowed to go up, did they, Robbie?"

"Nope."

"I feckin knew that you and my mother were in cahoots over something."

Luke winked and said that he'd be back later. "And by the way your mother wants you to wear something nice," he called out as he left.

Mammy came bustling down several hours later. I had just come back to the house after going to help Robbie unpack a new delivery in the shop (okay, what really happened was that Robbie said he'd got a new delivery in and that as he'd been instructed to guard me I was to go with him).

"Will I do?" I asked.

"You look lovely," she said, appraising my black and green top which I had accompanied with leggings and black pumps. "I suppose that's as close as we'll ever get to seeing you dress like a girl before the wedding."

I stuck my tongue out and followed her into the bedroom where she was getting ready to change her clothes.

"So what's going on then? Why all the secrecy and having Robbie guard me like I'm some sort of delinquent?"

"You're not a delinquent but you see I've found you and Robbie out in your secret. You actually like each other so I just thought I'd help out and facilitate your friendship."

"Shut up, Mother."

"Honestly, Gabriel is nowhere near as difficult as you are. He goes fishing with Robbie and has become quite popular with the locals since he and Darryl moved in together."

The noise of a car pulling up outside alerted me to the fact that we had company and to my amazement I looked out and saw that Frankie and Owen and all the children had just arrived.

"Are you in on it as well then, Frankie?"

"I'm sure I don't know what you're talking about."

When I walked into the hotel there was most definitely a party atmosphere there. The red carpet had been laid out and there were lots of people I didn't know walking around clutching glasses of champagne.

"You didn't have to hire rent-a-mob, Mammy. I'd have been quite happy with just you lot."

At this point Gabriel, who had just appeared dressed in a navy suit with a bright purple tie, started to laugh.

"Bless her! She thinks all this is for her. I know you're getting married soon, sweetie, but seriously you're not that important."

"Shall we show her?"

"I think we should."

I knew that Mammy had organised for a few of the other rooms to be reconstructed and put back to the way they were when Monroe Manor was still a family home in all its glory, and as I followed her up the stairs I could smell furniture polish and paint.

"Someone's been busy," I said.

Luke and Mammy stopped outside a door which was shut. Mammy put her hand on the handle and put a finger up to make an announcement.

"This, my dear Ruby, was done especially for you. There used to be an art room in Monroe Manor but most of the paintings, apart from the ones dotted around the foyer, were taken away and either put in museums or auctioned off after the house ceased to operate. I thought it was a lovely idea and asked some of our local artists if they would like to display their work here and they've agreed and this is the grand opening night."

With a flourish she opened the door and I stepped into the room. The walls were all adorned with work from different artists with a special area dedicated to my favourite – the one and only Sarah Larkin.

"Is she here?" I asked, trembling with excitement.

"We couldn't get hold of her but the manager at Caitlin O'Neill's art studio said that he would keep leaving her messages."

"Some of her paintings are very sad," I commented, looking at them. "I've never seen these before."

Two paintings had caught my eye. One entitled *Lost* and the other one called *Missing You*. I realised once I studied them that they were of the same child who had been depicted in the picture I had got for Christmas – only that had been a happier one featuring outstretched arms and a smiling little girl.

Chapter 63

After people had been given the opportunity to mingle and walk around the room, Aisling, who had been meeting and greeting people downstairs, came up and asked for everyone's attention.

"I would like to welcome you all to Monroe Manor where tonight we are delighted to unveil our newly restored art room where we plan to exhibit the works of some of our favourite Donegal artists."

A round of applause came after that and then Aisling silenced everyone again with her hand.

"Of course, that's not the only thing we're here to celebrate because as most of you know there is going to be a wedding here at the weekend and not just any wedding either as the bride and groom happen to be good friends of mine."

Everyone looked in the direction of Luke and me as I stared at the floor and blushed furiously.

"Ruby also happens to be the most enthusiastic appreciator of art I know, so this room is in her honour and from now on will be known as Ruby's Art Gallery."

"Oh my God," I whispered as my eyes filled with tears.

"You deserve it all," Mammy said as she hugged me.

"What room are you naming after me then?" Luke demanded, to much giggling. "I want my own room."

A large crowd had turned out to celebrate the opening of my very own room but the person who I most wanted to meet hadn't come.

"Maybe she didn't get the messages," Luke suggested.

"Or maybe she's out of the country or away on business or something," said Mammy.

"Listen, don't worry about it," I said happily. "I'm more than happy with the way things have turned out. I couldn't have been any more surprised or privileged. What an honour to have my name in conjunction with such talent! If you don't mind I'd like to have another walk around before we leave. I spent so much time talking to people earlier that I didn't get a proper opportunity to look at the exhibits."

I took my time and gazed at each individual picture, still not daring to believe that I could now do it any time I wanted as these wonderful pieces of work were exhibits in a hotel which my mother now owned (seriously, if you had said this to me a year ago I would have been recommending that you be locked up for being mad).

Frankie came and linked arms with me and I put my head on her shoulder.

"There's something very special about you, Ruby Ross. Everyone says it. Even people who don't know you were saying it tonight."

"Well, obviously they don't know me very well then, do they? Ferocious Ruby with the bad temper –"

"And the heart of gold."

Mammy had just come into the room and was beaming from ear to ear. "You'll never guess! Sarah Larkin just rang to see if it was too late to drop by and see what we've done."

"That's just the icing on the cake then," I breathed. "This is the most perfect night ever."

"*Ahem!*" Luke said noisily. "I think maybe your wedding night might be your most perfect night. It's not too far away and I don't want too much to have to compete with."

"She's here!" Aisling shouted from the bottom of the stairs.

I turned and looked again at the beautiful paintings that Sarah had created and my excitement grew tenfold. I couldn't wait to see her. Then my eyes fell on another painting, which I hadn't noticed before, that was untitled.

"Where did this come from?" I asked in confusion. "It wasn't here before."

"It was one that we forgot to put out earlier," Mammy explained. "I think it was hidden behind a crate and we didn't see it until we were tidying up."

The picture was of the same child, but younger, with her rosy cheeks and red ringlets and she was laughing and looking up with large beguiling dark eyes. It was simple yet so detailed and painted with so much expression that I couldn't take my eyes off it.

"Do you like it?" a softly spoken voice with a Donegal brogue asked.

I heard Mammy and Luke gasp and saw Frankie's shocked expression before I looked into the face of the stranger who was addressing me.

The brown eyes that looked intently at me nearly took my breath away.

"I do. I like it a lot," I said, noting that Sarah wasn't wearing her hat tonight and that her hair which was the colour of burnished copper was cascading down her back.

"I drew it many years ago. It's a picture of my daughter. I had to let her go but I've never forgotten her. I changed my name, you see. I had to start a new life and didn't want anyone knowing who I was. It was complicated. My sister . . ." Her voice trailed off and she seemed unable to speak.

She nodded towards the painting and, pointing, drew my attention to the initials that were there . . . GD.

"It was an early painting, you see, that I never had any intention of showing, done before I became Sarah Larkin, but I decided some time ago that I wasn't going to hide my early work away any more."

"Did you ever find your daughter?" I asked, slowly looking into the eyes that mirrored my own.

The words hung in the air until Sarah slowly reached out and took my hands in her own. It was electrifying, the result of feeling the inextricable bond between mother and child that was like an invisible cord forever linking them.

"I never lost her," Sarah replied quietly. "She's always been with me in my heart."

Epilogue

Frankie and I stood outside the front of the picturesque country church. Gabriel had just closed the doors lest our entrance be spoiled by anyone seeing us before they were supposed to.

"I've never seen you look so beautiful, Ruby," Frankie said, trying to keep her emotions in check.

"Don't you dare cry. The beautician will have a heart attack and Gabriel will kill you if you look like a startled panda walking up the aisle."

"I won't – but look at you! Rose Malone is worth her weight in gold. Something very special happened the day that your finger was drawn towards her in the phone book."

I looked towards my reflection in the glass-panelled door and still couldn't believe that it was me. My hair had been shaped and cut in a feathery style which framed my face and gave me cheekbones that I never knew I had and my headdress was a pearl tiara which was inset with rubies (naturally).

My dress was exactly what I wanted but not as I had ever pictured it to be. It was made from cream satin and had a rounded neckline which was edged with Victorian lace and the bodice, which had roses with ruby insets liberally scattered on it and was laced with ribbon at the back, accentuated my waist beautifully whilst the stiff skirt flowed out from beneath and ended in a small train which was also trimmed with lace. I wore drop pearl studs in my ears and was proud to wear the same mother-of-pearl cameo necklace that Mammy had worn the day she had married my father. Cream roses which had diamanté and ruby-coloured stones interspersed through them completed my outfit whilst on my feet I wore cream satin kitten heels which Gabriel had got specially covered in lace for the occasion.

Frankie's bridesmaid's dress was made from colour-altering fabric which had shades of both green and purple in it. It was halter-neck in design with a band of roses dipping to a V shape at the waistline and sculpted her figure perfectly whilst elegantly flowing to the floor with a slight train at the back. Her flowers were also cream and had green and purple diamanté throughout. She wore shoes that had been covered in the same fabric and her hair had been curled softly at the back and decorated at the front with ornate clasps.

Carly who was my flower girl and dressed in the same material as her mother, with her hair pinned and curled, stood beside Frankie brimming with pride and dancing with excitement.

My 'big day' would be perfect. I could feel it in my heart. The only thing missing was my daddy. I missed him more than ever and wished that he could have been part of it all. I knew that he would have been very proud of me and that he would approve wholeheartedly of my decision to marry Luke who not only was proving to be the perfect partner but also was extremely protective of my mother. I hadn't got around to asking for details about my birth father but was willing to take things one baby-step at a time and so far that philosophy was working well for me.

I breathed deeply as I heard the music change and knew that Gabriel would be opening the door any second as he had done during our rehearsal the evening before.

As I had anticipated, he appeared soon afterwards and waved us in with a flourish. I could see Luke standing at the altar with Owen by his side whilst my two ushers, Robbie and Donal, stood reverently at the back of the chapel.

I watched as Carly walked up the aisle with Frankie following her, treading in time to the dulcet tones of Chris de Burgh. Then it was my turn. At the base of the altar I was encircled from either side and as I glided towards my future husband in all my finery I felt enveloped in love.

I looked at the sea of faces that were smiling and nodding encouragement and could have burst with happiness. On one side I saw Ella, who was sporting a rounded tummy and Hammy who was holding Baby Celia Rose whilst Ben, who looked very handsome in his suit, Angelica, who looked fabulous in a red dress, and Frankie's parents looked on proudly. Mandy stood at the other side of the church, glowing with pride, beside her parents who so far looked sober and happy to be there. I also spotted Aisling and Darryl who were busily taking photographs.

When we arrived at the altar Luke took my arm and kissed me on the cheek but not before I looked to my right and left and tenderly thanked the two women who had both been instrumental in making me into the person I was today.

Tears of happiness coursed down my mother's cheeks as she kissed me and Sarah looked equally as emotional as she squeezed me reassuringly and then let me go, only this time it wasn't for good. This time she would be waiting for me, to share in the rest of my life.

"Who gives this woman to this man?" the priest asked.

After looking at each other and exchanging looks of mutual respect, Isobel and Sarah answered confidently, their eyes brimming with love: "We do."

THE END

If you enjoyed *Anyone for Me?*
by Fiona Cassidy why not try
Anyone for Seconds? also published by Poolbeg?
Here's a sneak preview of Chapter One.

Anyone *for* Seconds?

Chapter 1

It was the cold and frosty month of January but instead of being miserable because I suffered from SAD and depressed because as usual I was broke, I was rather pleased with myself. The source of my pleasure was the fact that I had just recently met the man of my dreams. His name was Owen Byrne and he was a lecturer at the college where I'd been temping as Public Relations Officer for the past two weeks. He was tall with brown hair and he'd got that distinguished sexy look that only a man who wears glasses can carry.

He said that someone advised him to get contact lenses and I told him no way, that I thought his glasses suited him. I think he was rather surprised by my conviction, especially when I made him take his glasses off, studied him, walked around him as a vulture would circle an object of prey and then said "Definitely not" in a purring voice.

I've always been rather obvious when it comes to my feelings. My mother used to chastise me as a teenager when I'd come home from the discos and tell her that I'd met "Him".

"Frankie McCormick, will you stop wearing your heart on

your sleeve?" she would say sternly, hands on hips, wearing her floral dressing gown and trying to inconspicuously (not one of her stronger attributes) smell my breath lest the demon drink had passed my lips. "Men don't like that sort of desperation. It makes them want to run away and hide."

Personally I didn't think my mother was qualified to talk about what men like or don't like. She'd had the same one for forty years, therefore had been out of the running for quite a long time. Things had changed substantially since my mother was dancing the two-hand reel and Daddy was walking her to the end of her lane.

Getting back to Owen though. He hadn't been hiding from me. In fact, the other girls in the office had been telling me that he'd been asking subtle questions about me.

"Was Frankie with you when you went for a drink last week?" he reportedly asked Ruby, my stalwart companion and best friend.

"No, she had to go home. No baby-sitter, you see."

"She has children?"

I was told that this was said with more than a little intonation of surprise.

Ruby proceeded to tell him about my "experience" which she peppered with expletives. She was not my ex-husband's biggest fan. Sometimes I thought she disliked him more than I did.

Ruby is best described as being an eccentric fun-loving dynamo with a heart of pure gold. With spiky bright-red hair and a temper to match she's easy to spot. We'd been friends for about twelve years. It was she who put in the good word for me which enabled me to get my job.

Ruby said that Owen then clammed up and wouldn't divulge any details apart from saying he was a single father. She made a big deal of letting him know that I was on the market as well.

I had made the mistake of telling Ruby that I thought that Owen was rather attractive. Okay, who am I kidding – I think my exact words were that he was "a total screw" and that "given half the chance I'd love to put all six foot two of him in my pocket and take him home to be my willing slave".

Ruby is one of those people however who is as subtle as a bag of flying boulders and, stopping short of telling Owen that I would straddle him bareback without a saddle, she let him know in no uncertain terms that I liked him.

"She had no baby-sitter last Friday night but I'd baby-sit for her if I thought that she would have a good night out with a man who would treat her well," she said coyly.

"Do you know any men like that?" Owen reportedly asked with a mischievous twinkle in his eye.

"From personal and disastrous experience, no, but Frankie is one of these tiresome girlies who insist on seeing the good in people and likes to give them the benefit of the doubt until they prove otherwise. She loves the Clark Kent look. Men with glasses make her all hot and bothered."

When she told me what she'd said I smacked her around the head with the paper plate that held my soggy salad sandwich. (It was Monday – the one and only day I am ever on a diet.)

"Rubbeeeee!" I admonished, cringing at the thought of what he must be thinking of me

"Frankie, men are stupid creatures who need things pointed out and spelt for them. They don't do well with this female habit of trying to drop hints."

"Well, no one could ever accuse you of trying to do that," I muttered.

"Straight to the point; that's me."

I couldn't stay cross with her for long though, especially when Superman himself, minus his cape and manky-looking Y-fronts, came to ask if he could take me out. He took my number and promised to phone me that weekend.

It was Friday and I left the office waving goodbye to him with my heart pounding.

I'd already convinced myself that it wasn't going to happen. (It's a method of self-preservation when you've been hurt, you see.) You tell yourself that you're not worthy, that he's only doing it to be nice and that he'll come up with a suitable excuse as to why he couldn't phone. Ruby told me that he had a daughter so I'd already painted the scenario that one of her legs would fall off or something equally dramatic would happen to completely eradicate me from his mind.

"Bye, Frankie," he called in a friendly voice. "I'll chat to you tomorrow night."

"Sure," I said in a cheerful tone, still wondering what his excuse would be on Monday.

It was Saturday morning and I was up with the lark. The children were downstairs watching what they call "the funnies" on television and I could hear them giggling in high-pitched voices as somebody got a bucket of gunge dumped on their head from a great height.

I was changing the beds and as usual finding nine-year-old Ben's toy cars everywhere. No matter how often I told him not to leave them lying around I always inevitably ended up standing on one of them (in my bare feet of course, so that it hurt more). His room was an explosion of red in honour of his beloved Liverpool. I hate football but got an intense kick out of the fact that he supported an opposing team to his father and could never be swayed no matter what Tony (die-hard Arsenal supporter) said to him.

I picked up his dirty football kit and put it in my linen basket. He played for the Swiftstown under-tens and wore his blue and white colours with pride.

Carly's room was much tidier. It was pink and decorated with brightly coloured wall stickers and hanging mobiles. Her DVDs of *Cinderella* and *Beauty and the Beast* and other fantasy princesses were neatly stacked at the side of her little white TV and her *High School Musical* poster had pride of place above her bed. She loved singing and I could hear her warbling in her six-year-old voice as I descended the stairs, grubby duvet covers in hand.

"Muummeee!" she shouted as she put her arms around my neck and swung. She was tall and gangly for her age with a head full of blonde curls and was as light as a feather.

Everyone always jokes that there must have been a mix-up at the hospital where Carly was concerned as we are nothing alike. I am five feet tall and not a centimetre more and have a bit of a spare-tyre thing going on around my middle. My blonde hair is not really blonde but everyone told me that it suited me the first time I got it highlighted so I keep getting it done. I have large eyes and am blessed with long eyelashes and buying the latest mascara is my favourite hobby as I like enhancing the good features I have. I am also told that I have a lovely smile but equally that I can deliver the foulest looks on the planet when the mood takes me.

"What are we doing today, Mum?" came the all-too-familiar question.

Saturday was our treat day when we went to the Popcorn Club at the cinema or to the swimming pool.

Saturday used to be the day when their father would spoil them until he decided to move to America with his new Californian wife who had the cheek to have legs up to her armpits and look like a coat-hanger.

Tony (aka The Arsehole) came home one day about four years before this and announced that he no longer loved me but hoped that I would understand that he had found a soul mate. Stella was the American stick insect's name. Tony met her through business and it was the start of a beautiful relationship. It was just a pity that the prick didn't remember that he was in one with me at the time.

My children no longer saw their father and he didn't seem to care. He and his new wife were expecting a baby, I had heard, and were all loved up. Tony's sadistic old hag of a grandmother took great pleasure in imparting this particular piece of information just as I was unloading my trolley in Tesco's the previous week. My first thought when I had digested the news was that I hoped that the baby had an unusually large head. Perhaps if the bimbo went through a tough labour she wouldn't be so keen to get pregnant by other people's husbands and her sprog wouldn't be nicking Ben and Carly's father either.

Saturday evening came and we were all pooped. My children loved saying or rather singing that word, should I say. We all loved the film *Father of the Bride*, you see, so the kids liked to indulge in a verse of "Every Party has a Pooper" and stick in "Mum" where George Banks' name should be.

The day had been hectic. We went to the circus at Ruby's request. Ruby was a child at heart and not having children of her own she often used mine as an excuse to do things that she should have grown out of years ago. She loved the circus so accompanying Ben, Carly and me was a good reason to go. The children had always called her Auntie Ruby and she was like one of the family. A very noisy, boisterous addition in fact.

"First one to bed gets a bottle of chocolate milk!" I shouted and heard the children scrambling to beat each other into their rooms. Of course they knew I had one sitting in the fridge for each of them but they didn't seem to care about that as I announced the competition.

An hour later and I had finally settled in front of the Saturday-night film with a glass of White Zinfandel. I was trying my best not to keep looking at the phone but I couldn't help it. It was sitting in the corner of the room mocking me by remaining silent.

I repeated the mantra over and over again in my head. *He's not going to phone. He's not going to phone. He's a man. He's not to be trusted and he's not going to phone.*

Midway through my inner speech the phone rang and I sloshed wine all over my jeans.

"Hello?"

"Hello, can I speak to Lois?"

"I'm sorry, you must have the wrong number," I said with bitter disappointment in my voice.

"That's a pity," the caller said. "Because it's Clark Kent here."

•◆•

If you enjoyed this chapter from
Anyone for Seconds? by Fiona Cassidy
why not order the full book online
@ www.poolbeg.com

See next page for details.

•◆•